# NO DARK
# PLACE

# NO DARK PLACE

## JOAN WOLF

HarperCollins*Publishers*

HarperCollins books may be purchased for educational, business, or sales promotional use. For information please write: Special Markets Department, HarperCollins Publishers, Inc., 10 East 53rd Street, New York, NY 10022.

FIRST EDITION

*Designed by Nancy Singer Olaguera*

Library of Congress Cataloging-in-Publication Data

Wolf, Joan.
    No dark place / Joan Wolf. — 1st ed.
      p.  cm.
    ISBN 0-06-019238-0
    1. Great Britain—History—Norman period, 1066-1154—Fiction.
  I. Title.
  PS3573.0486N6   1999
  813'.54—dc21                          98-35763

99 00 01 02 03 ❖/RRD 10 9 8 7 6 5 4 3 2 1

FOR MARIE WOLF, MY SECOND MOTHER

"YET CAN I NOT HIDE ME IN NO DARK PLACE."

—*Sir Thomas Wyatt*

# AUTHOR'S NOTE

The language supposedly spoken by the characters in this book is Norman French. What you are reading is a "translation" into modern English.

# 1

The line of knights parted silently as the boy led his bloodstained horse through their ranks, back toward the camp area where the wounded were being attended. The Battle of the Standard was over and won, but the Sheriff of Lincoln had fallen, and it was his body that was laid across the sweaty back of the huge black warhorse the boy was leading through the humid mist of a hot August day.

Men rushed forward to help as soon as the boy entered the encampment, but his face stopped them in their tracks, and it was he alone who reached up for the body of the larger, heavier man laying prone across the high-pommeled leather saddle.

He lifted the dead weight in his arms and stood there for a moment, holding it as if it were a sleeping child.

The black horse blew loudly, breaking the eerie silence of the surrounding men.

Then, "Is he dead, lad?" a voice asked gently.

"Aye," said the boy. He looked at the man who had spoken. "Take down the flag, Bernard, and spread it on the ground."

The man obeyed, and the boy stooped and gently laid the body of the only father he had ever known upon the red silk of Lincoln's flag.

The only evidence he gave of strain from the heavy

weight was the fine mist of sweat that broke out upon his brow and the muscle that flickered along one of his high cheekbones.

The sheriff's men looked grimly down upon the dead face of their leader. His uncovered brown hair was matted with dirt and sweat and blood. The helmet he had worn into battle was gone, nor was he wearing his mail coif. Someone had pushed it off to try to staunch the wound that had killed him.

A fruitless enterprise, obviously, as the man's whole skull was caved in.

"What happened, Hugh?" one of the other men asked. He spoke in a lowered voice, as if it might be possible to disturb the sleep of the man who lay on the ground before them. "Did you see it?"

"Aye, I saw it," the boy replied in a careful, steady voice. "Ralf and I were walking back toward the camp together when I stopped to get a drink from a stream. Ralf went on ahead of me, God alone knows why, and the next thing I heard was his shout. I looked up to see four Scots leaping out at him from within a small copse of wood. They had seen that he was alone and unhelmeted, and one of them had a mace." The boy drew a deep breath. "They were after his sword."

"Why did you not come to his aid?" a tall knight demanded angrily. "Surely he deserved that much of you!"

Other voices muttered at the speaker to keep quiet, but the boy replied with steely composure, "I was too far away. I ran to help him, of course, but by the time I arrived he had fallen."

Silence fell as all of the men looked at the body laying before them on the blood-red silk of Lincoln's flag.

"And did the four who killed him get away, Hugh?" asked the quiet voice of the man named Bernard.

"No," the boy said simply. "I killed them all."

The boy was twenty years old and this was his first battle, but there wasn't a man there who did not believe him.

"Why in the name of God did he not have his helmet on?" the angry knight cried.

"The noseguard had been bent and it was in the way of his vision," the boy replied.

The men stood under the misty sun, regarding with sorrow the fallen body of the sheriff.

Bernard pulled himself together. "We must get him back to Northallerton," he said. "He deserves a decent burial."

"Not here," Hugh said quickly. "I will take him home and bury him next to Adela. That is what he would have wanted."

One of the sheriff's men began to say something, but at a look from the boy's startling light gray eyes, he fell silent.

"All right," Bernard said quietly. "We will take him home."

They put the body of Ralf Corbaille on a hurdle and carried him back to the king's base camp at Northallerton. King Stephen had not been present at this first battle of the civil war that was brewing between him and his cousin, the Empress Matilda. This had been a fight between the northern English, reinforced by some southern troops, and the Scots under their king, David, who was uncle to the empress.

"I will need to have a coffin," Hugh said to the oldest and most faithful of his father's knights, Bernard Radvers. They were standing in the hall of Northallerton Castle, where the body of the Sheriff of Lincoln had been laid temporarily to get it out of the warmth of the emerging sunlight. "And I will need a wagon."

"Lad." Bernard looked at the boy he had known since he was eight and had first come to live with Ralf. Hugh was still wearing his mail hauberk, but he had taken off his helmet and mail coif and his thick black hair had fallen forward across his brow, almost to the level line of his brows.

His face was expressionless, as armored as his body. If Bernard did not know better, he would assume that the death of the Sheriff of Lincoln meant nothing to this youngster who was looking at him with such disciplined immobility.

Ignoring all the signs that forbade it, Bernard reached out and touched the boy's bare hand in a gesture of comfort.

Hugh's face never changed.

At least, Bernard thought, he did not pull away.

"I will see to the coffin," Bernard said. "Your duty is to see how many other of our men have taken harm."

At those words, there was a slight change in the gray eyes looking at him so levelly. Bernard understood that Hugh had been so concentrated on his own loss that it was a shock for him to realize that other men might be hurt.

Hugh tossed the ink-dark hair off his forehead and looked again toward the bier. Clearly he did not want to leave, but Bernard had used the authority word, "duty," and Hugh had been brought up to respond to its imperative call. "All right," he said reluctantly. "I'll go."

But he didn't move. He just stood there, staring with that slightly out-of-focus expression in his eyes.

"Hugh," Bernard said gently.

"Aye," the boy said again. "I'm going."

Bernard accompanied the boy out into the heat of the bailey courtyard and then stood his ground and watched as Hugh turned and walked away from him in the direction of the great wooden gate. The boy's head was up and his slim, light body moved forward purposefully under its mail coat.

*Dear God,* Bernard thought despairingly. *What is Hugh going to do without Ralf?*

It was then that it happened, the thing that was to change all their lives. A knight of about Bernard's age was crossing the bailey at the same time as Hugh. As they passed each other, the man glanced carelessly over at the boy, then stopped abruptly. His face was blanched as white as new-fallen snow.

He looked, Bernard thought, exactly as if he had seen a dead man pass by.

As Bernard continued to watch, the knight turned and took a few steps, as if he would follow Hugh, then stopped again. He didn't move again, just stood there, his eyes glued to the slender figure, who had been joined by a squire leading a horse.

Hugh vaulted into the saddle of his almost purely white stallion and rode through the open gate, heading in the direction of the Sheriff of Lincoln's camp.

The knight continued to stare after him. He was not wearing armor, and Bernard could see how rigid were his shoulders and back under his sweat-stained shirt.

The hair prickled on the back of Bernard's neck.

With a great effort of will, he forced himself to move forward to the side of the stricken knight.

The man turned to look at him. He had graying hair and brown eyes and narrow, aristocratic features. "Do you know who that boy is?" he demanded.

Bernard had never heard him speak before, but he knew instinctively that that husky, choked sound was not the stranger's ordinary speaking voice.

"That is Hugh Corbaille, the son of the Sheriff of Lincoln." He was relieved to hear that his own voice sounded normal. "Why do you ask?"

The other knight turned again, to stare after Hugh. "The son of the Sheriff of Lincoln?" he said slowly. "If that is so, then why is he the living image of Hugh de Leon, only son of the Earl of Wiltshire, who was kidnapped from his home some thirteen years ago?"

Hugh found few serious injuries among the men Ralf Corbaille had brought with him to the Battle of the Standard. The English had broken the Scots early, and the greatest part of the battle had consisted of chasing the panic-stricken enemy through the fields and woods of misty Yorkshire. Thousands of Scots had fallen, and very few English. The Battle of the Standard had been a rout.

But Ralf was dead.

*Why did he go on ahead of me like that?*

This was the thought that ran nonstop through Hugh's mind all the while he was going dutifully around the camp, talking to the men of Lincoln, assuring them that their officers would see them safely home, doing all the things that Ralf would have wanted him to do.

*If I had been beside him, this never would have happened. Why did I have to stop to take a drink?*

"Is it true that the sheriff has fallen?"

Over and over the question was asked, until Hugh thought that he would surely kill the next man who spoke those words. But over and over again he answered, calm, disciplined, reassuring. "All will be well. See to the wounded. We will be leaving for home on the morrow."

After what seemed to him an eternity, but was actually only two hours, he was able to leave the camp and return to the castle, where he could keep watch over Ralf as Adela would have wanted.

Bernard was there before him.

"I have seen to the coffin, lad," said the middle-aged knight, who had been Ralf's man for more years than Hugh had been alive. "It will be ready by this evening."

Hugh nodded.

Bernard opened his mouth, as if he would say something more, and involuntarily Hugh shut his eyes, willing the other man to go away and leave him alone.

There was the sound of a step, and Hugh felt a flicker of relief that his wish was indeed being granted. Then Bernard's voice sounded next to his ear.

"Let me unbuckle your mail for you and then I will leave you be. It is too hot for you to be wearing armor if you do not need it."

Hugh stood perfectly still and allowed the older man to play squire, unbuckling the mail hauberk and lifting it over his bare head. When finally he stood there in his sweat-stained linen shirt and leggings, Bernard said gently, "All right, Hugh. I'll leave you alone now."

Hugh stood mute as Bernard left the hall. When at last he was alone, he approached the body of the man who was lying on a low makeshift bier in the middle of the room.

It was cooler in the hall than it had been outdoors, but even so the unmistakable odor of death was in the air. Hugh looked down at the face and ruined head of his foster father, and a wave of unbridled fury surged through him.

*How could you have done this to me? How could you have gone away and left me like this?*

His fingers curled into fists, and for a moment gray spots danced in front of his eyes. He dropped to his knees and lowered his head to ward away the faintness.

*Damn you, Ralf.*

He gulped air into his lungs, furious at his own weakness.

His eyes fell on the crucifix that Ralf always wore on a chain around his neck. It was a symbol of faith that should be a comfort to Hugh in his hour of need. He knew what the priests would tell him. They would say that Ralf was at peace in Christ, that he had been reunited with Adela, the wife he had so dearly loved.

But none of this was a comfort to Hugh. All he knew was that Ralf had left him and he was alone.

Slowly he reached up his hand and closed his fingers around

those of the dead man. Even in the heat of the August day, Ralf's hand was cold.

This was the hand that had ruthlessly dragged him out of his hiding place that bitter January night and brought him home to Adela. This was the hand that had shown him how to hold a sword, and a bow. This was the hand that had only recently dubbed him a knight.

*Damn you, Ralf. Damn you, damn you, damn you. How could you have done this to me?*

A shudder passed through his body, then another one. His hand closed more tightly on the cold, unresponsive one of his foster father.

*In all these years,* Hugh thought in anguish, *I never once told you that I loved you.*

When Bernard went back out into the bailey after leaving Hugh in the hall, he almost walked into the strange knight whom he had encountered earlier.

"If you don't mind, I should like to talk to you for a minute," the man said. His voice sounded more composed than it had several hours ago. It also sounded determined.

Bernard shrugged, trying to conceal his uneasiness. "Go ahead." He began to walk slowly toward the gate and the man fell into step beside him.

"My name is Nigel Haslin," the knight said, "and I am here with the men of Robert of Ferrers, from whom I hold one of my manors. My chief feudal lord, however, is the Earl of Wiltshire, and it is of him that I wish to speak."

"Aye?" said Bernard, terse and wary and anxious not to give anything away. The courtyard was filled with men coming and going on errands for the different lords who had led the English army. Bernard and Nigel Haslin walked side by side through the bustle of purposeful activity, intent on their own conversation.

"That boy," Nigel said abruptly. "Where does he come from?"

Bernard ran hard, callused fingers through his short, graying hair. "I told you earlier. He is the son of the Sheriff of Lincoln."

"From birth?" the other man said.

Bernard looked at him somberly and did not reply.

Something flickered in the other man's brown eyes. "So," he said. "A foster son, then."

"In every way that counts, Hugh is the son of Ralf and Adela Corbaille," Bernard said emphatically. "He will tell you that himself."

At that, Nigel put a restraining hand upon Bernard's arm, forcing him to come to a halt. Bernard swung around in annoyance and the two men stood face to face in the middle of the busy courtyard. "And if he is more than that?" Nigel demanded. "If he is in fact the heir to a great earldom—and to vast estates in Normandy as well?"

"That cannot be," Bernard said emphatically. "Nor would it be fair to put such thoughts into his head. There is already an Earl of Wiltshire. All do know that."

A menial passed close behind them, carrying two buckets of water from the castle well.

Nigel said, "It is true that Guy de Leon is the present earl. He is younger brother to Earl Roger, the previous lord." The knight paused and his eyes hardened. "The one who was murdered."

"Murdered?" Bernard repeated with shock. "I never heard anything of murder."

Nigel's expression was grim. "Oh, it was hushed up. But the fact is that thirteen years ago, Earl Roger was stabbed to death in the chapel of Chippenham Castle. And on that same day, the earl's only son, Hugh, disappeared, believed to be kidnapped by the very man who had murdered his father."

Bernard's eyes were stretched wide with horror. "And who was that man?"

Two horses pulling a cart filled with hay came through the open gate of the castle bailey. With one accord, Bernard and Nigel veered out of the cart's way and headed toward one of the towers built into the bailey wall.

Nigel said, "We think it was a household knight named Walter Crespin. He disappeared from the castle on the day of the murder. Two days later, the deputy sheriff brought his body back to Chippenham. Evidently he had been the victim of outlaws in the forest."

"And the boy?"

"He was never seen again." Nigel looked Bernard straight in the eyes. "Until today."

Bernard shook his head. "You are mistaken. You must be mistaken." He frowned, causing the weather-scarred wrinkles in his forehead and at the corners of his light blue eyes to score even deeper into his face.

The men walked in silence for a moment. Then Bernard asked reluctantly, "How old was this Hugh de Leon when he disappeared?"

"Seven."

Once more Bernard felt the hairs stand up on the back of his neck.

Still, he said stoutly, "If the man who took him was killed, it is almost certain that the boy must have been killed as well."

"So we all thought," Nigel Haslin said. "But I tell you, that boy in the chapel is the living image of Hugh de Leon."

"Good God, man!" Bernard said impatiently. "Be realistic." He raised his hand to acknowledge the greeting of a man who was passing by. "When last you saw this Hugh de Leon he was but seven years of age. Boys change out of all recognition from seven to twenty. You know that! Perhaps there is a faint resemblance between our Hugh and yours, but you are stretching it beyond all reason."

The other knight shook his head. "Bones don't change, and I would know those facial bones anywhere. They are the bones of his mother, the Lady Isabel. And the eyes. They are not the sort of eyes that are easily mistaken. They were the eyes of his father and they are the eyes of his uncle, the present earl. Light gray fringed with black."

"You cannot be sure," Bernard said, still unconvinced.

"What hand does this Hugh Corbaille use to wield his sword?" Nigel asked abruptly.

A faint brown haze lay in the air of the bailey as the activity of so many men stirred the summer-dry earth underfoot. Bernard stared at the other man through the dust and did not reply.

"The de Leons are always left-handed," Nigel said. "In fact, the present earl is widely known as Guy le Gaucher."

Still Bernard did not reply.

"Your Hugh is left-handed, isn't he?" Nigel demanded.

Bernard stared down at the packed dry earth of the courtyard under his feet.

*What if this man is speaking true? What if Hugh really is . . . ?*

He bit his lip and said grudgingly, "What do you want to know?"

The hay wagon had stopped at the stable that lay along one of the bailey walls, and two stableboys were beginning to unload it.

Bernard and Nigel reached the cool shadow of the tall wooden tower and stopped.

Nigel said, "How old was Hugh when he came to be fostered in the sheriff's household?"

"The usual age," Bernard replied. "Eight."

"And where did he come from?"

Bernard scowled, shifting uneasily from one foot to the other. Should he say? But the story was well known. Nigel would discover it from another, if not from him.

"Ralf found Hugh starving in the streets of Lincoln," he said at last. "When the boy spoke to him in Norman French, he took him home to his own house. Ralf and his wife had no children, and Hugh became to them the son they had always longed for."

For a long moment, Nigel was silent, obviously mulling over what Bernard had just said. "And what did Hugh tell Ralf about his past?" he asked finally.

"Nothing," Bernard replied with palpable reluctance. "He has always said that he cannot remember."

The brown eyes regarding Bernard widened as Nigel took in the full import of that statement.

"My God," he breathed at last. Then, speaking urgently, "I must talk to him."

"This is not the time to approach Hugh," Bernard said adamantly. "Not while he is grieving for Ralf."

Nigel inhaled sharply. At last he said, "I suppose I can understand that." He frowned. "All right, I will give him time to come to terms with his grief, and then I will visit him. Where can I find him?"

"I don't know if I should tell you," Bernard said. "I don't even know if I should have spoken to you about him at all."

"Don't you understand?" Nigel demanded fiercely. "If this boy is who I think he is, he is by right the Earl of Wiltshire and Count of Linaux. Surely you would not seek to deny him such a heritage?"

Most of the morning mist had cleared and the sky overhead was a hazy blue. The air was hot and muggy, and the line at the castle well was a long one.

"And how will the present earl and count receive the news of a possible usurper?" Bernard asked shrewdly.

"Lord Guy has only daughters. There is no son to succeed him," Nigel said. "The way would lie open for Hugh."

Bernard raised skeptical eyebrows. "Do you really think that because he has no sons, Earl Guy would be willing to put aside his own claim in favor of a nephew he does not know? For that is what Guy would have to do if he recognized Hugh as his brother's true son. He would have to step aside."

Nigel's lips twitched, and he did not reply.

A man on a magnificent black horse attended by a guard of knights rode in through the bailey gate. Stableboys scrambled to take the horses.

Bernard said, "Before he could even think of approaching Guy, Hugh would first have to prove he is who you say he is."

"He wears his proof on his face," the other man returned.

Bernard went on as if he had not heard. "And, of course, there is always the possibility that Hugh will not want to prove it."

Nigel looked at him as if he were mad. "No man would turn his back on such a heritage."

And Bernard said wryly, "You don't know Hugh."

# 2

Ralf Corbaille's manor of Keal lay in Lincolnshire, a part of England Nigel Haslin was not overly fond of. The fen country of Lincolnshire might be beautiful to those who lived in it, but to a Wiltshire man like Nigel, the endless, flat, watery expanses were not only unattractive, they were a nuisance to travel across.

It was March 1139, seven months after the Battle of the Standard. Time enough, Nigel thought, for Hugh to have recovered from his grief. Time enough for him to be setting his sights upon the future.

The weeks and months had also given Nigel a chance to think more clearly about the wisdom of resurrecting a possible heir to the earldom of Wiltshire. He had been so stunned to see Hugh at Northallerton that he had acted instinctively in talking to Bernard Radvers. The last seven months had given him a chance to consider whether or not he would be wise to proceed in this matter, or if it would be more sensible simply to pretend that he had never seen the boy at all.

As Nigel well knew, Guy de Leon would not be at all happy to find that his nephew had miraculously risen from the dead. Furthermore, he would be furious with the vassal who dared to sponsor such a claimant.

On the other hand, there were many reasons why Nigel would like to see Guy replaced as his overlord.

For one thing, he strongly suspected that Guy had been involved in the death of his elder brother. Nigel had held his former lord in high regard and would very much like to see his murderer punished.

He also gravely disapproved of the dissolute way in which Guy lived.

And finally, he did not approve of Guy's refusal to declare his support for the king.

In short, Guy was the complete opposite of the brother he had succeeded. Roger de Leon's name had rung through all of the Christian world for his deeds during the late Crusade. It was Roger who had led the attack upon the gates of Jerusalem, the attack that had won the Holy City back from the infidels. Under Roger, Chippenham had been a model of morality and propriety. Roger, Nigel was certain, would have upheld his feudal oath to his overlord, King Stephen, and not been solely on the lookout for his own advantage.

Nigel would far rather owe his own feudal duty to Roger's son than he would to Guy.

And then there was Isabel.

What would it mean to her to know that her son was still alive?

When Bernard thought of her, and all her beauty, hidden away in that convent for the last thirteen years, his heart lifted with the hope that Hugh's return might also mean the return of his mother to the world.

It was late in the afternoon of a cold, blowy day when the party from Wiltshire finally saw the stockade fence of Keal rising in the distance. Gray clouds raced across the wide East Anglia sky as Nigel and the five men of his household guard who were accompanying him approached the manor.

By the time they reached the open gate, a man had moved to bar their way. The sentry was dressed in the leather jerkin and cross-gartered leggings of a man-at-arms and he wore a sword at his side.

Nigel identified himself and stated that he had business with Hugh Corbaille, whose manor he believed this to be.

Nigel was told to wait in the courtyard while the sentry

informed his master of the new arrivals. Before he left the courtyard, however, the sentry signaled to two of his fellows to come and
stand by Nigel's party.

Security was not taken lightly at Keal, Nigel thought approvingly.

While he waited, he looked around, judging the quality of the
property. As was customary in such establishments, barns and byres
lined the inside of the stockade fence, all of them looking to be in
very good repair. The house itself was also built of timber. Most of
it was two floors high, but attached to the main block was a three-
floor section that looked as if it was a more recent addition.

Oddly, even though night was coming on and the air was chill,
all the window shutters on the third floor were open.

The front door of the manor swung open and a man came out.
It did not take Nigel long to recognize Bernard Radvers.

Bernard crossed the courtyard and came to a halt in front of
Nigel's horse. "So," he said. "You have come."

"I said I would," Nigel replied calmly. "Is the boy within?"

"He has ridden out, but I expect him back shortly." Several
stableboys came running at Bernard's signal. "You and your party
must come inside," he said courteously. "You are weary and in need
of refreshment."

Nigel dismounted gratefully and followed Bernard to the stairs
that led up to the main door of the house. As in so many buildings
of this type, the living quarters were on the second floor, as the first
floor was used for storage.

Bernard pushed the door open and led Nigel and his following
into the chief room of the manor, the hall.

The first thing that struck Nigel's senses was the fresh, fragrant
scent of the room. He looked down and saw that the herb-strewn
rushes on the floor looked as if they had been freshly laid that day.

He sniffed appreciatively.

Bernard smiled. "Adela, Ralf's wife, was always a meticulous
housekeeper. Hugh was brought up in an immaculate house, and
clearly he has seen to it that Adela's ways are still followed."

Nigel nodded and let himself be led forward to the large fireplace in which two massive logs smoldered comfortably. A young
boy came from the far side of the room to help him remove his mail

coif and hauberk. In the far corner, his guards were also being helped out of their heavy mail garments.

He and his men had made the ride from Wiltshire in full armor, a precaution he always took when traveling in these unsettled times.

A boy brought cups of ale for Bernard and Nigel, and Bernard gestured his guest to one of the heavy carved chairs that were placed near the fireplace. The two men sat down on the comfortable cushions Adela had embroidered, sipped their wine, and regarded each other a little warily.

"Are you part of this household, then?" Nigel asked after he had gratefully swallowed his first draft of ale.

Bernard shook his head. "I am part of the garrison at Lincoln Castle still. I had business in this part of the county, though, and took the opportunity to stop by to see Hugh. I arrived but yesterday."

Nigel leaned back in his chair and stretched his legs toward the pleasant warmth of the fire. "Have you told him aught of what passed between us at Northallerton?"

"No." Bernard's pale blue eyes regarded him measuringly. "I was not sure if I would ever see you again."

"Well, as you see, I have come."

Bernard took a sip of ale and looked steadily at Nigel over the top of his cup. "Why?"

Nigel made an impatient gesture. "We have been over this ground before, I think. I have come because I believe this boy may be the heir to the earldom of Wiltshire."

Slowly, Bernard revolved his pewter ale cup in his hands. "I have done some investigating of the present earl since last we spoke," he said. "He is not a man likely to open his arms wide to a long-lost nephew desirous of usurping his place."

"I know that," Nigel returned calmly. "On the other hand, if King Stephen himself recognizes Hugh as Roger's son, then Guy will have no legal claim to the earldom."

Bernard gave the other knight a long, level look. "Why should Stephen want to recognize Hugh?"

"Stephen knows that Roger was murdered. Perhaps Hugh will be able to tell the king who was responsible for that heinous crime.

If it was Guy . . . well, Stephen will not allow a murderer to continue on as one of his earls."

"You forget one thing," Bernard said. His steady eyes regarded Nigel over his wine cup. "Hugh will not be able to name the murderer. He does not remember anything that happened to him before he came to Ralf."

Nigel looked skeptical. "Does he really not remember, or is he just saying that?"

"Believe me," Bernard said with absolute finality. "He really does not remember."

Silence fell as Nigel contemplated this statement.

Finally he said, "Well, even if Hugh cannot point a finger at Guy, there is still ample reason for Stephen to take up his cause."

"I don't see why," Bernard said.

Nigel leaned a little forward in his chair, trying to communicate his sense of urgency. "Stephen needs Wiltshire. If Hugh will promise to stand with Stephen, and if we can present some reasonable evidence that he is indeed Earl Roger's lost son, then I have no doubt that the king will support his claim over Guy's."

Bernard looked thoughtful. "Why should Stephen be so eager to get rid of Guy? Is he going to declare for Matilda?"

Nigel leaned back in his chair. "Guy will declare for no one," he said bitterly. "He will sit on the edge of the battle and, like a scavenger, look to grab up every scrap of the leavings for himself."

Before Bernard could reply to this harsh comment, the hall door opened and Hugh came into the room. His step was quiet, nor had the door made any noise when it opened, but every man in the hall was instantly aware of his presence.

It always amazed Bernard to see how effortlessly the boy could command attention.

There had been the faint murmur of voices in the hall before Hugh's entrance, but silence fell as the boy crossed the rush-strewn floor toward the two men seated before the comfortable fire.

Bernard felt his stomach twist as once again he beheld the too-thin face of Ralf's beloved foster son. Until yesterday, he had not seen Hugh since they had buried Ralf last summer, and he had been profoundly shocked to see that thin, nervy face, those shadowed gray eyes. He thought the boy looked as if he were at the end of his tether.

*I knew it would not be good for him to be alone here,* Bernard thought now grimly. *There are too many memories at Keal.*

But there were few alternatives for Hugh. He had inherited Keal as well as Ralf's two other, smaller manors, and this was where he was supposed to be.

Bernard said composedly, "Hugh, this is Nigel Haslin of Somerford Castle in Wiltshire. He has traveled a long way in order to speak to you."

Outside it must have begun to rain, because there was a fine mist of drops on Hugh's black hair. He unfastened his cloak and stood there in a leather jerkin and beautifully embroidered shirt. Bernard recognized Adela's talented workmanship.

A young boy came on quiet feet to take the damp cloak and put a cup of ale into Hugh's hand.

Hugh didn't drink, just stood there looking at Nigel, waiting.

Nigel shot a quick glance at Bernard. "This is not business that ought to be discussed in front of others," he said.

Hugh frowned.

"It's important, lad," Bernard assured him. "Why don't you take Nigel upstairs to the solar and talk to him there?"

For a long moment, Hugh didn't reply. At last he said softly, "Very well," and, without looking at either man, he turned and led the way to the stairs that went from the hall up to the third level of the addition.

There were two doors at the top of the stairs and Hugh opened one, which led into a large comfortable room with tapestry-covered walls and heavy, carved, cushioned furniture. At least the room would have been comfortable, Nigel thought, if all the windows had not been open to let in the cold, damp, rainy air. There was no fireplace in this room, just a tiled hearth place in the center that contained an unlit charcoal brazier. The floor was swept bare.

Hugh made no move to invite him to sit but stood there in silence, waiting.

Nigel looked at the beautiful, wary face in front of him.

He had to be Isabel's son. Those cheekbones . . . that mouth . . .

Nigel took a deep breath and began to speak.

The minutes went by like hours as Bernard waited for the two men to come back downstairs. But when Nigel finally returned to the hall, he was alone.

"Well?" Bernard said urgently as the other knight joined him in front of the warm fire.

Nigel's mouth was tight. "He doesn't believe me. He says it cannot be true."

Bernard heaved himself to his feet. "Was he upset?"

"Who knows?" Nigel said. "That is a boy who shows nothing on his face. All I can tell you is that he was adamant that he cannot possibly be the son of Roger, Earl of Wiltshire."

"You told him about the resemblance? About the left-handedness?"

"Of course I told him those things," Nigel responded impatiently. "He didn't listen. All he would do is deny it."

"Let me talk to him," Bernard said.

"He is where I left him," Nigel said a little bitterly. "He dismissed me out of hand."

Slowly Bernard climbed the stairs to the next level, bracing himself for what he was going to find. He owed it to Ralf to do his best for Hugh. He just wished he knew what the best thing was.

Hugh was standing in the middle of the room, staring down at the empty brazier, when Bernard came in.

The room was freezing. Without comment, Bernard went around closing the shutters.

"Adela would have had the brazier lit and the shutters closed," he said to Hugh's back.

"I told them to air it out today. I never sit here anymore," Hugh said.

The solar had been the gathering place for the family that no longer existed.

Bernard glanced toward the two doors that opened off the solar. They led to two bedrooms. One had belonged to Ralf and Adela and one had belonged to Hugh. From the previous night, Bernard knew that Hugh still used his bedroom. Privacy had always been of paramount importance to him.

Bernard said, "What did you think of Nigel's story?"

At that, Hugh swung around to face him. "How long have you known of this?" he demanded.

"He saw you at Northallerton and approached me," Bernard said.

"Why did you tell him about me?" Hugh asked furiously. "Why did you tell him about my memory?"

Bernard had been prepared for shock. He had not been prepared for this anger. "Hugh," he said carefully. "Think. It may just be possible that you are this Hugh de Leon. At any rate, you cannot dismiss the possibility out of hand."

"Aye, I can. I am Hugh Corbaille. I do not want or need to be anyone else."

Nigel refused to flinch before the flame of Hugh's anger. He said as reasonably as he could, "Before you were Hugh Corbaille you were someone else. You know that. I know that. Why is it so impossible that you were not this lost boy?"

Hugh pushed his still damp hair off of his forehead. "Because I would know it if I were. Do you think I would forget being the heir to such greatness?"

Bernard persevered. "You might have. Something happened to make you forget your past. That you cannot deny."

"I forgot my past because it was best for me to forget it. Terrible things happened to me . . . "

Abruptly the boy broke off. His eyes, huge and shocked, met those of Bernard.

"What terrible things, Hugh?" Bernard asked gently.

Hugh shook his head mutely and turned his back on the knight.

"I don't remember," he said.

And he didn't want to remember, Bernard realized at last.

It was time, Bernard thought, to speak a few home truths.

"You are wasted here, lad," he said bluntly. "If you had not been so young, it is highly likely that you would have been appointed sheriff after Ralf. You have the knack of leadership. Men look to you. From the time you were sixteen and Ralf first brought you to the castle with him, you have been a presence. There is more for you to do with your life than to collect rents and see that your lands are farmed."

Hugh shook his head but didn't reply.

"You are bored to death here," Bernard said. "Admit it."

Hugh said, "The present Earl of Wiltshire is one of the most powerful men in the land. It is mad to think that I could take his place."

Still speaking to Hugh's back, Bernard said, "You would make a good earl. It may even be in your blood."

As Hugh swung around to face him, Bernard said deliberately, "I never would have thought that Ralf could rear a coward."

Hugh's chin came up. His gray eyes glittered. He said levelly, "Don't try me too hard, Bernard."

Prudently, Bernard gave ground. "Just think about it, lad. That is all I ask of you. This is not an opportunity to throw away."

Hugh's body was rigid with resistance.

"Why are you so anxious to see me make a fool of myself?" he asked bitterly.

"I think this Nigel Haslin is honest," Bernard said. "I think his story is worth pursuing, at least for a little bit."

And to himself he added, *Anything is worth getting you away from here.*

"Will you think about it, at least?" he said.

There was a line like a sword between Hugh's straight black brows. "I will think about it," he said.

Trestle tables were set up in the hall for supper, and Nigel sat at the high table with Hugh and Bernard.

The only women in the hall were a few servants who sat at one of the lower tables. At the high table they were served by two young boys. As it was Lent, the main course consisted of a sauced mullet, which tasted deliciously fresh, to Nigel's surprise and delight. The three men discussed the latest news from court, the chief tidbit being that Stephen had succeeded in getting his brother, Henry, Bishop of Winchester, appointed papal legate, thus making him superior in rank to the Archbishop of Canterbury.

No further word was mentioned of the Earl of Wiltshire.

After supper was over and the trestle tables were being scrubbed with sand and removed, Hugh and the two older knights moved back to the fire.

In one of the corners, a man had taken out a lute and was strumming it.

Bernard said to Hugh, "Why don't you offer Nigel a game of chess?"

Hugh shot him an ironic look. "Why don't you play him, Bernard? I will be glad to look on."

Bernard turned to the visiting knight. "Are you a good player?" he asked.

"I am accounted so," Nigel replied comfortably.

"Play him," Bernard said to Hugh. "And give him a knight."

At that, Nigel sat a little forward in his chair. "That would not be fair."

"I play rather well," Hugh said.

Nigel's aristocratic nose quivered slightly with insult. "So do I," he informed the twenty-year-old sitting opposite him on the other side of the fire.

Hugh shrugged and called for the chess set. One of the boys who had served them at supper set the board up between the two men. Silence fell as the game began.

Twenty minutes later, Nigel, who was actually an excellent player, found himself in checkmate.

"I should have accepted that extra knight," he said slowly, staring at the arrangement of pieces on the board.

"Aye," Hugh said gravely. He stood up. "You can share my parents' bedroom off the solar with Bernard. He will show you the way. I will be going to bed myself once I make my evening rounds."

"Don't worry, I'll see to Nigel's comfort, lad," Bernard said easily. "His men can sleep here in the hall with mine and yours."

Hugh nodded and turned away from them, heading toward the door that led outside. He took his cloak from where it was hanging on a nail by the door, flung it around himself, and went out into the rain.

"Well?" Nigel said, turning to look at Bernard.

"Come upstairs," the other man said, "and we can speak in private."

# 3

When Hugh came back into the house, Nigel and Bernard were gone and the men who were to sleep in the hall were bedding down on the straw pallets that the servants had dragged out from their storage place behind the stairs. Hugh took the candle that had been placed next to the door for him and in silence crossed the mattress-strewn floor and mounted the stairs to the third level.

He felt a great rush of relief when he saw that there was no one in the solar. Bernard and Nigel Haslin had retired to bed; he would not have to face either of them again tonight.

He stood for a moment in the middle of the solar, looking around him by the flickering light of the wax candle he held in his hand.

How empty it was. How desolate. It had felt that way to him ever since Adela died. Even Ralf had not been able to completely fill the emptiness for him.

It still did not seem possible that they were gone, that he would never again feel Adela's fingers on his cheek, never again hear Ralf's deep, gruff voice . . .

Hugh shut his eyes, blotting out the sight of the room that had once been his home.

This had not been the place to which Ralf had brought him on that first night, of course. That had been the townhouse in Lincoln.

Hugh stood alone in the cold, empty solar, and it seemed that he could once again feel the touch of Ralf's hand, heavy on his shoulder, as the sheriff had dragged his eight-year-old self out of the hiding place he had found against the bitter cold of a winter night. Hugh had struggled mightily, but even though he had learned many dirty tricks during his time on the road, Ralf had known most of those tricks himself. And Hugh had been but eight years of age and weak with hunger, no match for the big, strong Sheriff of Lincoln.

He had cursed Ralf, first in English and then in his native Norman French.

Later he had discovered that it was the French that had stopped Ralf from taking him to the castle, which had been his original intention. Instead, impulsively, the sheriff had taken Hugh home to his wife for the night, to get the boy off the frigid winter streets of Lincoln and to find out who he was.

Adela had taken one look at the filthy bundle of rags that was Hugh and immediately called for a hot bath. Stunned and speechless, Hugh had found himself being scoured and scrubbed and then dressed in the clean clothes that Adela had borrowed from one of the household boys. Then she had sat him in front of the fire and fed him the first hot meal that he had seen in over a month.

He had eaten ravenously.

When Ralf would have questioned him, Adela had told her husband fiercely to hold his tongue. Couldn't he see that the boy was exhausted?

Then she had taken Hugh upstairs and tucked him into a warm, fur-covered bed in a room that he had all to himself. Before she left, she had bent and kissed him on the forehead.

"Never fret, my lamb," she had said. "I won't let any more harm befall you."

And she never had.

Hugh would have died for Adela, but she had thwarted him by dying first. It was the worst memory of his life: he and Ralf, each of them sitting on either side of her bed, watching as the fever ate her away. She had slipped away in the night without a word to either of them.

He had been seventeen when she died.

Three years later, he had lost Ralf.

The seven months since Ralf's death had been a torment to Hugh. Losing his foster parents had opened a great chasm of emptiness inside him that he was terrified to contemplate. Even during the years that he had lived with them, he had known deep down that he was balancing precariously on the edge of a precipice. But Adela had kept the terror away. At least, for most of the time she had.

*Why can't I remember?*

It was not a question he often asked himself. He had always known that it was safer not to remember. For thirteen years he had been content to live as half a person with half a life. It had been enough that he was the son of Adela and Ralf.

But they were gone now. They had died and left him alone.

Who was he, really? Who had he been before Ralf had found him starving in the streets of Lincoln?

He remembered some of what had befallen him before he reached Lincoln. He remembered the traveling mummers who had wanted to use him in their show. He remembered what one of the men had tried to do to him and how he had escaped from their clutches.

But of the time before that—nothing.

*Could what this Nigel had said possibly be true? Could I be this missing Hugh de Leon?*

All of his inner self rose up to deny it.

*Why am I so sure it isn't true?*

*Why am I so afraid?*

*Is it because I saw my father being murdered? Is that why I lost my memory?*

A drop of hot wax trickled down onto Hugh's hand, bringing him back to his surroundings.

Slowly he walked into his bedroom and began to undress. He had told his bodyservant he wanted no help this night.

He pulled his jerkin off over his head, and bent to unbuckle his boots. As he stood next to the bed in his hose and beautifully embroidered shirt, he shuddered, and it was not with cold.

The bedroom next door was occupied this night, but not with the people he loved.

He stripped off the rest of his clothes and got into his solitary bed.

*I don't know how much more of this loneliness I can stand,* he thought desperately as he burrowed his face into the embroidered pillow that Adela had made for him so lovingly.

*Perhaps it won't hurt to speak a little further with this Nigel Haslin on the morrow.*

There was no chapel at Keal and consequently the household met for the first time in the hall. The first meal of the day was always a simple one of bread washed down with ale, and then everyone dispersed to their morning chores before they reassembled again at noon for dinner.

"I must be back in Lincoln by evening, lad," Bernard said to Hugh as the three men sat over their ale cups at the high table.

Hugh had begun to pick up his cup, but now he set it back down again on the table. "Of course," he said with careful courtesy. "It was good of you to come to see me, Bernard."

The knight scowled. "I don't want to leave you here alone again," he said frankly. "It isn't good for you."

Bernard could almost see the shutters come down behind the boy's light gray eyes.

"This is my home," Hugh said.

"You may have another home," Bernard said deliberately. "That is, if you can find the courage to fight for it."

The boy's finely cut nostrils quivered with an emotion that could have been either anger or amusement.

"You must be desperate to get me away if you have to resort to insulting me," Hugh said.

It was amusement, Bernard realized.

"Listen to me, lad," he said, gripping his ale cup in tense, hard fingers. "The evidence presented here by Nigel is too persuasive for you to turn your back upon. You may very well be who he thinks you to be. You owe it to yourself to pursue the matter further."

Hugh looked away from Bernard and for a brief moment fixed his eyes on the scoured oak of the table at which the three of them were sitting. His profile gave away nothing. Then, slowly, he turned his head the other way and looked at Nigel Haslin.

"Why have you sought me out?" he asked. "What ill will do you harbor against Guy de Leon that makes you so urgent to see him replaced by an unknown like me?"

*Leave it to Hugh to thrust his sword right into one's most vulnerable spot,* Bernard thought with a mixture of humor and resignation.

Nigel, however, did not look dismayed by Hugh's challenge. He folded his hands on the table in front of him and replied with an air of frankness, "I will be honest and tell you that my chief motive in wishing to see Guy displaced is political. As you well know, the ill wind of civil war is blowing toward us in this land. While it is true that Matilda is the only legitimate child of our previous king, and while it is also true that Henry forced his barons to swear allegiance to her while he was still alive, yet there are many who do not wish to see a woman wear the English crown. Consequently, when the old king died and his nephew, Stephen, seized the crown for himself, most of the barons welcomed him."

Nigel's brown eyes flicked across Hugh's still face.

Hugh looked back and waited.

After a moment, when he realized that Hugh was not going to speak, Nigel forged on. "Matilda knows nothing of us here in England. When she was but a child, her father married her to the German emperor; then, after the elderly emperor died, she was married to Geoffrey, Count of Anjou."

At the word "Anjou," Nigel's voice hardened "Matilda's husband has no interest in England; he wants to be Duke of Normandy. It was not until Matilda's bastard brother, Robert, Earl of Gloucester, decided to champion her cause that she even contemplated making a play for the English crown."

Hugh drummed his fingers impatiently on the table. "All this may be true," he said, "but what has it to do with me?"

Nigel said flatly, "Stephen needs Wiltshire."

There was silence as Hugh digested this information. At last he inquired in a mild voice, "Is Guy going to declare for the empress?"

Nigel told him what he had told Bernard the day before. "Guy will declare for no one. He is like the vultures who hover over the dead on a battlefield, hungry to take the pickings for themselves."

Hugh leaned back in his chair and took a thoughtful sip of ale. "So you are Stephen's man?"

"Aye," Nigel returned.

Hugh said, in the same mild tone as before, "And to whom do you swear your feudal oath?"

A faint flush stained Nigel's cheeks. "The Earl of Wiltshire is my chief feudal lord, although I have a manor that lies under the lordship of Ferrers. It was my allegiance to Ferrers that brought me north to the Battle of the Standard."

Hugh lifted a slim black eyebrow and said nothing.

Nigel's mouth compressed into a hard, straight line. "You think I am betraying my feudal oath by speaking to you the way I have."

Hugh took another sip of ale, watched him, and didn't reply.

"I see I must open my whole mind to you on this subject," Nigel said.

"I think that might be wise," Hugh said softly.

Nigel took a long draft of ale, returned his cup to the table, and resumed speaking in a cautiously lowered tone.

"When Lord Roger was found lying in his own blood, in his own chapel, no one doubted for long that it was the knight Walter Crespin who was responsible for the knife thrust that killed the earl. It was soon discovered, you see, that Walter had left Chippenham shortly before the earl's body was found, taking the heir with him."

Hugh's half-lowered lashes concealed the expression in his eyes.

Nigel lowered his voice even more. "I have always wondered at the convenience of the attack that killed Walter," he said.

At that, Bernard leaned around Hugh to stare at Nigel. "Good God, man. Do you think he was killed deliberately?"

"By himself, Walter had no reason to kill Lord Roger," Nigel said. "He was but a simple household knight. What would he gain by such a dreadful deed?"

"You think he was working for someone else?" Hugh said.

"I do."

"And whom do you suspect?"

Nigel replied by posing another question. "Who is the one who gained the most by the death of Lord Roger and the disappearance of his only son and heir?"

"Guy," Bernard said emphatically. He pounded his fist once upon the table. "By God, you suspect that Guy was behind the death of his brother!"

"Nor am I the only one to have harbored such a thought," Nigel said grimly.

"There was no proof?" Bernard demanded. "No way of connecting this Walter Crespin to Guy?"

Nigel's smile held no humor. "Walter was conveniently dead, and it is not possible to question a dead man."

The two men looked at each other around the still figure of Hugh.

Bernard said, "Walter's body was returned, but not the body of the boy?"

"That is right. Although I am certain that he was meant to be killed as well, evidently he found some means of getting away."

At this, both knights fixed their eyes upon Hugh.

His beautiful face wore the still, reserved, utterly unapproachable expression that Bernard had always dreaded to see.

"A very interesting thesis," Hugh said. "It is a pity that you have no proof."

"You wear my proof upon your face," Nigel told him grimly. "No one who sees you can doubt who you are."

A muscle flickered along Hugh's jawbone.

"What do you propose I do?" he asked in the same cool voice as before. "Make an appointment to see my supposed uncle and ask him to recognize me as his long-lost nephew?"

Nigel's aristocratic nostrils pinched together with insult. "I am not so foolhardy as that."

Hugh's cold eyes looked at him. "What do you want me to do, then?" he repeated.

"Come with me to the king," Nigel replied. "If Stephen will recognize your claim, then you will have the legitimacy you need to challenge Guy."

Once more Hugh raised a skeptical eyebrow. "I rather think that King Stephen will require more proof of my identity than the assurance of one of Guy's discontented vassals that I look like the dead heir."

Anger flashed across Nigel's face, but before he could reply, Bernard cut in.

"The lad is right. There must be more voices than yours to represent his claim to the king."

Nigel set his jaw. "Then he must go to see his mother. If I was able to recognize him so immediately, she will be even quicker to do so."

The two men were so involved with each other that neither of them noticed the way Hugh had frozen at Nigel's words.

"His mother is still alive?" Bernard asked incredulously. "Why didn't you mention this earlier? Where is she?"

"In the Benedictine convent in Worcester," Nigel replied. "It is where she has resided since the death of her husband and the loss of her son." Nigel turned to Hugh and said emotionally, "She will be overjoyed to see you, lad."

The eyes he encountered were as bleak and cold as the North Sea in January.

"No," Hugh said.

Nigel's head snapped up. "What do you mean, *no*? Are you saying that you won't go to see your mother?"

"She is not my mother," Hugh said. "And I won't see her."

The two older men stared at him in astonishment.

Hugh stood up. "Why makes you so certain that my loyalty is pledged to Stephen?" he demanded of Nigel Haslin.

Nigel's voice became louder. "You fought for him at the Battle of the Standard!"

"I followed my foster father to the Standard, as was my duty. But Ralf is dead now."

Nigel leaped to his feet so that he loomed over Hugh. "You cannot seriously be thinking of declaring for the empress?"

"Stephen once swore allegiance to her," Hugh pointed out calmly.

"We all did!" Nigel cried. "Her father, the old king, forced us to."

Hugh shrugged.

"You cannot declare for the empress, lad," Bernard said. He too had gotten to his feet. "Ralf was Stephen's man. He had his manors of Stephen. You cannot expect to hold them from another."

"Perhaps I do not want to hold them," Hugh said. "Perhaps I would rather give them to you."

At that, Bernard's mouth dropped open with shock.

Hugh smiled at him. His smile was so rare that when it came

its effect was extraordinary. "You are growing old to be a landless knight, Bernard. Wouldn't you like to be the lord of Keal?"

Bernard recovered himself. "Don't be a fool, Hugh," he said sternly.

"You said yourself that I should get away from here," Hugh pointed out.

"I meant that you should go with Nigel! In the name of God, lad, how do you think you will support yourself if you give up Keal?"

"I have been thinking that perhaps I might try earning my living at the tournaments in France," Hugh said. He stepped away from the table. "Now, if you gentlemen will excuse me, I have some business I must attend to." He put his hand upon the carved back of his chair and asked with belated courtesy, "Will you be staying to dinner?"

Bernard set his jaw. "Aye," he said. "I will stay for dinner."

"So will I," said Nigel Haslin.

"How delightful," said Hugh.

The two older knights stood on the dais and watched the slender figure of their host as he strode to the door and went outside into the cold March morning.

Alone at the table, they turned to look at each other.

"Was he serious?" Nigel asked incredulously.

Bernard sighed. "One never knows with Hugh."

"I cannot believe he would prefer Matilda to Stephen!"

"He cannot declare for Matilda and continue to hold Keal and his other manors. He knows that. He was just trying to rile us."

"He was very quick to mention the tournaments in France." Nigel was seriously agitated. "It seems to me that he has been thinking about this."

"He won't go to France," Bernard said positively. "Adela would not have liked it, and Hugh never does anything that Adela wouldn't have liked."

The last of the breaking-fast tables had been stacked against the wall and all of the men had left the hall. Several serving girls were sweeping up the rushes on the floor.

Nigel rested his hand upon his belt, in the place where his sword would normally hang. He scowled. "Why would he refuse so to see the Lady Isabel?"

"I have no idea." Bernard gestured that the other man should resume his chair. When both were once more sitting, he asked, "Is there any way we can proceed with this business and leave out taking Hugh to see Stephen?"

"I am not prepared to hand Wiltshire over to the empress," Nigel replied very stiffly.

"I doubt very much that Hugh knows his own mind about who he will support," Bernard said. His pale blue eyes fixed the dark gaze of the other knight. "I can tell you this, though. Hugh was raised by the most honorable man I ever knew. He will make his choice based on his judgment as to what is best for the country, not on what is best for himself."

The serving girls were now sweeping the old rushes into the fire, which flared up with the addition of fresh fuel.

Bernard went on, "From what you have told me of Earl Guy, Hugh is by far the better man."

After a long moment, Nigel shook his head regretfully. "Hugh simply cannot challenge Guy without the backing of the king."

"What about the backing of the Church?" Bernard countered.

Nigel's eyebrows rose. "What do you mean?"

"If Hugh is able positively to name Guy as the man behind his father's murder, and if he can bring some proof to support his accusation, then Guy will be guilty of fratricide. Under those circumstances, the church will force him to forfeit his brother's property."

Nigel made an impatient gesture. "But you have told me that Hugh doesn't remember anything about his early life."

"Perhaps revisiting the scenes of his childhood will bring back his memory," Bernard said. His voice took on a note of gruffness. "Something terrible happened to that boy to make him forget the way he has. In truth, I begin to wonder if perhaps he might have been present when his father was killed."

"Good God!" said Nigel.

"Aye," Bernard said. "Such a sight might well cause a seven-year-old to blank out his memory."

Silence fell as the two men contemplated this harrowing thought.

Finally Nigel said, "What do you want me to do?"

"Convince Hugh to pay a visit to your home. He said earlier in scorn that perhaps you could arrange an interview between him and his uncle. Well . . . perhaps you can."

Nigel gave a short bark of laughter. "You want me to introduce Hugh to Guy as his lost nephew? That would be somewhat dangerous, I fear."

"No, I don't want you to actually introduce them. I want you to bring Hugh to Chippenham disguised as one of your own knights." Bernard gave Nigel a piercing look. "You can surely find some reason to pay a visit to Guy?"

"Well, aye . . . "

"Chippenham was the castle where the old earl was murdered. Isn't that what you said?"

"Aye. Chippenham has ever been the main castle of the earls of Wiltshire. It is where Hugh grew up."

"Then take Hugh there. It is possible that once he has returned to the scenes of his childhood, he will begin to remember things."

"Things that will lead to the truth about his father's murder?"

"Perhaps," said Bernard somberly.

After a minute, Nigel let out his breath in a long sigh. "We could try it, I suppose."

Bernard's eyes went to the door through which Hugh had exited a few moments before. He nodded slowly.

"The question is: How I am going to get him to agree to visit me?" Nigel said. "You must admit that he has proved markedly uncooperative thus far."

"He might agree to a visit if we give him time," Bernard said. "If he has actually been thinking of going off to the French tournaments, he is desperate to get away from here."

"He is not going to be easy to hide," Nigel warned. "Once Guy gets a look at his face, he will recognize him as Roger's son. We may very well be placing Hugh in grave danger."

The scent of herbs drifted to their nostrils as the serving girls began to sprinkle fresh rushes around the hall.

"He will be in worse danger if he remains here," Bernard said bleakly. "If we set him to unraveling a thirteen-year-old mystery, it will at least have the benefit of occupying his mind."

# 4

The forest stretched away darkly on either side of the track, but the road itself was wide enough for the late August sun to reach through the trees and reflect off the mail of Hugh and his party of four as they crossed into Wiltshire to begin the final stage of their journey. Purple-red foxglove blossomed along the edges of the road, and the sound of birds flying busily among the deep green branches of the trees accompanied the riders as they trotted steadily along the forest track. The smell of summer was still in the air.

Here and there the mounted company passed small assarts, cut out of the woods by poor farmers willing to work hard for a little land of their own. Otherwise there was just the forest, rich with game waiting to be hunted by some great lord.

*What am I doing here?*

The thought echoed through Hugh's mind as he rode his white stallion in the midst of the four knights Nigel Haslin had sent to escort him to Nigel's home for the visit Hugh had finally agreed to pay.

It had taken him five months to give in. When Nigel had first proposed that Hugh should come to Somerford, he had refused, as he had refused all the subsequent invitations delivered regularly by one of Nigel's knights.

The last invitation had come on the anniversary of

the Battle of the Standard, exactly one year after Ralf's death. It had caught Hugh at a particularly vulnerable time.

He had thought that after a year, he would be coping better with his life.

He wasn't. In fact, as the days went by, he felt himself growing more and more disconnected from Keal and the people in it.

For one thing, there wasn't enough to keep him occupied. He could run Keal, and Ralf's two other manors, blindfolded with his hands tied behind his back. Bernard had been right when he had said that Hugh was bored. In fact, he was beginning to feel like a sword left to rust in the corner of a castle storeroom.

It had been all right when Ralf was alive. Then they had spent only a part of the year at Keal. The rest of the time Ralf had lived in Lincoln, or traveled the shire administering the king's justice.

Hugh had gone everywhere with Ralf, had learned everything that Ralf could teach him. He had not needed to serve as a squire in some great lord's household. He had learned all about being a knight from his foster father, one of the finest men who ever lived.

The steady four-beat thud of horses trotting on dirt sounded in his ears. The escort of unfamiliar knights rode two abreast, before and behind him. The sun shone on the well-kept brown coats of the stallions in front of him.

*Why did I agree to go to Somerford?*

Hugh drew in a deep breath of the warm, forest-scented air. A small brown bird flew across the track holding a piece of twig in its beak. The twig was larger than the bird.

Hugh drew in another long, steadying breath, and answered his own question.

*Because you think it is entirely possible that you might actually be Hugh de Leon, rightful Earl of Wiltshire.*

It was a thought that had haunted him ever since Nigel had left Keal in March. No matter how hard he tried to push it away, it kept creeping back into the conscious levels of his brain.

He was afraid to find out about his past. On the other hand, he wasn't doing very well with his present, and the future looked even bleaker.

If nothing else, he thought, a visit to Somerford would be a diversion. And it had the added advantage of getting him away from Keal.

One of the knights of his escort, the youngest, pushed his horse forward to trot beside Hugh's.

"We are but a few hours from Somerford," the knight, whose name was Thomas, remarked cheerfully. "We should be there well in time for supper."

Hugh forced himself to smile into the round, freckled face that was beaming at him with such good will. "That is good news," he said.

"We've been lucky that the weather has held so fair," Thomas said next, and Hugh nodded and made a courteous reply.

They were an hour away from Somerford when the headache started. At first Hugh thought it was just the way the sunlight reflected off the mail of the man in front of him that was bothering his eyes. But then the pain moved into his forehead as well.

By the time the walls and high keep of Somerford Castle appeared in the distance, Hugh was in grave distress.

He said nothing to the men of his escort, just loosened his rein and let his stallion follow the other horses as they approached the great wooden stockade that surrounded the castle bailey.

A moat had been dug around the stockade and a drawbridge was let down across it. The guards in the small towers on either side of the bridge shouted a greeting to their fellows as the five mounted horses and one pack horse trotted over the drawbridge, between the high walls, and into the large bailey.

By now the pain in Hugh's head was like a firestorm. The sunlight hurt him unbearably and all he wanted was to get away by himself into some dark place.

His stomach heaved and he was desperately afraid he was going to be sick.

He clutched Rufus's mane with sweaty fingers and, balancing precariously, swung himself down from his saddle.

He took off his helmet, hoping that the lessened weight would help his head.

His mail coif felt as if it were grinding into his skull.

"Hugh! How pleased I am to welcome you to Somerford Castle."

It was Nigel.

Hugh opened his mouth and spoke. What he said must have been relatively sensible, for Nigel smiled and turned to lead the way up the hill and into the keep.

Hugh followed, clammy and shivering and sick, his head thundering with pain.

They entered through a large door, out of the hot sunshine and into a cooler hall.

Hugh shut his eyes.

When he opened them again, a young girl was standing in front of him. "My daughter, Cristen," Nigel was saying.

Hugh looked down into a pair of enormous brown eyes. They looked back clearly and then a quiet, low-pitched voice said, "You're ill. What is wrong?"

"It's nothing," Hugh said. "A headache. It has made me rather dizzy, that's all."

A small hand closed competently around his wrist. "Come with me," Nigel's daughter said.

Hugh went.

She took him across the hall, through two doors, and into a small bedroom.

"You must get out of that mail," she said. "I'll send someone to help you."

Hugh clenched his teeth against the bile he could feel rising in his throat. He would not be sick in front of this girl. *He would not.*

She handed him a bowl.

"Go ahead," she said practically. "You'll probably feel better once you clear out your stomach."

Unfortunately, at this point he had no choice. He gagged, and then the whole of his midday meal came burning up through his throat and into the basin.

When he was finished, she took the mess away from him.

"Here is William," she said quietly. "He will help you out of your mail. Then get into bed."

A young boy came forward and Hugh endured the removal of his mail coif and hauberk, his spurs and leather boots. Finally, when he was clad in only his shirt and leggings, he managed to say, "Thank you," and to crawl mercifully into bed.

The agony did not lessen. If anything, it was getting worse. He shut his eyes against the pale light in the room.

The quiet voice of Nigel's daughter said, "Try to drink this. It might help."

He would drink scalding pitch if it would help.

He pushed himself up onto his elbow and swallowed the liquid in the cup she was holding to his lips. Then he lay back down again.

"I have some cold cloths for your forehead," the girl said.

"Thank you. I'm sorry to be such a nuisance."

"Don't be foolish," she said, and placed something cold on his head.

He shut his eyes again. "Thank you," he said.

She didn't reply, but once again he felt her fingers on his wrist. This time she was feeling his pulse.

After a minute, she released his hand and said, "Are you often subject to headaches?"

"No," he replied in a voice that sounded very far away. "This is the first time."

"It will pass," she said reassuringly. "I have seen this kind of headache before and I promise you that it will pass."

"When?" he asked desperately.

"Within a few hours. Perhaps sooner."

The pain had begun to throb with the beating of his pulse. How could he stand hours more of this?

"Do you want me to go away?" she asked. "Or do you want me to stay?"

And Hugh, who had thought he wanted nothing more in the world than to be alone, heard himself saying, "Stay."

The headache lifted two hours later. There was the slight sensation of a hum in his head, and then, suddenly and absolutely, the pain receded and disappeared.

Slowly he opened his eyes. "It's gone," he said in amazement.

The girl, who had been sitting beside him, periodically replenishing the cold cloths on his forehead, stood up.

"Thank God," she said simply.

He moved his head back and forth on the pillow, testing to see whether or not the pain would return.

Nothing.

He drew in a deep, unsteady breath and let it out again.

"You will be all right now," the girl said. "I have seen these headaches before. When the pain finally goes away, it does not come back."

She reached out and removed the cold cloth that was still lying on his forehead.

Hugh looked up, and for the first time he really saw the girl who had been taking care of him.

She was young, sixteen perhaps, and she was lovely. Her face was a perfect, delicate oval, her nose was small and straight, her mouth was tender and yet it looked as if it could also be stern. But it was her eyes that caught and held him; huge brown eyes that looked at him with such directness, such honesty.

She looked at him as if she could see into his very soul.

And Hugh, who revealed himself to no one, looked back.

"I'm sorry," he said. "I don't remember your name."

"My name is Cristen."

He swung his feet to the floor and, slowly and carefully, stood up. She was small; the top of her head reached only to his mouth and he was not a tall man. Her shining brown hair was center-parted and hung rain-straight to her waist. It had the texture of fine silk.

"What is the time?" he asked. For some reason, he knew he did not have to make polite conversation with this girl.

"It is late, after nine o'clock."

He ran his fingers through his hair, which was damp from the cold, wet cloths. "What must your father think of me?"

"He thinks you were sick, and he will be happy to hear that you are better." She bent to lift a basket full of cloths from the floor. "Would you like me to send him to see you or would you rather wait until the morning?"

Hugh would much rather wait until the morning.

"If he wishes me to come to the hall, of course I will do so," he said.

She gave him a severe look. "You are not going into the hall tonight. If you wish to see my father, he will come to you."

"I shall be happy to see him if that is what he would like," Hugh responded stoically.

She read him unerringly. "Father Adolphus from Malmesbury Abbey is visiting us, so we will begin the day tomorrow with mass in the chapel at seven. I will tell Father you will see him then."

"Thank you," Hugh said. He did not try to disguise his relief. "You have been very kind."

"I will send a boy with water so you can wash," she said. "Do you wish something to eat?"

He shook his head, astonished that he felt no pain with the movement. "My stomach is still somewhat uneasy."

"Would you like me to fix you a potion for it?"

"Thank you, but no. I think all that I need is some sleep."

She nodded agreement. "I shall wish you a good night, then."

"My name is Hugh," he said gravely.

At that, she smiled. "Good night, Hugh."

And he, who so rarely smiled himself, felt his own lips curve in reply. "Good night," he said. "Cristen."

Hugh slept deeply and dreamlessly, only waking when a squire came into his bedroom with water and fresh clothes. He put on his linen drawers while he was still in bed and then he rose to wash in the basin of cold water the boy had brought.

After washing, he put on a clean shirt and hose. Over these went a crimson wool surcoat, with Adela's handiwork embroidered on its hem and the edges of its long, tight sleeves. Around his waist he buckled a plain leather belt and on his feet he slipped the soft leather shoes that were the proper footwear for indoors. He ran Adela's fine wooden comb quickly through his short black hair, then said to the squire, "Can you direct me to the chapel?"

"It is up the stairs," the boy told him. "If you will come with me, I will take you."

"Thank you," Hugh said, and allowed Nigel's squire to lead him out of the bedroom and into a room that looked as if it might be the family solar. They passed through another door that took them into the great hall. As he crossed the rush-strewn wooden floor in the wake of the servant, Hugh made himself look around, trying to distract himself from his dread of going into the chapel.

The hall was a large room with decent-sized windows thrown open to the summer air. Colorful rugs hung on the stone walls to keep out drafts. There was a large fireplace set into one wall, and two balls of gray fur lay curled in the rushes in front of the empty grate.

The castle cats were taking a rest from their rodent-catching duties, Hugh thought.

The high table was already in place for the morning's breaking fast, but the trestle tables for the lesser folk were still stacked along the walls.

The room smelled clean. Adela would have approved, Hugh thought.

"This way," the squire said, and Hugh put his foot on the sturdy wooden staircase that would take him to the third level of the castle.

He saw the open door of the chapel as soon as he reached the top of the stairs. Servants were filing in, but Hugh scarcely noticed them. He was too busy trying to repress the feeling he always got in his stomach whenever he entered a castle chapel.

"The master and Lady Cristen are already seated in the front," his youthful escort murmured, and obediently Hugh made his way down the narrow aisle. He stepped into the carved wooden pew next to Nigel.

His host gave him a grave smile and then turned his attention to the altar.

Hugh stared straight ahead, first at the carved crucifix that hung on the wall over the altar, then at the altar itself, covered with an embroidered linen cloth and topped with gold candlesticks and a carved wooden tabernacle.

The too-familiar feeling began to creep over him again: part terror, part anger, part utter desolation.

He was all right in a large church, but in a chapel . . .

*Why do I always feel like this?*

Instinctively he knew that he did not want to learn the answer to that question.

*The earl was killed in a chapel.*

He did not want to think about that, either. It was fruitless to think about that. He couldn't remember.

The priest had come out onto the altar. He faced the tabernacle, raised his hands and began to intone the prayer that always opened mass: "*In nomine patris . . .*"

The congregation, Hugh included, made the sign of the cross.

When mass was finished, Hugh filed out of the chapel with Nigel and Cristen.

"How are you feeling this morning?" his host asked, scanning Hugh's tense face with narrowed eyes.

"Much better," Hugh replied. "I apologize for arriving in such a pitiful state."

"You don't look well," Nigel said bluntly.

Hugh's nostrils pinched together. "I assure you, I am fine."

The three of them began to descend the stairs to the great hall, where the servants were busily setting up the trestle tables for the morning's breaking fast.

Halfway down the stairs, they were met by two dogs who came racing to shove their noses into Cristen's hands. The girl laughed, caressed their heads briefly, then turned to Hugh. "You must allow me to introduce you. This is Cedric," she nodded toward the shaggy brown mongrel with one torn ear that was pressing against her leg. "And this is Ralf."

Hugh felt his eyes widen at the mention of the name. He looked at the large, black-and-white, freckle-nosed dog and, unconsciously, his hand went up to encircle the gold cross he had worn around his throat ever since his foster father's death.

Nigel said with resignation, "My daughter should have a pure-bred, of course, but these are the dogs she wanted."

"There is always someone who will take a purebred," Cristen said briskly. "Cedric and Ralf need me."

She bestowed one more pat on each dog and then resumed walking down the stairs.

"Cristen rescued Ralf from being drowned in the river when he was a puppy and Cedric came wandering up to the castle walls one night, injured and crying, and she insisted that we take him in." Nigel's voice held a mixture of amusement and pride as he spoke of his daughter and her animals.

They had reached the bottom of the stairs and now they began to walk across the hall floor toward the high table. Hugh noticed that Ralf had a noticeable limp.

A servant stepped up to Cristen's side and she stopped to speak to him. "How is Berta this morning?"

The man smiled at her, revealing two missing front teeth. "She is feeling better, my lady. She wanted to come down to the morning meal but I told her she had best not stir until you gave her leave."

Cristen nodded. "You did well, Martin. I will go to see her after the breaking of fast."

"Thank you, my lady."

Hugh looked with curiosity into the small oval face of the girl who was walking beside him flanked by her dogs. "Are you a doctor then, Lady Cristen?"

She laughed. "No. I merely have some knowledge of herbs, and the castle folk find me helpful."

"Not just the castle folk," her father interjected. They had reached the dais by now, and he gestured Hugh to the chair on his right. "Cristen's skill as a healer is well known in all the surrounding countryside."

Hugh said, "So that is why you were able to take care of me so ably yesterday."

The two dogs established themselves with comfortable familiarity behind Cristen's chair. She said, "If you would like, Hugh, I will show you my herb garden after we have broken fast."

Hugh looked at her. "I should like that very much."

Hugh stood before the high table, waiting for Cristen to return from her visit to the sick Berta. The cats were gone from in front of the fireplace and the hall was filled with servants busily scouring the trestle tables and moving them back against the walls so they would not be in the way of the morning activities.

Sunlight slanted in through the open windows on the right wall, dappling the heads of the busy servants.

Thomas, the young knight who had been part of Hugh's escort, passed in front of him and offered a tentative smile. Grave-faced, Hugh nodded back.

*What am I doing here?*

It was the thought that had haunted Hugh ever since Ralf's death. Night after night, he had stood in front of the fireplace at Keal, staring at his own hall, at his own dependents, and the thought had risen in his brain.

*What am I doing here?*

Accompanying that question was the terrifying sensation that he had been separated from the rest of the people in the room by a wall of ice. He could see them clearly enough, but he could not communicate with them. No matter what he did, he could not break through the frozen wall that isolated him in such desolate loneliness. The despair that welled up inside him at these moments was almost unbearable. One day it would be truly unbearable, and what would he do then?

A warm hand touched his arm.

A white-tipped tail slapped against his leg.

He looked down into a pair of clear brown eyes.

"I'm ready," Cristen said. "Do you still want to see my garden?"

Hugh inhaled deeply. "Aye," he said. "I do."

# 5

The morning was pleasantly warm, with only a few fleecy white clouds floating across a serene blue sky. As Hugh walked down the castle stairs with Cristen, he looked around and for the first time actually saw the outside of Somerford Castle. He had been in no condition to notice much of anything yesterday.

Somerford had obviously been built as a traditional motte and bailey castle, although it had been added to as the years had gone by. The original wooden keep had been replaced by a three-story stone structure situated on a hill that overlooked a swiftly flowing stream, which Cristen informed him led into the River Avon a few miles away. Around the top of the hill, or motte, was a ten-foot-high wall that had also probably once been made of timber but was now built of local stone. Four guards stood duty on the four sides of the wall's sentry walk, which afforded them an excellent view of the surrounding countryside.

A sloping bridge that finished in a drawbridge led over a filled moat from the motte to the level lower ground of the bailey. Hugh walked across the bridge with Cristen, their feet, encased now in outdoor boots, making a hollow sound on the wooden planks. The dogs paced along at Cristen's heels, as close as shadows.

Looking around, Hugh estimated that the bailey of

Somerford probably covered about four acres. It contained the usual necessities of castle life: cookhouse, bakehouse, brewhouse, armory, barns and pens for cattle and horses, grooms' living quarters, and workshops for the skilled craftsmen who served the castle.

Nigel maintained a guard of resident knights, but Hugh thought that this castle was more a home than it was a military bastion.

All that might change with the coming war.

Unlike the inner wall surrounding the motte, which was made of stone, the outer wall of the bailey was constructed of the original wood. Hugh remembered passing over the outer moat and through the bailey drawbridge yesterday. He didn't remember anything else.

As they walked along, Cristen was greeted respectfully by each homespun clad workman they passed.

No, it was more than respectfully, Hugh corrected himself. It was fondly.

"My garden is this way," Cristen said to him as she led the way toward a part of the bailey that was blocked off by a five-foot-high wooden fence. He trailed after her like one of her dogs as she led the way into her private domain.

The first thing that struck Hugh as he walked through the gate was the heady, aromatic fragrance of the herbs. He looked around and saw row upon row of plants, all neatly laid out one after the other. Along the far wall of the garden there grew a profusion of rosebushes that were in full bloom. He could smell their perfume mixed in with the herbs.

Adela had loved roses.

Against another wall there stood a small wooden shed.

Cristen saw him looking at it. "The shed is where I dry my herbs and make my medicinal potions."

"You are young to be so knowledgeable," Hugh said.

"The garden was actually started by my mother. She was interested in herbs and healing and she passed her knowledge along to me."

She tipped her head up to smile at him. This morning she wore her hair plaited into two long braids and her sleeveless blue outer tunic was worn over a long-sleeved robe of red. It was too warm for a cloak.

"I need to boil up another cough mixture for Berta, if you don't mind waiting," she said.

"Of course not." He followed her to the shed and looked inside. Dried herbs hung from the roof and shelves lined the walls. They were filled with bottles, some already filled and stoppered, some still open, waiting to be filled. A small charcoal brazier stood near the door, and there was a bench along the wall beside it.

"Pull the bench into the sun and sit down, Hugh," she said. "This won't take very long."

He did as she suggested and watched her as she competently crushed some ingredients together and put them in a bottle with wine and honey.

"Most frequently I use crushed almonds and chestnut leaves for coughs," she said. "As Berta seems to be responding well to the mixture, I won't try to change it."

Hugh sat in silence, feeling the warmth of the sun on his back and shoulders. The shed and the garden seemed very peaceful, and he felt some of the chapel-induced tension begin to drain away. The dogs stretched out in the sun behind him.

Cristen took tinder and flint from its place on a shelf, lit the charcoal brazier, and placed the flagon she had filled on the heat. Then she came to join him on the bench.

"Have you ever met the Earl of Wiltshire?" Hugh heard himself asking.

"Aye," she returned. "I have met him a number of times."

Hugh gazed fixedly at the flagon on the brazier in front of him. "Tell me," he said, "is it true that I look like him?"

She answered matter-of-factly, "You have his eyes, Hugh, but the rest of his features are heavier than yours, more massive."

He continued to stare at the flagon. "Your father thinks I am the boy who was kidnapped from the castle thirteen years ago."

He did not know why he was talking to this girl like this, but for some reason he felt comfortable with her.

"I know," she said.

At last he turned to look at her. "Why did he invite me here, Cristen? What does he hope to gain by it?"

She smoothed her hands along the fine blue wool of her outer tunic. "Justice, I think," she answered. "My father has always thought that Guy was behind his brother's death. It has angered him to see a man whom he regarded as a murderer sitting in Lord Roger's place."

"Your father thought highly of Lord Roger?"

She smiled. "All the world thought highly of Lord Roger. He was a great crusader, you know."

"No," Hugh replied slowly. "I didn't know."

"Father has always thought it particularly shameful that such a man should be murdered in his own chapel."

Hugh's eyes narrowed. "Your father also wants an earl who will pledge Wiltshire to Stephen, and I told him that I was not sure that I could do that."

"Why not?" Cristen asked curiously. "Are you an adherent of the empress?"

Hugh shrugged. "I know little about the empress, but I think that her brother, Robert of Gloucester, would be a better king than Stephen."

"My father thinks Robert of Gloucester is a good man also," Cristen said agreeably. "But Gloucester is a bastard and so cannot be king. He is supporting the right of his half-sister and her son."

Hugh stretched his legs in front of him and didn't reply.

"What don't you like about Stephen?" Cristen asked.

Her voice was merely interested.

Hugh stared at his boots and replied, "He is indecisive, and at this point in time what England desperately needs is a king who is strong. Stephen needs to stop this rebellion before it starts, and he is not doing the right things to accomplish that end."

"He has taken all the castles that rebelled against him," Cristen pointed out.

"He has not taken Bristol and he needs to take Bristol. As soon as Gloucester returns from Normandy, he will make Bristol his headquarters, and Stephen cannot afford to give him that kind of advantage. Once Gloucester is established in Bristol, all of those castles that Stephen has taken will fall once more to the empress."

Cristen moved her foot back and forth on the dirt floor. It was a very small foot, Hugh noticed, and the boot she wore was scuffed.

Behind them one of the dogs began to snore.

"My father says that Stephen is very gallant," Cristen said.

Hugh returned grimly, "What we need at the moment is a king who is ruthless, not gallant."

"Ruthless is an ugly word."

"Civil war is even uglier. It is the little people who will be hurt the worst by such a war, the very people whom the king has sworn to defend."

Cristen sighed. "It always seems to be the little people who get hurt."

"Unfortunately," Hugh said.

The snoring behind them stopped as the dog shifted position.

Cristen said, "My father said that Gloucester and the empress will be coming to England any day now and that Stephen has posted troops at all the main ports to repulse them."

"They won't try to land at any of the main ports," Hugh said. "Gloucester is too clever for that."

Cristen got up to go and check on her potion. Evidently she judged it not yet ready, for she left it on the brazier and returned to the bench. She folded her hands in her lap and Hugh noticed that the tips of her fingers were stained with green from the leaves she had crushed.

"Where do you think they will land?" she asked curiously.

"It could be any of several places. Arundel, perhaps. Matilda's stepmother, Adeliza, holds the castle there."

"I don't like to think about it," Cristen confessed. "The whole idea of war is frightening."

"Aye," Hugh said somberly. "It is."

A comfortable silence fell between them. On the brazier the liquid in the flagon began to bubble.

Hugh inhaled the warm, herb-scented air.

"I don't know why I agreed to come here," he said slowly. "I have been thinking ever since I left home that I must be mad."

"Not mad," Cristen said. "Just confused, I imagine. It's a little overwhelming to be suddenly told you might be somebody else. And I think it's only natural to want to find out if it might be true."

She got up and went to take the flagon off the brazier, using a thick cloth to shield her hand from the bottle's heat.

He watched her for a while in silence.

Then, "Did your father tell you that I can't remember anything of my first seven years?" he asked.

"Aye," she said. Her back was to him as she carefully placed the hot flagon on a tile that stood next to the brazier. Her braids were bound by scarlet ribbons that matched her undertunic. The nape of her neck looked as tender as a child's.

"Have you ever heard of such a thing before?"

She turned around to face him. "Many people have little memory of their early childhood."

He didn't reply, just regarded her steadily.

"You must have remembered that your name was Hugh," she said.

"Perhaps it wasn't. Perhaps it was something else. Perhaps I am not this Hugh de Leon after all."

"There is always that possibility," she agreed.

Her large brown eyes were luminous as she regarded him.

"I think you need to find out," she said. "I think that's why you came here."

His face was bleak. "I think perhaps you are right."

Nigel stood in front of the blacksmith's hut holding the lead line of a large brown stallion, his eyes on Hugh and his daughter as they crossed the bailey together. As he watched, Cristen glanced up at the boy next to her and said something. Hugh flashed her a smile in response.

Nigel stared in amazement at that brilliant, youthful look and shook his head.

Cristen was working her magic again.

His daughter was another reason that Nigel would be happy to see Lord Guy replaced as Earl of Wiltshire. Three times in the last two years Guy had proposed matches for Cristen and three times Nigel had refused them.

All of Guy's choices had been men at least twenty years older than Cristen. More importantly, they had been men whom Nigel did not like, men who were Guy's followers, whom Guy had wanted to reward with the desirable honor of Somerford.

Cristen was seventeen and she should be wed, but she was his only child and Nigel was not going to hand her over, along with her dowry of Somerford, to a man he did not trust.

It was not always easy these days to find a suitable match for a daughter. Because of the Norman custom that decreed that all of a family's holdings be passed down to the eldest son, it was only the eldest son in a family who was eligible to marry. Penniless younger sons usually remained bachelors. This left a limited number of potential husbands for the daughters of the nobility, and competition was fierce. The convents were filled with girls whose families had not been able to give them a good enough dowry to purchase a husband.

But Cristen would eventually have Somerford, so Nigel knew he should have little trouble finding a husband for her. The trouble lay in securing the agreement of his overlord, Guy, to Nigel's choice.

If Hugh became Earl of Wiltshire, he would owe his position to Nigel. Under such circumstances, Nigel didn't think that Hugh would object to Nigel's choice of a husband for his daughter.

Cristen had seen him and now she changed course and began to walk in his direction. Hugh and the dogs followed her lead.

The forge was going and the sound of the smith's hammer rang out in the warm summer air. Nigel's favorite horse was being shod this morning and he had come to see that the shoeing went well. Byrony had been becoming increasingly more difficult for the blacksmith to handle.

As Cristen and Hugh came up to the forge, the big, dark brown stallion snorted and aimed a kick right at the smith's head.

With a sharp curse, the smith leaped out of the way.

"Oh dear," Cristen said. "Is Byrony up to his tricks again?"

"He hates getting shoes, especially on his hind feet," Nigel said. He looked at Hugh. "He's been this way ever since I bought him and it seems that every time we shoe him he gets worse."

Hugh watched for a few minutes as the blacksmith picked up Byrony's off hind and tried to hammer in another nail.

The horse kicked out again.

Again the blacksmith leaped out of the way and cursed.

"You're holding his foot too high and it's hurting him," Hugh said quietly.

The blacksmith, a stocky man wearing a leather apron, looked at Hugh truculently. "I been shoeing horses for fifteen years and more. I'm holding his foot like I always do."

"He is probably more sensitive than other horses, and he is not willing to suffer," Hugh said. "You need to work with him differently."

The blacksmith glared at Hugh.

Nigel said, "What do you suggest?"

"If I were you, I would begin by getting him used to having his feet picked up without pain," Hugh said. "Just lift them slightly for one or two seconds when you bring him back to his stable after a ride. Praise him. Give him a treat. Gradually you should be able to increase the amount of time he will allow you to hold them. Just be careful you don't lift them too high."

Nigel frowned skeptically.

"Why not try it?" Hugh said. "You have nothing to lose. The way you are going now, you soon won't be able to get a shoe on him at all."

"Hugh is right, Father," Cristen said. She rubbed Byrony's soft nose. "Poor fellow," she said. "Is Giles hurting you?"

The horse snorted, as if he agreed.

"Not as much as he is hurting me, my lady," the blacksmith said gloomily.

"The more you fight with him over this, the more frightened and defensive he will become," Hugh said.

"I suppose it's worth a try," Nigel conceded. "He's a good horse, but he will be useless to me if he can't be shod."

"If you want, I will work with him," Hugh said. "I have always gotten along well with horses."

"Very well," Nigel said after a minute. "Thank you, Hugh."

"Shall I finish this shoe, Sir Nigel?" the blacksmith asked. "There's only the one more nail to put in."

"Aye, finish it, but try not to lift his leg so high."

"Aye, Sir Nigel," the blacksmith returned even more gloomily than before.

By the time Giles finally managed to get the last shoe on Byrony, it was time for dinner. Nigel, Cristen, and Hugh left the blacksmith's hut and began to walk toward the bridge that connected the bailey to the castle.

"This afternoon I thought I would show you some of the farms that belong to Somerford," Nigel said to Hugh as they crossed the last part of the bridge, the drawbridge. The two men were walking side by side. Cristen was behind them with her dogs.

"That would be enjoyable," Hugh replied courteously.

"And tomorrow morning I will conduct a knightly practice session, which I hope you will join," Nigel went on. "We have been working hard for the last few weeks to prepare for the tournament."

Hugh's chin lifted. "Tournament?" he said. "What tournament are you talking about? Tournaments have been outlawed in England for years."

"Well, strictly speaking, it is not a tournament at all, although in many ways it mimics one," Nigel returned. "It is held every year at Chippenham Castle by Earl Guy in conjunction with the fair put on by the town in honor of their local saint."

The guards on the inner wall were changing. The men who had just been relieved of duty were descending the steps from the sentry walk to the courtyard.

Hugh said, "Surely you do not expect me to accompany you to this tournament?"

"Why not?" Nigel replied. "It will be the perfect opportunity for you to see your old home."

They stepped off the drawbridge onto the hard-packed dirt of the courtyard.

Hugh was frowning.

"You can go to Chippenham as part of my retinue of knights," Nigel said reasonably. "There will be no reason for you to stand out from the others. It is a perfect opportunity for you to see the earl and to judge for yourself whether or not I have exaggerated your resemblance to him. It will also give you a chance to visit the castle where you spent the first seven years of your life."

Hugh did not reply.

"You have nothing to lose and everything to gain," Nigel said.

Still Hugh said nothing.

Cristen moved up to walk beside him.

"I have to go, too," she said with resignation. "Lord Guy likes to have ladies present to admire all the manly exhibitions."

A corner of Hugh's mouth twitched with amusement.

"You don't sound as if you approve of these 'manly exhibitions,'" he said.

"Everyone sweats so much," Cristen said.

Hugh's mouth twitched again.

She added, "And the festivities in the castle hall tend to get rather boisterous."

"Guy's hall is well known for its debauchery," Nigel said disapprovingly. "He keeps a large household and there is always much gaming and intemperance. Chippenham was a very different place under the old earl. Roger was an austere, ascetic man. The two of them may look alike, but temperamentally no brothers could be more different."

"Cristen told me earlier that Earl Roger had been on crusade," Hugh said. "I did not know that."

Nigel sighed with faint exasperation. "It is the greatest pity that this present generation has forgotten the names of all the great men who retook Jerusalem for the church. Let me tell you, Hugh, that Roger de Leon, your father, was the one who first breached the gates of the holy city. He was a living legend among his own generation."

"I see," Hugh said. His face was closed and still.

"The last time we were at Chippenham, Father had to rescue me from the unwelcome embrace of a very large, very drunken knight," Cristen said. "This year, you can look after me as well, Hugh."

He smiled down at her. "I should be glad to," he said.

# 6

The rain held off until Simon of Evesham and his escort of five knights were almost at the doors of the Benedictine convent in Worcester.

"God's bones," Simon said to the young knight who rode by his side. "Ten more minutes and we would have escaped it." He scowled with annoyance and pulled the hood of his light wool cloak up over his head.

"I don't mind the rain," Philip replied. "I think it feels refreshing. The road has been so dusty that my throat hurts." He held his face up to the sky as if he would drink in the flow of water cascading from the dark clouds above.

Simon grunted and pulled his hood even further forward. "All I can say is that there had better be a good reason for my sister to have sent for me at such a time. I don't want to be away from Evesham for long. I expect to have news any day now that Earl Robert has landed."

There was a stream in front of them, with a narrow bridge that required their party of six to file across it one by one.

Ducks floated on the rain-dappled, greenish water and an old boat was moored along the far shore.

When they had reached the other side of the bridge and Philip was once more riding next to Simon, the young knight said, "It's been a long wait, almost a full year since the earl formally renounced his allegiance to Stephen and declared for Matilda."

"Aye, well, he had to settle his estates in Normandy before he could come back to England," Simon said.

The rain began to fall harder.

"You have no idea what Lady Isabel wants?" Philip asked. He was on comfortable terms with Simon, having served in the lord of Evesham's household since he was a child of eight.

"I have no idea," Simon replied grumpily. "My sister has communicated with me very rarely since she insisted on immuring herself in that convent. I cannot imagine why she is so insistent that she must see me now."

In the distance, Philip saw the spire of the abbey church appear over the trees. He pointed it out to his lord.

"We're almost there," he said. "You shall know soon enough."

Isabel de Leon's brother and his retinue rode up to the gatehouse of the convent just as the bells were ringing for vespers. The portress told them that they were expected and that rooms in the guest house had been prepared. She summoned grooms to take their horses, and a lay sister to show them the way to their quarters.

Simon could see Isabel after vespers in the cloister, the portress said as they prepared to follow the lay sister across the now-muddy courtyard. In the meanwhile, a cold collation would be served to them in the guest house hall.

"Thank you, Sister," Simon responded courteously. "Something to eat would be greatly appreciated."

After they had entered the guest house, Philip accompanied Simon to his room in order to relieve him of his mail. Worcester was officially under the governance of Stephen, and it was wise for any person who might be suspected of favoring Earl Robert and the empress to tred carefully in this part of the world. Simon's whole party had ridden from Evesham wearing mail shirts under their surcoats.

The room Simon had been given was scarcely luxurious, containing only a bed, one chair, and a small table with a plain pottery washbasin, a pitcher with water in it, and a solitary cup. Philip glanced out the single small window as he waited for Simon to drink some water.

The stone of the abbey buildings looked silvery in the steadily falling rain. He looked across the courtyard at the church and imagined the nuns in their places for vespers, hidden from public view behind a carved altar screen.

Philip knew very little about his lord's sister except that she had once been married to the Earl of Wiltshire and that after his death she had chosen to reside in a convent rather than to marry again. The lords of Evesham had always been patrons of the abbey of Worcester, which was why she had been sent to this particular institution.

In all these years, however, Isabel had never taken the vows that would have made her a nun. For the last thirteen years she had been content to live as a humble lay sister, working with her hands, doing menial tasks that Philip knew his lord disapproved of.

Simon put down the cup from which he had been drinking and said, "I am ready for you to undress me, Philip."

They had brought no squires with them, so it was Philip's place to perform a squire's service for his lord.

The young knight went to Simon, unbuckled his belt, and lifted off his sword. Next Simon raised his arms so that the blue wool surcoat could be lifted over his head, revealing the mail shirt he wore beneath. Philip laid aside the surcoat and began to unfasten the shoulder buckles that held the mail hauberk in place. Once that was off and Simon was standing in just his linen shirt and leggings, he knelt to undo the spurs that were strapped to his lord's boots.

There came a knock upon the door and Philip went to open it. A young girl stood there holding a pitcher of water and a towel. He thanked her courteously, took the items, and went to pour the water into the basin so that Simon could wash.

Once Simon was dressed in fresh clothes, Philip went to the room he was sharing with the other knights and one of them helped him take off his own mail. Then they all went down to supper in the small dining hall of the guest house, where they were the only guests in attendance.

After supper was over, the same young girl who had brought the water earlier arrived to escort Simon to his sister. Philip and the other knights stayed behind in the dining hall, finishing their wine and talking in carefully lowered voices.

None of them was completely comfortable being lodged in a convent.

Finally, after the wine was done, two of the knights announced that they were going to go to the stables to check on the horses. The rain had stopped and Philip, who wanted an excuse to get out into the cool evening air, decided to go along with them. He was at the door of the dining hall when he was intercepted by a young novice dressed in a shapeless brown wool dress, who told him that his lord wished him to come to the cloister.

The girl was wearing high wooden pattens to protect her feet from the mud, and Philip followed her across the yard and around to the cloister at the back of the church.

The Worcester Abbey cloister formed a perfect square of stone arches around an open courtyard. Sitting in the middle of the courtyard upon a stone bench were a man and a woman.

The evening sun slanted over the west archways of the cloister and fell on the grass of the courtyard, which still sparkled with drops from the rain that had fallen earlier. The air smelled fresh and clean. Philip crossed the courtyard and came to a halt in front of the two on the bench.

"You wished to see me, my lord?" he asked respectfully.

"Aye," Simon returned. He turned to the woman beside him on the bench and said, "This is the knight I told you about, Isabel."

For the first time Philip turned his eyes to look at Simon's sister.

He saw a face that, while no longer young, was still heartbreakingly beautiful. Isabel's veil concealed the color of her hair, but her perfectly arched eyebrows were a glossy black. Her eyes were dark dark blue. The merciless light from the setting sun exposed fine lines at the corners of those eyes, but nothing would ever detract from the perfect bone structure that lay beneath her delicate fair skin.

Her eyes were regarding him searchingly, and there was a definite look of strain in their dark blue depths. He met her gaze squarely and tried not to look as dazzled as he felt.

She turned back to her brother and said a little doubtfully, "He is very young, Simon."

"He is a very competent young man, Isabel," Simon replied.

Philip stood in front of them and waited.

After a minute she said, "I had hoped you could go yourself."

"It is impossible." Simon sounded grim. "I expect to hear from Earl Robert any day now. I cannot be away from Evesham."

A faint frown dented the skin between her perfect eyebrows.

"Are you absolutely certain that you want to do this, Isabel?" Simon asked. "Frankly, I think Nigel Haslin is so desperate to replace Guy with a new earl that he is seeing in this boy only what he wishes to see. There is small likelihood that Hugh is still alive after all these years."

"Nigel would not have sent to tell me about this boy if he was not certain that he is my son," Isabel said. Her voice was quiet, but Philip could hear the emotion that she was trying to keep in check. "He is a kind man, Nigel Haslin. He would not seek to torment me with a pretender."

"Isabel . . ." Simon said wearily.

"I have never believed that Hugh was dead," Isabel said. "They never found his body."

"If he was alive, he would have tried to reach you," Simon said.

"Perhaps not." Isabel's voice was full of pain. "I was not a good mother to him, Simon. It is quite possible that he did not trust me to take care of him." She looked down at the tips of the brown leather shoes that peered out from beneath her brown wool skirt. "I did not take very good care of him when he was a child."

"You did the best that you could," Simon said gruffly.

She shook her head.

Simon sighed. "I suppose you will not rest easy until we have sent someone to identify this boy."

She swallowed. Philip had to restrain himself from reaching out a hand to comfort her. "No," she said. "I won't."

"Very well," Simon said resignedly. He looked at Philip. "The situation is thus. Thirteen years ago my sister's husband, the Earl of Wiltshire, was killed in the chapel at Chippenham. That very same day, her son, the heir to the earldom, disappeared. We believe he was kidnapped by the man who killed the earl. Several days later, the body of the kidnapper was returned to Chippenham, the apparent victim of outlaws on the road, but nothing has ever been heard of Hugh."

Philip had always known that there were strange circumstances surrounding the death of the previous Earl of Wiltshire, but he had never heard the full story before.

"Jesu," he breathed. Then, remembering that he was in a convent, "I beg your pardon, my lady."

Isabel said nothing.

Simon grunted. "The Lady Isabel has just received word from one of the Earl of Wiltshire's vassals, a man named Nigel Haslin, that he has discovered a boy whom he thinks may be my nephew, Hugh. Nigel has asked the Lady Isabel to send someone whom she trusts to see if he can identify him."

"And is there such a man?" Philip asked.

"Aye," Isabel said. "The priest who was chaplain at Chippenham during the years that Hugh was a child." Unmistakable pain deepened the lines in her face. "He knows my son well. He will know if this boy is indeed Hugh."

Philip said diffidently, "How old was your son when he was kidnapped, my lady?"

"Seven," Isabel said.

Philip hesitated, glancing at Simon. Simon's face was stoic, giving nothing away.

"Boys of seven can change beyond recognition in thirteen years," Philip said gently. "It is entirely possible that it will be impossible to say for certain whether this boy is your son or no."

Isabel shook her head sharply. "Bones don't change," she said, "and Hugh looked just like me."

After a moment, during which he tried in vain to picture a male Isabel, Philip asked, "What do you wish me to do?"

"Father Anselm is presently serving in the cathedral at Winchester," Isabel said. "I want you to escort him to Nigel Haslin's home of Somerford Castle, where he can meet with Hugh. Father Anselm will know if this boy is truly my son."

"But my lady . . ." Philip looked once again to his lord, and once again encountered that stoic, unhelpful face. Simon clearly did not approve of this plan, but just as clearly he was going to go along with it.

Philip began carefully, "If this boy is indeed your son, as he claims to be . . ."

At that Simon finally spoke. "You don't understand, Philip. The boy makes no such claim. It is Nigel who thinks he is the heir to Wiltshire."

Now Philip was thoroughly bewildered. "You have the right of it, my lord. I don't understand."

"This Hugh was the foster son of the Sheriff of Lincoln," Simon explained. His voice took on a noticeably sarcastic note. "Evidently the sheriff found him starving in the streets of Lincoln when he was a child and took him in. He told the sheriff that he did not remember who he was."

Philip stared. "He did not remember?"

"That is what he said. That is what he still says."

"It is perfectly possible that he is telling the truth," Isabel said sadly. "There is no reason for him to want to remember, and many reasons for him to need to forget."

"I find it hard to believe that one would forget that one was the Earl of Wiltshire and the Count of Linaux," Simon said grimly. "I don't want you to get your hopes set upon this boy, Isabel. It is most likely that he is some clever pretender playing on Nigel Haslin's desire to rid himself of Lord Guy."

Isabel bowed her head and said softly, "For fourteen years I have done penance for my wrongs to my son, and for fourteen years I have prayed that he would be returned to me. Perhaps God has finally answered my prayers."

Simon made an impatient gesture. "All right, Isabel. We will send the priest to look at this boy. But I want you to promise me that if Father Anselm returns to you and says that he is not Hugh, you will accept the priest's judgment."

Isabel's beautiful face was very pale. "Father Anselm wants Hugh to be alive as much as I do," she said. "I will believe what he tells me."

Philip traveled to Winchester by himself. Over his hauberk he wore a simple brown surcoat, and if he was stopped, the story he had prepared was that he was a knight in the service of Nigel Haslin. Winchester was a city that was firmly in the grasp of King Stephen; the Bishop of Winchester was in fact Stephen's brother. It would not be conducive to Philip's health for anyone to find out that he was a knight of the household of Simon of Evesham. All knew that Simon was going to declare for Earl Robert and the empress.

This was another reason that Simon had sent Philip to escort the priest and had not come himself. Philip's face was unknown in Winchester; Simon's was not.

As the young knight rode through the rolling country north of Winchester, the September forest was filled with white plovers and skylarks, and the chalk stream of the River Itchen flowed gently southward on its peaceful way to the Channel. Philip's thoughts, however, were not as pleasant as his surroundings.

He was on a fool's errand. Simon knew it. Philip knew it. Apparently the only one who did not know it was the Lady Isabel.

Philip hoped to God that this priest would be sensible enough to know it, too.

This young man whom Nigel Haslin had produced in the hopes of pushing Guy le Gaucher out of his earldom must be very clever indeed, Philip thought. What a stroke of genius, to say that he did not remember who he was. It was a perfect excuse for not knowing the answers to questions that Hugh de Leon would be expected to know. Philip could almost admire such cleverness, if it were not going to result in such obvious pain to the Lady Isabel.

She must have been scarcely more than a child herself when Hugh was born. And to have spent the last fourteen years locked away from the world, doing penance for some imagined wrong she had done to her son! It did not bear thinking on.

*I would like to wring this pretender's neck,* Philip thought fiercely. *And Nigel Haslin's as well, for allowing political considerations to bring that woman pain.*

The afternoon was cool and bright when Philip entered the city of Winchester through the Kings Gate, which lay right beside the cathedral close. He gave a coin to a youngster who was standing in the busy cathedral courtyard and told him to hold his horse. Then he began asking around for Father Anselm.

At last he found the priest saying confessions in a carved booth in the rear of the cool dark church. There were three old women already waiting outside the confessional, and Philip got into line behind them to wait his turn.

The incense Philip had smelled when he first entered the church was overlaid by the overpowering smell of garlic that emanated from the old lady standing in front of him. Philip tried to breathe through his mouth and was much relieved when it was her turn to enter into the confessional booth.

She took forever.

How many sins could one old woman commit? Philip thought impatiently, shifting from one foot to the other in an effort to get comfortable.

The woman who had joined the line behind him heard the clink of his mail shirt and gave a fiercely disapproving snort. Obviously she did not approve of him wearing mail inside the house of God.

Philip folded his arms, bent his uncovered blond head, and stared moodily at the tips of his dusty boots. He thought that he would have to get the priest to meet him after he was finished here. He was damned if he was going to whisper the Lady Isabel's commission through a confessional screen.

At last the old lady came out from behind the curtain, blessing herself and already muttering her penance. She passed Philip in a cloud of garlic, and he pushed back the red velvet curtain and entered the confessional himself.

The old lady had left her smell behind.

"Aye, my son," a soft voice said from the other side of the screen. "You have come to make your confession?"

The priest sounded surprised. Philip thought that he was probably the first male he had seen in his confessional in a while.

"No, Father Anselm," he said. "I have come in search of you. I have a commission for you from the Lady Isabel de Leon."

Silence.

Philip waited.

At last, "Lady Isabel?" the disembodied voice said waveringly.

"Aye, Father. It is important. Can we go somewhere and talk?"

"I must remain here for another half an hour," the priest said. His voice still sounded breathless. "After that I can meet you at the front door of the cathedral."

"Very well," said Philip. "My name is Philip Demain and I will be there."

As Philip left the confessional, he got a very self-satisfied, *I told you so* kind of look from the old lady who was waiting to go in behind him. Obviously she thought that he was leaving so quickly because the priest had refused to hear his confession due to the fact that he was desecrating the church by wearing armor.

Philip gave her a pleasant smile.

She looked affronted.

He decided he would go and get something to eat before returning to the cathedral to meet the priest.

Half an hour later Philip stood in front of the great carved wooden doors of Winchester Cathedral. With a cup of ale and an eel pie in his stomach, he was feeling a bit more in charity with the world.

The cathedral doors were open to the September sun and a tall priest wearing a long brown robe and sandals came through them. It did not take him long to pick out Philip.

"Philip Demain?" he asked as he came up beside the young knight.

"Aye," Philip said.

"I am Father Anselm," came the simple reply.

The priest was as tall as Philip, which was not something that often happened. Unlike Philip, however, he was very thin, almost emaciated, and his dark eyes had a haunted expression that was not entirely comfortable to look upon. He appeared to be somewhere in his early forties, younger than Philip had expected.

"We can go into the cathedral garden, if you like," Father Anselm said in a voice that was a little stronger than the one Philip had heard in the confessional.

Philip nodded and followed the priest around the side of the great gray stone church and into the grounds of a small, neat herb and flower garden that lay against the cathedral walls. There was an empty stone bench placed along one of the paths, and the priest led him to it. The three other benches in the garden were filled with people, all of whom were speaking in low voices.

From the garden one had a good view of the two hills that looked down on Winchester, St. Giles Hill, which lay on the east bank of the Itchen, and St. Catherine's Hill, which lay to the city's south.

"So," Father Anselm said, "you have come from the Lady Isabel?"

"Aye, Father, she has sent me with a commission for you."

The priest nodded. His haunted brown eyes were fixed unwaveringly on Philip's face. "How . . . how is she?" he asked.

Philip was surprised, not so much by the question as by the urgent manner in which it was asked.

"She is well, Father," he replied after a minute. "She is resident in the Benedictine convent in Worcester and has been there for the last fourteen years."

The priest wet his lips with his tongue. "Aye," he said. "I know." He seemed to make an effort to pull himself together. "So," he said resolutely, "what commission does Lady Isabel have for me?"

Philip told him. Then he quickly reached out his hand to steady the man, who had gone so pale that Philip was afraid he might faint.

"Hugh?" the priest said. His voice was a mere thread of sound. "Nigel Haslin thinks that he has found Hugh?"

"Aye, Father. He has asked Lady Isabel to send someone to Somerford to verify the man's identity."

Older men might refer to Hugh as a boy, but Philip, who was his exact age, never would.

"Can it be possible?" Father Anselm said with palpable wonder. "Could God be that good?" The priest's great dark haunted eyes lifted toward the sky. "After all these years, can He have actually given Hugh back to us?"

The scent of flowers and herbs was rich in the mild September air. The sun was warm upon Philip's uncovered head. He felt his face freeze at the priest's words.

"You must prepare yourself to be disappointed, Father," he said as gently as he could. "There is little likelihood that Hugh could have survived for all these years."

The priest did not even hear him. Instead he clasped his hands together in an attitude of prayer. "Can it be possible?" he repeated in the same wondering voice as before. "At last am I to be given the chance to make up for all the wrong that I did to that boy?"

# 7

The weeks before Nigel and his following left for the tournament at Chippenham were hectic. Every day the men were out on the practice field, wrestling, tilting at the quintain, practicing their archery and their horsemanship. When they were not using their arms, they were polishing them, or repairing them, or having the smith make them new ones.

The men of Somerford were determined not to be disgraced by their performance at Chippenham. All of Guy's other vassals and their retinues would be there, and the men of Somerford desired to shine the brightest.

One thing became very apparent, however, as the days went by. It was going to be very difficult to hide Hugh among the large company of Nigel's men—at least if he was going to take part in any of the exercises.

He was too good. He stood out from the rest of them like a steel sword in the midst of a line of wooden pikes.

Nigel was astonished. He had not expected such prowess from one who was so young and so lightly built.

But Jesu, the boy was strong. And even more impressively, he had the speed and balance of a cat.

He beat all of Nigel's men at wrestling and archery.

He beat all of them at swordplay.

To see him manage his horse, without reins, with seat and legs only, was a thing to bring tears to a man's eyes.

"How can I possibly hide him?" Nigel said to his daughter one day as she stood next to him at the edge of the practice field, watching Hugh ride at the quintain.

He hit it perfectly, dead on, ducked so that his body was hanging off the side of his horse, and galloped on.

"You can't," Cristen said with amusement.

"I was not planning to bring him to Earl Guy's notice quite so emphatically," Nigel said.

"Do you know, Father, I rather think that once we reach Chippenham, what happens to Hugh is going to be out of your hands."

He gave her a grim look. "You think it is Guy who will be calling the tune?"

"No," Cristen said, with the same amusement she had shown before. "I think it will be Hugh."

One of Cristen's jobs was to procure the provisions and the fodder they would need for moving a large group of men and horses to Chippenham. It was less than a day's ride to Guy's castle, but Nigel liked to bring his own hay for his horses. One year he had been given moldy hay by the earl and he had never forgotten it.

At last, all was in order. All the mail was polished until it shone—helmets, shields, hauberks, swords. All the spears were sharpened. The hay was loaded on the wagons. The men's clothing was clean and mended (another job that had fallen to Cristen and her ladies). There was no reason at all for Nigel's men not to make a good show at his overlord's tournament.

The night before they were to leave, Cristen and Hugh went for a walk down to her garden. She wanted to pack her medicine bag full of remedies, as some of the men always got hurt.

"I cannot believe that there is actually a mêlée at this tournament," Hugh said as he sat on the bench in the evening twilight watching her work. "At such a time, and in a land threatened by war . . ." He shook his head. "It is irresponsible."

"It is always irresponsible to throw away men's lives in play," Cristen said severely.

He smiled at her. "Women ever think thus."

"That is because women are intelligent," she shot back.

He cocked an eyebrow, continued to smile, but prudently made no reply.

"Lord Guy gets away with the tournament by saying it is part of the town fair," Cristen said. She put her medicine pouch on the wooden table and opened it. "But it is not part of the fair at all. The townspeople have nothing at all to do with what happens at the castle."

"I suppose that Stephen is still hoping to woo Guy to his side and that is why he has not put a stop to it," Hugh said.

"You suppose right." Cristen chose a flagon from one of the shelves, checked to see that it was fully stoppered, and packed it carefully in her pouch.

"Another example of Stephen's weakness," said Hugh.

Cristen looked up from her packing. "What would you do if you were Stephen and you found yourself in this situation?" she asked curiously.

"I would order Guy not to hold the tournament," Hugh replied promptly.

"And if he did not obey?"

"Then I would declare that he had forfeited his earldom to the crown."

Cristen took a brown jar from the shelves. "Guy is not about to hand over Chippenham to Stephen, Hugh."

"I would bring an army to take it away from him."

Cristen slowly put down the glass jar and stared at him.

"Stephen cannot have his barons acting as autonomous rulers of their own lands," Hugh said. "If he allows that, then he is not a king."

"Chippenham is an extremely well-fortified castle," she exclaimed.

"There is no castle so well fortified that it cannot be taken."

She frowned, then began to measure some leaves from the jar into a small bottle. When she had finished, she looked up again at the boy on the bench. The setting sun was shining on his black hair, and as she watched he tossed it off his forehead in a gesture that had become very familiar to her. Her frown deepened. "You obviously have little respect for Stephen. Have you decided that you prefer the empress, then? Would you declare for her if you became the earl?"

He took her question seriously, as he always did, and replied thoughtfully, "Actually, I would probably do the same thing Guy is doing, but for a different purpose. I would stay neutral to try to hold a balance between Stephen and the empress. I would stay neutral to try to accumulate enough power to one day bring about a peace."

She was not surprised to find that he had obviously been thinking about this.

She lifted her delicate brows. "Then you would act–how did you put it–as an autonomous ruler of your own lands?"

He grinned at her. "Aye," he said. "I would. Because Stephen wouldn't have the guts to stop me." The smile faded. "But I'll tell you something, Cristen. I wish to God he had."

Fifty members of Nigel's household accompanied him to Chippenham. Twenty of the company were knights; the rest consisted of pages and squires and Cristen and her ladies.

The spirits of the men were high as they rode out of the gates of Somerford under their lord's blue and white flag. The sun shone on polished helmets and hauberks and shields, and the sheen of the horse's coats almost equaled the brightness of the men's armor. The day was chilly, with a wind that whipped color into riders' faces. The flags flew bravely. The jingle of spurs and armor could be heard all along the road as they passed.

The tournament held by Guy was of a very small scale, numbering in the hundreds, not the thousands such as appeared at the great tournaments in France. Still, it was the only tournament most of Nigel's knights would ever fight in, and their blood was hot to prove their prowess. A tournament was a quintessential competition of males, performed under the admiring eyes of beautiful ladies, who were present in order to excite the warriors to ever greater heights of valor.

Cristen despised it. Every year since the Chippenham tournament had started, at least one knight had been killed in the mêlée. Even though killing was not the purpose of the fighting, an unhorsed knight was in great danger of being trampled to death by the iron-shod hooves of the powerful destriers the knights rode.

Every year Cristen begged her father not to participate in the mêlée, and every year he told her that it was his duty to lead his men on the field of honor.

Cristen, who had the job of binding up all the wounds encountered on the field of honor, thought rather that it was a field of fools.

Her opinion, however, was shared by no one else who attended the festivities at Chippenham. Even the ladies watched avidly, not at all put off by the dust and the blood and the danger. In fact, they seemed to love it.

This year Cristen had a new worry to add to all of those she already bore.

Hugh.

What was going to happen when he saw Chippenham again? Would it trigger his memory, as her father hoped it would?

What was going to happen when Earl Guy saw him?

Was Hugh going to be safe?

As with all great castles, a large area outside the walls of Chippenham had been cleared when it was built so that no one could approach it unseen, and it was on this great open field that the tournament was to be held. Hugh was riding next to Cristen when Nigel's party came out of the woods onto the field and he had his first view of the castle in the distance.

It was an impressive sight. Surrounding the keep was a massive stone battlemented curtain wall, with twin gate towers on the wall that faced the field. From these towers, and from the crenelated crests of four other towers set at the corners of each of the four outer walls, flew a crimson flag displaying the de Leon signature of a golden boar.

Cristen looked at Hugh to see what his reaction to the sight of Chippenham might be.

He was staring at the flag, his face perfectly still.

"The boar has been the symbol of the Earls of Wiltshire since the time of Guy's father," she said quietly.

After a moment, he nodded. Then he picked up his helmet, which he had been carrying in front of him on his saddle, and fitted it on his head over his mail coif. The noseguard effectively hid his face from view.

A number of red-and-gold-striped pavilions were set up all along the edges of the field for lodging the tournament guests. The castle itself, even though it was large, was not capable of accommodating over 800 extra people with any degree of comfort.

A single horseman was riding across the field to greet Nigel's party. Cristen recognized the rider as Guy's steward, and relayed that information to Hugh.

"He will be welcoming us to Chippenham," she said. "Then I expect he will have someone show us to our tents."

Hugh nodded again.

The men and women were lodged in separate pavilions, and Cristen and her ladies were forced to follow the knight who had been sent to escort them. She parted from Hugh reluctantly.

She hated this tournament and wished they had not come.

The inside of the pavilion was as Cristen remembered it from past years. Beds were strewn all over the floor, with silk gowns and fur-trimmed cloaks heaped upon them. Small chests with mirrors and jewelry were placed on the floor next to many of the beds. A group of women had come in before Cristen and her ladies, and they were chattering and primping, making ready to sally forth again.

Cristen was not hungry, but she knew that her father and his men would be gathered around the food being cooked in the castle bailey, and she was anxious to see Hugh again.

The girls Cristen had brought were excited and anxious to leave the pavilion and get out into the crowd. After they had washed off the dust of the ride and attended to their needs, they exited from the tent, where they were met by two of her father's pages, whom he had sent to keep an eye on them.

"Well, Brian," Cristen said to the hazel-eyed boy of twelve who had leaped forward as soon as he saw her. "Are you going to escort us to the feast?"

"Aye, my lady," he said. "Lord Nigel said that we were to make certain that we brought you to him."

Cristen began to walk across the field, her ladies behind her, the pages on either side of her. The ground was dry under her feet; it had been unusually rainless for the last few weeks. Cristen hoped the weather would hold until the end of the tournament. One year it had poured, and the horses sliding in the mud had made for even more injuries than usual.

A man crossed in front of her and stopped, forcing her to come to a halt.

"Lady Cristen," he said, and bowed elaborately. "What a joy to see you again."

"Sir Richard," Cristen said sedately.

Richard Evril was one of the chief knights of Earl Guy's household. Cristen knew that Guy had wanted her to marry him and that her father had refused the match.

The man smiled, showing stained teeth. He was big, with broad shoulders and the beginnings of a paunch showing under his bright yellow tunic.

"Are you going to get some food?" he asked.

"Aye," Cristen said. "We are meeting my father."

He offered her his arm. "Allow me to escort you to him."

Behind the knight's back, Cristen could see Brian scowling. She could not refuse Sir Richard's arm without showing extreme discourtesy, however.

"Thank you," she said, and gingerly laid her small hand on his brilliant blue sleeve.

"You are looking as lovely as ever," he said jovially as they began to walk across the field.

"Thank you," Cristen said again. "Tell me, Sir Richard, whom can we expect to see at the tournament this year? Have all the usual vassals come?"

"Indeed, aye," he returned. And he proceeded to tell her in detail about everyone who was participating.

At last they were walking across the drawbridge that led from the field over a filled moat. The gate towers rose on either side of Cristen, and for a moment she felt panic tighten her stomach.

She could not rid herself of the feeling that she was walking into a trap.

"Sir Nigel is over there, my lady," Brian said helpfully.

"Oh, good," Cristen said. She forced herself to smile up at the knight beside her. "Thank you for your escort, Sir Richard, but my pages will take me to my father now."

He scowled, obviously not pleased with his dismissal.

"I was hoping to sup with you, Lady Cristen."

Cristen didn't want him to see Hugh. It was a foolish feeling, she knew. Hugh hadn't come here to hide, after all. But this knight was too close to Lord Guy. He would notice the resemblance.

"I believe my father was planning to sup with only his own household this evening, Sir Richard," she said firmly. "Tomorrow, perhaps."

The man's scowl deepened.

Brian stepped to her side. "I will escort you now, Lady Cristen," he said.

She smiled into the boy's flashing hazel eyes. "Thank you, Brian. Good evening, Sir Richard."

They crossed the flat bailey to the place where Nigel and his men were gathered around one of the five smoking firepits, where enough meat to feed almost a thousand people was being roasted. The inner walls and great stone keep of Chippenham loomed above them.

The meal on the first day of the tournament was always informal. Lord Guy's pages, dressed in scarlet surcoats with gold trim, were circulating with heaping platters of oxen, boar, venison, lamb, rabbit, and all kinds of fowl. Other pages were going around with flagons of wine. There was fine white bread as well, and sweets.

"Cristen!" Sir Nigel roared, waving a hand in which he clutched a piece of meat on a bone.

Cristen came up beside him. "Hello, Father."

"Was that Richard Evril I just saw you with?"

She sighed. "Aye, unfortunately."

"He insisted on escorting the Lady Cristen, my lord, but I stayed right behind her," Brian said.

"Good lad," Nigel grunted. "I don't like that man."

"What man?"

It was Hugh, coming up behind her.

"Richard Evril," Nigel said. "He is one of Guy's chief knights; he's been with him forever. Guy wanted to marry him to Cristen, as a matter of fact, but I refused."

Hugh looked revolted. "That old man? How disgusting."

"It is very common for older men to marry young girls," Nigel said repressively. "You must know that, Hugh."

Hugh was looking across the packed courtyard, trying to locate Sir Richard, but the knight had disappeared. He turned back to Cristen. "Was he the man who tried to kiss you last year?" he demanded.

"No," Cristen said gloomily. "That was someone else."

"You had better stay by me," he ordered. "It seems you are in some danger in this place."

"It's because everyone drinks too much," Cristen said. She eyed the flagon of wine in Hugh's hand.

"It's my first," he said austerely.

He certainly looked sober, Cristen thought. He had taken off his mail like the rest of the men and was garbed in a dark green overtunic with an undertunic of dark blue. The air was warm from the heat of the fires, and he had opened the laces at his throat, revealing the cross and chain he always wore. His eyes were somber.

"What do you want to eat?" he asked her now. "I'll get it for you."

"Some of the fowl, I think," she said. "And a little bread."

Hugh stepped away from her and lifted a hand to a circulating page. The boy, who had been simultaneously signaled by two older men, came to Hugh's side immediately.

"The lady wishes some fowl," Hugh said.

The boy offered Cristen his platter of meat. She chose what she wanted, smiled, and thanked him. He ducked his head and rushed off to answer other summonses.

Nigel offered his daughter a cup of wine. She shook her head. "I'll share Hugh's."

A smile dented the corner of Hugh's mouth. "Don't you trust me?"

"It is not that at all," she said repressively. "It is that I cannot hold my meat and bread and a cup of wine at the same time."

"Hmmm," he said.

"What events will you enter tomorrow, Hugh?" Nigel asked.

"What is on the program?" Hugh replied.

"There is a horsemanship competition, and wrestling, archery, and tilting at the quintain. The last is more for the squires than for the knights, however."

Hugh offered Cristen a sip of his wine.

"What is the horsemanship competition?"

Cristen took a dainty swallow and returned his cup to him.

"They set up an obstacle course with barrels, gates, a bridge, that sort of thing. Everything is hung with brightly colored flags, which makes it a bit scary for the horses. Last year Guy even had a few small jumps."

"It doesn't sound too difficult," Hugh said.

"No, well, the difficult part is that you have to carry a sword in one hand and a shield in the other and tie your horse's reins on his neck."

Hugh's straight black brows rose. "Ah. That does make it more interesting."

"You and Rufus would probably do very well in that competition, Hugh," Cristen said.

She liked the horsemanship competition. It was fun to watch, and no one got hurt.

"Aye," Hugh said. "We might."

She gave him a hopeful look. "It's much cleaner than the wrestling."

He looked amused. "Aye, I imagine that it must be."

"Shall I enter you for the horsemanship, then?" Nigel asked.

"Why not?" Hugh said lightly, and Cristen breathed a sigh of relief.

"Can a knight enter more than one competition?" Hugh asked.

"Of course," Nigel said. "They take place one after the other—except for the tilting at the quintain, which goes on all day."

"Do you participate yourself, sir?" Hugh asked courteously.

"Aye," Nigel said. "I like to compete in the archery."

Nigel was a very fine bowman.

He gave Hugh a wry look. "Will you do the archery as well, Hugh?"

Hugh was better than he was.

The boy shook his head. "If you are going to compete, then I will cheer for you."

Nigel, who had won the archery for the last four years, was a little embarrassed at how grateful he was for that response.

After supper was finished, all of the knights and ladies and squires and pages retreated to their tents for a good night's rest. Or at least, that was what they were supposed to do.

In reality, the ladies' tent was busy all night long, as women went in and out, keeping the assignations they had made during suppertime. Lying awake, her sleep disturbed by all the coming and going, Cristen wondered bitterly if any of Guy's vassals could boast of a faithful wife or daughter.

*What terrible marriages they must have,* she thought sadly. She herself had been fortunate in being the product of one of the few happy unions that she knew of. In fact, it often seemed to her that women of the lower classes, whose marriages were made for compatibility and not for land, had a better life than the women of the aristocracy, who all too often were married to much older men with whom they had little or nothing in common.

She thought of Sir Richard, and shuddered.

Thank God she had a father who cared about her happiness. She was well aware that most girls were not in such a fortunate situation.

*If I were married to Sir Richard, maybe I would cheat too,* she thought grimly.

Unbidden, her thoughts turned to Hugh. What was going to happen on the morrow?

# 8

When Philip and Father Anselm finally reached Somerford Castle on a warm September evening, they found it virtually deserted.

"They are all gone to the tournament at Chippenham," the men at arms who were manning the outer gate told them.

Philip knew about the tournament, but he hadn't realized that it was going to interfere with his mission.

"Here's a coil," he said to the priest, who was riding beside him on the horse Philip had rented for him in Winchester. "I hadn't counted on this."

"Has the boy known as Hugh Corbaille gone to Chippenham with Sir Nigel?" Father Anselm said to the men at the gate.

"Aye," one replied. "All the knights went. And Lady Cristen and her ladies as well. It's a great tournament, you know. All of Lord Guy's vassals participate."

"Hugh will bring home prizes, too," the other man at arms said approvingly. "He's that good."

The pretender had evidently wormed his way into the good graces of the entire castle, Philip thought sourly.

Father Anselm looked at Philip. "Then we must go to Chippenham as well."

Philip frowned. "Is that wise, Father? Would it not be better for us to await their return here at Somerford?"

"No," the priest said positively. "The Lady Isabel must not be kept in doubt for any longer than is necessary."

Philip couldn't disagree with that. The sooner she discovered that this man was not her son, the sooner she would regain her peace of mind.

"All right," he said. "But it is too late to start for Chippenham now."

"You can spend the night at Somerford," one of the gatekeepers said promptly. "Lady Cristen would never turn away a priest."

"Very well," Philip said. "Thank you, that is what we will do. And in the morning we will leave for the tournament."

The grounds in front of Chippenham were ablaze with color when Philip and Father Anselm rode out of the surrounding woods the following afternoon. Men and boys and horses were scattered everywhere on the dry, packed earth of the tournament field. Striped pavilions glowed in the sun, and the scarlet flags of the Earl of Wiltshire vied in brilliance with the colors of the flags of all of Wiltshire's vassals.

On the section of the field nearest to the woods, a quintain had been set up and, one after another, boys were tilting at it recklessly. Hoots or cheers greeted the results, depending on how successful each contender was.

A large number of boys appeared to be hitting the ground as they misjudged their hits and the quintain swung back and swatted them out of the saddle.

The part of the field nearest to the castle walls had been roped off and set up as an obstacle course, which a single horse and rider were attempting to negotiate. Wooden stands had been erected along one side of the course, and this was where the ladies were sitting. The brilliant colors of their gowns and veils glowed in the golden September sunshine.

Philip signaled to a squire who was leading a horse across the field in front of them. "Hey there! Can you tell me where I might find Sir Nigel Haslin?"

"Most of the knights are watching the horsemanship contest," the boy replied.

Philip looked at the crowds of men standing around the roped-off obstacle course. Then he turned to the priest at his side. "Would you know this Nigel if you saw him, Father?"

"I think so," the priest said.

They dismounted, found a page to hold their horses, walked across the dry and dusty field to the crowd around the obstacle course, and began to search for Nigel. Both men were dressed in plain riding clothes, and Father Anselm wore his hood pulled up to cover his tonsure. The church had banned all tournaments, and if it was seen that he was a priest they were sure to attract the kind of attention they did not want. As it was, two men of their unusual height were noteworthy enough.

They found Nigel ten minutes later, standing with a group of his men near the stands that held the ladies.

"Sir Nigel," Father Anselm said.

Nigel's head swung around.

"The Lady Isabel de Leon sent me," the priest said softly. "My name is Father Anselm. I was Lord Roger's chaplain and I knew Hugh well when he was a child."

Nigel's brown eyes searched the priest's face. "I think I remember you."

Father Anselm bowed his hooded head. Then he glanced at Philip. "This is Philip Demain. He is a knight of Simon of Evesham's. He fetched me from Winchester and brought me here."

Nigel's brows had snapped together at the mention of Simon's name. He was well aware of Isabel's brother's allegiance to Robert of Gloucester. "I see," he said stiffly.

"We are here to see if Father Anselm can identify this man you have taken up as Lady Isabel's son," Philip said coolly. "Once we have done that, we will be on our way again. In the meanwhile, if you will allow us to pass as members of your retinue, we would be grateful."

"Of course," Nigel said, even more stiffly than before. "Although I must say, I hardly expected that you would follow me to Chippenham."

"I do not wish to keep the Lady Isabel waiting any longer than she must," Father Anselm said. "You can imagine her anxiety."

Nigel's aristocratic face softened. "Of course. Of course." He gestured toward the obstacle course. "Hugh is riding in the competition. You will have to wait until he is finished before you can meet him."

Philip crossed his arms over his chest, spread his legs a little and settled himself to watch the man and horse presently on the field.

"We will wait," he said.

He watched while six men and horses went through the obstacle course, to the accompaniment of encouraging cheers from the knights of their retinues.

They had varying degrees of success. One horse-and-rider combination came to grief at the small bridge that was decorated with many strings of fluttering flags. Every time the knight brought his horse up to the start of the bridge, the stallion would shy away. After three such refusals, the pair was disqualified.

A second contestant had trouble with the series of three small, brightly painted jumps, which had a multitude of flags hanging off their standards. The horse went over the first jump, but stopped dead in front of the second, snorting and pawing and shaking his head. The knight circled him around and headed him at the first jump again, and this time he refused that. The knight tried again, with the same results. He was disqualified.

A third contestant got across the bridge and the jumps, but failed to get his horse through the tunnel that had been made from what looked like an immense circular barrel. It was dark inside the tunnel, and the horse refused to enter. They were dismissed.

Three of the contestants made it around the entire course. The horses walked in places, in places stopped and looked as if they would refuse, but, with some verbal and physical encouragement from their riders, eventually they obeyed and went on.

Then a man on a roan stallion came onto the course.

The men around Nigel all cheered.

"He's one of ours," Nigel said to Philip. Turning toward the field, he called, "Come on, Geoffrey. Show them how the men of Somerford can ride."

The roan trotted out onto the course and went through the maze delineated by the first set of barrels.

Philip, watching, thought that this pair was having the best ride of any that he had seen. The roan was slow and cautious, but he kept going forward. He stopped at the bridge and looked long and hard at the flags, but when the knight pricked him with a spur, he went. He hopped over the jumps one at a time, not in one fluid motion, his nose almost on the rails, he was looking so hard, but he went. He walked through the barrel as if he were treading on eggshells, but he went.

The men of Somerford were delighted.

"Our lord won the archery contest earlier," one of them confided to Philip. "And one of our knights came in third in the wrestling. If we can win the horsemanship, the men of Somerford will have taken the day."

"Well, from what I have seen, that was certainly the best ride yet," Philip said courteously.

Privately, he thought that he could have done better, but he was prudent enough to hold his tongue.

"Of course," another man said, "Hugh has yet to come."

"And when shall we have the joy of seeing him?" Philip said with lethal courtesy.

"Right now," came the reply, and Philip turned his eyes to the horse-and-rider combination coming through the opening in the ropes that was the start of the obstacle course.

The horse was a white stallion, not overly large but muscular and very fit-looking. The rider did not look to be overly large, either. His face was hidden by the noseguard on his helmet.

The horse paused for a moment, then began to trot forward.

His step was springy and forward. His ears were pricked with interest. The man on his back carried his sword in one hand and his shield in the other and rode in the way of all knights, legs straight down under him as if he were standing on the ground. His mail glittered in the sun.

The horse trotted smoothly through the different lines set up by the barrels, his hind legs stepping well up under him, his back swinging with relaxation. Still keeping the same steady pace, he approached the bridge and, without a moment's hesitation, trotted over it. There were more barrels, this time set up in circles, and the stallion veered perfectly left to enter between them.

There was no sign of movement on the part of the rider. Other men had kicked, had used their spurs, but this rider sat perfectly quietly. To all outward appearances, the horse was acting on his own.

Then they were at the jumps. The stallion trotted forward. He leaped the first. The rider stood a little more in his stirrups, but otherwise did not change position. The horse, still holding the same steady pace, jumped the second and then the third pole. He turned at the end of the line and headed toward the tunnel.

As he approached the strange circular barrel, for the first time he showed a sign of nervousness. His ears, which had been pricked forward, flicked back toward his rider twice.

They reached the edge of the barrel, where the horse had to step up onto the wood and commit himself to going through.

Philip thought he saw an infinite hesitation on the part of the white stallion. His front feet touched the wood, then his back feet, and then he was trotting through, a little more quickly, perhaps, than he had been trotting before, but nevertheless trotting.

Back out again into the sunlight, there was only one more formation of barrels, a figure eight, to go through, and they were finished.

For a moment there was silence in the audience. Then it was as if everyone let out a collective breath. And then came the cheers.

Despite himself, Philip was impressed. It took an extraordinary kind of communication between rider and horse to get an animal to perform like that. Philip wasn't fool enough to think that the horse had done it on his own.

"We've won! We've won!" the man behind him was exulting. "No matter how much the judges might want to give the prize to another, they cannot do it. Not with that kind of performance!"

Philip agreed. No one else had come close to that ride.

Evidently, the judges agreed also. Three more knights rode after Hugh, but it was an anticlimax and everyone knew it. It took the judges exactly two minutes to come to their decision.

Lord Guy himself stepped onto the field from his place in the front row of the stands to award the prize—a handsome new saddle.

"Hugh Corbaille of Somerford, come forward to accept your prize!" the knight who accompanied the earl blared forth.

From amidst the crowd of horsemen waiting by the opening in the ropes, a lone rider came into the ring. The white stallion glistened in the sun, his muscles moving smoothly under his polished coat. Just before they reached the earl, the man on his back lifted his hands to remove his helmet. He was not wearing his mail coif, and his uncovered black hair shone in the brilliant sunlight. He stopped the white horse in front of Lord Guy. The two men looked at each other.

Beside him, Philip heard the breath ratchet in Nigel Haslin's throat.

Philip looked at the face of the man on the white stallion and felt his heart kick once, hard, against his ribs.

He had wondered what a male Isabel would look like. Now he knew.

"Jesu," he heard the priest beside him mumble, as if in prayer. "It is Hugh."

It had to be, Philip thought blankly. The man wearing that face had to be Isabel's son. There could be no other explanation for such a resemblance.

He turned his eyes to the earl, who was standing in front of the white stallion, flanked by a knight and a page holding the saddle. Guy was staring at Hugh as if he was seeing a ghost.

Hugh sat his horse like a statue, and looked back.

A rustle of uneasiness ran through the crowd. The noise seemed to break the spell that was holding Guy frozen, and he stepped forward. He put a hand on the white stallion's bridle and looked up at his rider. His lips moved.

Hugh answered.

"Dear God," Nigel breathed. "What can they be saying?"

"I imagine he wants to know who the hell Hugh is," Philip said.

Then Guy signaled to the page, who came forward to present the saddle to Hugh. He leaned from his horse to lift it in his arms. He nodded to Guy. Then, as if on his own volition, the white stallion backed up and whirled, and the two of them cantered off the field.

For a long moment, no one spoke.

Then, "Judas," Philip said. "That was a scene."

"I must find Hugh," Nigel said, and he began to push his way through the crowd.

"Let's go," Philip said to the dazed-looking priest at his side, and the two tall men followed close upon the heels of the lord of Somerford.

* * *

Cristen didn't know whether to laugh or to cry.

"Did he have to be quite so dramatic?" she grumbled as she got to her feet and prepared to leave the stands with her ladies.

"Lady Cristen!"

She shut her eyes for a moment in dismay. When she opened them again, there was Sir Richard standing in front of her.

"Who was that boy?" the knight demanded.

She opened her eyes wider. "What boy, Sir Richard?"

"You know who I am talking about," he replied angrily. "The boy who just won the horsemanship contest. He came to Chippenham with your father."

"Didn't you hear his name?" she said in feigned surprise. "He is Hugh Corbaille, the son of Ralf Corbaille, he who was Sheriff of Lincoln before he was killed at the Battle of the Standard last year. Hugh has been visiting us."

Sir Richard showed his stained teeth in a smile that was not pleasant. "I see," he said. "And where did your father meet this Hugh Corbaille?"

"I believe you will have to ask him that yourself," she returned pleasantly. "Now, if you will excuse me, Sir Richard, my ladies and I would like to retire."

He gave her a narrow look out of flat, slate-blue eyes.

"I will see you later," he promised. "At the feast in the castle."

She forced a smile, then turned, beckoned to her ladies, and began to thread her way through the remaining crowd, away from the vicinity of Sir Richard, who she was sure had been an emissary from the earl.

Hugh rode Rufus directly to the stabling area that had been allotted to the men of Somerford.

He was trembling.

It was one thing to have heard that he looked like Guy, but to look into a pair of eyes that were a mirror image of his own . . .

He had seen the naked shock in those eyes when Guy had seen Hugh's face. It had been the shock of recognition.

Hugh balanced his new saddle on Rufus's withers and dismounted. His knees felt weak as he landed on the ground.

One of the squires came running. "I saw your ride, Hugh!" He was panting with excitement. "It was wonderful!"

"Thank you," Hugh said automatically.

"I'll take care of Rufus for you," the boy said. "Don't worry about him. He'll get a good rubdown and a nice feed. He deserves it." The squire patted the arched white neck of the stallion. "He is a splendid horse."

Hugh lifted down his new saddle and stood for a moment as Rufus was led off. He didn't know what he should do.

The trembling was getting worse.

He didn't want to return to the pavilion. He didn't want to deal with congratulations or with the excitement of the knights of Somerford as they celebrated their victories.

He didn't want to see anyone.

He wished Cristen was here so he could talk to her.

Several men he didn't know came up to him as he stood there and began to ask him about how he had trained Rufus. He managed to answer somehow, and then he started to walk in the direction of the pavilion where he knew Cristen was lodged. He was still carrying his saddle.

"Hugh!"

It took him a moment to recognize Nigel's voice. He looked over his shoulder and saw the lord of Somerford hurrying after him. He stopped.

Nigel came up beside him, followed by two very tall men.

"I have some people who wish to meet you," Nigel said.

They were not far from the ladies' pavilion and the only people near them at the moment were a few pages who were scurrying around on errands for their mistresses. Most of the company was still clustered around the obstacle course.

The two big men loomed behind Nigel. One was as young as Hugh himself, and this was the man Nigel introduced first. "This is Philip Demain, Hugh. He is a knight of Simon of Evesham's."

With a great effort, Hugh pulled himself together. He looked at the young knight.

Philip's hair was the color of the sun, his eyes the blue of a summer sky. His shoulders were immensely broad and he was at least five inches taller than Hugh.

Hugh nodded at him.

"And this is Father Anselm." Nigel's voice was suspiciously gentle. "He was Lord Roger's chaplain, Hugh. He knew you when you were a child."

Hugh stared into the thin, dark face of the hooded man. Great, haunted brown eyes looked back at him.

"Hugh," the man said hoarsely. "My God, Hugh. After all these years, you have come back to us."

Hugh had no recollection of ever seeing the man before.

Sweat broke out on his forehead.

"I . . ." He inhaled deeply and tried again. "I'm afraid I do not know you, Father."

The priest stepped closer to Hugh and laid a hand on his arm. It took an immense effort of willpower to keep from pulling away.

"I have come as an emissary from your mother, the Lady Isabel," the priest said.

Hugh pulled his arm away and stepped back.

"My mother was Adela Corbaille," he said sharply.

The priest was shaking his head. "No, my boy. Your mother is Isabel de Leon."

The young knight spoke for the first time. His voice was very deep. "You look just like her," he said. "It's uncanny."

Suddenly, Hugh was dizzy.

*I will not faint,* he told himself fiercely. *I will not faint.*

He blinked and struggled to control his too-rapid breathing.

Then deliverance arrived.

"Here you are, Hugh," said Cristen. "I have been searching for you."

He turned to her. She took one look at his face and knew he was in trouble.

"I need Hugh's help, Father," she said to Nigel. "Do you mind if I borrow him for a while?"

There was a moment's silence while Nigel looked at his daughter. Then he said quietly, "Of course not, my dear. I will see you both later."

Cristen put her hand firmly on Hugh's arm and began to steer him away from her father and the two tall men.

Without a word, Hugh turned and went with her.

*  *  *

They walked in the direction of the pavilions, Hugh carrying his new saddle under his left arm, Cristen on his other side. The sun was hot and Cristen stopped in the shade cast by the first pavilion, turned and scanned his face.

"Are you all right?" she asked softly.

He shook his head as if dazed. "His eyes . . . he does look like me, Cristen. He does."

She nodded. "I know, Hugh."

"I didn't really believe it until I saw him."

He was standing perfectly still, not even seeming to notice the weight of the saddle resting on his hip.

She reached out and touched his shoulder. The dazed look left his face and his eyes focused on her. "I don't remember," he said. There was anguish in his voice. "I don't remember the priest, or this place, or Guy, or anything!"

She replied gently, "Perhaps you never will, Hugh. You have lived with that gap in your life for fourteen years. Perhaps you will have to live with it forever."

"But don't you see?" he cried. "If it is true, and I am his son, then I must find out what happened. My father was murdered! I cannot just let that go, Cristen. What kind of a man would I be if I just let that go?"

His words struck her to the heart.

"But what can you do?" She had not expected this reaction, and she tried very hard to keep her voice calm. "His death happened fourteen years ago, Hugh. How can you possibly find out the truth of it after so long a time?"

His nostrils quivered. "I have to try. My father was a crusader and he was murdered in his own chapel. I owe it to him to try to find his killer."

A shadow fell upon them and, startled, they both jerked their heads around. One of Nigel's squires was standing there.

"Would you like me to take that saddle from you, Hugh?" the boy asked respectfully. "I will put it with the rest of Rufus' gear."

Hugh blinked and for the first time seemed to realize that he was holding the saddle.

"Oh, of course." He grasped the saddle with both hands and handed it over. "Thank you, William."

"You were splendid, Hugh," the boy said with a grin. "Everyone is talking about your ride."

"Are they?" Hugh's voice was wry.

He and Cristen stood together in silence and watched as William went off with the saddle. Then Hugh drew a deep breath and seemed to gather himself together.

"Well," he said, "I suppose I . . . "

His words trailed off.

She looked up at him worriedly. "What is it?"

He nodded fractionally toward the front of the pavilion. "Who is that? Do you know?"

Cristen glanced in the direction Hugh had indicated and saw a solitary knight standing by the water pails that were lined up in front of the pavilion. The man's face was rigid with barely controlled emotion, and he was staring at Hugh with hard and glittering eyes.

She looked back to Hugh. "I don't know."

"I think he is the man who won the wrestling today," Hugh said. "One of Guy's knights, I believe."

Cristen turned and openly gazed at the knight. Realizing that he had been seen, the man bent, picked up a pail of water, and disappeared quickly into the pavilion.

"He probably recognized your resemblance to Guy," Cristen said.

Hugh was frowning. "Aye."

Fear caught Cristen by the throat. "He didn't look very friendly, did he?"

"Perhaps he saw the same thing that Guy did when he looked at me this afternoon," Hugh said.

"What is that, Hugh?"

In a grim voice, Hugh replied, "Retribution."

# 9

Supper for all the visiting knights and ladies was held in the Great Hall of Chippenham's keep that evening. Philip went to the castle with the knights of Somerford while Father Anselm, who would not be able to keep his tonsure covered indoors, stayed behind in the pavilion. Young Brian was to bring him food from the supper that was being served in the bailey for the squires and pages.

As they approached the castle, Philip scanned it with the appraising eye of a potential attacker.

From what he could see, Chippenham's defenses were formidable indeed. The outer wall of the castle, the curtain wall, had to be at least fifteen feet thick and was reinforced by towers at all the corners. Such a wall would be well able to withstand most available siege artillery, he thought.

The men of Somerford passed between the gate towers, under the raised portcullis, and into the outer bailey. This courtyard contained ample stabling as well as the usual storehouses and buildings for workmen and castle defenders. There was even enough room in the large bailey to house additional troops, should they be necessary for the castle's defense.

Nigel's men crossed the bailey in the direction of the castle's inner walls. These walls were also built of thick stone, with a second gate barred by another iron portcullis. A square tower stood at each of the four corners of these inner walls.

Inside the second set of walls was the keep, a square, stone edifice, four stories high, with four towers that rose another two stories above the main building.

If ever a castle looked impregnable, Philip thought grimly, Chippenham did. Whoever commanded such a fortress was well nigh untouchable. The only tactic that could force such a bastion to surrender would be the starvation of its defending troops.

Led by Nigel, who had Cristen on his arm, Philip and the men of Somerford walked up the stone ramp that led to the main door of the keep. This door led into the second floor of the forebuilding, a three-story square block that jutted out from the west end of the main part of the castle.

Philip was not unfamiliar with this style of keep. Robert of Gloucester's castle, which he had visited upon a number of occasions, was built very like Chippenham. The first floor of such a castle was usually given over to storerooms, the second floor to guardrooms, and the third floor to the Great Hall. The fourth floor and the towers usually held the family solar and bedrooms.

Sure enough, after ascending one flight of stairs, Philip found himself stepping out of the enclosed staircase (which could be defended by a few men against an army) and into Chippenham's Great Hall.

Trestle tables crowded the floor of the immense room, whose high ceiling had louvered holes set into it to allow the smoke generated from the enormous hearth to escape. The noise level in the hall was already high, as men sat around the tables, drinking ale and reliving the exploits of the day while waiting for the meal to be served.

The seats at the high table were still empty, waiting for the earl and his retinue to arrive.

Nigel and Cristen moved away from the group of Somerford knights to take their places at one of the higher tables with Guy's other vassals and their ladies. Philip and the rest of Nigel's men went to find a table at the lower end of the hall, among the knights of the other retinues.

Hugh went with them.

Philip managed to arrange matters so that he was seated next to

Hugh when the Somerford men found empty places at one of the trestle tables.

As they took their seats on the bench, Philip turned to Hugh and asked quietly, "Does any of this look familiar to you?"

Hugh's face was completely shuttered. His profile might have been carved in stone.

"No," he said.

Philip eyed him curiously. "You really don't remember anything about your childhood?"

"No," Hugh said again. This time a telltale muscle clenched along his jaw.

Philip continued to regard the closed face of Isabel's son.

Hugh might have inherited his mother's perfectly sculpted bones, but by some strange alchemy of nature, his beauty was completely male.

Hugh's light gray eyes, which were not Isabel's, turned and looked at him straightly. "Do I really look so much like her?" he said.

"Aye," Philip returned. "You do."

Hugh's lashes dropped.

"What did Guy say to you this afternoon when he was awarding your prize?" Philip asked.

Hugh shrugged. "He wanted to know who I was."

He accepted a cup of ale from one of the pages who were circulating among the tables and took a long drink.

"I can imagine that he did," Philip said with a cynical smile. "He must know what his brother's wife looks like. Hers is not a face you would easily forget."

Hugh didn't reply.

The scent of roasted meat filled the hall even though the food had not yet been brought in. Evidently it had already been carried up to the pantry from the kitchen building. It would not be served, however, until the earl had taken his place.

Philip took a sip of his ale.

"Did Nigel send word to the Lady Isabel about me?" Hugh asked in a carefully detached voice.

"Aye. She is in the Benedictine convent at Worcester, and has been for the last fourteen years. Since her husband was killed and you were lost, in fact. After she received Nigel's message, she sent for her brother, Simon of Evesham, and Simon and I went to visit her. I got the task of bringing the priest to Somerford to identify you." Philip shrugged his big shoulders. "In fact, we didn't need the priest. I could have done it myself. Anyone who has seen the Lady Isabel would recognize you."

Hugh was slowly revolving his cup on the table in front of him. Philip could not see his eyes.

"Why did Simon send the priest? Why didn't he come himself?" he asked at last.

"My lord is anxiously awaiting word from Robert of Gloucester," Philip said. "We expect to hear news any day now that the earl has landed with his sister."

The gray eyes flicked around to his face.

"Simon is going to support the empress, then?"

"He is Robert's man. He will support whomever Robert supports."

"I see," said Hugh.

"Whom do you support, Hugh?" Philip asked, trying to sound casual. "Are you Stephen's man, like Nigel Haslin?"

A large group of knights came into the room, laughing and talking raucously. They began to search among the tables for places to sit.

Hugh watched them absently.

"My allegiance is of no matter," he said. "My foster father was the Sheriff of Lincoln, and a man to be reckoned with, but I am only the holder of a few small manors. My allegiance can make little difference to either side."

"It will make a great deal of difference if you are the Earl of Wiltshire," Philip said bluntly.

Hugh's eyes were fixed on one of the knights who had just come in.

He said, "Even if I am Roger's son, I see little chance of claiming my inheritance from Lord Guy. He appears to be well entrenched."

Philip looked at the knight Hugh was watching. He was a man who looked to be in his late twenties, tall, with distinctive chestnut hair.

"Who is that?" Philip asked curiously.

"I don't know," Hugh replied.

At that moment, the knight's eyes swung toward them as if he felt their gaze. His whole face hardened when he recognized Hugh.

For a brief moment, the two men stared at each other across the noisy room. Then one of the knight's companions put a hand on his arm to steer him toward a table. He broke the eye contact with Hugh and turned away.

"Judas," Philip said. "I think you have an enemy there."

"He does not look like a friend," Hugh agreed.

"I'd find out who he is, if I were you," Philip recommended.

Hugh nodded and lifted his ale cup.

A dog's sharp yelp cut through the noise of the hall. Evidently someone had trodden on his tail.

Philip returned to his original topic of conversation. "If you had the backing of Robert of Gloucester, you might stand a chance of displacing your uncle."

Hugh took a sip of his ale and did not reply.

"Earl Robert is a fine soldier," Philip went on. "With him to back you, you would not be powerless."

"So is Stephen a fine soldier," said Hugh. He took another sip of ale.

A roar of laughter came from the men seated farther down the table from them.

Philip snorted. "Stephen can fight, I will give you that. He just cannot *keep* at anything for very long. If he decided to support you and besiege Chippenham on your behalf, he would last outside the gates for no more than two weeks. Then he would lose interest and march away."

Someone shouted a question to Hugh. He shot back an answer, which produced another roar of laughter. Then he turned back to Philip and said regretfully, "You are probably right."

"He is a usurper," Philip said firmly. "Matilda is the only legitimate child of our old king. It is she—and her son after her—who should be England's ruler. Not Stephen."

"Stephen has been consecrated by the church," Hugh pointed out. "He was not doing a bad job as king until Robert of Gloucester decided to challenge him."

"He has not the right," Philip said stubbornly.

"Both sides have some part of the right," Hugh said. "To speak true, Philip, I am not overly interested in who has the greater right. I am interested in who will be the better ruler for England."

The noise in the hall was rising to a riotous level. If the food didn't come soon, half of the company would be drunk before the feast even started.

Philip was outraged. "You don't care about justice?" he demanded.

Hugh said, "I care about England. I do not want to see us plunged into a civil war. It will be devastating."

Philip drummed his fingers impatiently on the table. "Wiltshire is the bulwark that sits between Stephen's holdings in the east and Earl Robert's holdings in the west. The loyalty of the Earl of Wiltshire is crucial to both sides in this conflict."

"I realize that," Hugh said quietly.

Philip leaned his bright head closer to the ink-black one of the man seated beside him. He lowered his voice. "Come with me to meet Lord Simon," he said.

Hugh turned toward him, lifting an eyebrow. "So he can try to talk me into asking support from Earl Robert?"

Philip said grimly, "So that he can explain to you how vital it is for you to assume your rightful role as Earl of Wiltshire. So that he can tell you that the Earl of Gloucester will certainly support you, if you in turn will promise to support him."

Hugh looked faintly amused. "Do you know, Sir Nigel invited me to visit Stephen with him for the exact same reason?"

Philip set his jaw. "Nigel Haslin is not your blood kin. Simon of Evesham is your uncle."

"Is he?" Hugh said bleakly.

"Aye," Philip said. "He is."

At this point there was a blare of horns and Lord Guy, dressed in a splendid tunic of emerald green, entered the hall. A golden-haired woman wearing a purple gown walked beside him, her fingers daintily perched upon his arm. They were followed by a small retinue of knights, among whom was Sir Richard Evril.

"I don't know what your life has been like for the last fourteen years," Philip said to Hugh, "but as of this day you must make up your mind to take up the responsibilities you were born to."

After a tense moment of silence, Hugh replied, "If I am in fact the son of Roger de Leon, then my first obligation is to discover who is responsible for murdering my father."

Philip stared at the remote, perfect profile of the man sitting next to him, and did not have a reply.

Cristen thought the feast would never end. The tables sagged under the huge amounts of food set upon them. Immense platters of roast pork and roast venison, pheasants, pigeons, swans, peacocks, and larks as well as a wide variety of fish covered the boards. The trenchers that the guests used as plates were of fine white bread, not the usual stale stuff from the day before. The majority of the knights in the hall were being served ale, but at Cristen's table, wine was the drink being offered and it was being imbibed a bit too freely, she thought disapprovingly.

Even her father was celebrating the Somerford victories by drinking too much.

She fretted that she had not been able to sit with Hugh. He had been deeply upset this afternoon after his double encounter with Guy and Roger's old chaplain. She was not even able to see him over the heads of the hundreds of men crammed into the noisy hall.

"Sir Nigel."

Cristen looked around to see one of Lord Guy's squires standing next to her father.

"My lord would like to speak with you," the squire said.

Nigel had been laughing uproariously at a joke, but at these words, his face sobered. He rose slowly to his feet. "Of course," he said.

Cristen watched her father cross the floor to the high table, where a place had been made for him to sit next to Lord Guy. Nigel seemed steady on his feet, she thought, and prayed that he was sober enough to answer Guy's questions carefully.

There was no doubt in her mind that Guy wanted to know about Hugh.

A man sat down next to her. With a great effort of will, she repressed a shudder of distaste. It was Richard Evril.

"Lady Cristen," the knight said jovially. "You are looking lovely as always."

"Thank you," Cristen said.

"My lord is still curious about the young man who won the horsemanship contest today," Sir Richard said. "If he has been staying with you, you must know something about him."

"Is Lord Guy so curious about all the men who won the contests today?" Cristen asked ingenuously.

"He is only curious about the one who bears such a noticeable resemblance to himself," Sir Richard said grimly. "What do you know about him, Lady Cristen?"

Cristen replied with composure, "He is the lord of several manors in Lincolnshire. His father, Ralf Corbaille, left them to him when he was killed last summer."

"This Ralf Corbaille—was he the boy's true father?"

Cristen hesitated. "He was his foster father, I believe."

"Who was his true father, then?" Sir Richard asked sharply.

"I do not know," she said.

Sir Richard's slate-blue eyes narrowed. "Are they large manors?" he said.

Cristen stared at him in confusion.

Sir Richard repeated impatiently, "These manors owned by Hugh Corbaille—are they large?"

"Oh," Cristen said. "No, I don't believe they are very large."

"Then he is not a candidate for your hand?"

Cristen stared at the heavy knight repressively. "This is not a subject that you ought to be discussing with me, Sir Richard."

The knight's pudgy cheeks flushed with anger. "Come, girl, don't play the innocent with me. Before you set your heart on a handsome face, let me remind you that your father must have the permission of his overlord before you can wed. And I doubt very much that Lord Guy will give his consent for you to marry a man who owns but a few small manors in Lincolnshire."

He said the word *Lincolnshire* in the same tone as he would have said *pigsty*.

"And how many manors do you own, Sir Richard?" Cristen asked sweetly.

The broken veins in the knight's nose turned a brighter red. "Don't get saucy with me, my girl."

"It was you who wished to sit beside me, Sir Richard," Cristen replied.

She willed him to go away so she could turn her attention to what was transpiring between her father and Lord Guy at the high table.

"You have grown impertinent, Lady Cristen," the knight said

grimly. "It is not a pretty thing to see in a young girl. Your husband will have to teach you some manners."

"If my conversation does not please you, you have a remedy," Cristen said tartly.

The knight surged to his feet. "Very well. But you will regret speaking to me with such a lack of respect."

The lord of Minton Castle, who was sitting on Cristen's other side, turned, gave Sir Richard a hard look, and said, "Is everything all right with you, Lady Cristen?"

Cristen gave him a reassuring smile. "Aye, my lord."

After shooting her one more angry look, Sir Richard left, returning to the high table to make his report to Lord Guy.

"I don't like that man," Fulk of Minton said.

"Neither do I," Cristen replied.

The man on the other side of Fulk reclaimed his attention by asking a question about the next day's mêlée.

Finally Cristen was able to turn her eyes to the high table. She was in time to see her father get to his feet. Nigel recrossed the crowded floor and resumed his place next to her. He looked as if the conversation with Guy had rendered him completely sober.

"What did Lord Guy want?" she asked in a low voice.

He put his mouth close to her ear, so only she could hear his reply. "He wanted to know about Hugh, of course."

"What did you tell him?"

"I told him that I knew nothing about the boy other than the fact that he was the foster son of Ralf Corbaille. I told him that if he wanted an explanation of Hugh's startling resemblance to the de Leon family, he would have to talk to Hugh himself."

"Father . . ." Cristen's voice was not quite steady. "Father, Hugh still doesn't remember anything about his childhood. Perhaps he never will."

"I think he remembered the flag," Nigel said. "He may not admit it, but I think he did."

"Oh, God," Cristen said despairingly. "What have we done, bringing him here to this place?"

"I am trying to give him back his life, Cristen," Nigel said.

Cristen stared at the uneaten food on her trencher, and did not reply.

# 10

After the banquet was over, the knights filed out of the Great Hall to return to their pavilions. The mêlée was to be on the morrow, and before they went to sleep all the participants wanted to check once again the fit of each piece of armor and harness, go over hauberks of interlinking rings to make certain that none of the links were weak, inspect helms and sword hilts to make sure the joints were firm, and examine the noseguards on their helmets to make sure they were properly attached.

Hugh went through the same routine as the other men, although he spoke very little and appeared preoccupied. Finally he was able to crawl into his pallet next to the tent wall, where he lay awake for hours, with all of the images of the day flashing compulsively through his mind: Lord Guy, who had looked at him out of such chillingly familiar eyes; the priest, who had recognized him instantly; Philip Demain, who had sworn he was the image of Isabel de Leon.

*What could have happened to me all those years ago?* Hugh thought in frustration and fear.

*What was so dreadful that it caused me to lose my memory?*

He had a premonition that he knew the answer to that question. He thought of his reaction every time he entered a castle chapel, and he had a sickening feeling that he might actually have seen his father killed.

*I must find out the truth,* he told himself as he lay sleepless on his straw pallet, surrounded by dozens of other slumbering knights. *If a mere vassal like Nigel Haslin feels it his duty to seek justice for Roger de Leon, then how much greater must be the duty of a son?*

For he was Roger's son. He had to be. The resemblance was clearly too great to be passed off as a coincidence.

Then there was the de Leon flag. The golden boar. It had stirred something in him, some wisp of familiarity.

Or was he only imagining such a response?

Hugh flung a restless arm across his eyes.

The knight on the pallet next to him was snoring loudly.

*If I am to fight tomorrow I must get some sleep,* Hugh thought desperately.

But it was a very long time before he finally managed to drift into an uneasy slumber.

He awoke to pain.

He lay very still for a minute, listening to the sounds of the other knights in the pavilion as they rose from their pallets and began to dress.

The pain was in the back of his head, not in his forehead as before. It stabbed like a knife every time he moved.

*It's starting again,* Hugh thought in panic.

"Come on, Hugh," Thomas said jovially as he came to stand beside Hugh's pallet. "Time to get up and prepare for the mêlée."

Hugh lifted his head. Agony banded his skull from ear to ear across the back of his head.

Very slowly, being careful to move his head as little as he possibly could, Hugh arose and put on his clothes. Then he went out of the tent to look for a page.

The sunlight stabbed his eyes.

"Brian," he called to the boy, who was bustling past him carrying a well-polished sword. "Will you go and get the Lady Cristen for me? Tell her I am not feeling well."

The boy's hazel eyes widened in alarm. "You're sick, Hugh? But we need you today in the mêlée."

"Get Lady Cristen," Hugh repeated desperately.

The boy turned and ran off, the sword still held in his hand.

Hugh stood perfectly still. The pain was beginning to move higher in his head. His stomach was uneasy.

One of Nigel's knights joined him. "Breaking fast is in the bailey," he said. "Are you coming with us, Hugh?"

"Not just yet," Hugh said.

The knight stared at him. "You look very pale."

"I'm not feeling well," Hugh said. "Lady Cristen is coming. Perhaps she will have something to help."

"You drank too much last night," the knight said with a grin. "Don't worry, the Lady Cristen will have something for you. I've called on her myself in similar circumstances."

Hugh managed a shadowy smile in response.

He stood there in the brutal sunshine, agony pounding through his head, waiting for her.

The knights left to break their fast.

A few squires scurried around, busy with equipment and with stealing surreptitious looks at Hugh's immobile figure.

Then, finally, she was there.

"Hugh?"

"My head," he said, turning it very slowly to look at her out of heavy eyes. "The pain has started again, Cristen."

"Dear God." She put her hand on his arm. "Come inside out of the sun."

Eyes half-shut, he allowed her to lead him back into the pavilion. "Lie down," she said. "How is your stomach?"

Cautiously, he lowered himself to his pallet. "Uneasy."

From somewhere, she produced a bowl. "Here. Use this if you have to." She knelt on the ground next to him and opened up her medicine bag. "I packed my betony potion just in case this happened. I don't think it will make the headache go away completely, Hugh, but it might help with the pain."

By now the headache had moved into his forehead and was hammering against his temples with agonizing regularity.

He pushed himself up on his elbow and drank the medicine she gave him. Then he lay back down again, his eyes shut.

"The mêlée," he said faintly.

"You can't fight in this condition," she said.

She was right. At this point, he wasn't even capable of standing up, much less sitting on a horse.

His stomach heaved.

"Oh, God," he groaned. "Where is that bowl?"

She handed it to him, and he vomited what was left in his stomach of last night's dinner.

His head pounded harder.

He lay back down again. Cristen's gentle hand smoothed his hair off his sweaty forehead.

"I don't want anyone to see me like this," he said desperately.

"There's nowhere else to go, Hugh."

He groaned.

She said firmly, "No one will bother you as long as I am here."

He opened his eyes and looked up into her face. His eyes were almost black with pain. "You can't stay here in the knights' pavilion!"

"Of course I can stay," she returned. "The men will be back only to get into their armor and then they'll be heading for the stables to collect their horses. They'll be out of here in fifteen minutes. Don't worry, it will be all right."

But word had already passed among the Somerford men that Hugh was sick, and after breakfast Nigel came immediately to Hugh's pallet to ask Cristen what was the matter with him.

She looked up from her place on the ground next to Hugh's bed. "He is ill, Father," she said matter-of-factly. "Much too ill to participate in the mêlée, I'm afraid."

Nigel glanced over her head at Hugh's face. The boy's eyes were shut and his face was white and drawn with pain.

"What is it?" he asked his daughter in a lowered voice.

"I'm afraid something he ate last night must have disagreed with him," she returned. "He can barely stand, Father. You will have to do without him today."

Nigel scowled. He hated to part with his best knight. He looked again at Hugh's face and knew he had no choice. The boy did indeed look dreadfully ill.

"You can't remain here, Cristen," he said to his daughter gruffly. "We need you at the mêlée in case someone gets hurt."

"I have every intention of coming to the mêlée, Father," she said.

Hugh half-opened his eyes and looked up at Nigel. "I'm sorry, sir," he said.

"It's not your fault, boy," the older knight replied bracingly. "But Judas, we shall miss you."

Hugh managed a faint smile before he closed his eyes again.

Fifteen minutes later, the pavilion was empty once more.

"Is it any better at all, Hugh?" Cristen asked softly.

"I think the medicine is helping," he replied. His voice sounded stronger and a little color had come back to his face.

"Lady Cristen . . . "

She looked up to find one of the Somerford knights standing behind her.

"May I talk to Hugh for a moment?" he asked.

Cristen frowned.

Hugh said, "What is it, Geoffrey?"

Cristen rose to her feet. "I have to get dressed for the mêlée, Hugh," she said reluctantly.

"Go ahead," he replied. His eyes opened fully and held hers. "There's nothing more you can do here. And I really do think the medicine is helping."

She smiled at him, then turned to give an admonitory stare to the young knight standing behind her. "Don't talk for too long, Geoffrey."

"I won't, Lady Cristen," he replied earnestly.

With palpable reluctance, Cristen left the pavilion to go and array herself in her best finery in order to attend the mêlée.

Philip was glad that Father Anselm had insisted they follow Hugh to Chippenham. This was the only chance he would ever get to watch a tournament mêlée, and he was thrilled at the prospect.

Of course, it would have been even better if he could have participated in the fight himself. Unfortunately, it was out of the question for him to ask Nigel Haslin to add an unknown knight to his team, so Philip was forced to content himself with looking on.

This particular mêlée would have two hundred men on each of the two sides, which would be led by Lord Guy's vassals, each of whom had come to the tournament with a team of twenty knights. These teams had been grouped together by Lord Guy to form two opposing armies. Guy himself had forty knights participating in the mêlée, but he had divided his men so that twenty were assigned to either side, which kept the numbers even.

The action of a mêlée consisted of one side hurling itself upon the other, just as in a real battle. The goal was to unhorse as many knights as possible, to the point where the opposition could no longer hold together and was forced to flee the field in chaos.

Of course, Philip knew that the Chippenham tournament was negligible compared to the great tournaments that were staged in France. There, thousands of men fought on each side, and the field itself was immense, often encompassing a village or a vineyard where opposing knights could be driven and surrounded and made to surrender. Another difference between Chippenham and the French tournaments was that the knights participating in the French tournaments did not do so solely for the honor of their team. They came, as to war, in order to take weapons, harnesses, and horses, and to capture men for ransom. If a knight was skillful enough, much money was to be made in France.

The tournament at Chippenham was for honor only. But the participants took it with deadly seriousness, and the spectators did so as well. The wooden stands were filled with ladies dressed in brightly colored silk and samite, vigorously waving scarves that bore the colors of their teams. Lord Guy presided from the center of the stands, the same golden-haired lady who had been with him the previous evening once more at his side.

Philip was surprised that the earl was not on the field at the head of his own men, but a squire standing nearby told him that Guy never participated in the battle itself.

"He is the judge," the squire said a little scornfully. "He decides when to separate the sides during the fight, and when the mêlée is over, he chooses the best knight from among the winning team."

"And how is the winning team chosen?" Philip inquired.

The squire grinned. "Whichever team has the most men still on the field at the end of the day is the winner."

Philip and Father Anselm had stationed themselves in one of the lists, which were barricades at the side of the field behind which men could seek safety after they had been unhorsed. Any knight who tried to pursue a man into the lists would be heavily penalized.

Philip watched with eager anticipation as the two sides began to line up at the far ends of the open field. He searched for and found the blue and white flag of Somerford among the army to his right, then he trained his keen, farsighted gaze on Nigel's men as they began to form up into two lines of ten, one behind the other.

Suddenly, Philip frowned.

"I don't see Hugh," he said to Father Anselm.

The priest looked in the direction of the Somerford men.

"You're right," he said after a minute. "He isn't there. Unless he is riding another horse?"

"Wait a minute," Philip said. "Here he comes now."

As the two men watched, the white stallion that had swept the honors in the horsemanship contest the day before came cantering up to the Somerford team and moved into the place of honor next to Nigel.

The front line was the most dangerous as well as the most honorable place to be. If a knight in the front line was unhorsed, he faced the possibility of being trampled by the horses of his own side, which were directly behind him, as well as by the horses of the opposition.

The two sides continued to form up at the edges of the field, the team of each vassal making a definite unit within the larger group. The individual teams would fight as a company, striving to preserve their formation and to keep their ranks close. In the mêlée, individual honor was less important than holding together with one's comrades. Victory fell most often to the team that exhibited the most discipline and self-mastery.

Finally it seemed as if the lines of horsemen looming on the far edges of the field were in order.

A page carrying a horn stepped forward from beside Lord Guy and blew a blast upon his instrument.

The horsemen began to move forward.

The ground under Philip's feet vibrated with the thunder of four hundred horses coming at full gallop. Knights rode side by side, knee perilously close to knee, shield and reins and tilted lance balanced in skillful hands. The lances were the first weapons that would be used. Once they had shattered, which they did relatively easily, the knights would switch to the great broadswords that hung at their belts.

The sun shone on the helmets of the advancing knights and glinted off the polished metal in dazzling sheets of light. The leveled lances flashed and the brightly colored flags of the different teams streamed in the breeze created by the speed of the charging horses. Philip kept his eyes on the knight on the white stallion as he rode shoulder to shoulder with Nigel Haslin in the front line of the Somerford team.

The two sides met in the center of the field with an audible shock of collision. Philip could hear the clash of lance against lance and lance against mail hauberk. Most of the fragile weapons shattered and fell to the ground with the first or second encounter. The war cry of each vassal sounded through the now-dusty air as knights unsheathed their swords and began to hack away.

Unhorsed men were hurled into the air. Riderless horses galloped madly away from the combat, snorting and sweating, frantic to find safety.

After the fight had gone on for a while, the horn that had started the mêlée blasted once more. Slowly, with obvious reluctance, the two sides disengaged and pulled back to their points of origin at the edges of the field, milling around and counting up their losses.

As soon as the mounted knights had retreated, squires dashed onto the field to pull those who had fallen out of the way. If this had been a real war, of course, there would have been no retreat and the unhorsed men would have met certain death under the hooves of the great stallions who were still carrying on the battle.

Five knights were brought into the list where Philip and Father Anselm were stationed. Philip checked the devices on their sleeves and saw that none of them were men of Somerford.

One of the knights was moaning in pain, bent over and clutching his middle. Philip figured he probably had some broken ribs. A second had a broken arm. The other three were merely bruised and shaken.

All had gotten their injuries as a result of being run over by horses.

The two sides were forming up again and all of the men in the lists, even the man with the broken ribs, turned to watch the next encounter.

The horn sounded and on they came again, two great waves of horsemen, long shields on one arm, broadswords in the other. Some of the men had slung their shields on their backs so they had two hands free to swing their swords. They did this because the broadsword was actually more of a concussion than a cutting weapon. While the mail the knights wore protected them from being sliced by the blade, the hauberk of interlinking rings could not prevent a man from having his bones crushed by the powerful blow of a massive broadsword, especially if it was swung two-handed by the knight wielding it.

Each side had lost about a fourth of its men in the first encounter. The remaining knights appeared to have lost none of their ardor for battle, however, and galloped eagerly forward, side by side, until the front lines of one side reached the front lines of the other.

Once again they came together with a loud clanging of swords, of men shouting, of horses screaming as their riders were swept away and they were left to fend for themselves.

Philip tried to keep his eye on the white stallion that carried Hugh. It was difficult, as the trampling of the many hooves had raised a cloud of dust around the entire mêlée. It seemed to him as if the men of Somerford were maintaining their formation in better order than the men of the other vassals, but he couldn't be certain.

Once again the horn blew. Once again the horses wheeled and retreated to the edges of the field. Once again the squires rushed forth to retrieve the unhorsed men left lying on the field. More men were carried into the list where Philip and Father Anselm were stationed.

It happened on the third charge. Philip, whose eyes were glued to the white stallion, saw the incident very clearly. The two sides met with the now-familiar shock of noise, and Hugh pitched sharply forward over the shoulder of his stallion. He disappeared under the hooves of the horses who were coming behind him.

Philip's stomach clenched.

"Hugh's down," he said to the priest, who was standing next to him.

"Oh no," said the Father Anselm. "Oh, my dear God, no."

The white stallion, riderless now, came galloping out of the mass of fighting men and stopped on the edge of the field to look around, as if bewildered. A squire belonging to Nigel Haslin darted out to catch his bridle and lead him away.

Philip watched the fighting with a feeling of helpless horror. It was impossible to find Hugh. He had gone down in the middle of the line and been instantly surrounded. It had happened so quickly that his own men had been past him before they could even realize he was on the ground.

The fighting went on for a much longer period of time than had been allowed before. Finally, when Philip had despaired of Guy's ever ending the battle, the horn blew again and the now seriously depleted sides retreated once more.

One of Nigel's squires raced onto the field and began to look through the fallen bodies, searching for Hugh.

Philip felt his blunt fingernails pressing into his palms as he watched the squire's progress. At last the boy dropped to his knees next to one of the inert bodies. Five seconds later, he stood up again and signaled for help. Cristen came running onto the field to join him. She knelt in the dust next to the fallen knight, totally oblivious of her fine silk gown.

The fallen man did not move.

"Judas," Philip croaked. "He's been killed."

"He can't be dead," the priest replied in anguish. "God would not be so cruel, to give him back to us only to take him away again like this."

"He went off right at the beginning of the charge," Philip said. Anger shook his voice. "And he went off his horse in a forward motion, Father. I saw it happen." He turned to look at the priest standing beside him and said, his anger even more evident than before, "He went off as if he had taken a blow from behind, not from in front."

The priest's eyes swung around to meet Philip's. "What are you saying?"

The answer was grim. "I'm saying that Hugh was struck down by someone on his own side."

The priest stared at him in horror.

The squire who had first reached Hugh was now running across the field in their direction. He reached the list and spoke across the barrier directly to Father Anselm. "Is it true that you're a priest?"

Father Anselm answered without a moment's hesitation. "Aye."

"We have need of you," the squire said. There were tears in his hazel eyes. "Will you come?"

"Aye," said Father Anselm once more and, putting his hand on the barrier, he vaulted over it onto the field and strode across the trampled earth in the direction of the fallen man.

# 11

It wasn't Hugh.

That was the first thing Father Anselm saw as he knelt beside the knight lying lifeless on the trampled earth. The bruised young face looking up at him did not belong to Hugh.

"He's dead, Father," Cristen said. She was holding the young knight's hand. "Can you give him the last rites?"

"Aye," said the priest. "He has not been long on his journey."

He made the sign of the cross, and all of those in the vicinity dropped to their knees and did likewise.

The serene blue sky looked down peacefully as Father Anselm recited the Latin prayers for the dead over the crumpled body laying so quietly on the bloodstained field of Chippenham. When he had finished, they lifted Geoffrey onto a hurdle and carried him away.

Once the sad cortege was out of sight, the horn blew and the mêlée began once again.

"I saw it happen."

It was two hours later and Philip was talking to Nigel outside the pavilion where the Somerford knights were lodged. He repeated to Geoffrey's lord what he had said earlier to Father Anselm. "He went forward over his horse's shoulder, as if he had received a blow from behind, not before."

There was a white line down the center of Nigel's thin, aristocratic nose. He said, "It was my men who were behind him."

"Guy had twenty men on your side," Philip said. "Was it possible for one of them to get behind Geoffrey in the rush of the charge?"

Nigel was pale under his tan. "I suppose it could have happened. The third charge was much more disorganized than the first two." His lips tightened. "His armor was so crushed from the horses' hooves that it is impossible to tell if he took a sword blow from behind."

Two of Nigel's knights walked past, somber-faced. They cast a quick glance at their lord, then went on into the pavilion.

"It was meant for Hugh," Philip said. "Whoever did this meant to kill Hugh."

"Aye," Nigel said. "That is how it must have been."

"Why wasn't he there?" Philip demanded. "Why didn't he fight in the mêlée?"

Nigel replied wearily, "Hugh was ill this morning, and then Geoffrey's roan came up lame. That would have left our team two men short and so Geoffrey asked Hugh if he could ride Rufus in the mêlée. Hugh said that he could."

A group of knights belonging to another of Guy's vassals approached the pavilion, spurs jingling, dusty helmets tucked under their arms. They were laughing and talking in loud voices. One of them pointed to Nigel, and they all respectfully moderated their tones.

"If I thought it was Hugh on Rufus, then you can be certain that others did likewise," Philip said grimly. "Hugh's illness saved his life."

The two men looked at each other.

"Where is he now?" Philip asked.

"I don't know. He's not in the pavilion. I just looked."

"Where have they put Geoffrey?"

Nigel's eyes widened with enlightenment. "Lord Guy had him taken to the castle chapel."

"The chapel," said Philip. "Isn't that where . . . ?"

"Aye," said Nigel. He swung around in the direction of the castle. "Let's go."

Without hesitation, Philip followed.

He didn't want to do this, but he had to. He had to see Geoffrey, and Geoffrey was in the chapel.

Because of him, Geoffrey was dead.

Hugh knew that as surely as he knew that Adela had loved him.

Geoffrey had borrowed his horse this morning, and because of that, Geoffrey was dead.

Guy had killed him thinking he was Hugh.

He walked like a sleepwalker, across the torn-up field of Chippenham, through the gate in the immense stone wall, across the outer bailey, and through the gatehouse of the inner walls, the Somerford insignia on his sleeve affording him immediate access to the castle. There had been but one fatality at the tournament, and everyone knew that it was one of Nigel's men who had fallen.

Oblivious to the eyes that were watching him, Hugh climbed the steep stone ramp that led to the castle entrance. Once inside the small hall, he automatically turned to his left, entered the fore-building, and began to climb the stairs to the third floor, where he knew the chapel was located.

The familiar sick, frightened feeling began to tighten his stomach.

The stone staircase was cold.

He stepped out onto a wooden-floored landing. Two massive doors confronted him. Both were closed. Without thought, he stepped to the door that led to the chapel and opened it.

Geoffrey's broken body had been carefully straightened and laid upon a bier in front of the altar. Candles flickered at his head and his feet.

The chapel smelled faintly of old incense and damp.

There was a window in the shape of a half-circle set in the stone wall over the altar. It was open and the late-afternoon sunlight was pouring through it, falling on the altar, which was carved of dark wood and covered with a crisp white embroidered cloth.

Hugh stared at the window and, deep within the recesses of his memory, something stirred.

He began to shiver.

With a great effort of will, he forced himself to walk to the bier and look down at Geoffrey.

*My fault,* he thought. *It's all my fault.*

The shivering grew stronger.

Feelings of guilt.

Of terror.

The image of a man's body sprawled on the floor, almost in the exact same place where Geoffrey now lay.

Blood.

*My fault. My fault.*

By now the shivering had grown almost uncontrollable. He couldn't breathe.

Hugh lifted his shaking hand and smashed his fist against the corner of Geoffrey's bier. The hair on his forehead stirred with the force of the blow.

The immediate, sharp pain helped to clear his head. He was breathing as if he had run twenty miles.

He forced his eyes to focus on Geoffrey's quiet face.

Never again would Geoffrey know the simple joys of riding his horse in the autumn sunshine, of singing songs around the massive fireplace at Somerford, of donning his armor and working out on the practice field with his fellow knights. At the age of twenty-three, Geoffrey was dead.

Because of Hugh.

*But I am no longer a helpless seven-year-old,* Hugh thought grimly as he stared down at the quiet face of the dead young knight. *Now I am a man. Now I am someone to be reckoned with. Now I am capable of retribution.*

After a few moments, he turned on his heel and left the chapel. Never once did he notice the figure of Father Anselm, on his knees in a darkened corner.

Philip and Nigel met him as he was coming out of the forebuilding.

"Hugh!" Nigel cried. "We've been looking for you."

Hugh's face was pale, but otherwise he had himself under strict control. "I have just been to see Geoffrey."

They were standing at the bottom of the stone ramp that led to the castle entrance, and now Nigel glanced around to make sure no one was near enough to overhear them. When he was assured that it was safe, he continued in a low voice, "Philip here saw the whole incident and he is convinced that Geoffrey was hit from behind, not from before."

Hugh's expression did not change.

"Do you understand the implications of this, Hugh?" Nigel said. "Only our own men knew that it was Geoffrey and not you riding Rufus."

"I understand very well," Hugh said. "You are saying it is I who should be lying dead in that chapel, not Geoffrey."

"That's right," Philip said grimly.

"It was done by Guy's order, I'm sure of it," said Nigel. "He had some of his men fighting with us. Both sides were greatly depleted by the third charge. It would not have been difficult for one of his men to have gotten behind Geoffrey."

"I have little doubt that that is what happened," Hugh said. "Geoffrey was too good a horseman to have been unseated at the very beginning of a charge."

His voice was cool. Philip would have thought Geoffrey's fate was of no consequence to him were it not for the pallor of his self-contained face and the shadows under his eyes.

Of course, they might have been the result of his illness.

"What was the matter with you this morning?" Philip asked abruptly. "You seem perfectly all right now. What was it that kept you from participating in the mêlée?"

The look in Hugh's gray eyes froze the blood in his veins.

"I was ill," Hugh said.

Philip, who was a brave man, found that he did not have the nerve to inquire farther.

After a moment of distinctly uncomfortable silence, Nigel attempted to carry on. "Then you were in the chapel just now?"

"Aye," said Hugh.

He looked at Nigel, his face as cold as winter ice.

Nigel, who wanted to ask if he had remembered anything, found that he couldn't say anything.

"If you will both excuse me," Hugh said. "I have something I must do."

The two men stood and watched Hugh's slender figure as he made his way across the inner bailey and out between the twin gate towers.

"What do you think happened while he was in the chapel?" Philip asked when Hugh was no longer in sight.

"Something that he doesn't want to talk about," said Nigel. "Which means, I think, that he is starting to remember."

Cristen had also seen Geoffrey go down and she had come to the same conclusion as Philip. The blow that had felled Geoffrey had come from behind and had been intended as an execution.

She said as much to Hugh when he sought her out after he had returned from his visit to the chapel.

"Aye," he said. "I believe you, Cristen."

They were walking together along the horse lines, where the hundreds of visiting horses had been picketed to be taken care of by their own grooms. Hugh was going to check on Rufus, and on Geoffrey's lame roan as well.

"Geoffrey's death was Guy's doing, Hugh, not yours," Cristen said now, quietly.

The black stallion they were passing stamped his rear off leg and swished his tail irritably.

"He was killed because someone mistook him for me," Hugh said.

"Aye," she agreed. "Lord Guy recognized you."

Hugh said in a strange voice, "Evidently he has."

In reply, she slipped her hand into his.

They walked for another few feet along the line of tethered horses. The great war stallions, tired from their day's exertions, munched on piles of hay while grooms brushed the dust out of their once shiny coats and picked the dirt out of their hooves.

Gray clouds were blowing in from the west, covering the blue sky of early afternoon. The smell of horses filled the air.

Hugh said in the same strange voice he had spoken with earlier, "I am Hugh de Leon, Cristen, aren't I?"

"Aye," she said matter-of-factly. "I believe that you are."

A groom cursed as one of the stallions swung around on him with bared teeth.

"I think I knew it all along," Hugh said.

Her fingers tightened around his.

He drew in a long, shuddering breath. "I remembered the chapel."

"Did you?"

"I remembered the window, at any rate. I remembered the way the sunlight used to come through it. I remembered the way the dust motes used to dance in the air."

He didn't want to tell anyone, even her, about the brief vision he had had of a dead man in front of the altar.

He inhaled deeply once again. "So now I must decide what I should do next."

"The first thing you must do is get away from Chippenham," she said decisively. "You're not safe here, Hugh. That has been made abundantly clear."

With his boot he kicked a wisp of hay that had blown in front of them. "I think I shall go with Philip Demain to pay a visit to Simon of Evesham," he said. "If Simon formally recognizes me as the son of Roger and Isabel, then Guy will have to pay attention to me."

"For God's sake, he has already paid attention to you," Cristen cried. "He tried to kill you!"

"No." Hugh shook his head. "He tried to kill an obscure knight who came to Chippenham in the company of one of his vassals. It will be a very different thing for him to try to kill his brother's son."

Cristen began to shiver.

He dropped her hand and reached his arm around her shoulders, as if he could give her some of his warmth. "Try to understand. This is something I have to do. If Guy is indeed responsible for my father's death, then he must be made to pay for it. He already owes a debt for Geoffrey."

Cristen tilted her head to look up into his face. "Why go to Simon, Hugh? Why not go to your mother?"

He stiffened. "Simon has power," he said. "Isabel has none."

A faint line appeared between her delicate brows. "Still . . . you are planning to go to see her? It will give her such joy to know that you are alive."

His high cheekbones looked as if they might push out through his taut, pale skin. She was close enough to him to feel that he was trembling.

"I . . . I can't," he said after a while.

"Why not?" she asked softly.

He didn't answer.

"Hugh?" she said. "Why not?"

"I don't know," he returned at last. He stared down at her, his eyes glittering. "I don't know, Cristen. All I know is that I dare not see her again."

Guy le Gaucher looked around his packed hall, his eyes searching for one particular figure. When he didn't find it, he turned and spoke to the man who sat on the far side of the woman whose place was beside him.

"Where is the boy?" he demanded. "For that matter, where are Nigel Haslin and his daughter? I don't see them anywhere in the hall."

Sir Richard Evril replied, "Shall I find out?"

"Aye," said Guy. "Do that."

Guy sat in brooding silence, drinking his wine and staring at the boisterous scene before him. His golden-haired companion tried to get his attention by leaning against him, but he ignored her.

*If that boy has gotten away . . .* he thought in fury.

It took Sir Richard ten minutes to discover that Nigel Haslin and all his knights had departed from Chippenham several hours earlier.

Guy was livid. "What about the body that lies in my chapel? Did they leave it?"

"They must have left it," Richard said. "Certainly no one saw it being removed. If they had, they would have reported it to me."

"Go and check," Guy said.

Sir Richard looked as if he were going to object. The food was being served and he was hungry. One look at Guy's face changed his mind, however, and without further comment he left the table to go to the chapel.

He was back before Guy had had a chance to take more than a few bites of the roast swan that was on his trencher.

"It's gone," Richard said. His veined cheeks were red with

anger. "They took the body away and no one reported it to me."

Guy slammed his hand down on the table and the blonde lady next to him jumped.

"I want that boy back here," he said in a low, menacing voice. "I don't want him showing that face around the countryside. If Simon of Evesham gets a look at him .. . ."

"You can always say he is a bastard, my lord," Richard said reasonably. "It is true that he has the de Leon eyes, but there is no proof that he came by them honestly."

"You fool," Guy snarled. "First of all, my dear brother was far too righteous ever to stray from the sacrament of holy matrimony. In truth, the great crusader had the soul of a priest." Guy's voice was full of contempt. "He only married to keep me from becoming earl."

The blonde lady sitting next to him laughed knowingly. "You certainly don't have the soul of a priest, my lord."

"Shut up," Guy said.

She shrank into herself and was quiet.

"Even the holiest of men may be tempted by a beautiful woman," Richard insisted.

"You don't understand," Guy said impatiently. "That boy may have the de Leon eyes, but the rest of his face is a mirror image of my sister-in-law. That is why Nigel Haslin picked him up, of course. He saw the resemblance and thought to use the boy against me. Nigel has always suspected I had something to do with my brother's death." He glared at the woman next to him. "Which I didn't!"

"Of course not, my lord," she said hastily.

Guy narrowed his eyes in a way that made him look remarkably like Hugh. "I have no intention of turning my honors over to an upstart boy, even if he is my nephew. I will hold what is mine, no matter what it costs to do so."

"What do you think he is going to do next?" Sir Richard asked.

"I think Nigel will take him to Stephen," Guy said. He set his jaw angrily. "Which means that I must get to Stephen first."

# 12

Nigel was enormously relieved when he reached Somerford safely. All during the ride he had been blaming himself bitterly for his carelessness in taking Hugh to Chippenham.

*I should have realized that Guy was bound to strike out at the boy,* he thought as he walked wearily up the ramp to the door of his castle. *He killed to get the earldom. What a fool I was not to realize that he would kill again to keep it.*

He looked at his daughter, who was walking beside him.

"I feel like a fool, Cristen," he said. "It is my fault that Geoffrey is dead."

She said to her father what she had said earlier to Hugh. "The fault is Guy's, Father, not yours."

"That's too easy a way out," he said tiredly. "It is I who bear the responsibility of taking Hugh to Chippenham. And all that was on my mind when I did so was that perhaps he would remember something if he saw the place where he passed his childhood. I never thought seriously about Guy's reaction. I was only thinking of Hugh's."

They passed through the door, which was being held open for them by a page, and entered the Great Hall.

Cristen was immediately attacked by her dogs, who leaped around her in ecstasy.

"Manners, manners," she admonished them, but her hands were caressing two eager heads and scratching two blissful sets of ears.

"Watch out they don't knock you over," Nigel warned.

She laughed and knelt down to be closer to her welcoming party. "I missed you, too," she said to shiny black Ralf. "And I missed you as well," she added to the rapturous shaggy brown ball that was Cedric.

Nigel had moved along to the fire, which was burning brightly in welcome for the lord of the castle, lowered himself to the largest chair, and called for a cup of wine. It was nine o'clock at night and the day had been a long one. Nigel was feeling every one of his fifty-five years.

A group of returning knights had come in the door after Nigel and Cristen, but their numbers were depleted, as Hugh and some others had taken Geoffrey's body into Malmesbury, to see him properly disposed in the abbey church.

Finally Cristen was able to quiet her admirers enough to come and join her father by the fire.

She sat in one of the high-backed chairs and a page brought her a cup of wine, which she sipped gratefully.

"That was quite a coup the men pulled off, managing to extricate Geoffrey's body without any of Guy's men knowing what they were doing," she said with admiration.

"Aye," said Nigel. "Two of them held his arms around their necks and carried him away from the castle seated on their crossed hands. They told the guards that he was one of the men who had accompanied them to pay their respects to Geoffrey, but that he had drunk too much earlier and had passed out."

"Thank God his body had not yet begun to stiffen," Cristen said.

"Aye," her father agreed. He leaned back in his chair, stretched his legs before him, rested his chin on his chest, and said sorrowfully, "Poor Geoffrey. He was a fine lad. I dread having to tell his mother that he is dead."

"I know," said Cristen.

One of the dogs nudged her thigh. Automatically, she stroked his head.

Behind them, the knights who had returned with them were

speaking in low voices as they unpacked their gear. Cristen's ladies had already retired to their solar on the next floor.

"Your idea to take Hugh to Chippenham was not entirely without merit, Father," she said quietly. "He did remember something."

Nigel's head jerked up. "He did?"

"Aye." She continued to stroke Ralf's black head. "He told me that he remembered the chapel."

Nigel stared at the small, pure oval of his daughter's face. She was wearing her long brown hair in braids and they fell across her shoulders all the way down past her waist. One of them almost touched the dog's head.

"He wouldn't tell me anything at all," Nigel said.

"It is that he is more comfortable with me," she said easily. "I think it is less difficult for him to talk to women than to men. He loved his foster mother a great deal, you see."

She didn't say anything to her father about Hugh's refusal to meet his natural mother.

Nigel put his hands on the carved oak arms of his chair. "And did he see fit to confide any of his future plans to you?" he asked, a slight edge to his voice.

"Just that he was going to pay a visit to Simon of Evesham," she replied serenely. "Evidently Philip Demain asked him to go back with him."

At that, Nigel pushed himself upright in his chair. "Simon of Evesham is a supporter of the empress!"

Both dogs looked at him, reacting to the tone of his voice. Ralf laid his ears back and growled softly in his throat. Cristen patted him reassuringly.

"Set your mind at rest, Father," she said, her voice as reassuring as her pat to Ralf. "I don't think Hugh is interested in politics at the moment." Her face was grave. "I'm sorry to say that at present, his sole interest appears to lie in avenging the death of his father."

Nigel's eyes, the same color as his daughter's but not nearly as large, were fixed on her face. "Are you saying that he has finally admitted that he is Hugh de Leon?"

Cristen said simply, "Aye, he has."

Nigel pounded his fists on the arms of the chair. "That is wonderful!"

"I don't know," Cristen said.

He scowled at her. "Surely you couldn't wish him to continue as he was? As Hugh Corbaille he owned three small manors in Lincolnshire. As Earl of Wiltshire he will be the overlord of *forty-three* manors—in Wiltshire, Dorset, Somerset, Hampshire, Surrey, Buckinghamshire, Hertfordshire, and Oxfordshire!"

She withdrew her hand from the dog. She looked very small in the big chair, almost like a child. The expression on her face was not at all childlike, however.

She said, "But he is not the Earl of Wiltshire yet, Father, and in order to gain that title he will have to overcome Lord Guy—who is a formidable adversary, as we have discovered to our sorrow."

"I realize that, my dear," Nigel said. "But the king is desperate to control Wiltshire. The support of the Earl of Wiltshire, like that of the Earl of Chester and the Earl of Essex, are prizes that both Stephen and the empress will be vying for with all the largesse that is in their gift."

Cristen smoothed her hand along one of her braids. "Have you thought that it is possible that Guy will sell his backing to Stephen in order to gain Stephen's support against Hugh? Guy is the man presently in possession of the earldom, remember. It will be almost impossible to dislodge him if he has the backing of the king."

Nigel scowled. "Guy is staying aloof from this fight."

"He was staying aloof before he knew about Hugh," Cristen said. "Now that he knows there is a challenger for his title, he may well offer to sell his support to Stephen in exchange for the king's promise of assistance against Hugh's claim."

Nigel's scowl deepened. "Then we must get to Stephen first."

Cristen said, "Hugh is right. First he must go to Simon of Evesham to have his claim validated. By the time he does that, however, it may be too late to go to Stephen."

Nigel cursed. Then he muttered apologetically, "Sorry, my dear."

Cristen leaned her head back against the carved wood of her chair. Her face looked strained. "I'm afraid, Father," she said. "I'm afraid for Hugh."

Ralf pushed himself under her feet so that he was serving as her footrest.

"I will tell you something about Hugh, Cristen," her father replied. "He is the most thoroughly competent young man I have ever been privileged to meet. Believe me, he can take care of himself."

"In the field he can," she returned grimly. "But his fighting skills won't save him from a knife in his back."

"No." Nigel's face was perfectly sober. "That will be the job of his friends."

By the time Hugh returned to Somerford, Nigel had gone to bed and Cristen had retired to the family solar. As Hugh was sleeping in one of the bedrooms that led off the solar, and not in the hall with the other knights, he entered the family refuge to find her sitting in front of the brazier, which had been lit against the chilly autumn night.

"You saw Geoffrey safely to the church?" she asked quietly as he shut the door behind him.

"Aye." He took the chair next to hers and stretched his cold hands out to the brazier.

"Father is going to ride over to Bradly to see his family tomorrow morning. They may wish to bring his body home for burial."

"Aye," he said again.

She sighed. "He blames himself for Geoffrey's death."

"Your father blames himself?" He stared at her in shocked surprise. "It was my fault, not his!"

"It was as much my father's fault as it was yours, Hugh," she replied. "He blames himself for bringing you to Chippenham without foreseeing what Guy's response might be." Her eyes were on his hands, which were still held out toward the brazier. "You, on the other hand, blame yourself for getting sick and letting Geoffrey borrow your horse."

He continued to stare at her. The hands he was holding out to the fire were rigid. "You don't think it was either of our faults?" he demanded.

At last she turned her eyes to meet his. "I can understand why you both feel guilty about Geoffrey," she said. "Whenever someone is connected to the death of another, it is only natural to feel some degree of guilt." Her voice was quiet, her face grave. "Believe me,

Hugh, when I tell you that I understand this. I feel guilty every time I'm called in to help someone with my herbs and I fail."

There was a line sharp as a sword between his brows. "That's ridiculous. You try to help. There is no reason for you to feel guilty if you fail!"

"I understand that with my reason." The light from the brazier illuminated the peach-colored glow of her suntanned cheeks. "But I feel guilty that my knowledge isn't enough. It isn't a rational feeling, I realize that, and I don't let it stop me from trying again. Nonetheless, it's there."

There was a long silence while Hugh continued to look at her.

At last he moved, leaning his dark head against the back of his chair. "You are saying that it's natural for me to feel guilty about Geoffrey, but that I shouldn't let it cripple me," he said.

She regarded him, her great brown eyes filled with beautiful clarity. "Aye," she said. "That is what I am saying."

His face was very still. "That is what Bernard said when I let Ralf walk ahead without me. Strange how it never seems to be my fault when the people around me get killed."

She said, "My mother caught the illness she died of from me."

An expression finally flickered across his face. "Jesu," he said. "What a selfish monster you must think me."

She shook her head. "No. You're just human, Hugh. And that means you feel guilty. Isn't that what original sin is all about?"

*I felt guilty in that chapel and it had nothing to do with original sin.*

But he didn't say it. He knew the feeling was connected somehow with the image of the body he had seen lying on the chapel floor. He didn't understand what he had seen and felt, but he knew that somehow he was going to find out. No matter how terrible his past had been, he couldn't live without it any longer.

He gave Cristen a faint smile. "All right," he said. "I understand what you are saying."

She smiled back. "Talk to Father Anselm," she recommended. "He was a member of the Chippenham household when you were young. He should be able to answer some of your questions."

He wasn't even surprised that she had divined his thoughts. She had done it too often before.

He nodded. "I will."

All of a sudden, she yawned, showing an expanse of pink mouth and white teeth. He smiled. "Go to bed," he said. "You must be exhausted."

She wrinkled her nose at him. "I am."

She didn't tell him that he must be tired as well. Cristen never said the wrong thing.

She stood up. "Good night, Hugh."

Courteously, he stood as well. "Good night, Cristen."

He watched her small, straight-backed figure as she crossed the solar floor and opened the door that led to her bedroom. She went in without looking back.

A few minutes later, Hugh made his way to his own room. The squire who was sleepily waiting inside brought him water and helped him out of his clothes, and in short order he was sliding naked into the comfortable bed.

He had been prepared for sleeplessness, but to his great surprise he fell into deep slumber immediately and slept soundly through the night.

Philip Demain was sleeping in the Great Hall along with Father Anselm and Nigel's resident knights. The third floor of the castle was reserved for the ladies, and Somerford was not big enough to have a large number of private bedchambers.

As Philip settled himself comfortably on the straw mattress that was to be his bed for the night, he reflected complacently that his mission had been a success. Not only had he been able to identify Hugh as the son of Roger and Isabel, but Hugh was going to accompany him back to Evesham to show himself to his uncle, Philip's lord. No doubt once the visit to Simon was accomplished, he would go on to Worcester to see his mother.

Philip said now to Father Anselm, who was lying on the mattress next to his, "You will be accompanying us back to Evesham, Father, won't you?"

"No," the priest surprised him by saying. "I will be returning to Winchester. I have duties at the cathedral there that I cannot neglect."

The two men had found a corner to themselves, thus gaining a modicum of privacy from the rest of the knights. Philip said now, his voice pitched softly so that no one but the priest would hear him, "But . . . I had thought you would want to spend some time with Hugh. If he is to regain his memory, he needs to have someone who can tell him stories about his childhood. My own lord cannot do that. He scarcely knew Hugh when he was a child."

There was a long silence. Then the priest said in a strained voice, "Believe me, son, it is better for Hugh not to remember."

Philip pushed himself up on his elbow and tried to see the priest through the darkness of the hall. All he could make out, however, was a shadowy outline lying on top of the mattress.

He said, "Why should you say such a thing? Here is a man who is the son of one of England's greatest crusaders. His mother is the most beautiful woman I have ever laid eyes on. He is the rightful heir to the earldom of Wiltshire. Judas," said Philip with a rough laugh, "I wish I were in his position!"

"No," the priest said with great somberness. "You don't."

Philip leaned a little closer to the priest, trying to see his face. "I don't understand you. It's true that his father was killed in a dreadful way. Hugh's kidnapping was dreadful as well, but he was found and nurtured by fine people. Judas, it's not as if he had been abused!"

The priest said in an uneven voice, "It is true that God was looking out for Hugh when he put him into the hands of Ralf Corbaille."

Philip continued to stare at the priest through the dark. At last he said firmly, "I think you should come to Evesham with us. Hugh told me that he is committed to solving the murder of his father. He will have questions to ask that only someone who was a member of Roger's household will be able to answer."

The priest surprised Philip by jerking upward to a sitting position. "He wants to find Lord Roger's murderer?"

Philip replied in a reasonable voice, "It's only natural that he should feel that way, Father. He is the man's son, after all."

Father Anselm reached out in the dark and closed his fingers around Philip's arm. "He mustn't," he said hoarsely. "Tell him to leave it alone. Roger is dead and nothing can bring him back. Tell Hugh to leave it alone!"

The priest's long fingers were pressing into the hard muscles of Philip's upper arm.

"Don't you understand the necessity of such a search?" the young knight said, lifting his right hand to pry those painful fingers away. "If Hugh can prove that Guy was involved in the death of his own brother, then the church will take Roger's honors away from Guy. A murderer is not allowed to benefit from his crime, and fratricide is one of the worst crimes that one can imagine."

"I understand the consequences of such a search far better than you," Father Anselm said darkly. "Hugh must leave the manner of Roger's death alone. Let him seek to win his earldom in some other way."

The priest's fingers loosened of their own accord and dropped away from Philip's arm.

"What do you know that you are not telling?" Philip demanded harshly. "Do you know who killed Lord Roger?"

The priest flopped back down on his mattress. "Everyone knows who killed Lord Roger. It was Walter Crespin, the same man who kidnapped Hugh."

"If that is true, then why are you so adamant that Hugh should investigate the matter no further?"

The priest groaned. "Ask me no more about this, Philip."

Slowly, Philip lowered himself back onto his own mattress. "Hugh is unlikely to stop his pursuit of the truth just because I tell him to," he said.

Silence fell. Philip was just drifting off to sleep when Father Anselm said, "Is Hugh going to visit his mother?"

"Of course he will visit his mother," returned Philip sleepily.

"Then I will come with you to Evesham," the priest said. "My duties at the cathedral will have to wait a little longer."

# 13

Nigel rode to the manor of Bradley the following morning, to bring the news of their son's demise to Geoffrey's family. Geoffrey's mother was heartbroken, but Geoffrey's father took the news philosophically. Geoffrey was a younger son, and in the feudal world of the twelfth century, younger sons were expendable, particularly when there were five of them.

Then, too, Geoffrey had lived at Somerford since he was eight years of age. Nigel probably knew him better, and mourned him more deeply, than did his father.

Consequently, Geoffrey's father's decision to leave his body where it was came as small surprise to anyone. As soon as Nigel returned to Somerford from Bradley, he went into Malmesbury and made the necessary arrangements for the funeral. The following day, the family and the knights of Somerford filled the abbey church to say their reverent farewells to the young man who had been one of their own.

Cristen knelt in the first pew, with her father on one side of her and Hugh on the other. After communion, she bowed her head, the host still held devoutly on her tongue, and prayed with heartfelt fervor. Her prayer was not for Geoffrey, however, who was safe now with God, but for Hugh, whom she knew was in deadly danger.

*Dear Lord, give Hugh the wisdom to do what is the right*

*thing in this tangle that faces him. Guide him and be ever close by his
side. Give him the strength to face whatever it is that must be faced, and
most of all, Dear Lord, keep him safe. Amen.*

They came out of the church into a gray, overcast day. The
weather matched the mood of the mourners as they followed
Geoffrey to the churchyard, which was situated just outside the
walls of the abbey, and saw his coffined body lowered into the
freshly dug earth.

Thomas was crying. One of the older knights put an arm
around the young man's shoulders to comfort him.

Nigel's head was bowed. His face was lined with grief.

Hugh's face was perfectly shuttered. He stood a little apart from
the others, watching as the gravedigger threw shovelfuls of earth on
top of Geoffrey.

Cristen's heart ached for him, but it was to her father's side that
she went.

"It's time to go," she said.

He turned to her wearily. "Aye."

He took her arm and began to walk away from the grave. The
rest of the knights followed behind them.

"Hugh," she heard one of them say.

"I'm coming." Hugh's voice sounded close to normal, but not
quite.

"It's not your fault, Hugh." It was Thomas speaking, his voice
recognizable even though it was clogged with tears. "I was the one
who suggested that Geoffrey ask to borrow your horse."

Evidently Nigel's knights had also come to the conclusion that
Geoffrey's death had not been accidental.

"Next we will be blaming poor Rufus." Hugh's voice sounded
closer and Cristen knew that he had finally joined the rest of the
knights.

One of the other knights asked, his tone cautious, "Is it true
that you are the lost son of the old earl, Hugh?"

After the briefest of pauses, Hugh's reply drifted to Cristen's
ears: "It seems that I am."

Thomas said, "Well, if ever you want help in dislodging Lord
Guy, you have only to call on me."

"And me!" said another voice.

A chorus of "And me's" followed as Nigel's knights eagerly pledged themselves to avenge the death of their comrade.

Nigel murmured to Cristen, "It seems that I am losing the loyalty of my own household guard."

Oddly enough, he didn't sound angry about such a defection; on the contrary, he sounded pleased.

Hugh left for Evesham the following day. Cristen said her farewells in the family solar.

She did not want to see him ride away.

"I'll be back. You know that," he said. He was holding both her hands in his own hard, callused grasp.

"I'll be here," she replied simply.

He hesitated, then bent and kissed her on the forehead.

A squire opened the solar door.

"Sir Nigel sent me to tell you that the horses are waiting, my lord," he said.

Cristen saw the surprise flare in Hugh's eyes at the title the squire had bestowed upon him.

"Word has evidently spread through the ranks," she said with a smile. "It's their way of saying that they're on your side."

He nodded abruptly, squeezed her hands once, and dropped them.

"I won't say goodbye," he said.

"If you need me, send and I will come," she said.

His mouth quirked. "I always need you," he said, turned on his heel, and walked swiftly out of the room.

It rained during the whole ride to Evesham. Hugh huddled under the hood of his cloak and remembered the terrible headache that had attacked him when he had first arrived at Somerford.

*Please, God, don't let that happen now,* he prayed.

There would be no Cristen at Evesham to take him in charge and hide him away.

The miles fell behind them and his head remained clear. Philip Demain and Father Anselm rode with him, and he was enormously grateful that neither of them tried to talk to him about anything but the exigencies of the journey.

It was late in the afternoon when Philip said, "Evesham is just a few miles away."

Fifteen minutes later, their small cavalcade ascended a gently sloping, grassy, treeless incline, and there before them, looming out of the rain and the mist, was a large gray stone castle. Like Somerford, it had obviously once been a motte and bailey castle that had been converted into something more substantial by using local stone. The thick walls that surrounded it were broken up by five towers.

"Have the Matard family held Evesham for many years?" Hugh asked Philip.

"Since the time of the Conqueror," Philip answered proudly. "Your heritage is a proud one, my lord. A son of Roger de Leon and Isabel Matard need bow his head to no man in England. Or in Normandy, for that matter."

"I am not 'my lord' quite yet," Hugh said mildly.

"Let us see what my Lord Simon has to say about that," Philip replied.

When Hugh and Philip and Father Anselm walked into the Great Hall of Evesham, the trestle tables were being set up for supper.

"Lord Simon is in the solar," Philip was informed by one of the pages, who was carrying out his duty of putting the great saltcellars on each of the individual tables.

"Alan." Philip summoned another one of the pages who was in the hall. "Go and tell Lord Simon that I have returned from Somerford and that I have brought someone with me."

"Aye, sir," the page returned. He cast a quick, curious look at Hugh, put down the flagon of ale he had been carrying, and ran to the wooden staircase that led from the hall to the next floor of the castle.

As Hugh stood with his two companions waiting for the page to return, he surveyed his surroundings.

The Great Hall of Evesham was larger than the hall at Somerford, but smaller than the one at Chippenham. The servants and pages were working cheerfully together, making ready the many tables for the evening meal. Several dogs roamed about, eager for supper to be served so that they could dine on the castoffs.

Hugh's fastidious nose detected the fact that the rushes should have been changed yesterday.

The page had returned. "My lord said to come up to the solar," he said to Philip.

They crossed the floor to the staircase, Hugh and Father Anselm trailing after Philip.

The door to the solar at the top of the stairs was open, and Philip stepped aside, gesturing for Hugh to go in first. He did so, entering into a richly furnished room, which was lit by the mellow light of the late sun coming in at the two windows. Hugh's eyes immediately located the room's single occupant, a man sitting on a carved bench that was placed against the wall close to one of the open windows

"Well, Philip?" the man said.

"Go to him," Philip said to Hugh in a low voice.

Hugh made his way across the floor, detouring around the brazier that stood in the center of the room, and came to a halt in front of his uncle.

"My lord," he said.

Simon Matard stared at Hugh, his face wearing the shocked expression that Hugh was becoming all too familiar with when people first saw him.

"God's blood," Simon said.

There was no reply to that, so Hugh said nothing.

Simon got up slowly from his bench. Slowly he reached out and put his hand under Hugh's chin and turned his face from side to side. Finally he said, his voice choked with emotion, "You are the living image of my sister."

"So everyone tells me," Hugh said, his own voice calm and collected.

He looked at Simon, evaluating the other man the way he himself was being evaluated.

Simon Matard of Evesham was no taller than Hugh, although he was somewhat thicker in the torso. His hair was mostly silver, but enough of the original color remained to show that it had once been black. His eyes were grayish-blue, but he had the same high cheekbones that Hugh saw in the mirror every day when he shaved.

"I didn't believe it," Simon said, still staring at Hugh. "I sent someone to Somerford simply to placate my sister. I never for one moment believed that the man Nigel Haslin was harboring could really be her son."

Hugh said somberly, "I didn't believe it either, until Guy nearly fainted when he saw me."

"Oh, my boy," said Simon. His usually brisk voice quivered slightly. "This is like a miracle, to have you back."

And he stepped forward to enfold Hugh in a warm embrace.

Hugh tolerated it. He didn't return it, but neither did he pull away.

At last Simon's arms dropped. He stepped back. "Where have you been all these years?" he demanded. "Why didn't you let us know that you were alive?"

"I was in Lincolnshire, being brought up as the foster son of Ralf and Adela Corbaille," Hugh replied. "I didn't let you know because I have no memory of my life before Ralf adopted me." He paused. "I still don't."

Simon's eyes narrowed. "Nonsense. I never heard of such a thing."

Hugh's mouth set. "Nevertheless, it is true. I had no idea of my original identity until Nigel Haslin accosted me at Northallerton after the Battle of the Standard."

The sun slanting in the window was falling on the top of Hugh's head, making a pool of shining ebony out of his hair.

"You don't remember being taken away from Chippenham?" Simon demanded.

"No."

Silence fell as Simon Matard regarded Hugh with speculative eyes. At last he said, "Well, the important thing is that you are here now. And as it turns out, you could not have arrived at a better time for us."

Hugh lifted an eyebrow. "Oh? How is that?"

Simon started to say something, then changed his mind. "We'll talk about it later. As for now, supper is being served, and if you have been traveling all day, I'll wager you're hungry."

"That we are, my lord," Philip said.

For the first time, Simon's eyes left Hugh's face. He noticed Father Anselm standing next to Philip and said, "Is this the priest you took to Somerford, Philip?"

"Aye, my lord," said Philip. "May I present Father Anselm, of the cathedral of Westminster."

"You are welcome to Evesham, Father," Simon said courteously.

"Thank you, my lord."

One of the doors that led off the solar opened, and a woman came into the room.

"Are you ready to go down to supper, my lord?" she said to Simon. She noticed Philip and gave him a smile. "It is good to have you back with us, Philip."

"Thank you, my lady."

"My dear," Simon said, "let me introduce you to my nephew, Hugh de Leon, Isabel's long-lost son."

"Is it true then?" The women turned to look at Hugh and her hazel eyes widened with recognition. "Aye," she said slowly, "I see that it is true indeed."

"My wife, the Lady Alyce," Simon said to Hugh.

"I am pleased to meet you, my lady," Hugh said courteously.

She gave him a warm smile. "How happy your mother will be to see you!"

Hugh drew a deep breath and tried not to let his rejection of that idea show on his face.

Apparently he was successful, for the Lady Alyce laid her hand upon her husband's arm and said, "Shall we, my lord?"

The two of them moved toward the door, and Hugh and Philip and Father Anselm fell in behind them.

Supper was amiable enough. Hugh was placed at the high table next to one of Nigel's daughters—his cousin, he supposed. He was so accustomed to thinking of himself as solitary that it was a shock to realize that he had a cousin.

Juliana Matard was a pretty girl of about fifteen, and she spent the entire suppertime plying him with questions he couldn't answer.

"I really don't remember, my lady," he said for about the fifteenth time as a page refilled his cup with wine.

"But it's so *strange*," she said. She had already made this remark several times before.

There was a bustle of activity near the door and Hugh looked with relief at the young man who had just come in and was striding across the floor in the direction of the high table. Any interruption that would get him away from Juliana's interminable questions was welcome.

"Father!" the young man said to Simon. He was not wearing mail, and his close-cut hair was black as coal. "The news just came to Moreton and I thought I would carry it to you myself. Earl Robert has landed with the empress and is riding west. He should be in Bristol sometime tomorrow!"

Simon was elated at the news brought by his son. Even the information that Gloucester had landed with only a small force of 140 knights did not daunt him.

"He could not have come with a large force," Simon said. "Stephen has all of the large ports under close watch. It was only sensible for him to put in at a little port like Arundel. When I think of it, it's a perfect place for a secretive entry by a small group."

Simon, his son, Gilbert, Hugh, Philip, and several older knights were gathered together in the room where Hugh had first met his uncle, discussing the news that Gilbert had brought. The ladies had disappeared into their own bower, leaving the solar to the men.

Bright color flamed in the cheeks of Simon Matard. "We have been waiting for so long!" he said.

"Is the empress coming to Bristol with her brother?" Hugh asked Gilbert.

"Not yet," Gilbert replied. He rubbed his hand across the top of his close-cropped head. "My information was that the earl left her in Arundel, which is commanded by her stepmother, Adeliza, and set out immediately with a small escort for the west. He did not wish to waste time rousing his supporters."

"And supporters he has in plenty," Simon said fiercely.

The charcoal fire flickered in the darkening room. The candles had not yet been lit.

"He left the empress in Arundel?" Hugh said in surprise.

"Arundel is a strong castle placed on a good defensive site. It is not easy to approach by land," Philip said. "I had occasion to visit there once. She will be safe in Arundel."

Hugh looked toward the shadowy face of the young knight who had been his escort. The brightest thing in the room was Philip's hair.

"Even if Stephen besieges it?" Hugh said.

"Stephen is far more worried about Earl Robert than he is about the empress," Simon said. He laughed. "As well he should be. Without him, she is nothing. Without her, he is still our lord whom we will follow to the death."

"That may be so," Hugh said mildly, "but without the empress, Robert of Gloucester is merely a subject in rebellion against his king. He needs his sister if he wishes to give his cause legitimacy."

Simon scowled at him. Clearly any criticism of Robert of Gloucester was not going to be tolerated in Simon's presence.

The door opened, admitting a page with a taper. "My lady sent me to light the candles, my lord," he said to Simon.

"Go ahead," Simon said impatiently.

Silence fell on the group as the page went around the room, lighting the fat candles that were placed on the various tables. When the boy had finally left, Gilbert asked, "What are you going to do, Father?"

Simon's reply was instantaneous. "Go to Bristol myself and offer the earl my services. What else?"

Gilbert and Philip grinned. Clearly the prospect of action pleased them.

Simon's eyes passed to the contained face of his nephew. "Will you come with us, Hugh?" He quirked a well-arched gray eyebrow. "Make it a family affair."

Hugh did not reply.

Simon pressed on. "If you want to reclaim your earldom from Guy, you will need help, and Stephen is most likely to support the man in possession." His lip curled with contempt. "It is ever Stephen's inclination to take the easiest way. Promise Wiltshire to Earl Robert, and he will help you win it back from that murdering bastard who holds it now."

Still Hugh said nothing.

"Will you come with us?" Simon said again.

Hugh lifted his straight black de Leon eyebrows. "Why not?" he said lightly.

"Good lad!" said Simon, and once more a grin split Philip Demain's face.

# 14

The castle at Bristol was strongly built and strongly defended by Gloucester loyalists, which was the reason that Stephen had decided not to attempt it during the year before Earl Robert's return to England. It received its lord with a warm welcome, and for the remainder of the war it would serve most effectively as the chief base of his operations.

The earl was in one of the smaller rooms off the Great Hall when the arrival of Simon's party was announced to him. Simon was escorted to him, with Hugh at his side.

Robert, Earl of Gloucester, the greatest noble in England after the king himself, was a squarely built man of middle height. His brown hair and short beard were streaked with gray, and his brown eyes looked levelly and intelligently at Simon and Hugh as they came into the smallish room, whose walls were hung with embroidered tapestries of the hunt. The tapestries were not only there to lend beauty to the room; they also provided protection against the damp and cold of the stone walls.

"My lord," said Simon. He went immediately to kneel in front of his feudal lord, who was seated on a backless bench that had high, elaborately carved sides. "How glad I am to see you returned to us."

"Thank you, Simon," the earl replied. His voice was

of the middle register, calm and quiet. There was nothing at all about him that was remarkable. Even his green tunic was merely serviceable.

His eyes never once flicked toward Hugh.

"I have come to offer you my sword and the swords of all those who follow me," Simon said.

"I am pleased to hear that, Simon." The earl's face remained grave. "Every sword is welcome to our cause."

"Men will soon be pouring in to join you," Simon said firmly. "You shall see."

"All of my feudal vassals have been quick to voice their support," Robert said. "I greatly appreciate their loyalty."

He gestured to Simon to rise.

Simon got to his feet a little slowly. He was no longer a young man. "Of course your vassals will support you, my lord. But . . . what of the other barons and earls?"

Robert's face hardened infinitesimally. "The two greatest men who have come forward are Miles, Constable of Gloucester, and Brian fitz Count, who has pledged us the fortress of Wallingford in the Thames Valley. Wallingford is virtually impregnable itself, and its location will be invaluable to my sister's cause. It poses a direct threat to Oxford and will be a menace to communications with London for any royalist force operating in the upper Thames region and beyond."

Not a large contingent, Hugh thought, and outside Robert himself, it contained none of England's greatest magnates. It would be a considerable coup if Robert could add the Earl of Wiltshire to his list of adherents.

"My lord," said Simon. His voice indicated that he, too, was disturbed by the lack of Robert's support. "I bring you someone whom I think you will be very interested to meet." He gestured to Hugh, who had been standing a few steps behind him. "Come forward, Hugh."

Hugh moved forward until he was standing beside Simon, directly in front of the seated earl.

"This is my nephew, Hugh de Leon," Simon announced. "He is the son of my sister and Roger de Leon, the previous Earl of Wiltshire."

Silence fell as Robert stared at Hugh, his brows contracted. At last, "I thought Roger's son was dead," he said.

"So did we all," Simon replied. "It is nothing short of a miracle that he has been returned to us. I do not know if you have heard the full story, my lord, of how my sister's husband came to die . . . "

Hugh lifted his eyes to the figures embroidered on the tapestry hanging on the wall behind the earl and listened with half an ear as Simon recounted once again the tale of Roger's murder and his own kidnapping.

The great deerhound had been most cunningly done, he thought, as he regarded the sequence of the hunt that made up the panel hanging over the earl's head.

"I did not know this," Earl Robert replied when Simon had finally finished. "I knew that Roger had been killed, of course, but murdered . . . ?"

A little unwillingly, Hugh returned his attention to the conversation.

"Aye, my lord, murdered," Simon said grimly.

"But why was this not made public knowledge?" Robert demanded. "The murder of an earl is a matter of the utmost gravity."

Simon shifted a little on his feet. "The murderer was killed himself, my lord, taking his secrets with him. There was little to gain by making the matter a public scandal. We thought that Hugh was dead, you see. It was not until one of Roger's vassals discovered him at the Battle of the Standard that we learned otherwise."

Robert's eyes fixed themselves upon Hugh. "Why did you not make yourself known sooner?" he said sternly.

Hugh hated this, hated having to reveal his disability over and over again to strangers. "I remembered nothing of my past," he said tightly. "I still don't."

Robert's incredulous stare was the twin of all the stares Hugh had been the target of whenever he made this revelation.

"You don't remember?" Robert said in disbelief.

"No," said Hugh icily. "I don't remember."

"There can be no doubt about who he is, my lord," Simon put in hastily. "He wears his heritage on his face."

Several high-backed chairs had been grouped around a square

table at one end of the room, and now Robert of Gloucester rose from his bench and moved toward them, signaling Simon and Hugh to follow.

Hugh admired the earl's adroitness. The move gave him time to think.

When they were seated at the table, Robert and Simon facing each other with Hugh between them, the earl turned to Hugh. "So," he said, "you are Roger de Leon's son."

"Aye," said Hugh. His face gave away nothing.

Robert leaned back in his chair and rested his hands upon the arms. "Roger de Leon was one of the heroes of my youth," he said reminiscently. "Did you know that his deeds at the taking of Jerusalem and Ascalon rang throughout the whole of the Christian world? And after, when so many of the leaders of the Crusade did naught but squabble greedily among themselves over the spoils of war, Roger alone stood aloof. He was content to be a Knight of Christ; he needed no other reward for his valor."

Hugh watched the earl and said nothing.

Robert went on, "All of this happened years before you were born, of course." His voice took on a censorious note. "Like most of your generation, you probably know little about the campaigns of the Crusade and the men who fought them."

Hugh's face never changed. He did not reply.

The earl allowed the silence to go on for a few more moments. Then he said, "I met your father once, when he first returned to England after his elder brother's death." His eyes narrowed. "You do have his eyes."

Hugh said, "So I have been told."

"Who is the one responsible for the murder of so great a man?" Robert demanded. "No mere household knight would have dared such a thing on his own."

Hugh's hands were folded quietly on the tabletop in front of him. "I intend to find out the answer to that question, my lord," he said.

Robert frowned. "Where was his brother when Roger was killed?"

Hugh's fingers tightened infinitesimally. "That is also something I intend to find out."

The earl's intelligent eyes were steady on Hugh's face. "I could help you," he said.

Hugh's expression did not change.

"You are intelligent enough to realize that my sister's cause would benefit greatly if we could add Wiltshire to our list of adherents," the earl said. "I will make you an offer that will be to our mutual benefit, Hugh de Leon. I will make you the Earl of Wiltshire if you will promise to throw your support to us."

Simon might not have been in the room, so concentrated were the other two upon each other.

"And just how do you propose to do that, my lord?" Hugh asked, his voice very soft.

Robert leaned a little forward in his chair. His eyes were locked on Hugh's. "We'll begin by taking some of the castles that Guy controls and putting our men in charge of them. That will be a challenge that Guy cannot ignore. He will have to try to retake them. If we are lucky, we'll be able to capture him." Slowly, Robert leaned back in his chair, his eyes never leaving Hugh's. "Once we have Guy in our hands, you will be able to discover just how involved he was in your father's death." Robert's lips tightened. "I confess, I would like to know the answer to that question myself."

"And if Guy goes to Stephen for redress?" Hugh said. "If it is the king himself who comes against those castles you have taken?"

"We will have to meet Stephen at some time or another," Robert said. "And Wiltshire is worth the gamble."

Simon's party stayed in Bristol for two more days, then left to return to Evesham. Hugh managed to depart without making any commitment to Robert of Gloucester. Simon was not happy about this indecision, but Gloucester himself was clever enough not to press too hard.

He knew he had dangled a very attractive bait. He was willing to give the fish time to bite.

It was a misty, drizzly morning when Simon's party set out from Bristol. They had traveled several hours when a heavy rain began to fall and Simon decided to put up at an inn in Gloucester rather than continue on to Evesham in the bad weather.

The inn Simon chose was crowded with other travelers who had been caught by the rain, but Simon, by far the most noble guest, was able to command two rooms, one for himself and one for his men.

Hugh spent the evening in the tap room with Philip, drinking ale and politely warding off the advances of the barmaids, who supplemented their income by plying the world's oldest profession.

Philip pretended to be hugely insulted by the girls' obvious interest in Hugh.

"I am not accustomed to having my manly charms so slightly regarded," he grumbled.

As he had a girl on each knee when he made this remark, no one paid him much attention.

Hugh, who had his chair to himself, snorted.

One of the girls ran her fingers through Philip's golden hair. "How's about another drink, luv?" she asked.

"I'll get it," Hugh said. "Your hands appear to be full at the moment."

Philip grinned.

The tavern was warm and steamy. It smelled of wet wool and too many male bodies crammed into too small a space. Philip, watching, saw Hugh's nose wrinkle in distaste as he waved his hand to signal that he wanted three more flagons.

While the innkeeper was drawing the ale, another of the tavern girls approached Hugh. As Philip watched, the girl rubbed her ripe body against him and said something.

Hugh shook his head and said something back to her.

A sulky look came over the girl's pretty face.

Hugh patted her on the arm in a friendly fashion, and reached for his flagons of ale.

"What's the matter with your friend, luv?" one of the girls who was sitting on Philip's knee asked. "Doesn't he like women?"

"A good-looking lad like that, it'd be a crime if he didn't," the other one said.

"I'm insulted," Philip complained. "Here you are, sitting on my knees, and you're talking about another man."

Cooing, both girls turned their attention to him.

Hugh threaded his way through the noisy crowd, put the flagons of ale upon the table without spilling a drop, and said to Philip, "I'm going to bed."

Philip and his girls watched his slender figure disappear up the stairs to the bedrooms.

Philip said to his companions, "Don't feel too rejected. He already has a girl."

"Lucky thing," the girl on his left knee replied, then she leaned forward to kiss him on the mouth.

When Philip finally came upstairs to the bedroom he was sharing with Hugh and Simon's other knights, he was alone. The rain had stopped earlier and moonlight was coming in through the open window of the crowded room, making it bright enough for Philip to see that Hugh was still awake.

He was lying on his back, one arm flung over his head, his open eyes on Philip.

"The girls thought that maybe you fancied men instead of women," Philip informed him as he stripped off his tunic.

"If it made them happy to think that, then let them," Hugh said unconcernedly.

Philip sat on his straw mattress and began to unlace his boots. "Why are you still awake? Regretting the voluptuous pleasures you so carelessly passed up?"

"They probably all had the pox," Hugh said.

"They probably did," Philip agreed. "But it wouldn't have hurt you to buy them a drink and let them sit on your lap."

"I hope you had sense enough not to do anything more than that."

"I'm not a randy enough fool to fall into the sack with a tavern girl," Philip said impatiently.

"I'm glad to hear that."

"You didn't answer my question. Why are you still awake?"

Hugh made a face. "Listen to that cacophony. Who can sleep in the midst of so much noise?"

The rest of the knights were deeply asleep and snoring lustily from all the ale they had drunk.

"You're spoiled," Philip said. He put his boots to the side and prepared to stretch out in his shirt and hose. "Not everyone grew up with the luxury of a bedroom of his own, like you. You get used to the snoring."

"You do?" Hugh sounded unconvinced.

"I thought perhaps you might be thinking about Gloucester's offer," Philip said.

Hugh's response was unexpectedly candid. "I have been."

"And have you decided what you are going to do?"

"Not yet. I need to talk it over first."

"Nigel Haslin is Stephen's man," Philip warned. "He'll try to talk you into going to Stephen."

"It's not Nigel I want to talk to," Hugh said. Then, when Philip tried to ask another question, Hugh shut his eyes, rolled over on his side, and told Philip to go to sleep.

The sun was shining when they arose the following morning, but none of Simon's knights appeared to appreciate the brightness of the day.

"Too much ale," Hugh diagnosed solemnly when he saw Philip wince as he stepped out of the shadow of the inn into the merciless light of the yard.

Hugh himself had had scarcely any sleep at all, but he looked alert and rested compared to the rest of Simon's party.

Simon himself had gone to bed early in his own private room, and he was full of energy and ready to start for Evesham. His pain-wracked knights trailed along behind him to the stableyard, mounted up, and rode stoically through the streets of Gloucester, heading for the road that would take them home.

Simon kept his horse next to Hugh's and spent the entire ride trying to talk him into accepting Gloucester's offer. Hugh spent the entire ride returning noncommittal replies to Simon's arguments.

He was very glad to reach Evesham, where he hoped he would be able to escape, if only briefly, from Simon's insistent presence.

The Lady Alyce was waiting in the Great Hall to greet them when they walked in.

"You are welcome home, my lord," she said to Simon and held her face up to him for the kiss of peace.

Then she turned to Hugh.

"I have a wonderful surprise for you," she said. Her eyes were sparkling like a young girl's. "Guess who has come to visit?"

Hugh looked back at her blankly. He hated guessing games and had no reply.

"Your mother!" Alyce said triumphantly.

Hugh froze.

"I sent to Worcester to tell her you were here and she arrived yesterday. In all that rain!" Alyce was bubbling on, completely oblivious to Hugh's reaction. "She was so anxious to see you that she couldn't wait."

Simon spoke into the silence. "Isabel is here?"

Alyce gave her lord a radiant smile. "She is upstairs, my lord." She turned back to Hugh. "I promised her I would send you to see her the moment you returned."

The silence in the hall was catastrophic. Finally even Alyce noticed that something was wrong.

"I will take you to her myself," she said, but with less confidence than she had spoken before.

Hugh's face was as white as parchment. Then, still without speaking a word, he turned on his heel and walked out of the hall.

The people he left behind stood for a moment as if they had been glued into place. Then Simon cursed and started after him.

The horses they had ridden from Bristol had not yet left the bailey, and Simon was in time to see Hugh leap onto Rufus's back and ride out through the inner gates of the castle.

"God's bones," he said through his teeth.

"That bastard." It was Philip Demain, standing at his side. "Do you want me to go after him?"

"No," Simon said in a flat voice. "Let him go."

Philip shoved his hand through his hair. "What the hell is wrong with him?" he demanded.

"I don't know," Simon said. Unlike Philip, he did not appear to be angry. He merely looked bleak. "Judas. I am going to have to tell Isabel what happened."

The lady Alyce accompanied her husband to Isabel's bedchamber and listened in fulminating silence while he told his sister that Hugh had left the castle.

Alyce waited for Isabel to cry out with dismay. Instead she sat silent, staring at her brother. The only sign she gave of distress was that all of the color drained from her face.

"I'm sorry, Isabel," Simon said in a gruff voice. "Alyce should not have invited you so precipitately."

"And why not, I should like to know?" Alyce demanded, defending herself. She glared at her husband. "Who could have suspected that Hugh would behave in such a fashion? What in the name of God is wrong with that boy?"

"I'm sure he had his reasons," Isabel replied in a steady voice.

Alyce stepped forward with some notion of taking her sister-in-law into her arms to comfort her.

There were no tears in Isabel's dark blue eyes, however. Her face was white, but she had herself under strict control. Only the trembling of her hands in her lap betrayed her feelings.

"I should have waited for him to come to me," was all she said. Her face told Alyce not to embrace her. "It was my fault for behaving too rashly."

"I don't think it's rash for a mother to want to see the son she thought was dead," Alyce said angrily.

"He was not ready," Isabel replied. Her skin looked parchment-thin over her perfect bones.

Alyce used her husband's favorite oath. "God's bones, what did he have to be ready for? You're his mother!"

"Quiet, my lady," Simon said. "Isabel is upset enough already."

Abashed, Alyce reined in her temper. Simon was right. "I did not mean to shout at you, Isabel," she said.

Isabel gave Alyce a shadowy smile. The sun pouring in the window illuminated her face, revealing the fine lines around her eyes and her mouth.

"Is there aught we can do for you?" Alyce asked.

"I would like to see Father Anselm, if he is here," Isabel said.

"I'll send him to you," Simon said. "And now that you have finally returned to Evesham, I hope that you will remain with us."

She shook her head. "No, Simon, I shall return to Worcester in the morning."

"You don't have to pray for him any longer, Isabel," Simon said grimly. "I can assure you that he is very much alive."

Her face, if possible, looked even more ghostlike than it had before. "For all these years I have been praying for myself," she said. "*I* was the one who needed Hugh to be alive. Now the time has come for me to pray for him."

\* \* \*

*Stupid woman,* Hugh thought as he cantered Rufus away from the walls of Evesham. *To bring her there, without telling me. Stupid, stupid, stupid.*

His heart was hammering, his breathing was coming fast, and it was not due to the pace at which he was he was riding.

He continued to vilify the Lady Alyce for the next fifteen minutes while he cantered Rufus along the wide, well-kept road that would take him south, to Somerford. The vale of Evesham stretched around him on all sides, with its abundant fields that belonged to Simon's honor, but Hugh was completely unaware of the richness through which he was passing.

At last, his bodily functions began to regulate themselves and his brain began to function once again. He slowed the white stallion, who had already made one journey today and would tire quickly if Hugh continued to push him.

It had been pure instinct, to turn and run when Lady Alyce had made that announcement.

Now instinct gave way to thought.

What must they think of him at Evesham? How was he ever going to explain his action?

How could he explain it to himself?

*I can't explain it. I just know that I can't see her. Not yet.*

It was the only explanation that he could find, this instinctive feeling he had about not wanting to see his mother.

For she was his mother. She must be. Everyone said how much he looked like her.

*The living image of Isabel.*

He closed his eyes and longed for Isabel to be Adela. His love for his foster mother had been total and uncomplicated, as hers had been for him.

This had not been the kind of relationship he had known with his own mother. He knew that. If it had been, he would not be feeling the way he was.

If Isabel had been Adela, he would have rushed up those stairs and thrown himself into her arms.

Instead, he had run away.

*I ran away.*

He never ran away from anything. It was one of the laws he

lived his life by. It was why he had forced himself to go to Somerford, even though the rational part of him had said to remain safely at Keal.

But he had most certainly run away from Isabel.

Why? What had happened in his childhood that made him so fearful of seeing his mother?

He didn't want to find out.

*Still running away,* he thought, and his lips compressed into a thin hard line.

He wrenched his mind away from what had happened at Evesham and looked for the first time at the countryside through which he was passing.

The road had left the Vale of Evesham and become a forest track, closely hemmed in on either side. He was riding through Gloucestershire now, with Wiltshire lying just to his south.

He thought of the offer Earl Robert had made to him.

He wanted to find out who had killed his father and he wanted to be the Earl of Wiltshire.

But he knew he would rather achieve both those aims on his own.

# 15

It was dark by the time Hugh reached Somerford, which was situated in the very northern part of Wiltshire, close to the border of Earl Robert's territory. If Hugh accepted the earl's offer, Somerford would most likely be one of the first castles that Robert would try to take.

Supper was finished and the tables already cleared away when Hugh walked into the castle's Great Hall. Servants were carrying platters and basins to the buttery to be washed, while others were raking the rushes so that they lay evenly on the floor. A group of Nigel's knights were gathered in front of the leaping fire. Thomas was playing his lute in accompaniment of Reginald, who was singing a French love song in his mellow baritone. A few knights played at dice, while others were mending harnesses and listening to the music.

Hugh sniffed the air appreciatively, smelling the faint, pleasant aroma of the herbs that had been sprinkled in the fresh rushes.

Reginald saw him first, stopped his singing, and shouted a greeting. Hugh went to join the men by the fire.

After exchanging greetings with the knights, he inquired, "Is Sir Nigel in the solar?"

"Sir Nigel is not here," Thomas returned. "He left

shortly after you did, to pay a visit to Marlborough. We expect him back shortly, however."

Hugh slowly pulled off his gloves. He was not wearing mail, as Simon's party had traveled back and forth to Bristol unarmed. Simon had had no fear of attack so deep in the Earl of Gloucester's own territory.

"I see," Hugh said, trying not to let his disappointment show.

"The Lady Cristen is here, though," Thomas went on.

Hugh's disappointment magically disappeared.

"She is upstairs with her ladies," Thomas said. "Shall I send a page to tell her that you have returned?"

"Aye," said Hugh. "Do that."

He stood with the men in front of the fire, listening idly to Thomas's music while the page ran upstairs to fetch her. It seemed a very long time before he heard the sound of the dogs' nails scratching on the wood of the floor above. They came galloping excitedly down the stairs, and then, finally, Cristen herself appeared.

If someone had asked him what color tunic she was wearing, he wouldn't have been able to answer. All he saw was her face, her eyes, and the delicate flush of color in her cheeks.

He went to meet her.

"Hugh." She held out her hands. "Welcome back."

He took her small, competent hands into his own and for the first time since that dreadful near-encounter with his mother, he felt the world steady itself under his feet. He managed a smile. "I'm sorry to arrive at such an inconvenient hour."

She wrinkled her straight little nose in dismissal of such foolishness. "Come along with me into the solar and I'll have some food brought to you," she said briskly.

Ralf was whining softly and butting his head against Hugh's knee. Hugh looked with mock sternness into the eager black face that was lifted to his. "Do you require some attention?"

The dog's tail, which was tipped at the end with a splash of white, making it look as if it had been dipped in a pot of whitewash, wagged frantically. Hugh bent and scratched him behind his ears, in the exact spot he liked the most.

Ralf sighed with pleasure.

Cedric, more timid than his companion, looked longingly at Ralf's ecstasy.

"Play fair," Cristen said with amusement. "It's Cedric's turn now."

Obediently, Hugh transferred the ministrations of his long, clever fingers to Cedric.

Proper recognition having been accorded to her dogs, Cristen was ready to move to the solar. Hugh and the animals accompanied her.

The page Cristen had sent ahead of them had already lit the candles and was in the process of lighting the charcoal brazier when they came in the door.

Hugh said, "Can it be possible that you have grown another inch in the week that I have been gone, Brian?"

The boy flushed with pleasure. "Perhaps not quite an inch, Hugh. But I *am* growing."

"You certainly are," Hugh said admiringly. "You'll top me soon."

Brian stood up straighter. Then he stiffened and his flush of pleasure was replaced with the brighter red of embarrassment. "I'm s-sorry, my lord," he stuttered. "I did not mean to be overly familiar."

"Don't be an ass," Hugh said easily.

Brian grinned.

"Food, Brian," Cristen said gently.

"Aye, my lady!"

At last the food had been brought, the wine had been poured, the brazier was glowing, and they were alone.

"What happened?" Cristen asked.

While he ate he told her about his meeting with Simon and their subsequent visit to Robert of Gloucester. He finished by telling her about the earl's offer.

Silence fell as he sat back in his chair, a cup of wine between his fingers. He had eaten every scrap of food that Brian had brought.

"He must need Wiltshire badly," Cristen said at last.

She was sitting in her usual chair, with her feet resting on an embroidered footstool. She needed the footstool, else her feet wouldn't touch the floor. The dogs lay on either side of the stool;

Ralf's chin was actually propped right on it, with his nose touching her small leather slipper.

"He does, of course," Hugh replied. "He was disappointed, I think, by the response to his arrival. Except for Wallingford, which was pledged to him by Brian fitz Count, all of his support is in the west."

"Well, he certainly did his best to tempt you."

His look was wry. "Get thee behind me, Satan . . . ?"

Her face was grave. "Earl Robert has a few adherents in this part of the world, Hugh. Father went to Marlborough because Stephen was there, besieging the castle. John Marshall, the castellan, has declared for the empress."

Hugh's eyes glittered with sudden alertness. "Oh?"

"The king isn't there any longer, however. I received word from Father yesterday that he has raised the siege and taken his forces south, to besiege the empress in Arundel. Father sent the knights of his own escort to accompany the king."

Hugh leaned his dark head against the back of his chair and looked thoughtful.

"In the same letter, Father told me that Guy had also come to Marlborough."

Hugh's shoulders tensed.

Cristen's brown eyes were solemn. "I don't know what happened between Guy and Stephen. Father will probably be able to tell us when he returns. I expect him tomorrow or the day after."

Hugh took a sip of his wine. "If Stephen succeeds in capturing the empress and sending her back to Normandy, this war will be over before it begins."

Ralf yawned.

"That's your opinion," Hugh said sternly to the dog, who stared back for a moment, then closed his eyes.

"That might not be a good thing for you," Cristen pointed out in a neutral voice. "Earl Robert's offer to support you only has value if there is a war."

They looked at each other.

Finally he said, "I wasn't raised by a great feudal lord, Cristen. I was raised by a man who had some respect for his country."

She smiled at him, as if he had given her a great gift.

Some of the tenseness left his body.

Cedric turned and bit at the top of his tail.

"You had better not have fleas, Cedric," Cristen said.

The dog gave her an adoring look.

Cristen turned back to Hugh. "Something else happened while you were at Evesham. You were very upset when you arrived, and it wasn't about Earl Robert's offer."

Hugh lifted his brows in mock outrage. "Don't I have any privacy at all?"

She smiled at him again. "Not from me."

He sighed and then, in a flat, expressionless voice, he told her about what Lady Alyce had done, and his own disastrous response.

When he had finished he sat looking at her stoically, awaiting her judgment.

She leaned toward him and said in an aching voice, "I'm so sorry. Oh, Hugh, I'm so very, very sorry."

She didn't say what she was sorry for, but he knew it was for his pain, and he was comforted.

He managed a crooked smile. "The people at Evesham must think I'm insane."

"Who cares what the people at Evesham think?" she said fiercely.

He put his wine down and ran his fingers through his hair. "I need to talk to someone who lived at Chippenham when I was a child, Cristen. Do you know the names of any of my father's household knights? They must have been loyal to him. Perhaps I can trace a few of them."

"Father will know," Cristen said. "We'll ask him when he returns."

They talked for a little longer and then Hugh retired to his solitary bedroom, enormously appreciative of the quiet and the privacy after the noise and the cramped quarters of the night before.

Since Nigel wasn't at home, Cristen had one of her ladies spend the night with her, for the sake of propriety. For her sake, Hugh hoped that Cristen's companion didn't snore.

It was three more days before Nigel finally returned to Somerford, and when he did he was not alone. Henry Fairfax of Bowden, another of Guy's vassals, accompanied him.

The lord of Bowden was a man of about thirty-five, tall and

fair-haired and ruddy of complexion. He had been at Marlborough in Guy's train and so was privy to the deal that the earl had struck with Stephen. Nigel told Hugh all about it as they walked through the bailey on their way to the mews. Henry Fairfax was an avid falconer and had asked to see Nigel's birds.

"It is as I feared," Nigel said to Hugh. The two of them were walking together, with Cristen and the lord of Bowden several steps in front of them. "Fairfax has told me that Stephen promised to confirm Guy in his earldom if Guy would rally his feudal levies for Stephen when the king calls upon him."

"No surprise there," Hugh said noncommittally.

There was a strong wind blowing from the west, and all the Somerford flags were streaming straight out. As they passed the fish pond, Hugh noticed that even the surface of the water was rippling from the stiff breeze.

Nigel said gruffly, "What happened at Evesham?"

"Simon took me to see Robert of Gloucester, who made me the identical offer that Stephen made to Guy," Hugh said.

The breath hissed between Nigel's teeth.

"And what was your answer?" he demanded.

The wind was blowing Hugh's black hair, which needed to be cut. "I didn't give him an answer."

Nigel walked along in silence, his head lowered as he fixedly regarded the dirt of the bailey yard. "I'm sorry, lad," he said at last. "I bungled things by taking you to Chippenham. I forced Guy's hand in a way that I never intended to happen."

Hugh disagreed. "On the contrary, it was the right thing to do. I needed to go to Chippenham."

He noticed how the wind was blowing Cristen's red tunic flat against her slender body.

"You are the rightful earl!" Nigel exploded. "Everyone who sees you must know that!"

Hugh answered patiently, "It doesn't matter if I am Roger's son or not. Earldoms have changed hands before this, sir. You know that is true. And Guy has been the earl for fourteen years. My face isn't going to change that."

There was a moment of frustrated silence. "Are you giving up, then?" Nigel demanded.

There was humor in Hugh's voice as he answered, "I never give up. Perseverance is one of my few virtues."

Nigel stopped walking. "Well, then, what are you going to do? Accept Gloucester's offer?"

Hugh replied quietly, "Before I do anything, I need to know how my father died."

After a moment, Nigel's scowl lifted and he began to walk forward again. "I'm a fool. Of course. The best way to depose Guy is to prove him a murderer."

"Aye. And to do that, I need to talk to someone—preferably several people—who lived at Chippenham when I was a boy. I was wondering if you knew where I might find some of my father's old household knights, sir. Perhaps they might be able to shed some light on what happened all those years ago."

Nigel frowned. "Roger's knights? To the best of my knowledge, lad, most of them are still at Chippenham."

Hugh was stunned.

"Still at Chippenham?" he repeated, staring at Nigel in amazement.

"Aye. Guy had no following of his own. He was a younger son, remember. He brought a few friends with him when he became the earl, but otherwise he kept on Roger's household guard."

"My father's knights transferred their allegiance to Guy?"

Hugh's amazement was so profound that Nigel began to feel uneasy. "Why does that surprise you so?"

"Well, for one thing, it must mean that Roger's own knights did not suspect Guy of having a hand in his death!"

"Not necessarily," Nigel said. "It is not easy for a landless knight in these times, Hugh. There are few men who would forsake a comfortable place in an earl's household, no matter what they might suspect in their hearts."

"No honorable man would serve his lord's murderer," Hugh snapped.

"You wouldn't. I wouldn't. But necessity is a hard mistress, lad."

There was a sharp line between Hugh's brows. He did not look convinced.

"At any rate," Nigel said, "if you wish to speak to some of Roger's old knights, you have not far to look for them. Of course, many of them will have grown too old for service, but I'm sure a few still remain at Chippenham."

Cristen's laugh floated back to them. She was smiling up at Henry Fairfax.

For some reason, this put Hugh out of temper.

"Did you question that Father Anselm?" Nigel asked. "He was Roger's priest. He might be a good source of information."

Hugh flushed as he thought of the manner of his leaving Evesham. "I didn't have the chance," he said shortly. "I will do so eventually, but first I think I shall go to Chippenham."

"And just how do you plan to gain entrance to Chippenham?" Nigel asked with heavy sarcasm. "Introduce yourself to Guy as his nephew and ask if you might pay a visit to your old home?"

Hugh looked amused. "A brilliant idea," he said. "I believe that is precisely what I shall do."

Nigel groaned.

"I rather think that he will let me come," Hugh said. "He'll feel more comfortable with me under his eye than knowing I'm running loose around the countryside."

"He'd feel more comfortable if you were dead," Nigel said bluntly.

Hugh shook his head. "He won't harm me. He can't afford to have it whispered that another de Leon came to an untimely end at Chippenham. He must know that he has been suspected of doing away with his brother."

"Don't you understand?" Nigel said impatiently. "Guy is one of the greatest territorial magnates in all of England. He is an immensely powerful man, Hugh. He administers his palatinate free from any vestige of royal control. Within his own lands, he wields the power of life and death. Furthermore, he is arrogant and hot-headed. He has frequently been known to act first and think later."

They had almost reached the mews.

"I cannot guarantee your safety if you go to Chippenham," Nigel said.

"I am not asking you to guarantee my safety, sir," Hugh said calmly.

Nigel swore.

Cristen and Henry Fairfax had already reached the mews, and

Cristen was introducing the falconer to Henry Fairfax when Hugh and Nigel came up to them.

Nigel looked at his guest, clearly making an effort to focus his mind on a topic other than the one he had been discussing with Hugh.

"I don't have very many birds, Fairfax, but I think the ones I do have are quite fine."

The big man said indulgently, "Lady Cristen has been telling me that she does not care for the sport."

"She never has," Nigel said ruefully.

"I have a very pretty little merlin," Fairfax said. "A perfect bird for a lady. If I may, I will send it over for Lady Cristen. Perhaps she will change her mind about hunting once she sees my Faence."

He gave Cristen a charming smile.

Hugh scowled. Who the devil did this man think he was, offering Cristen a hawk?

Cristen said firmly, "Hunting for meat is one thing, Sir Henry, but killing for sport is not something of which I will ever approve."

Fairfax looked amused. "Your daughter is very tenderhearted," he said to Nigel indulgently.

Hugh gave him such a hostile look that if Fairfax had seen it, he might have been tempted to draw his dagger to defend himself.

"Come, Pritchard," Nigel said to his falconer. "Let us show Sir Henry our birds."

Hugh's dislike of Henry Fairfax increased as the day went on. He hung around Cristen so closely that Hugh scarcely got a chance to speak to her himself. And Nigel seemed to approve, actively encouraging the man to spend time with his daughter.

By the time supper was finished, Hugh was ready to skewer the man.

The crowning insult came when the four of them were sitting around the brazier in the solar and Nigel said, "You won't mind if Sir Henry shares your room tonight, will you, Hugh?"

"Not at all, sir," Hugh said between his teeth. "In fact, he may have it to himself. I'll be glad to sleep in the hall with the knights."

"That won't be necessary," Fairfax said with the genial charm that Hugh found so nauseating. "I don't mind sharing."

*Well, I do.*

Adela's training held firm, however, and Hugh did not speak his rude thought aloud. Instead he gave a long, lethal look to Nigel's hated guest and said, "I shall be perfectly happy in the hall."

Fairfax shrugged.

Cristen gave him a worried look.

"Suit yourself," Nigel grunted.

When the group around the brazier finally broke up, Hugh went back to the hall, took one of the straw mattresses, and dragged it away from the beds of the other knights.

"Where are you going, Hugh?" Thomas said. "You'll be warmer if you stay with us."

"Do any of you snore?" Hugh demanded.

Every eye went immediately to Ranulf.

"I thought so," Hugh said. "It will be quieter over here."

Ranulf did indeed snore magnificently, but it was not the noise that kept Hugh awake. It was the image of Fairfax's blond head bending over Cristen.

He scowled fiercely into the dark.

"Hugh."

He didn't know if she actually spoke or if he heard her voice in his mind, but he opened his eyes and saw her kneeling next to him. She was holding a candle and shading its light with her hand.

"Come with me to the pantry," she breathed. "I have to talk to you."

He rose soundlessly and followed her to the small service room where the food brought from the kitchen was arranged on platters before the servants took it into the hall to be served. Cristen put her candle down on one of the scoured wooden benches and turned to face Hugh.

"What's the matter?" he said. A thought struck him and he went rigid. "That dolt Fairfax wasn't trying to bother you, was he?"

"Nay, that's not it." She shook her head. Her hair was done in two loose plaits and hung over her shoulders and down the front of her green velvet robe.

"What the devil is your father thinking, letting that fellow hang all over you?" Hugh demanded next.

"He wants to marry me, Hugh," she replied. "And Father thinks it's a good match."

Hugh was thunderstruck.

"He wants to marry you?"

"Aye."

"Well, he can't!" Hugh said fiercely.

She looked at him.

"You're not going to marry anyone but me."

The single candle did not give them much light to see each other by, but he thought he could see her eyes glisten.

"You can't marry me," she whispered. "You're my feudal lord."

"I'm not your feudal lord yet," he said. "Besides, what does that have to do with anything?"

"An overlord does not marry the daughter of one of his vassals, Hugh."

"I shall marry whomever I choose to marry," he replied with splendid arrogance. "And I choose to marry you."

It was the only time she had ever heard him sound young.

A note of doubt crept into his voice. "Don't you want to marry me, Cristen?"

"Of course I want to marry you," she said.

The doubt left his voice. "Come here," he said, and held out his arms.

She walked into them and lifted her face. His mouth came down on hers.

His kiss was not tender, it was hard and hungry and fiercely possessive.

His passion did not frighten Cristen. She slid her arms around his waist, pressed herself against his hard young body, and kissed him back.

It was Hugh who finally separated them.

"We have to stop this or I won't answer for the consequences," he said. His voice was shaking.

Cristen pulled the front of her robe together with unsteady hands.

"I'll talk to your father tomorrow," Hugh said. His light eyes glittered in the semidark.

"No," Cristen said. She took a deep breath to steady herself. "Don't say anything to him yet."

"Why not?" he demanded. His eyes narrowed. "I don't want

that obnoxious fellow laying his hands on you, Cristen."

He looked and sounded dangerous.

"He won't do that. He's too much of a gentleman."

Hugh snorted contemptuously. "I wouldn't count on that."

"Listen to me," Cristen said urgently. "Now is not the time to speak to Father about us. He won't let me marry you the way things are now."

"What do you mean, *the way things are now?*"

"Father thinks you are in danger, Hugh. He won't let me marry a man who is a target for an arrow in the back."

He dragged his hand through his hair. "All right." His voice was taut. "I suppose I can understand that. But what about this Fairfax fellow?"

"I will tell Father that I don't like him and that I won't marry him."

"What if he insists that you do?"

"He won't."

"But what if he does?"

"A parent cannot force a woman to marry against her will, Hugh. The pope has ruled quite clearly on that issue."

There was a white line around his compressed mouth.

"I won't marry him," she said softly.

He let out his breath. "All right."

"Find out the truth about your past," Cristen said. "For your own peace of mind, you need to know it. Then, when all is made clear, we will go to my father."

He scowled at her. "Don't let that blond giant lay a finger on you."

She smiled. "I have the dogs."

Finally his face relaxed and he smiled back. "I love you," he said. "I knew it the first time I met you. Do you remember? I had that headache and you asked me if I wanted you to stay with me and I said that I did."

"I remember," she said.

"I never want anyone near me when I'm ill, but I knew I wanted you."

"I love you, too." She stood on her toes, kissed him on the mouth, then turned to pick up her candle.

"Come," she said. "I had better get back to my room before someone misses me."

# 16

Hugh wrote to Lord Guy, telling the earl who he was and asking if he could pay a visit to his old home of Chippenham. Nigel's messenger returned with Guy's reply the following day.

"What does he say?" Nigel asked. The messenger had found the two men at the blacksmith's forge, watching while Nigel's stallion was shod. Hugh had been patiently working with the horse, holding his feet for longer and longer periods until he was able to stand quietly for five minutes at a time. This was his first shoeing and he was behaving very well.

Hugh slowly rerolled the parchment upon which Guy's letter had been written. "He says he finds my claim of identity dubious, but that I am welcome to visit Chippenham if I wish."

The stallion swished his tail irritably and Hugh said, "Put his foot down, Giles, and give him a rest."

"Of course he is not going to admit your identity," Nigel said scornfully. "To do so would be to throw his own legitimacy into question."

"There is also the minor problem that I don't have any proof," Hugh pointed out.

Nigel grunted. "Your face is proof enough."

Hugh gave the stallion a treat and patted his thick, arched neck. "Not for Guy," he said.

"If your memory returned and you could answer questions about your childhood, then your claim would have validity."

Hugh rubbed the back of his own neck as if it ached. "Aye, I suppose that is so."

The air was filled with the acrid odor of burnt hoof. The stallion looked at Hugh and blew softly through his nostrils. Hugh said, "All right, Giles, you can try again."

The blacksmith lifted the stallion's rear foot and Nigel said, "I am going to accompany you to Chippenham. You will need someone to watch your back while you are there."

"You cannot accompany me," Hugh said. He was watching intently as the blacksmith fitted a shoe to the stallion's hoof. "You are Guy's vassal and simply by finding me you have done enough to anger him. It would not be wise to oppose him further." Abruptly Hugh switched his attention from the horse to Nigel. "You yourself have been at pains to point out to me exactly how much power Guy wields. You don't want him to send an army against Somerford, sir."

"He won't do that," Nigel said. "I haven't openly opposed him in anything. And I would never forgive myself, lad, if something happened to you that my presence might have prevented." He smiled ruefully. "My daughter wouldn't forgive me, either."

Hugh looked unconvinced.

"I am not asking you if I might come, Hugh," Nigel said pleasantly. "I am telling you."

Abruptly Hugh's face lit with his rare, radiant smile, the one that made him look as young as he actually was. "Thank you, sir," he said. "I shall appreciate your assistance. You can point out to me which of my father's knights are still at Chippenham so that I may question them."

The Somerford household was at supper when the knights whom Nigel had sent to accompany Stephen's army to Arundel returned home. They brought the astonishing news that not only had Stephen raised the siege, but he had agreed to give the empress a safe conduct to join her half-brother, the Earl of Gloucester, in Bristol.

Hugh was incredulous. "*He let her go?*" he said to the mail-clad knight who was standing in front of the high table addressing them.

Matthew was one of Nigel's oldest retainers and his seamed,

weather-beaten face was grim as he replied, "Yes, my lord. He let
her go. Bishop Henry and Count Waleran of Meulan were to
escort her to meet her brother."

Even Nigel looked shaken by such news.

"What could the king have been thinking of, to do such a
thing?" Cristen asked in amazement.

"I believe his thinking is perfectly clear, Lady Cristen," Henry
Fairfax said in a pompous, patronizing tone. "By raising the siege
of Arundel, the king has freed his forces. This will enable him to
concentrate them on Earl Robert, who is his real enemy." He gave
her the sort of smile one would give to a small child whom one was
instructing. "Surely you can appreciate the chivalry of the king in
choosing Robert as his main target, and not a lady."

"His chivalry is misplaced, to say the least, if its result is to
plunge the country into civil war," Cristen replied tartly.

Fairfax looked first startled and then annoyed. Clearly he did
not relish being contradicted by a woman.

Hugh said coldly, "What the king has done in releasing
Matilda is to give Gloucester the moral claim he needs to make his
cause a just one. What the king has done is to give Gloucester and
his sister a solid, compact base in the west and Wales. What the
king has done is to open the door to chaos."

By now Fairfax was looking angry. "I rather think that the king
has a better grasp of what is best for the country than does a young
knight such as yourself, Corbaille."

Hugh looked at him.

Fairfax's already ruddy skin flushed a brighter red.

"You are disrespectful," he said angrily.

Hugh said, each word dropping like a chink of ice into the vast
silence of the hall, "It is difficult to respect a man who acts as stu-
pidly as Stephen does."

"What do you think he should have done?" Fairfax demanded.
"Captured Matilda and thrown her into chains? Or perhaps you think
he should have had her executed? I can imagine what the Church
would have to say about that!" He leaned his upper body toward
Hugh, who was sitting on the other side of Nigel, and said nastily,
"Tell me, Corbaille, what would *you* have done if you were Stephen?"

"It isn't difficult to answer that question," Hugh said. As Fairfax grew hotter, Hugh was growing colder. "I would have captured Matilda and put her on a ship back to Normandy."

"That would have been best," Nigel agreed unwillingly. "I cannot see that allowing the empress to go free was a good move, Fairfax."

Sir Henry scowled to find himself under attack from yet another quarter. "Stephen has a big heart," he said. "It is one of his most admirable traits."

Hugh lifted an ironic eyebrow. "I would rather have a king with a big brain."

By now Fairfax's face was scarlet. "I don't know who you think you are, Corbaille . . ." he began furiously.

Hugh grew very pale. His light eyes glittered between their dark lashes. He stared at the older man for a long moment of silence before he replied evenly, "My name is not Corbaille, it is de Leon. And I can tell you who I think I am, Fairfax. I think I am your rightful overlord, the Earl of Wiltshire."

Henry Fairfax retired to his bedroom early, still fuming at Hugh's opposition and suspicious of his claim of identity. After Fairfax had gone, leaving Nigel and Cristen alone together in the solar, he told her that while he was at Chippenham he would ask Lord Guy's permission for her to wed with the lord of Bowden.

Cristen was sitting in her usual chair, her feet resting on her footstool, her dogs on either side of her. "But I don't wish to marry Sir Henry, Father," she replied calmly. "I don't like him."

Nigel was sitting in the large, high-backed chair with carved lion's paws for armrests that was next to hers. At her reply, his head snapped around and his brows drew together. "Don't like him?" he repeated. "Nonsense. What is there not to like about him? He's a fine-looking man, and, I might add, a careful steward of his own property. He is the sort of man who will look after you and Somerford the way I want you looked after."

"He patronizes me," Cristen said.

"Nonsense," Nigel said gruffly, his frown deepening.

She shook her head decisively. "It's not nonsense, Father. You heard him yourself this evening. He talks to me as if I were a child. I may not always be correct, Father, but I do claim the right to make my own moral judgments. *You* have always accorded me that honor."

Nigel looked at his daughter. She seemed so small and delicate as she sat there, almost lost in her chair, but he knew better than anyone that there was steel in Cristen's backbone. The servants of Somerford adored her, but they also respected and obeyed her. They had done so since she had taken over as chatelaine when her mother died seven years before.

"You must marry someone, Cristen," he said reasonably, "and good matches such as Henry Fairfax don't grow on trees. His first wife died last year and he is in the market to replace her. The addition of Somerford to his honor would greatly enhance his stature. You would be a lady of some consequence if you married him."

"I don't like him," Cristen repeated. "He's too big. His face is too red. And he patronizes me." Her eyes sparkled with indignation. "Did you hear him call me *tenderhearted* because I said I disapproved of hunting for sport? I disapprove of hunting because I find it morally repugnant, Father, not because I'm tenderhearted!"

"Cristen . . ." Nigel gave her a worried look. He bit his lip. "I trust you are not placing your hopes in Hugh."

Her eyebrows lifted, two fine aloof arches over her inquiring brown eyes. "My hopes?"

"I trust you are not hoping to marry Hugh," he said bluntly. "I can see how close the two of you have grown, but it will not do, Cristen. His situation at present is too precarious for him to be able to offer you any stability. And if he does succeed in winning his rightful place, he will be your overlord."

"I know that, Father," she said serenely.

He looked at her in frustration.

Her brown eyes were full of sympathy. "Poor Father. Am I such a trial to you?"

"You are not a trial at all," he said gruffly. "You have always been my greatest joy. It is of the utmost importance to me to see you happily married."

"I would never be happy married to Henry Fairfax," she said positively.

"You haven't given him a chance."

She sighed. "He's the worst sort of combination, Father. A man who isn't clever and thinks he is. I also suspect that he's a bit of a bully. And I do not take well to being bullied."

Nigel slammed his hands down on the lion's-paw armrests of his chair. "Is that what you want me to tell the man? That you think he is a stupid bully?"

Her full, serious mouth quirked. "I don't think that would be terribly tactful."

"Well, what am I to say, then?" Nigel was clearly disgruntled. "I don't want to insult him, and he will be insulted if you refuse him."

"Tell him I don't want to leave you," she said. She smiled at him. "It will be the truth, Father."

He tried to hide his pleasure. "You're seventeen years old," he complained. "Many girls are married at fifteen, Cristen."

She slid out of her chair and came over to give him a hug. "You should go to bed," she said. "You and Hugh are to leave for Chippenham tomorrow."

"Humph," he said.

She kissed his cheek. "Good night, Father."

"Good night, Cristen."

He watched her trail off to her room, a worried frown between his brows.

Hugh awoke the following morning with a headache. Cristen ruthlessly evicted Henry Fairfax from his room and installed Hugh in his old bed.

"There must be something going wrong inside my brain," Hugh said to Cristen tightly as she changed the cold cloths she was putting on his forehead. "I never had headaches before."

She gently put the new cloths into place and said composedly, "I think they will go away once you find out the truth about yourself."

The window shutters had been closed to keep out the light and no candles had been lit, but even in the dimness she could see how pale he was. The muscles in his face were tense with pain.

His lashes lifted. His eyes were much darker than usual. "Do you think the headaches have to do with my . . . search?"

"Yes, I do."

In fact, she was convinced of it. He had managed to survive in his identity of Hugh Corbaille by denying his past. Now that his past had caught up with him, however, the fear of facing it was tearing him apart.

No wonder he had headaches.

He said wretchedly, "I think I'm going to be sick."

She held the bowl for him.

"*I hate this,*" he said intensely when he had laid back down again.

She understood that it was not just the pain he was talking about. It was the humiliation of being ill.

"You're not perfect," she said calmly. "You can become ill just like anyone else."

"What time is it?" he asked.

She looked at the hourglass. The last two headaches had lasted for eight hours.

"You have four more hours to go," she said.

His lashes flickered.

*Four more hours of agony,* she thought despairingly. *It isn't fair, Dear Lord. Haven't You already given him enough to bear?*

"My lady." It was Brian at the door. "Sir Nigel sent me to tell you that Sir Henry is leaving."

"All right," she said. "I'll come."

Brian left and Cristen stood up. "I told Father last night that I wouldn't marry Sir Henry," she said to Hugh's pain-tensed face.

He managed a smile. "Good."

She bent and kissed his hair above the compress. "I'll be back," she said softly, and left to make her farewells to a very indignant lord of Bowden.

The headache held true to form and lifted eight hours after it had begun. A pale and tired-looking Hugh was able to join the household for supper, although he ate very little.

Nigel, warned by Cristen, said nothing about Hugh's illness. After supper, Cristen's ladies joined the knights in front of the fire in the Great Hall, and everyone sang to the accompaniment of Thomas' lute. Then, after the ladies had retired, Hugh remained in the hall to play a game of chess with Matthew.

The solar was dark when Hugh entered, and the doors to both Nigel's and Cristen's rooms were closed. Hugh went into his own room and told the squire who was waiting for him that he would undress himself. Once the squire had gone, Hugh returned to the solar.

He stood in the middle of the room, his eyes fixed on her bedroom door, and willed her to come out.

It took her thirty seconds.

She had on her green velvet robe and her shining hair was tucked behind her small ears, spreading in a smooth fan to her waist. She held a finger to her lips and pointed to his room. On silent feet the two of them went inside and closed the door behind them.

He reached out and took her into his arms.

She leaned against him and closed her eyes.

"You got rid of Fairfax all right?" he asked tensely.

"Aye."

He put his cheek against the silky round top of her head. Her hair smelled of lavender. "Good."

"Hugh," she said. "I understand that you must go to Chippenham, but please promise me that you will be careful."

"I promise," he said huskily.

"If anything should happen to you, I might find myself married to Henry Fairfax after all."

His arms tightened around her. "Never."

She pulled back a little and looked up into his face. Her skin was as perfect as a baby's, he thought, it was so closely textured and pure.

He bent his head and kissed her.

Her head tipped back and her hair streamed like a silken mantle down over his wrists. Her lips opened under the pressure of his and the kiss became deeply erotic.

When he finally tore himself away from her, he was breathing hard and a pulse was beating rapidly in his throat. "I wish we were already married," he said fiercely.

She felt his need, and all her instinct was to give him what he desired. "Do we have to wait until we're married?"

His mouth compressed into a hard, straight line. "Yes," he said. "We do."

She didn't answer.

He touched her cheek. "No matter what happens, I can bear it as long as I have you."

"You'll always have me," she said.

He smiled. "Aye," he said. "I know."

# 17

It was a mild, golden October day when Hugh and Nigel set off the following morning for Chippenham. The trees in the forest were brilliant with changing colors and the road they followed was for the most part good and broad, narrowing only in a few short stretches as they passed through a valley. Hugh and Nigel did not wear mail themselves, but they were escorted by six of Nigel's knights, who carried the blue and white flag of Somerford and were dressed in full armor.

It was midafternoon when the great walls of Chippenham came into sight. Hugh looked once again at the scarlet flag with its device of the golden boar and felt something in his chest tighten. His face was expressionless, however, as they rode up to the gatehouse and were admitted into the bailey.

They surrendered their horses in the inner courtyard to two of Guy's grooms and were escorted by one of the knights on guard up the stairs to the Great Hall.

There they found Lord Guy. He and his knights and a group of ladies had just come in from a pleasant few hours of hunting in the forest, and they were drinking wine and laughing and talking loudly in front of the fire.

The laughter and the talk died down as Hugh and Nigel crossed the floor.

Guy moved to meet them.

For a long silent moment, Hugh stared into a face that, except for the startling eyes, did not remotely resemble his. Guy's cheekbones were broad and flat, not high and sculpted, his jaw was longer than Hugh's, his lips fuller.

At the moment, his eyes were cold and dangerous-looking, even though a genial smile played around his lips.

"So," he said. "Hugh Corbaille who says he is my long-lost nephew."

"I think you know that I am," Hugh said softly.

Guy shrugged. "It doesn't matter one way or the other. There is nothing here for you at Chippenham. King Stephen himself has confirmed me in my title as earl."

"So I have heard," said Hugh.

Guy's eyes moved to Nigel and then back again to Hugh. "Why have you come here, then?"

"I am a man who has lost his past, my lord," Hugh said in the same soft tone he had used before. "I need to recapture it in order to make myself whole. I ask only that I might spend some time here in this castle where I grew up, that I be allowed to talk to some of the people who lived here when I was a child."

"It will do you no good," Guy said grimly.

"Perhaps not, but I need to try."

The earl shrugged. "Then do so. There is nothing here I wish to hide from you, Hugh *Corbaille*."

"Thank you, my lord."

Once more the cold gray eyes flicked toward Nigel. "And welcome to you also, Nigel Haslin."

Guy's voice was edged with steel.

Nigel bowed. "My lord."

Guy gestured toward the group around the fire. "Come and meet your hostess, my cousin, the Lady Eleanor."

Hugh walked beside his uncle toward the people who were staring at him, some surreptitiously, some openly. Guy was no taller than he, but was far more massively built. From the swell of his belly, it was clear that the earl enjoyed his food, but his neck was muscled, his shoulders broad and powerful, and he looked like a man to be reckoned with.

The golden-haired woman who had been beside Guy during the tournament came forward.

"My dear," Guy said, "allow me to introduce Hugh Corbaille, who will be visiting us for a while. And I believe you already know my vassal, the lord of Somerford."

The woman, who looked to be in her middle twenties, smiled at Hugh. Her eyes were round and blue, her nose was short and upturned, and she had a dimple in her left cheek.

Her teeth were not good. Hugh thought of Cristen's pink mouth and perfect white teeth, and smiled politely at the lady Eleanor.

"Will you join us for some wine?" she asked courteously. "You must be thirsty after your journey."

"Thank you, my lady," Hugh said, and moved to join the group in front of the fire.

The first person he saw was the chestnut-haired knight who had evinced such hostility toward him upon their previous encounters.

Hugh walked right over to him and said, "I am Hugh Corbaille."

There could be no doubt about the emotion that was looking at him out of the knight's pale green eyes. It was hatred, pure and simple.

The chestnut head nodded abruptly. "Aubrey d'Abrille," he said.

"Have we met before?" Hugh inquired softly.

"I do not think so." The knight's voice was quiet also, although his eyes were savage.

"You appear to know me, though," Hugh said.

"I do not know a Hugh Corbaille," the man replied.

The two pairs of light eyes locked together.

Hugh was in no doubt that he had an enemy in this man, although he still didn't know why.

"Sir Hugh?" said a sweet, feminine voice.

He broke eye contact with Aubrey d'Abrille and turned to the girl who had come up beside him. Out of the corner of his eye, he saw the chestnut-haired knight break away from the group and stride away across the floor.

* * *

They remained around the fire for another hour and then the lady Eleanor conducted Hugh and Nigel to a small bedroom, which they were to share, and left them to change their clothes for supper. William, the squire Nigel had brought to see to their needs, moved quietly around the room, putting things away while Hugh and Nigel talked by the unshuttered window.

"Who is this Lady Eleanor?" Hugh asked.

Nigel snorted. "If she's his cousin, it's a very distant connection. He installed her at Chippenham two years ago, after his wife died."

Pensively, Hugh scanned the scene outside the window. It afforded a good view of Chippenham's extensive kitchen garden.

"All of the knights we just met were too young to have been here in my father's time," he remarked.

"There are some older knights in the household, though," Nigel said. "We will probably see them at supper."

Hugh nodded and turned his back on the window.

"Do you have any memory of which bedroom used to be yours?" Nigel asked.

Hugh shook his head. His face was looking strained.

Nigel lifted his hand to pat him on the back, then dropped it again as he remembered how much Hugh disliked to be touched.

He turned instead to William. "Get us some water, lad, so that we may wash."

William straightened up from the wooden chest where he was arranging their clothes. "Aye, my lord," he said.

When Hugh and Nigel had washed and put on fresh tunics and hose and house shoes, they descended once more to the Great Hall, which was being readied for supper.

*This must be what it used to look like when I was a child,* Hugh thought as he stared at the room in front of him, struggling to summon up a memory. The trestle tables had all been set up and the servants were putting out the saltcellars, steel knives and silver spoons.

Hugh's eyes traveled slowly from the great fireplace along the high stone walls, and came to a stop at one of the tapestries featuring a knight on a horse.

It looked familiar.

*Of course it looks familiar,* he thought irritably. *I've probably seen dozens of such tapestries in my life.*

But there was something about the way the horse's feet were placed . . .

He was distracted by the sound of a feminine voice addressing him.

"You are the knight who won the horsemanship contest at the tournament, are you not, Sir Hugh?"

"Aye." Hugh forced his attention to the girl standing in front of him. Her hair was deeply auburn and her eyes a clear, azure blue. She gave him a dazzling smile, showing perfect, pearly white teeth.

"It was wonderful to see how at one you were with your horse," she said admiringly.

"Thank you, you are very kind," Hugh replied. He remembered meeting her earlier around the fire, but he had absolutely no recollection of her name.

"I believe you are to sit beside me at supper," she said, as if she were conferring a great favor upon him. Her long lashes fluttered. "I should be so interested to hear how you trained your marvelous horse."

*Might as well make a clean breast of it,* Hugh thought.

"I'm sorry," he said, "but I don't remember your name."

A flash of annoyance flickered across her lovely face. Then she gave a tinkling laugh. "It's Cecily, my lord. Lady Cecily Martaine."

"Lady Cecily," Hugh said gravely.

Nigel was watching this byplay with a distinct gleam of amusement in his eyes.

"Is your father Robert Martaine of Linkford?" he asked the girl.

Reluctantly she removed her eyes from Hugh's face. "Aye, Sir Nigel. I came to Chippenham last year to serve the lady Eleanor."

"I see," said Nigel.

People had begun to drift toward the tables and Cecily laid a proprietary hand on Hugh's sleeve. "Come," she said, "and I will show you where you are to sit."

They were not seated at the high table with Guy, but instead were placed at one of the trestle tables near the front of the hall. Hugh was disappointed to see that the other knights at the table were all under the age of thirty.

Hugh looked around for Aubrey d'Abrille and saw him sitting on the other side of the room.

The horn announcing dinner blew. Servants with ewers, basins, and towels attended to the guests so they could first wash their hands. Due to the fact that people shared dishes and ate with their fingers, Norman etiquette decreed that hands and nails must be kept scrupulously clean at table. A well-bred person also wiped his spoon and knife after use, and wiped his mouth before drinking as well.

The lady Cecily flirted outrageously with Hugh for the entire meal. It annoyed him intensely, as he wanted to be able to look around the hall to determine which of the men present might be of an age to be useful to him, and instead he was forced to pay attention to this pest of a girl.

Hugh had been brought up by Adela to be courteous to women, and he was courteous to Lady Cecily. But in his heart, he wanted to strangle her.

The final course was served and at last supper was over. Guy announced that after the tables had been cleared there would be dancing.

"How lovely!" Lady Cecily exclaimed, clapping her hands and flashing her perfect teeth.

"Aye," Hugh said glumly.

Nigel was talking to a middle-aged woman whom he seemed to know, and Hugh was forced to stand with Lady Cecily while the floor was cleared. She talked gaily the whole time. In fact, all the men and women were talking gaily. And loudly. It appeared to Hugh that quite a bit of wine had been drunk at supper.

He saw no sign of Aubrey d'Abrille. The knight had apparently left the hall.

Finally the last table was removed, and Lord Guy moved onto the floor holding the lady Eleanor by the hand. He moved lightly for such a heavy man.

Lady Cecily seized Hugh's hand and pulled him out to join the rest of the company. They spread out, forming a large circle in the middle of the rush-strewn floor.

Once the circle had been completed, and the alternating men and women were holding each other by the hand, Lord Guy asked genially, "Who will have the courtesy to sing for us?"

The music for dancing was always provided by the human voice.

One of the younger knights intoned a song for the leading voice and after a moment the rest of the company joined in. The men bowed, the ladies curtseyed, and the circle began to move. The dancing had begun.

Hugh went through the motions, his hand clasping the warm hand of the Lady Cecily, his feet moving automatically to the steps that Adela had taught him so many years before.

He did not sing.

After the first dance had finished, he became aware that one of Guy's knights was staring at him.

The man was no longer young. His hair was still brown and his belly was still flat, but his weather-beaten face gave away his forty and more years.

Hugh felt a surge of excitement. Perhaps this was the man he was looking for.

He deliberately made eye contact with the knight, who, instead of being embarrassed at being caught staring, looked directly back. Unlike Aubrey, however, there was no hostility in this man's gaze.

"Why is Alan fitzRobert staring at you, Sir Hugh?" Cecily asked.

A muscle twitched along Hugh's jaw. This girl was proving to be a definite nuisance.

"I don't know," he replied calmly.

"It's probably because of your eyes. Did you notice that you have the same color eyes as Lord Guy?"

"I noticed," Hugh said.

Her azure gaze was blatantly curious. "Why is that, do you think?"

"I have no idea."

She pouted.

Hugh wanted to go and talk to Alan, but Cecily was sticking to him like a leech.

"Perhaps I have met this Alan before and I don't recall him," he said. "If you will excuse me, Lady Cecily, I will go and speak to him."

"Oh, I'll come with you," she said gaily.

Hugh had had enough. With a mental apology to Adela, he said, "Thank you, but I prefer to go alone."

Color flushed into her ivory skin. He noted with perfect objectivity that she was a very pretty girl.

"You are discourteous, sir," she said stiffly.

"I beg your pardon," Hugh said.

He bowed and turned away, leaving her standing by herself against the wall.

When he saw Hugh crossing the floor in his direction, the knight named Alan jerked his head slightly in the direction of the door, then turned and left the hall.

Hugh followed.

The knight was waiting for him on the landing outside. "Come downstairs to the guardroom with me," he commanded.

"All right."

The landing was lit by a flambeau stuck into an iron holder on the wall. Alan lit a torch from the flambeau, held it aloft, and led the way down the stairs to the floor below, where the guardroom was located.

The vast room was deserted, as all of the knights were upstairs at the dancing. The flickering light from the torch allowed Hugh to see the array of swords and shields that hung upon the bare stone walls. Several trestle tables containing pieces of harness and armor were scattered about the floor. A wooden bench upon which straw mattresses and blankets had been set ran around the entire room. Trunks containing the clothes and belongings of each knight were stored under the bench.

Chippenham was large enough to have a separate room for the knights to sleep in.

Alan held his torch so that its light fell directly on Hugh's face. "Who are you?" he demanded.

Hugh stood lance straight under that burning gaze. "I am Hugh de Leon, the son of Roger and Isabel," he replied steadily.

The knight's breath hissed through his teeth. "I thought so."

He swung around and took the torch to one of the tables, lit the candle that was on it, then brought the torch back out to the landing, where he thrust it into an empty iron holder. Then he came back into the guardroom.

His eyes searched Hugh's face. Even in the dimness, Hugh could see a muscle twitch in his cheek.

"Where have you been for all these years?"

Hugh answered him honestly, giving a brief summary of what had happened to him since he was taken from Chippenham.

Still speaking with dogged steadiness, he told Alan about his memory loss.

"I have never heard of such a thing," the knight said.

The single candle lit only the part of the room in which they were standing. Everything else was in deep shadow.

Hugh was white about the mouth. "Nevertheless, it is true."

The knight took a step closer. "Why in the name of God have you come here? Surely you must see how dangerous it is! Your very existence is a direct threat to Guy's position."

Hugh held the man's eyes with his own. "I have come because I can no longer live with only half a life," he said. "I need to find out who I really am. I came here to try to find someone who might help me do this." His whole being was intent upon the lean man standing in front of him, backlit by candlelight. "Lady Cecily told me your name was Alan fitzRobert. You were one of my father's knights, were you not?"

For a long moment, Alan did not reply. Then he admitted, "Aye, I was."

"And you switched your allegiance to Guy after my father was killed?"

Hugh had tried to keep his voice dispassionate, but something of what he was feeling must have seeped through, because the knight's lips tightened. He said, "Guy offered me a place and I knew nothing against him, so I took it."

The smoke from the torch on the landing drifted in the door and assailed Hugh's nostrils. His heartbeat accelerated as he said the words he had come to Chippenham to say.

"I have come here for one other reason, Alan. I have come to find out who murdered my father."

The older knight suddenly looked very weary. "I was afraid of that," he said.

"Why should you be afraid?" Hugh demanded. "Because you are Guy's man?"

Alan's voice sounded as weary as he looked. "Guy did not murder your father, Hugh. He was killed by one of his own knights."

"I don't believe that," Hugh said fiercely. "No simple knight would have reason to kill an earl—unless he was paid to do it by someone else!"

"Oh, Walter Crespin had reason, Hugh," Alan said. "It was no mystery to any of us knights why Walter would want to kill Earl Roger."

Hugh had learned long ago how to guard his face, but the shock of this reply showed in his eyes.

"Tell me," he said at last. "I need to know."

The knight shook his head in denial. "Why not leave well enough alone, boy? You have made a good life for yourself . . . "

"No." All the force of Hugh's formidable will was trained on the man facing him. "Tell me."

Once more Alan's eyes traced Hugh's face. "You look so much like your mother," he said, seemingly at random.

Hugh felt as if a hand was closing around his chest, cutting off his breathing. "Does my father's death have something to do with my mother?"

Alan took a step backwards.

Hugh followed him. For the third time he said, "Tell me."

"Why don't you ask these questions of the Lady Isabel?"

The knight had backed up to the point where his legs were pressing against the bench belonging to one of the tables.

Hugh said, "I haven't seen my . . . I haven't seen Isabel. I can't see her until I know."

Some of the anguish Hugh was trying to conceal finally got through to the knight. Silence fell as they looked at each other.

Then, "All right," Alan said with resignation. "Perhaps it will be best for you to know. Once you learn the truth, perhaps you will be satisfied that Guy had nothing to do with your father's murder and will leave here while you are still alive."

Hugh was quivering all over, like a bow that has been strung too tightly. He nodded.

The knight gestured toward the table behind him. "Come and sit down, Hugh. This is not a pleasant tale I have to tell."

# 18

They sat facing each other across the table, a candle between them. On the table lay a bridle that someone had taken apart to clean.

"I saw you win the horsemanship contest at the tournament," Alan said. "Even when you were a child you had a way with horses."

Hugh's face never changed.

"Do you have a scar on your right knee?"

Suddenly Hugh felt dizzy. His stomach heaved and bile rose in the back of his throat. He swallowed it down and focused his eyes even more intently on the other man's face. "Aye," he managed to get out. "I do."

"You got that when you were four years old. You climbed onto your father's stallion when no one was looking, and he threw you. We were afraid you might have smashed your kneecap, but it was just a cut."

Hugh had a sudden, desperate wish that Cristen were here beside him. He said, "I don't remember."

Alan looked at the stark young face in front of him and said gently, "Are you certain you want to hear this, Hugh?"

"I have to," Hugh said. He took a deep, steadying breath. "I have to."

The knight sighed. "All right. If it is the only thing that will get you away from this place . . . "

He folded his big, scarred hands on the table in front of him and began to talk.

"Your father was forty-two years of age when he returned from the Holy Land. His fame as a crusader was great. Did you know that?"

Hugh nodded tensely.

"His elder brother had died, leaving no sons, and so Roger inherited the earldom. Of course, one of the first things he had to do when he returned was to marry and get sons to come after him. He chose to marry Isabel Matard."

Hugh dropped his eyes to the bridle pieces on the table. He picked up the brow band and rubbed it between his fingers. "Go on," he said, his voice low.

"Remember this, Hugh," Alan said. "Your mother was fifteen years old when first she came to Chippenham as Roger's wife. She was sixteen when she bore you."

*Cristen is seventeen*, Hugh thought. *My mother was younger than she when I was born.*

Alan said pensively, "Your mother . . ." He stared at his loosely clasped hands. "How can I make you see how beautiful your mother was?"

The light from the candle between them flickered on his down-looking face.

"All of us knights were in love with her, of course. How could we not be?"

He fell silent, as if he were conjuring up for himself the image of Isabel as she once had been.

Finally he lifted his eyes to look at Hugh. "Roger wasn't in love with her, though. I think he had spent all of his passion on the Crusade. There was nothing left in him to give to a woman. He was a cold man, Hugh. A very cold man."

Hugh's fingers tightened convulsively on the brow band.

"Once you were born, and he had done his duty to the succession, it was as if your mother didn't exist for him." Alan hesitated. "I think he felt that she made him impure."

"Impure?" Hugh said, clearly startled.

Alan went back to staring at his clasped hands, avoiding Hugh's gaze. He nodded. "Your father had been planning to join the

Templars before he was called home from the east. It is a pity he was unable to do so; he would have been a good fighting priest. Unfortunately, he was not a good husband."

Hugh forced his fingers to loosen their death grip on the bridle piece. "I see," he said.

Alan reached out and slightly moved the position of the candle so that it did not cast so much light on his face. He said, "At that time, Ivo Crespin was one of the knights of Roger's household."

"Ivo?" Hugh said. "I thought his name was Walter."

"Ivo was Walter's brother."

Hugh stiffened, as if bracing himself for a blow.

"Ivo was a splendid young man." For the first time since they had met, a faint smile touched Alan's lips. "You loved him. He used to let you ride in front of him on his horse. He was the one who first taught you how to shoot a bow."

Hugh forced himself to breathe evenly, trying to slow the hammer beats of his heart.

"Ivo was deeply in love with your mother," Alan said, "and she loved him back."

Once more Hugh's fingers tightened on the bridle. Sweat broke out on his forehead.

Alan's voice went relentlessly on. "We all knew it and we all held our tongues. Ivo was well liked by everyone and no one blamed your mother for trying to find some happiness with him. She was very lonely, Hugh."

Hugh tried to say something and failed.

Alan said sadly, "Then Roger found out."

Hugh's eyes clung desperately to Alan's face.

"You must understand Roger's position," the knight said. "It is every married man's greatest fear, that shame will come to him through his wife. In these great castles, with so few women and so many men . . . "

Alan made a very Gallic gesture with his hand.

"What happened?" Hugh croaked.

Alan clasped his hands once again and went back to looking at them. "We warned Ivo in time for him to get away, but he wouldn't go. He wouldn't leave your mother to face Roger's wrath alone. He made a mistake and he stayed."

Hugh's knuckles were white, he was holding the bridle so tightly.

Alan said quietly, "Your father had him taken prisoner and forcibly evicted from Chippenham. But before Ivo was taken away, Roger castrated him."

Hugh made a sound, which he quickly tried to suppress.

The lines in Alan's face looked as if they had been carved by a knife. He said, "Once he was away from Chippenham, and left alone, Ivo killed himself."

Hugh bowed his head and stared blindly at the scarred top of the table. "That is . . . a terrible story," he managed to say at last.

"It was very ugly," Alan agreed. "But now you see, Hugh, why Walter Crespin would want to kill Earl Roger."

"Aye," said Hugh, his voice unsteady.

"It took him over a year to exact his revenge. But when Roger was found dead and Walter was missing . . . well, we none of us had any doubt as to what had happened."

Hugh nodded. His fingers moved on the bridle piece.

"I don't know why he took you with him," Alan said. "Doing that only punished your mother. I suppose we will never know what was in his mind."

"Perhaps he wanted to punish her. Perhaps he blamed her for what happened to Ivo," Hugh said.

"None of us blamed your mother," Alan replied emphatically. "And as for punishment—your father had seen to that."

"Hugh's head jerked up. "What did he do to her?"

"He isolated her. He isolated her so that such a thing would never happen again. Worst of all, he kept you from her. He saw her as corrupted, you see, and he was afraid that she would corrupt you as well."

An image flashed before Hugh's mind: Ralf standing with his hand on Adela's shoulder and she looking up at him with a smile on her face.

He shut his eyes.

*What kind of blood do I have running in my veins?*

With a tremendous effort of will, he forced himself to speak calmly. "So you are telling me that Guy had no part in the murder of his brother?"

Never again would Hugh refer to Roger as his father. His allegiance was to Ralf, who had been a good man.

"That is what I am telling you, Hugh. I know that rumor has implicated Guy, and I suppose it is only natural that people should look to place the blame on the man who benefited most from Roger's death and your disappearance. But Guy is innocent of this deed. Roger was not killed for gain. He was killed for revenge."

Hugh put his hands on the table and pushed himself to his feet. He felt bruised all over, as if he had taken a vicious pummeling from someone's fists.

"I thank you for telling me this," he said carefully. "It was something I needed to know."

The knight rose also and came around the table to stand next to Hugh.

"You will leave here, then?"

Hugh's voice was harsh. "There seems to be little reason for me to remain."

Alan hesitated. Then he said, "I am sorry, Hugh. I'm sorry I had such an ugly tale to tell you."

He reached out to put a comforting hand upon Hugh's shoulder.

Hugh flinched away from him.

Alan's hand dropped.

"Go away before Guy can strike at you," the knight said.

"Guy has no reason to fear me," Hugh said bleakly. "He has had the king confirm him in his earldom."

Alan shook his head in disagreement. "You are Roger's son, and as such you will always be a threat to him. Leave Chippenham, Hugh. Nigel Haslin did you no favor when he told you who you are."

Hugh picked up the candle from the table, turned, and strode out of the room. Alan could not hear the sound of his feet in his soft shoes as he ascended the stairs, but he knew that Hugh was running.

Hugh did not return to the Great Hall. Instead he continued on up the stairs, to the floor on which his bedroom was located.

He prayed that Nigel would not be there, that he would have a chance to compose himself before he had to face Cristen's father.

The room was empty. Even William must still be downstairs with the other squires.

*Thank God*, Hugh thought.

He shut the door behind him and pain, sudden and violent, knifed through the left side of his head.

He stood like a statue, hoping it was just a momentary thing. Before this, his headaches had always started slowly.

The pain was white-hot and seemed to emanate from a muscle in the lower left part of his skull. It stabbed upward, behind his left eye, all the way up into his forehead.

Hugh stood at the door, rigid and quivering. *No*, he thought. *Not now. Please, not now.*

The pain did not stop.

Hugh closed his left eye and stumbled across the room toward the trunk where William had stored their belongings. Cristen had given him a packet of herbs to use in case of such an emergency. His hand was shaking as he pulled the packet out from beneath his folded clothes. He poured himself a cup of water from the pitcher standing on the room's single small table, and mixed the herbs into it.

He drank it all.

Then he went over to the bed and lay down, his arm flung over his eyes.

He was still lying like that when William came into the room a half an hour later.

"Hugh!" the squire said in surprise. "I did not know you were here. You should have sent for me."

"It's all right," Hugh said. "I'm not feeling well, William. Will you get me a basin in case I am sick?"

"Of course," the squire said soothingly. Clearly he thought that Hugh had drank too much. "I'll be right back."

He brought Hugh the basin and twenty minutes later, Hugh was sick in it. He desperately wanted to tell William to go away and leave him alone, but the boy was Nigel's squire and Nigel would want him when he came in.

An hour later, the lord of Somerford pushed open the door of the bedroom.

"Hugh," he said angrily when he saw the supine figure on the bed. "I was worried to death about you! Why didn't you tell me you were going upstairs?"

Hugh didn't answer. He was at the point where he simply couldn't.

"I think he's had too much to drink, Sir Nigel," William said in a low voice. "He's been sick to his stomach."

Nigel went over to the bed and leaned over Hugh, sniffing. "There's no smell of wine on his breath."

He straightened up. "Jesu Christ, could he have been poisoned?"

"No . . ." Hugh's voice was a mere thread of sound. "I just . . . have a headache. I've had them before. Cristen knows."

"A headache?" Nigel stared down at the part of Hugh's face that was not sheltered by his arm. "Is that the sickness that stopped you from riding in the mêlée?"

"Aye."

"Jesu," said Nigel. His voice softened. "What can I do to help you, lad? Is there something you can take?"

"Just . . . leave me in peace," Hugh said. "It will go away in its own time."

Nigel stood in silence, looking down at Hugh's shielded face. "Do you want to get out of your clothes?" he asked.

"No."

Nigel rubbed his own eyes. "All right." He turned to his squire. "Help me with my own clothes, William, and then you may go to your rest."

Once he was undressed, Nigel slipped carefully into the big bed he was sharing with Hugh.

Hugh never moved.

"I wish there was something I could do to help you, lad," Nigel said.

No answer.

Nigel sighed, turned on his side, closed his eyes, and composed himself to sleep.

The headache lifted in the middle of the night. It had both come and gone more quickly than the previous ones.

Hugh lay on his back, his eyes staring sightlessly into the dark. He felt utterly wrung out.

Now that he was able to think again, the story he had heard from Alan ran over and over through his mind.

*Castrated*, he thought.

All of a healthy young man's horror filled his soul at such a thought.

*I wonder why it took Walter Crespin over a year to avenge his brother?*

After half an hour of thinking, Hugh slipped out of bed, careful not to wake Nigel. The room was very cold, as the shutters still had not been drawn across the window. There was enough moonlight for Hugh to see his way across the floor. Nigel scarcely stirred as Hugh opened the bedroom door and stepped out into the hall.

A flambeau was burning in the hall outside, and Hugh reached up and lit the candle he had picked up in the bedroom on his way out. Then he began to make his way down the spiral staircase.

Chippenham was quiet. There was no guard stationed on the landing inside the front door, and Hugh made his way unimpeded into the castle forebuilding, where the chapel was located.

The heavy chapel door creaked as Hugh pushed it open. It was pitch-dark within, and Hugh held his candle in front of him as he walked up the center aisle.

He stood in the place where Geoffrey's bier had been placed and looked at the altar.

It was freezing in the chapel, but under the tunic and fine white shirt he had worn to supper, Hugh was sweating.

The familiar feelings of terror and guilt began to sweep over him.

*I have to do this*, he thought.

He shut his eyes and stood there, ramrod stiff, straining to remember.

Inside his brain he heard the sound of a single high-pitched scream. Was it himself he was hearing?

His breath came hard and painful, hurting his chest. The hand that was not holding the candle was clenched into a fist at his side.

*I was here when it happened*, he thought. *I know that I was here.*

Had he been kidnapped because he had seen what had happened? Had Walter taken him because he was a witness to Walter's murder of Roger?

*It's all my fault. It's all my fault.*

If that was what had happened, then why did he feel so guilty?

"Oh God," Hugh said out loud. "Why can't I just *remember?*"

A few minutes later Hugh left the chapel, closing the heavy door behind him.

An unexpected breeze chilled his fingers. His candle went out. A fraction of a second later, he was on the floor and rolling.

The heavy *thud* made by a dagger burying itself deep in wood sounded clearly in the small passage.

Someone had thrown a knife at the place where Hugh had just been standing and it had pierced the chapel door.

Hugh crouched in the spot where he had finished his roll, perfectly immobile, trying to not even breathe. Someone had extinguished the flambeaux that illuminated the staircase, and the landing was pitch dark.

He knelt there in the blackness, listening.

The sound of someone breathing came out of the darkness to his right. The would-be assassin was on the chapel side of the landing, about ten feet away from him.

This meant that Hugh was closer to the stairs.

Cursing the fact that he had left his dagger in his bedroom, Hugh balanced his weight on his toes and prepared to make a dash for his life.

A step sounded on the wooden floor, then came the sound of the dagger being ripped out of the wood of the door.

By then, Hugh was at the staircase, racing down and down in the inky darkness, keeping his feet by instinct alone.

He didn't stop at the Great Hall but continued on down to the floor below. At this hour, the guardroom would be filled with sleeping knights, making it far safer than the empty hall above.

Flambeaux lit the section of the staircase that connected the hall and the guardroom, and Hugh hurled himself downward toward safety.

He tumbled into the guardroom, which was in darkness, pressed himself against the cold stone wall, and waited.

The only sound he heard was the snoring of the knights.

He waited some more.

After about ten minutes, he moved cautiously to the wall, where he had seen a sword hanging earlier in the evening. He reached up, felt the cold steel blade, moved his hand to the hilt, and removed the sword from its hanger.

Once he was armed, he moved back to the door and stepped out onto the landing of the staircase.

No one was there.

He reached up and removed a flambeau from its iron holder. Holding the sword in his left hand and the flambeau in his right, he retraced his way up the stairs until he had reached the level of the Great Hall.

All was silent.

No one bothered him as he crossed the Great Hall and went on up the staircase that would lead him back to the room he was sharing with Nigel.

Once Hugh was safely back in bed, he crossed his arms behind his head and stared, wide-eyed, into the dark.

He had not thought that Guy would be stupid enough to attack him in Guy's own castle. He remembered Nigel's words on this subject, however. *Guy sometimes acts first and thinks later.*

Whether it was Guy or one of his henchmen, someone had clearly intended to remove Hugh from the world this night.

Hugh frowned, thought some more, and decided it would be wisest to say nothing of the incident outside the chapel to Nigel, who would only berate him for being fool enough to venture out on his own.

At last, as the first streaks of dawn were staining the sky, he turned on his side, closed his eyes, and prepared to try to get some sleep.

The following morning before breaking fast, Hugh sought out Alan.

"I have one more question for you," he said to the knight, who was standing before the fire in the Great Hall waiting for the tables to be set up.

"What is that?" Alan asked warily, lowering his voice so he could not be heard by those around him.

"Who found Roger's body in the chapel?"

Alan looked surprised. "Why, it was the priest," he said. "Father

Anselm. We reckoned that your father must have been laying there
for at least an hour. That was what gave Walter the time to get away."

"I see," said Hugh. "Thank you."

Lady Cecily, full of smiles and chatter, sat beside him at the
breaking of fast. After the meal was finished, Hugh got rid of her
by the simple expedient of saying that he was going to the garde-
robe. Instead, he went out into the courtyard.

He walked around to the back of the castle, to where the
kitchen garden he had seen from his window was located. Next to
the kitchen garden was a small walled-in pleasure garden.

He had known it would be there.

Slowly he walked to the gate of the garden and let himself in.

There were no flowers this time of year. The beds were full of
bare stalks and the rosebushes were all wood. Hugh shut his eyes
and the sweet scent of summer blossoms drifted to his nostrils.

He opened his eyes and stared at the wooden bench that was
placed in the middle of the garden. A picture formed in his mind of
a woman sitting there in the sun. A little boy came running down
one of the paths, and she stood up, bending down to him, her arms
outstretched. The child ran right into her arms.

Hugh smelled the scent of roses.

His lips formed the word *Mother.*

He stood there for a long time, staring sightlessly at the empty
bench. Then he turned and walked out of the garden, back to the
castle to look for Nigel.

He went first to the Great Hall, where he was accosted by Sir
Richard Evril, who informed him in a very clipped tone that Lord
Guy desired to speak to him. He followed Richard up the stairs,
through a small, sparsely furnished anteroom, and into what was
obviously the family solar, where Guy awaited him.

The earl was standing at the unshuttered window, looking out,
when Hugh came into the room. For a long moment he didn't
move, making Hugh stand and regard his back. Finally he turned
around. Slowly, he looked Hugh up and down.

"I thought we should have a little talk," he said at last.

Hugh looked back at the man who had twice tried to kill him,
the man who was responsible for the death of Geoffrey, and didn't
reply.

"What were you doing in the pleasure garden?" Guy said abruptly.

Hugh remained where he was by the door. "Trying to see if I remembered it," he said.

"And did you?"

"Aye," Hugh said. "I believe that I do."

There were dark pouches of dissipation below Guy's gray eyes, but the eyes themselves were clear and alert. "Hear me, Hugh Corbaille," he said in a hard voice. "I have thrown in my lot with Stephen. I didn't want to choose sides, but you forced me to it. Stephen may be weak in some things, but he will support me—with arms, if he has to. Wiltshire is too important for him to give it up."

"That is so," said Hugh. His expression was contained, giving nothing away.

Guy took a step away from the window into the room. He put his hands on the back of a carved chair and stared at Hugh over it. "I am telling you this because I know that your mother's family is of the empress's party." Guy leaned a little forward. "I have summoned you here to give you this warning. Do not go to Mathilda to uphold your claim."

The day outside the window was gloomy and overcast. The light in the solar was dim. The two men stood for a moment in silence, looking at each other across the bare wooden floor.

"And if I do?" Hugh asked.

"You will regret it," Guy replied in a hard voice. "My own feudal army equals anything Robert of Gloucester can put in the field. And Stephen will aid me as well." The gray eyes narrowed dangerously. "If it comes to a fight between us, you may well end up dead, Hugh. Think on that before you do something rash."

"Is that a threat?" Hugh asked softly.

Guy's full lips were set in a hard, implacable line. "You may take it that way if you wish."

Hugh moved forward one step, bringing him fractionally closer to Guy. He stared into the eyes that were so like his own and demanded, "Did you have anything to do with the death of your brother?"

Guy held his gaze unflinchingly. "I did not. If you came here seeking vengeance, I am not the man you want."

The two pairs of gray eyes held for a long, strained moment. Then Hugh slowly nodded.

There was the slightest relaxation of tension in Guy's face. "I have been the Earl of Wiltshire for fourteen years," he said. "You will not supplant me, even if you are my brother's son."

"If I am no threat to you, then why have you twice tried to have me killed?" Hugh inquired. His voice was merely curious.

Guy's eyes flickered with surprise. "What are you talking about?"

"The knight who was killed at the tournament was riding my horse, and there are those who will swear he was downed by a blow to his back, not his front."

"Nonsense," Guy said impatiently.

"Someone fighting on his own side killed Geoffrey," Hugh said. "And you had a number of men fighting on his side."

"I don't know where you have gotten this ridiculous notion, but I had nothing to do with the death of Nigel Haslin's knight!" Angry color flared in Guy's face. "Look to one of his own companions if you suspect he was betrayed. Perhaps one of his fellow knights held a grudge against him. But don't try to lay his death at my door!"

Hugh looked thoughtfully at the flushed, angry face of his uncle. Guy glared back at him.

Hugh said, "Someone tried to kill me last night."

Guy's whole face hardened. "How?"

"I went to the chapel in the morning hours. I wanted to see if I would be able to remember anything. When I came out, someone was waiting for me with a knife. I was lucky to get away."

"You didn't see who it was?"

"The landing was pitch dark. He had extinguished the flambeaux."

Guy cursed.

Hugh said neutrally, "As far as I know, you are the only person who would benefit from my death."

"I am not an assassin," Guy said furiously. "And as far as *I* know, you are making these stories up in order to discredit me."

"Your reputation is rather vulnerable," Hugh agreed.

"I had nothing to do with Roger's death," Guy said grimly.

"Someone killed him," Hugh said.

Guy made an impatient gesture with his hands. "It was the knight. Why can't you just accept that and let well enough alone?"

"Because I am like a dog who has buried a bone and can't find where he put it," Hugh said wearily. "I must keep digging and digging until I find what I want."

"Well, you will not find me," Guy said.

"Then you have nothing to worry about, do you?" Hugh replied pleasantly. He rubbed the back of his neck as if it ached. "I will be leaving Chippenham this afternoon, Uncle, so let me take this opportunity to say farewell to you."

"Don't hurry back," Guy said sarcastically.

Hugh gave him a long, level look, then turned and left the room.

# 19

The wind increased while the Chippenham household was at midday dinner, and by the time Hugh and Nigel started out on their return home, the temperature had dropped fifteen degrees. Both they and their escort were chilled to the bone by the time the walls of Somerford came into view.

Hugh had been silent for almost the entire ride, and Nigel did not attempt to force a confidence. From the expression on Hugh's face, he had known he would meet with little success.

In fact, for the first time since he had met Hugh, Nigel was wondering if he had done the right thing in telling the boy who he was. Now that Guy had won the king's backing, it did not look as if Hugh had any chance of winning the earldom that was rightfully his. It seemed to Nigel's discouraged mind that the only thing that his disclosure had done for the boy was to bring him grief.

It was growing dark by the time Nigel's party rode through the outer gate of Somerford. Grooms came running to take their horses, and Nigel and Hugh went wearily up the castle ramp and into the Great Hall.

Supper was finished and the tables had already been cleared away. The household knights sat around the fire, engaged in their usual pursuits of chess and dice. Thomas was plucking the strings of his lute.

Heads turned as Hugh and Nigel, followed by the knights of their escort, came into the room. One of the knights by the fire sent a page running up the stairs to relay the news to Cristen and her ladies that the lord of the castle had returned. Nigel and Hugh moved to stand by the fire and Nigel held out his cold hands to its warmth.

A few minutes later, the dogs came racing down the stairs. They were followed by Cristen.

Nigel turned from the fire when he saw his daughter. "How are you, my dear?" he asked, smiling at her. "Has all gone well in our absence?"

"I am fine, Father. Everything at Somerford is fine." She reached up to kiss him on the cheek. "It is good to have you home."

"Thank you, my dear."

"Welcome home, Hugh," Cristen said, turning to the slim silent figure who was letting the dogs sniff his hands.

Hugh nodded.

*Jesu*, Nigel thought. *Is the boy ever going to talk again?*

"You must be hungry," Cristen said practically.

"Aye," Nigel replied. "I think we all could do with something to eat and drink. It was a long, cold ride. It almost feels as if it might snow."

By now Hugh was patting the dogs. He said nothing.

He ate the bread and meat that he was served, however, and drank a cup of ale. Cristen talked easily the whole while, detailing the things that had happened while they were gone.

"Emma Jensen came to see me about a bad cough her eldest son has developed," she said. "I gave her some of my elixir of hore-hound. I hope it helps."

"I'm sure it will," Nigel said comfortably. "Your potions are always efficacious, my dear."

"Not always." For the first time, Nigel saw her shoot a worried look at Hugh. He remembered the boy's words to him the previous night about his headaches. *Cristen knows.*

Hugh put down his ale and finally spoke. "I hope you won't mind if I go to bed, sir. I am rather tired."

He looked more than tired. He looked exhausted.

"Go ahead, Hugh," Nigel said. "We'll see you in the morning."

"Good night, Cristen," Hugh said.

For the briefest of moments, the eyes of the two young people met. Then Cristen said softly, "Good night, Hugh."

Hugh walked to the door that led to the solar and family bedrooms. He went inside, closing the door behind him gently.

"Dear God, Father," Cristen said. Her face was pale. "*What happened?*"

"I don't know," Nigel said wearily. "He came to me this morning and said that we had to leave Chippenham. He's scarcely said a word since." Nigel hesitated, then added, "He was awake all night with a headache, Cristen. I could tell that he was in a great deal of pain. He told me he's had them before."

She bent her head and replied, her voice very low, "I think this whole business of trying to remember his past is tearing him apart."

Nigel said harshly, "All the while that we were riding home I was thinking that I should never have told him who he was, that I should have simply let him go on being Hugh Corbaille. He was better off so."

At that she lifted her head and shook it in emphatic disagreement. "If being Hugh Corbaille had been enough for him, he wouldn't have come here, Father. You were right to tell him. No matter how painful it may be, he needs to rediscover his past. It's the only way he can make himself whole."

Nigel rubbed his eyes. He felt almost as exhausted as Hugh looked.

Cristen got to her feet and went behind him to massage his shoulders.

"Aahh," he said with grateful pleasure. "That feels good."

The rest of the knights around the fire had gone on with their activities, although all ears were intent on the conversation between Nigel and Cristen.

Thomas said abruptly, as if he could contain himself no longer, "If Hugh is truly the son of Lord Roger, then isn't he *entitled* to be the Earl of Wiltshire?"

"He is entitled by right of inheritance," Nigel returned somberly. "But the king has the final say in such matters, Thomas. And it seems that the king is supporting Guy."

There was a grumble of discontent among the knights.

"Guy was responsible for his brother's death," Ranulf said. "He should not be allowed to profit from murder."

"There is no proof that Guy had aught to do with Roger's murder," Nigel pointed out.

Again came the grumble of discontent.

Cristen removed her hands from her father's shoulders and signaled to one of the pages. "Take the dogs for their last visit outside, will you, Brian?"

Brian whistled and Ralf and Cedric obediently trailed after him to the door.

Cristen said briskly, "I am going to bed, Father, and I recommend that you do the same. You look tired."

Nigel braced his hands on the carved arms of his chair and pushed himself to his feet. "I am tired," he admitted.

He offered her his arm and, after bidding good night to the knights, the two of them crossed the floor to the door that led into the solar.

Cristen's maid was waiting for her in her bedroom, and she helped Cristen out of her over- and undertunics and into her velvet robe. Then she brushed out the girl's long hair and plaited it loosely into a single braid.

"Thank you, Emily," Cristen said with a smile. "You may go to your own rest. I will see you in the morning."

"Good night, my lady."

After the girl had left, Cristen went to the door to make certain that Brian had returned the dogs. They were both curled in their usual places by the solar brazier. Ralf lifted his head to look at her, then closed his eyes again to go back to sleep. Cedric never stirred.

Cristen turned back into the room and got into her bed under the covers in order to keep warm. She turned the hourglass on her bedside table and started the sand falling. In a half an hour's time, Nigel should be fast asleep. She would give him an hour, just to be sure.

She lay in bed, staring at the ceiling, thinking. Outside it had begun to rain. She could hear the drops bouncing off the packed earth of the courtyard beneath her window.

When all the sand had run from the top of the glass into the bottom, Cristen got out of bed, picked up the candle she had left burning, and let herself out into the solar.

This time both dogs raised their heads when they saw her.

She ignored them and crossed the floor to the door that led to Hugh's bedroom. She pushed it open without knocking and went inside.

The room was dark. The only sound she heard was the drumming of the rain against the closed shutters. She held her candle in steady hands and looked toward the shadowy, silent bed.

"Hugh?" she said softly.

"What are you doing here?" His voice sounded harsh and strained.

She carried her candle over to the small table that was next to the bed. Hugh pushed himself up on his elbow and looked at her out of shadowed eyes. His hair was tousled, his shoulders bare.

She sat on the edge of the bed and regarded him gravely. "What happened at Chippenham?" she asked, her voice very quiet. "Why did you return so quickly?"

For a long moment she thought he was not going to answer her. Finally he said reluctantly, "I had a conversation with one of Roger's former knights." Exhaustion was etched in every line of his face, but she knew he had not been sleeping. "What he said was enough to cause me to doubt that Guy is guilty of his brother's death."

The single candle flickered in a sudden draft, then burned steadily once again. The rain still drummed steadily against the closed wooden shutters of the room.

"What did he tell you, Hugh?" Cristen asked.

He pushed himself upright, so that he was sitting with his back against his pillows. He pushed his hair out of his eyes. The bedcovers were pulled up to his waist, but his upper torso was bare. The light from the candle shone on the gold cross he wore around his neck.

He was so slender that it was always a surprise to see how well-muscled he was.

"Where's your bedrobe?" Cristen asked practically. "It's cold in here."

He made an irritable gesture. "I don't need it."

She looked around, then stretched toward the bottom of the bed, reaching out an arm. She grabbed the worn red velvet robe that Adela had made for Hugh's sixteenth birthday and handed it to him.

"Put it on."

He took it from her and impatiently flung it around his shoulders.

"Now," she said. "Tell me what happened."

Speaking in an emotionless monotone, he told her what he had learned from Alan. He stopped, however, before he had quite reached the end.

There was a faint frown between Cristen's delicate brows. "So Ivo stayed to try to protect your mother?" she prompted.

He nodded. His lips were folded into a tight, tense line.

"Hugh?" Her voice was gentle but implacable.

"He stayed," Hugh agreed. Then, visibly controlling all his sense of horror, he managed to get it out. "Roger castrated him, Cristen. After that, once he was left alone, Ivo killed himself."

"Oh my dear God," Cristen whispered.

Hugh's eyes were so dilated that they looked almost black. "So you see, Walter Crespin had good reason to kill Earl Roger. And you can also see why Roger's knights transferred their allegiance so easily to Guy. They knew that Guy had had nothing to do with his brother's death. Nor had they any cause to feel overly loyal to their former lord."

Cristen reached out and took his icy hands into her own warm clasp.

"Aye, I can see all of that," she said quietly. "But what I don't see, Hugh, is why Walter would want to kidnap you."

"I think . . ." His voice quivered. His hands clutched hers. He stopped and when he spoke again, his voice was steadier. "I think I was in the chapel when Roger was killed. I remember . . . things. Perhaps I was taken because I knew too much."

"Oh, Hugh," Cristen said. Her voice was full of an aching sadness. "This is so much for you to bear."

"I have you," he said hoarsely. "I can bear anything, Cristen, as long as I have you."

They stared at each as the seconds ticked by unregarded. Then he pulled her forward, into his arms.

There was desperation in his embrace. His face was buried in the warm fold between her neck and her shoulder. His lips moved on her bare skin. Their touch burned like fire.

"Cristen." His voice was like a groan.

She slid her arms around him and held him close. He was quivering like a bow that has been strung too tightly. "It's all right, Hugh," she said. "It's all right."

His lips moved from her throat to her mouth. His kiss was hard and urgent with need. She yielded to it, yielded to him and the almost frantic passion that was driving him.

She loved him so much. She didn't mind it that he hurt her, she was only fiercely glad that she was able to give him this release that he so desperately needed. When he finally lay still against her, she cradled him against her breast, buried her lips in his black hair, and whispered, "Go to sleep, Hugh. Go to sleep, my love."

Long after he had fallen into the deep sleep of utter exhaustion, she lay awake, listening to the rain beating against the shutters and thinking of what he had told her and of what it might mean.

When Hugh finally awoke, the candle was almost burned out and the rain was still pelting against the shutters. He felt the softness of Cristen beside him and remembered instantly what had happened.

Cautiously, he raised himself on his elbow and looked at the sleeping face of the girl laying beside him. Her long lashes lay quietly on her cheek and her loosened hair streamed across the rumpled bed covers.

He shut his eyes in pain.

*What have I done?*

He remembered his frantic possession of her just hours before, and his mouth was taut with pain.

*How could I have done that to Cristen?*

When he opened his eyes, she was stirring, as if she had sensed his distress. He watched her, his heart hammering. If she should turn from him in revulsion, he would want to die.

Her lashes lifted and she looked at him. The first expression he saw in her great brown eyes was surprise. Then, as her memory returned, the surprise turned to a look of guilt.

"Are you angry with me?" she asked.

He stared at her in utter stupefaction. "It is I who should be asking that question of you," he said at last.

She shook her head in disagreement. "It was my doing. I could have stopped you if I had wanted to." She smiled tentatively. "I didn't want to, you know."

He looked at her for a minute in silence and then the glimmer of an answering smile softened his grim young mouth.

"We will have to get married now," he said.

She reached her hands up to touch his face. "So we will," she agreed. "So we will."

It was an hour before dawn when Cristen finally left Hugh to creep back to her own room. This time the dogs got up to come and greet her when she came into the solar. She patted their heads without speaking, then slipped through the door into her bedroom.

The rain was still drumming against the shutters. Her bed, unoccupied for most of the night, was cold. She was sore between her legs.

But she was happy. Something irrevocable had happened between her and Hugh this night. Now they truly belonged to each other.

*I can bear anything as long as I have you.*

He had said that to her and she knew it was true. It had been like that between them almost from the moment they had met. He had never been a stranger. It was almost as if she had recognized him, as if they had known each other before and were only waiting for the time when they could come together again.

Beneath her joy, however, ran an irresistible current of fear.

What was the truth about Roger's murder?

She had not said this to Hugh, but she could not help but wonder why, if Walter Crespin had killed the earl to avenge his brother, he had waited a full year to do it.

*Perhaps it was done in a moment of uncontrollable anger,* she thought. *It must have been. There could be no other explanation for murdering a man in front of his son.*

But Cristen could not rid herself of the conviction that there was more to the story than they already knew. Hugh had told her that he was going to seek out Father Anselm, who had been the one to find Roger's dead body in the chapel.

"I need someone to corroborate Alan's tale about Ivo," he had said as they lay together after a second, heartstoppingly tender lovemaking. "There is always the possibility that he told me that terrible story in order to get me to exonerate Guy."

Cristen's brain agreed that Hugh needed to seek out the priest. It was her heart that feared for what else he might learn.

# 20

Hugh met Cristen at the breaking of fast in the hall. The two of them exchanged a single, veiled look before attending assiduously to their bread and ale.

The rain had finally stopped, although the hall was gloomy due to the lack of sunshine. Nigel asked Hugh if he would like to join the rest of the knights on the practice field that morning.

Hugh finished chewing his bread, then said, "Actually, sir, I have been thinking that I might return to Evesham."

These words made Nigel look grim. At the moment, the king was in the Thames Valley besieging Wallingford Castle—a difficult task, as Brian fitz Count was well enough supplied to hold out against him for years. The result of Stephen's attempt to blockade Wallingford was that the west was left wide open to the Earl of Gloucester, who had been recently joined by his sister—courtesy of Stephen.

Considering all this, Nigel thought he knew the reason for Hugh's sudden desire to revisit Evesham. He said in a hard voice, "You are going to accept Gloucester's offer to support your claim to the earldom, then?"

"No," Hugh said. "I desire only to speak to Father Anselm, and he was at Evesham when last I saw him."

He took another bite of his bread.

Nigel watched him. The terrible strained look the boy had worn all day yesterday was gone, and he was eating as if he were truly hungry.

Nigel asked cautiously, "Why do you wish to speak to the priest?"

Hugh drank some ale. "I want to see if he can corroborate a story I heard at Chippenham."

Nigel stared at Hugh's face. It might be more relaxed than it had been yesterday, but it was as unreadable as ever. "What story was that?" he dared to inquire.

"I would rather not say until I know that it is true," Hugh replied pleasantly. He rinsed his fingers in the bowl of water that had been provided for that purpose.

For some reason, Nigel found himself shooting a look at his daughter. She was feeding a piece of bread to one of her dogs. Her face was as unrevealing as Hugh's.

Nigel had a feeling that he was venturing into dangerously deep waters.

He cleared his throat. "I have been thinking, lad, that perhaps you and Guy might come to an understanding that you would recognize his right to the title if he would formally recognize you as his heir. He has no sons. after all . . . "

His voice petered out under the ironic look in Hugh's gray eyes. "I thought you wished to see Guy replaced because you held him responsible for the murder of Lord Roger—and of Geoffrey as well."

Nigel revolved his ale cup in his fingers and replied wearily, "Roger and Geoffrey are dead and nothing can bring them back. The way things have fallen out thus far, I think that it might be wisest for you to settle for what you can get, Hugh. Certainly it would be safer."

"I have to know the truth," Hugh said with a burst of sudden, fierce intensity. "Can't you understand that? If it turns out that Guy had nothing to do with Roger's or Geoffrey's death, then perhaps I would consider the course you have just named. But first I must know the truth!"

Nigel couldn't answer him.

Pale sunlight slanted in through the east windows of the hall. The clouds were evidently lifting.

Cristen said, "Perhaps you could send a few of the knights to Evesham with Hugh as an escort, Father."

"I don't need an escort," Hugh said.

"Yes, you do," Nigel contradicted him.

Hugh's mouth set in a stubborn line. Before he could object farther, however, Nigel said, "I would never forgive myself if something happened to you, Hugh. You must allow me to safeguard your journey."

"Of course he will allow you to do that, Father," Cristen said.

Silence from Hugh.

Finally he said, "Thank you, sir. You are very kind."

Nigel sighed with relief and leaned back in his chair. "When do you wish to leave?"

"Immediately, if you don't mind."

"I will tell Thomas and two of the other knights to make ready," Nigel said.

"Thank you," Hugh said again.

Nigel pushed back his chair and stood up.

"I will go to my herb garden and get you some more of my headache potion," Cristen said.

"I'll come with you," Hugh replied.

They stood inside the shelter of the herb garden shed, holding each other close.

"I wish we could get married right now," he said fiercely.

"I know."

He rubbed his cheek against the silky brown hair on the top of her head. "Your father's idea may not be a bad one after all. If I could get Guy to name me as his heir, then we would be able to marry."

"We'll see," she said. "First you must find out the truth you need to know. After that we'll think about Guy."

"All right." His arms around her tightened. "I wish I didn't have to leave you."

She wanted to cry and fought very hard not to.

"I know," she said again.

"I'll talk to this priest. He will know if Alan's story was true."

"Hugh . . . what if your mother is still at Evesham?"

She felt him shiver. "Then I will see her. I can't keep running away from her forever."

"If Alan's story was true, then I think she is very much to be pitied," Cristen said.

Hugh's shivering increased. "Aye. I suppose so."

She tipped up her head and kissed him on his jaw. "Let me mix up that headache potion for you to take with you."

Reluctantly, he loosened his arms. "All right."

She went to the shelves and took down a stoppered bottle. He watched her small, competent hands as they mixed the medicine.

"What I could really use is something to keep me from getting sick to my stomach," he said. "There's nothing more humiliating than heaving up your guts in some stranger's house."

"I'll give you a flagon of barley water as well."

She had almost finished when they heard the sound of feet pounding down the path outside the shed. The door of the shed opened and Brian's flushed face peered in.

"Hugh! A rider has just come from Malmesbury with news that the king is besieging the castle. His army is there right now!"

Hugh's startled eyes flew to Cristen. The formerly prosperous little town of Malmesbury was but a few miles to the northwest of Somerford. They had buried Geoffrey in the abbey churchyard there shortly before one of Gloucester's men, Robert fitz Hubert, had captured the castle and burned the town. The castle was still held by fitz Hubert for the empress.

"Go with Brian," Cristen told Hugh. "I'll come as soon as I've finished here."

He flashed her a smile and was out the door.

The visitor who had brought them the news was one of the monks from the abbey. He was talking to Nigel in front of the fire in the Great Hall when Hugh came in.

Nigel signaled for Hugh to join them.

"This is Brother Justin, Hugh," Nigel said. "Abbot Theobold sent him to inform us of what is happening in Malmesbury."

"I thought Stephen was besieging Wallingford," Hugh said.

"Aye, so did we all," Brother Justin replied. He was a man of about fifty, but tall and lean and strong-looking. "Apparently he decided that Wallingford was too much for him and turned west.

First he stormed and took the castle at South Cerney, which Miles of Gloucester's son-in-law had fortified to serve as a link between Gloucester and Wallingford." Bitterness edged the monk's voice. "Then he turned toward Malmesbury."

"Both South Cerney and Malmesbury castles are within the borders of Wiltshire," Nigel said to Hugh. "Do you think that the king has attacked them in order to put Guy in his debt?"

"Aye," Hugh returned cynically. "And I suspect that Stephen has every intention of collecting on that debt one of these days."

Nigel turned back to Brother Justin. "Is there aught that we can do for the town, Brother?"

"Abbot Theobold was hoping that perhaps you could take in some of the townspeople until the siege is finished," the monk replied. "Many of them have taken refuge in the abbey, but we have not the space nor the provisions to shelter everyone who is fleeing the bombardment."

"Of course we will help," Nigel said. "Those poor townsfolk! They had just started to rebuild Malmesbury after fitz Hubert burned it such a short time ago."

"Thank you, Sir Nigel," the monk said gratefully. "I will tell my abbot of your gracious offer."

At this moment, Cristen came into the hall.

"Here is my daughter," Nigel said, raising his hand to beckon her over. "You must allow her to offer you some refreshment, Brother, before your return journey."

"Thank you, Sir Nigel," the monk said again. "You are very kind."

"Cristen, will you see to it that Brother Justin has something to eat and to drink?" Nigel said as she joined the men in front of the fire.

"Of course, Father."

He answered the question in her eyes. "It seems that the townsfolk of Malmesbury need a refuge from the siege. Many of them have fled to the abbey, but there is not room enough there to accommodate all who have begged for shelter. I have said that we would take in some of them until the siege is lifted."

"Of course we will," Cristen said with warm sympathy. "What horrors those poor people have been through this last month!"

"Aye," Brother Justin said grimly.

"Come with me, Brother," Cristen said, and led him off in the direction of the pantry. They were trailed by the dogs.

Hugh said flatly, "It is Bristol all over again. The strategic importance of Wallingford is incalculable to the empress. It is imperative that Stephen take it. He cannot hope to reduce either Bristol or Gloucester with Wallingford sitting astride his lines of communication."

Nigel looked unhappy. "Wallingford is a redoubtable bastion, Hugh."

"So it is. That is why it is so valuable to the empress and why it is so vital that Stephen take it."

"He has left a strong enough garrison behind to keep it in check," Nigel pointed out.

"It is not enough," Hugh said shortly.

Nigel sighed. He very much feared that Hugh was right, although he did not like to say so.

He changed the subject.

"How would you like to ride to Malmesbury with me today?" he asked.

Hugh looked instantly wary. "Why?"

The question surprised Nigel. Hugh was not usually dense. "I must go to see the king and this seems a perfect opportunity for you to meet him," he explained.

The wary expression on Hugh's face did not lift. "What would be the point of that, sir?"

Nigel stared at him in exasperation. "The point is for him to meet you in person, to see you for himself." He tried an encouraging smile. "Who knows? Perhaps you will impress him so much that he will name you Earl of Wiltshire over Guy."

Hugh snorted with disbelief.

"You cannot lose by meeting him, Hugh," Nigel said reasonably.

Behind them some of the servants were sweeping up the old rushes from the hall floor. Others were carrying out basins and chamberpots to be emptied in the river. Most of the knights had already gone out into the courtyard.

Hugh said, "May I ask by which name you plan to introduce me to the king?"

"By your real name, of course," Nigel said. He was starting to get angry. "Hugh de Leon."

Hugh shook his head. "It's not a good idea. My identity is in limbo right now. I've ceased to be Hugh Corbaille, but I've not yet established myself as Hugh de Leon. I think I had better wait until I have a name before I meet the king."

"You have a name," Nigel said. "You are Hugh de Leon." He was growing more angry by the minute. "You know you are."

"Think for a moment about what you are proposing, sir," the twenty-one-year-old told him kindly. "The king will not thank you for introducing me to his notice. He has made a commitment to Guy and in return he has received the support of Wiltshire—which he badly needs. As far as Stephen is concerned, I am a nuisance at best. At worst, I am a threat."

Nigel's lips pinched together. He hated to admit it, but what the boy said made sense. Unfortunately.

"I am afraid that you are going to side with Gloucester," he admitted.

"I'm not ready to side with anyone just yet." Hugh's face was somber. "I have too many personal questions that need to be answered before I can begin to think of my future in political terms."

There was a moment's silence before Nigel said reluctantly, "Perhaps you are right." His voice strengthened. "However, with the king's forces only miles away, it is folly for you think of leaving for Evesham."

Hugh looked unconvinced.

"You have just told me that you don't wish to meet Stephen yet," Nigel pointed out. "If you are stopped by one of his men, you will most certainly end up doing just that."

It was Hugh's turn to say reluctantly, "Perhaps you are right."

"Well, I'm glad to hear I'm right about something for a change," Nigel grumbled.

At that, Hugh grinned. Nigel stared in surprise at the boy's face. He thought of the remote, closed look Hugh had worn all day yesterday. He thought of his daylong silence.

What had happened to change him from that to this?

\* \* \*

Nigel took an escort of knights and rode into Malmesbury to offer his homage to the king. Hugh and the rest of the knights went out hunting to bring in extra meat for the expected influx of refugees from the besieged town. Under Cristen's direction, the castle servants put up tents in the outer bailey to shelter the new arrivals. The bread ovens went into full-time production. In the kitchen, the cook and his staff roasted pork, beef, mutton, and poultry on a spit, and prepared stews and soups in the great iron cauldrons that hung over the fire. The alewife and her staff began to work to replace the store of ale that would most certainly be drunk by the refugees.

When Hugh and the knights finally returned from the hunt, their pack horses laden down with the carcasses of deer and wild pigs and fowl, they found the bailey crammed with men, women, and what appeared to be hundreds of children.

"Judas," Thomas said to Hugh. "That is a lot of mouths to feed."

"It certainly is," Hugh agreed. "I can see that we will be busy these next few days."

One of the squires came running up to them. His round face was beaming. "The king is coming to spend the night!" he shouted to the knights as a group. "Sir Nigel just returned from Malmesbury with the news."

A ripple of excitement ran through the ranks of the knights.

Hugh frowned. This was a development he had not foreseen and did not like. He took Rufus to the stable and took care of the stallion himself, as all the grooms were busy trying to make room for the king's horses. Once Rufus was groomed and fed and watered, Hugh made his way up to the castle.

The tables had already been set up in the Great Hall. Servants were scurrying around, putting down the benches and sprinkling dried herbs through the fresh rushes on the floor. Hugh asked one of the pages who was carrying the great saltcellar that went on the high table if he knew where Cristen was.

"I think Lady Cristen is in the kitchen, my lord," came the reply.

Hugh decided that he did not want to attempt the smoke and the confusion of the kitchen just now. He went into the solar, hoping he might find Nigel.

The solar was empty, but the door to Nigel's bedroom was open and William came out carrying Nigel's dagger to be polished. The squire grinned at Hugh. "Have you heard, Hugh? The king is coming to dinner and to stay the night!"

"I've heard," Hugh said.

Nigel heard his voice and called out through the partially open bedroom door, "Come in, Hugh. I want to talk to you."

For the first time, Hugh entered the bedroom that belonged to the lord of Somerford, which had once also belonged to his wife. It was a large room, with an immense bed covered with quilts, fur coverlets, and pillows. The heavy velvet curtains that enclosed the bed at night, both for privacy and for protection from drafts, were pulled back at the moment. Several large wooden chests, a chair, and two large stools with arms completed the furnishings.

Nigel was standing beside one of the chests, on top of which a rich, fur-lined robe was neatly folded. Clearly he was arraying himself in his best clothes for the occasion of the king's visit.

Hugh said, "Perhaps I should have gone to Evesham after all."

Nigel shook his head. "It wasn't safe."

Hugh cocked an eyebrow and didn't reply.

"You can sit with the knights at dinner," Nigel said. "There will be no reason for Stephen to notice you. I will give the king my bedroom, of course, and I will sleep in yours. You can spend the night in the hall as you did when Henry Fairfax visited." Nigel adjusted the lace at the throat of his immaculate white shirt. "There will be no reason for the king to think you are anyone other than one of my household knights."

"Perhaps it would be safer if I ate and spent the night in the stable," Hugh said.

Nigel lifted the robe from the chest and smoothed his hand along the soft fur. "Aren't you curious to see Stephen, at least?"

Hugh looked amused.

"You must be," Nigel said irritably.

"Of course I am," Hugh agreed. "I just do not want to be the cause of any embarrassment for you."

"The king won't ask for you. There is no reason for him even to know that you are here," Nigel said. "Just stay in the midst of the knights and you will be perfectly safe."

It was cold in the bedroom and Nigel shook out the cloak and settled it over his shoulders.

"All right," Hugh agreed mildly.

"Stephen is an impressive man, Hugh," Nigel said. "I think he will surprise you."

The amused look came back to Hugh's face. "Will he?"

William came into the room with the polished dagger ready to be thrust through its leather holder at Nigel's belt.

"I'll change my own clothes and get out of your way, sir," Hugh said.

"Very well." Nigel's voice was gruff. "I hope to God this dinner comes off all right. I never thought I would be entertaining the king!"

Stephen arrived an hour later, accompanied by his main military commander, the Fleming, William of Ypres, and a number of lesser lieutenants. Hugh saw him for the first time when he came into the Great Hall and took his place at the high table between Nigel and Cristen.

Stephen was indeed an impressive-looking man. In his fifties, he was yet tall, fair, handsome and splendidly built. Hugh watched as he bent his leonine head toward Cristen and made some comment. She smiled in reply.

Like Nigel, Cristen had dressed in her finest garments in honor of the king's visit. Her smoothly brushed hair was topped by a golden circlet from which fell a gauzy veil. She was wearing a fur-lined mantle over her deep red tunic.

Hugh thought she was the loveliest thing he had seen in all his life.

"The king looks younger than I thought he would," Thomas said. Hugh was sitting with a group of the younger knights in the middle of the hall.

"He seems very amiable," Lionel commented.

Hugh took a sip of his wine and said nothing.

"This should be a feast to remember," one of the other knights confided. "They were cooking in the kitchen all morning long."

It was a feast indeed. Cristen and her staff did Somerford proud, serving up a meal that was every bit the equal of the meals Hugh had eaten at the earl's castle of Chippenham.

He ate hungrily. It was amazing the way his appetite had come back after last night. Even the mushroom stuffing, which he did not usually like, tasted good to him.

The main part of the meal was over and the servants were in the process of serving the sweetmeats when one of the pages who were waiting on the high table came to tell Hugh that the king desired to meet him.

Hugh dropped his eyes to mask the flash of anger that shot through him.

*I thought I could trust Nigel not to do this!*

His face expressionless, he made his way around the tables and approached the high table. Stopping in front of Stephen, he went down on his knee.

"Your Grace," he heard Nigel saying, "this is the young man you asked about."

Hugh shot a quick look at Nigel's face and realized that this introduction was Stephen's doing, not his.

"You may rise," Stephen said.

Hugh stood and looked at the king, who was seated far above him.

Stephen regarded him across a tray of sweets. "So," he said, "you are he who claims to be the son of Roger de Leon."

He sounded merely interested.

"Aye, Your Grace," Hugh said.

The king leaned back in his chair as if he were perfectly relaxed. "Sir Nigel has told me that you were raised by my faithful servant, Ralf Corbaille, Sheriff of Lincoln."

"Aye, Your Grace," Hugh said again.

Stephen's blue eyes scanned Hugh's face. "And I am to understand that for all the years that you lived with the sheriff, you did not know who you really were?"

"That is correct, Your Grace."

Hugh was doing his best to disguise the anger he felt at this forced meeting, but from the sudden frown on Stephen's face he was afraid he had not been completely successful.

Then Stephen asked the one question that Hugh did not want to answer: "And where does *your* allegiance lie, Hugh? With your anointed king or with the rebel, Gloucester?"

"Are you asking that question of Hugh Corbaille or of Hugh de Leon, Your Grace?" Hugh replied steadily.

Stephen's gaze sharpened. He might be an indecisive man, but Hugh could see that he was not stupid.

"I am asking both of you," the king said.

Hugh clasped his hands lightly behind his back. "Hugh Corbaille is the owner of three small manors who owes his feudal duty to the king, Your Grace," he said. "At the moment, Hugh de Leon owns nothing except his sword."

Stephen's graying golden brows drew together. "If you are indeed Hugh de Leon, your mother's brother is one of Gloucester's chief supporters," he said grimly.

"And my father's brother is one of yours," Hugh returned.

"Let me remind you of this, Hugh whoever-you-are," Stephen said. "All of England's earls hold their honors solely at the will of the king. And I have named Lord Guy to be Earl of Wiltshire."

Hugh bowed his head. "I perfectly understand, Your Grace," he said softly.

Stephen's frown deepened. This interview was not going the way that he had planned. This boy, with his de Leon eyes, was perfectly courteous, perfectly respectful, but . . .

Stephen waved his hand in royal dismissal. "You may return to your supper, Hugh Corbaille."

He emphasized the last name, the name that was pledged to him.

"Thank you, Your Grace." Hugh knelt once more, then backed away from the high table. Before he turned to make his way back to his own table he shot a quick look at Cristen.

She was looking very grave.

He tried to look reassuring.

Then he had to turn away and go back to the knights.

# 21

One of the reasons Nigel had found it so easy to persuade Hugh to delay his visit to Evesham was that Hugh had had visions of spending a few more nights with Cristen.

That had been before the king's visit, of course.

As it was, Hugh spent the night in the Great Hall with the rest of the knights, listening to Ranulf snore and thinking about his interview with Stephen.

*How did the king know I was at Somerford?*

Guy must have told him that Nigel was the man who had discovered Hugh and introduced him into Chippenham, Hugh thought, as he lay on his straw pallet in the dark and chilly hall. Stephen could not have been certain that Hugh was still present at Somerford, but if the king had asked for him directly, then it wouldn't have been possible for Nigel to lie.

*It could have been worse,* Hugh told himself philosophically. *I might not have made a friend of the king, but neither did I make an enemy.*

At this point, however, he was truly stuck at Somerford until the king had left the district. If Stephen suspected that Hugh was planning a visit into Gloucester's territory, the king might very well arrest him.

Stephen would have to return to the siege of Malmesbury on the morrow, Hugh thought with a resur-

gence of hope. The king could not remain here at Somerford indef-
initely. He would have to return to his troops.

That would mean that Hugh would get his bedroom back. And
once everyone was asleep, he and Cristen . . .

With one part of his mind, Hugh knew that what he had done
with Cristen, and what he planned to keep right on doing, would
be perceived by others as grossly immoral. He knew others would
think that he had betrayed Nigel's trust and his hospitality by bedding his daughter under her father's own roof.

But what he felt for Cristen and she for him transcended all the
standard moral tenets of church and of society. He could no more
keep away from her than he could keep from breathing the air that
he needed to live. They belonged to each other.

They would marry. As soon as he learned what he needed to
know about his past, they would marry. Then they would never be
separated again.

The king left Somerford the following morning and the siege of
Malmesbury continued. Finally, after eight days of being under
constant fire, Robert fitz Hubert and his castle garrison surrendered. Conveniently for him, Robert was cousin to Stephen's commander, William of Ypres, and it was the Fleming who arranged
for Robert's release. To no one's surprise, once the former castellan
of Malmesbury was free, he rode west to join with the Earl of
Gloucester.

After his two successes in north Wiltshire, Stephen moved
twenty miles south to Trowbridge, a well-fortified castle belonging
to Miles of Gloucester's son-in-law, Humphrey de Bohun. There
the king began the laborious task of building siege engines to batter
down the walls.

Shortly after Stephen had left the district of a devastated
Malmesbury, Hugh prepared to ride northwest to Evesham in
hopes of catching up with Father Anselm.

"I wish I could go with you," Cristen said as they clung together
in the night.

"I wish you could, too," Hugh replied. His lips were buried in
her hair and he inhaled the scent of lavender that always clung to
its brown silkiness.

"If you need me, send and I will come."

He laughed shakily. "Your father might have something to say about that."

"It doesn't matter," she said starkly. She pressed closer to him in the bed. "Nothing matters now except us."

"Aye," he said. He closed his eyes and relished her nearness with every pore of his body. "And that is what will keep me sane."

He thought of this conversation the following morning as he mounted Rufus in the outer bailey and prepared to move off with the three knights Nigel had insisted on sending with him.

Cristen had not come to see him off.

"I can't bear to see you ride away from me," she had said last night.

"It's all right," he had said. "It's all right, my love. I will be back. I promise I will be back."

Hugh and his escort rode north to Gloucestershire and from thence they turned west, toward the vale of Evesham. It was November now and the weather had turned cold. Under their mail, Hugh and the knights wore several layers of wool shirts, and around their shoulders they wore warm wool cloaks.

Fortunately, it did not rain. The wind was sharp and chill, but the sun shone most of the time. The forest trees were almost bare and the paths were covered by the leaves that had fallen during the last month. As they passed the scattered assarts that small farmers had cut out of the woods, they could smell the fragrance of burning charcoal.

Hugh remembered the last time he had made the journey from Evesham to Somerford. He had been running from his mother then. He still did not know why he had this feeling about her. As Cristen had said, if Alan's story was true, she was very much to be pitied.

*Did she love me, I wonder?* Hugh thought. *Or was I too much of a reminder of the husband she did not like?*

It didn't matter if Isabel had loved him or not, Hugh told himself firmly. He had had Adela. She had been more than mother enough for him.

It was late in the afternoon and the gray of evening had started to set in, by the time Hugh and his party reached the walls of

Evesham. The knights on gate duty recognized him and let him in. With a trepidation he tried to deny even to himself, Hugh approached the formidable stone walls of the castle.

He hoped she wasn't there.

Philip Demain couldn't believe his eyes when Hugh walked into the Great Hall of Evesham.

*The incredible nerve of the man! After the way he had behaved to Isabel, to return here as if assured of a welcome!*

Philip simply couldn't believe it.

Simon had been sharing a cup of wine with a group of his knights in front of the fire, and he too looked amazed when he saw who had come into his hall.

"Hugh," he said in astonishment.

Everyone seated by the fire watched in silence as the slim young man crossed the floor. The only sound in the huge hall was the roaring of the fire and the clinking of his spurs.

Hugh stopped when he was still a few feet away from Simon. "My lord," he said respectfully. "I am sorry to have arrived unannounced like this. If I am not welcome, I will go away."

He was carrying his helmet under his arm. His fine-boned face that was so like his mother's was framed by his mail coif. His skin was red from the cold.

Philip longed to make a cutting remark to him, but there was something about Hugh's expression that warned him off.

"I did not expect to see you here again," Simon said. His own face was stern. "You left us so . . . precipitously . . . the last time you visited."

"I am sorry for that," Hugh said.

"It is not me to whom you owe an apology," Simon said grimly. "It is to your mother."

Philip saw a flash of quickly suppressed emotion flicker across Hugh's guarded face. "I realize that," he said quietly. "Is she still at Evesham?"

"Unfortunately, she is not," Simon said. "She went back to the convent in Worcester right after you left us."

Philip, watching Hugh closely, saw the relief that he could not quite disguise.

"I see," he said.

The scene in the hall had frozen into a tableau. The squires, who were playing dice around one of the trestle tables, had stopped their game. The pages, who were sitting on a bench along the wall kicking their heels and waiting to pour more wine for the knights, had ceased their low chatter. The knights around the fire sat in dead silence, staring at Hugh.

"Why have you come here?" Simon asked his nephew. "Was it just to offer your apologies?"

Against all the laws of hospitality, he was keeping Hugh, who was still dressed in full mail, standing while the rest of the men around the fire remained seated, wine cups in hand.

Hugh did not seem at all discomposed by his position. He stood easily, his feet a little apart, one arm cradling his helmet, the other hanging loosely at his side. He still wore his gloves.

He said, "Actually, I came to see Father Anselm, sir. Is he still at Evesham?"

"No, he is not. He left to return to the cathedral in Winchester two days ago."

Hugh's expression never altered. "I see. Well, if I may beg your hospitality for the night, I will be on my way again in the morning."

Simon's eyes narrowed. "You are going to go to Winchester?"

"Aye," Hugh replied simply.

Simon frowned. Then he waved toward the squires who were gathered around trestle table throwing dice. They, like everyone else in the hall, had stopped all activity and were silently watching Hugh.

"Someone come here immediately and disarm my nephew," the lord of Evesham said impatiently, as if it were the squires' fault that Hugh had been kept standing.

Two squires jumped up and ran to assist Hugh. For a long minute the only noise in the hall was the jingle of sword belt and spurs being removed, the rattle of a mail coat as it was pulled over the head.

Finally Hugh stood before them in his wool shirt and padded leather jerkin. There was a faint mark around his neck where the mail coat had chafed him.

"Sit down," Simon said, waving toward a stool that was placed next to his own high-backed chair.

Hugh obeyed. He sat easily, making it look as if the backless stool was the most comfortable seat in the world.

"We heard that the king was besieging Malmesbury," Simon said. "Is it true?"

"Aye," Hugh replied. "Robert fitz Hubert and his garrison surrendered a few days ago."

Simon waved to a page to bring Hugh some wine.

"We heard that as well," Philip said in a hard voice.

With a courteous nod of thanks, Hugh accepted a cup of wine from the page.

"Where is Stephen now?" Simon asked. "Do you know?"

He stared at his nephew as if he were issuing a challenge.

Hugh sipped his wine and replied calmly, "I believe he has gone to Trowbridge."

It was clear from the expression on his face that Simon had already known that.

"I would have returned to Evesham sooner, but with Stephen in the neighborhood, I did not feel it was wise for me to attempt a trip into Gloucester's territory," Hugh said.

Simon grunted his agreement. "If you had been caught, he would most probably have arrested you."

Philip said, with barely concealed hostility, "Did you meet the king while he was at Malmesbury? Somerford is only a few miles away, I believe."

The light gray eyes lifted to meet his. They wore an ironic look and Philip had the uncomfortable sensation that Hugh knew exactly what he was thinking.

"As a matter of fact, I did meet him," Hugh replied.

"God's bones," said Simon. He blew hard through his nose. "What happened? Did he ask you to swear allegiance to him?"

"Aye, he did."

Simon looked grim. "And did you so swear?"

Hugh took a sip of wine. "No," he said. "I did not."

The men around the fire regarded him with open disbelief.

"Then why aren't you under arrest?" Philip demanded.

A page came quietly forward with a flagon of wine and refilled one of the knight's cups.

"I didn't exactly refuse to swear allegiance to Stephen, either,"

Hugh replied mildly. "I . . . er . . . avoided the subject."

He took another swallow of his own wine.

"How did you manage to do that?" Simon asked incredulously.

Hugh rested his wine cup on his knee. "I told him that as Hugh Corbaille I owed him allegiance for my three manors in Lincolnshire, but that as Hugh de Leon I owned nothing and so had nothing to swear allegiance for."

The stares of the knights slowly turned to grudging admiration. Philip scowled.

"That was clever," Simon said.

Hugh did not reply.

"Why do you want to see Father Anselm?" Philip demanded.

Hugh lifted one level brow. "I want to talk to him."

"About what?"

Now Hugh's stare was frankly inimical. "I believe that is my affair, not yours."

Simon waved his hand impatiently. "Enough of this brangling! Did Stephen tell you that he would continue to support Guy as Earl of Wiltshire?"

"He did," said Hugh.

Simon looked pleased. "Well, then, it must be plain to you that your only chance of winning back your rightful place is to join with us."

"Perhaps," Hugh said mildly. "However, I am not ready to think of that yet. First I must speak to Father Anselm."

Simon's face was suddenly grave. "Why must you talk to the priest, Hugh?"

His voice sounded strangely heavy.

Hugh kept his level gray gaze trained on his uncle's face and did not reply.

"Why not just leave it alone?" Simon went on. "Digging up the past never did anyone any good. The present is challenge enough, I should think."

Hugh shook his head.

After a moment, Simon sighed. "All right." The heaviness had not left his voice. "If you must talk to the priest, you must talk to the priest."

"Thank you," Hugh said.

After another half an hour of general conversation, mostly about Stephen's prospects of succeeding with his siege of Trowbridge, Simon got to his feet and announced, "I'm for bed. "

The rest of the men stood with him in courtesy.

Simon looked at his nephew. "You had better come upstairs with me and greet the Lady Alyce, Hugh. She will tell you where you are to sleep."

Hugh looked faintly apprehensive. "Very well, sir."

Philip was glad to see that something could shake that formidable composure.

"She is not happy with your behavior," Simon said.

"No, sir," Hugh said resignedly.

Simon beckoned. "Come along then."

As the lord of Evesham moved toward the stairs, two of the squires who had been playing dice leaped to their feet and followed behind him.

Hugh had planned to leave for Winchester the following morning, but when he awoke it was to find that a storm had swept in from the west. Rain was falling in torrents and the wind was whipping it in sheets against the western wall of the castle.

It was not a day to travel.

The following day was still overcast and rainy, but the wind had died down considerably. At midday Hugh decided that it would not be unreasonable of him to ask Nigel's knights to attempt the weather.

He would have preferred to send them back to Somerford and travel on to Winchester alone, but he had promised Cristen that he wouldn't do that.

Thomas was sick. He protested that he was perfectly able to ride, but his skin was flushed and hot and he obviously had a fever. Since he absolutely refused to be left behind, Hugh felt he had no option but to remain yet another day at Evesham.

Two days suffering the reproachful looks of Lady Alyce and the unabashed curiosity of his cousin Juliana were a penance he supposed he deserved, but it wasn't pleasant.

Finally the weather lifted and Thomas's fever abated. Hugh was actually in the courtyard, preparing to leave, when a messenger from Earl Robert came galloping into the outer bailey with news for Simon.

Hugh went back into the castle to find out what was happening.

"I bring you good news, my lord," the messenger was saying triumphantly as Hugh entered the hall. "Earl Robert wishes me to tell you that Miles, Constable of Gloucester, has led an army to Wallingford and defeated and captured the garrisons that the king left there to hold Brian fitz Count in check!"

Simon was delighted. "That is great news indeed!"

*I knew it,* Hugh thought disgustedly. *Stephen should never have left Wallingford until he had taken it.*

He thought of the ruination of Malmesbury, of the devastation that Stephen's army was wreaking around Trowbridge, had already wreaked at Wallingford. Now Miles had also laid waste to Wallingford and was marching back west, to destroy as many of Stephen's strongholds as he could while the king was tied up at Trowbridge.

The empress had only been in England a little over a month, and already the damage was extensive.

"Sit down," Simon was urging Gloucester's man. "Have something to eat and tell us everything that you know." He turned to Hugh and motioned imperatively. "Join us, Hugh. You will be interested to hear this tale."

Hugh hesitated briefly, then nodded.

He supposed he could leave for Winchester tomorrow.

Hugh actually did manage to ride away from Evesham the following day. The weather was decent, Thomas was well, and no messengers came galloping in with war news.

They had reached Burford when Rufus lost a shoe. By the time Hugh had located a blacksmith and had the stallion reshod to his satisfaction, it was late afternoon. Reluctantly, he decided that they might as well spend the night at the local inn and start off again once more in the morning. If they rode hard all day, they would reach Winchester by evening.

In the morning, as Hugh and his escort of knights were having a morning meal of bread and ale in the taproom of the inn where they had spent the night, they heard the first rumor that Miles of Gloucester was heading for Worcester.

The garrison at Worcester was loyal to Stephen and the rumor was that Miles intended to sack the city and take the castle for the empress.

Hugh froze when he heard those words.

His mother's convent was in Worcester.

When finally he could get his lips to move, he turned to Thomas and said, "There's been a change in plans. We're riding back to Worcester."

Thomas took one look at Hugh's face and all of his questions died. "All right, Hugh," he said.

Hugh stood up. "We're leaving now."

The three knights had to run to keep up with him as he strode out of the taproom.

# 22

Hugh and his escort were yet some ten miles from Worcester when they saw the first signs that the rumors of imminent attack had been true.

Livestock were loose upon the road. Sheep wandered aimlessly along the forest path, and within the trees they saw domestic pigs rooting for food. At one point, a loose horse galloped past them, nostrils flaring, eyes showing white with fear.

Then they saw the refugees. Men, women, and children carrying their belongings on their backs streamed along the road in search of refuge in some manor, castle, abbey, or town where they could remain until they judged it was safe to return to their despoiled city.

The news Hugh gathered from the fleeing residents was not encouraging. The attack against Worcester's walls had come early in the morning, with Gloucester's troops finally breaking into the city on its north side. The soldiers had driven off all the town's livestock, murdered and maimed its inhabitants, and set fire to the town.

"They kidnapped many of our women, too," one of the refugees told Hugh indignantly. "They even took some of the nuns from the convent!"

Hugh felt his blood grow cold.

*Isabel would tell them who she was,* he thought, desperately trying to reassure himself. *They wouldn't dare harm a sister of Simon of Evesham!*

But the refugees said that the soldiers were drunk. Who knew what could happen during the rape and pillage of a city by drunken troops?

Hugh urged Rufus into a gallop, impelled by a sense of urgency that would not be denied.

He had to get to Worcester and find his mother.

They encountered no soldiers as they drew near to the city.

*The raiders must have finished their work and gone,* Hugh thought grimly.

He smelled the burning even before Worcester's walls came into view.

Hugh and his escort entered the city through the battered-down north gate. Everywhere they looked there was devastation. Fires raged on every street. Groups of citizens had organized to put them out, and Hugh and his small company passed by lines of firefighters throwing water on the roaring flames. The women and children who had remained in the city helped to pass the buckets along. The wet smoldering ashes of a number of houses testified to the fact that the firefighters had already been successful in some places.

Hugh asked one of the women passing buckets if she could tell him the location of the Benedictine convent. She directed him to the south of the city.

Hugh tried not to think as he and Nigel's three knights rode through the streets of the devastated city. The fear that he was too late, that his mother might be . . .

*I won't think of it,* he told himself sternly. *In just a few more minutes I will know for sure.*

As soon as they rode past the unoccupied convent gatehouse and into the small Benedictine enclave, it became brutally clear that even the sanctity of this holy place had been violated. Fires raged at all the wooden outbuildings and the nuns, dressed in smoke-stained habits, scurried about trying to put them out. They were assisted by a number of men of the town.

In a voice that he tried to keep steady, Hugh asked one of the nuns if she knew aught of Isabel de Leon.

"I haven't seen her," the nun said distractedly. "You had better speak to the prioress." And she directed him to the church.

"You go, Hugh," Thomas said. "We'll stay here and help with the fires."

Hugh nodded and turned Rufus in the direction of the convent church.

The day was growing dark and the interior of the church was dim as Hugh came in. He stopped for a moment inside the doorway to let his eyes grow accustomed to the lack of light. After a moment he saw a nun, standing still as a statue in the center of the nave.

Hugh looked slowly around the church.

The altar was empty. No gold candlesticks. No gold tabernacle. No gold chalices. The rug that had covered the altar steps was gone, exposing the lighter-colored wood that it had once hidden. Even the stations of the cross, which had once hung upon the stone walls, were gone.

*Perhaps the nuns hid everything,* Hugh thought. But from the desolate look of the still and silent figure in the middle of the nave, he did not think so.

Hugh removed his helmet and walked slowly toward the solitary prioress. She watched him come without comment. He stopped in front of her and instinctively bowed his head. She looked at him, waiting. Her face, framed by her wimple, was smooth and pale, the color of her eyes indecipherable in the dim light of the church. Her age could have been anywhere from fifty to seventy.

Hugh said quietly, "Reverend Mother, I have come in search of Isabel de Leon. Can you tell me where I might find her?"

"She's not here," the prioress said.

Hugh stopped breathing.

"Her brother came and fetched her away the day before the attack," the prioress went on.

Hugh felt momentarily dizzy, so intense was his relief.

*Thank you, God,* he thought.

He inhaled deeply, willing the world to steady itself around him.

"I am glad to hear that," he said.

"Lord Simon offered to escort all of the sisters to safety, but I refused." The prioress's voice was bitter with self-recrimination. "I felt that we could not desert the city at such a time, that it was our duty to remain. If we gathered together in the church, I was certain we would be safe. The soldiers might steal from us, I thought, but surely they would respect the habit of a nun."

"They did not?" Hugh asked in the same quiet voice he had used before.

"They were drunk and wild," the prioress said. "They took all of our sacred objects and—as if that were not bad enough!—they took some of our novices, those that were young and well-favored." For the first time her voice quivered. "They laughed at me when I protested."

Hugh did not know what to say.

"It was well that Isabel left when she did," the prioress said. "She is no longer young, but she would not have been ignored by those crazed men."

"I am so sorry, Reverend Mother," Hugh said. "You have been through a terrible ordeal. Is there aught I can do to help you?"

For the first time the prioress seemed to register Hugh's face. She stared at him and her eyes widened.

"You look like Isabel," she said in wonder.

"Aye," Hugh replied. He inhaled deeply, then, slowly and carefully, he let the breath out. "I am her son."

"Her son?" the prioress echoed. "The one who was lost when her husband was killed?"

"Aye," said Hugh again.

The prioress looked at him thoughtfully. She did not reply.

"Is there anything I can do for you, Reverend Mother?" Hugh repeated.

She roused herself from her contemplation of his face. "No," she said. "I think your need is to see your mother."

Hugh drew another long, steadying breath. "Aye," he said starkly. "I think you are right."

It was almost evening and Hugh decided it would be wise to wait until the following day before setting out for Evesham. He had no desire to run into a band of drunk and rowdy soldiers in the dark.

He and his men worked far into the night helping to put out the fires in the convent outbuildings. After a few hours' rest on the floor of the guest hall, which had been stripped bare even of its bedding, they rose to a dark and overcast sky.

The stench and desolation of Worcester the day after the attack was depressing in the extreme. Anger against Gloucester was running at fever pitch in the town, but Hugh was not naive enough to think that Gloucester's men were the only ones capable of such savagery. He had seen Malmesbury when Stephen had finished with it. He knew what the countryside around Trowbridge must look like with the king laying siege to the castle.

It was the face of war.

Hugh had been trained in the arts of war since he was a young child. He was a knight. War should be his natural milieu.

But Hugh had also been brought up by Ralf Corbaille, who had taught him that the first duty of a knight was to protect the powerless.

The citizens of Worcester had been powerless yesterday. The garrison had defended the castle, but there had been no one to protect the people in the streets or the nuns in the convent.

They were burying the dead as Hugh and his escort rode out of the ruined city and headed northwest toward Evesham.

*It is time for me to see her.*

This was the thought that ran through Hugh's mind during the whole of the cold, damp ride to Evesham.

*If something had happened to her at Worcester, I might have lost my chance ever to see her again.*

As they rode along, Thomas and the other two knights talked together about what they had seen in Worcester.

Hugh rode in silence.

Seven miles before Evesham, a sharp shaft of pain stabbed through the left side of his head.

*Please,* he thought despairingly. *Not now.*

But the pain continued. As before, it seemed to emanate from a single throbbing muscle in his neck, shooting up behind his eye and into his forehead.

He made the knights stop so that he could drink the barley water Cristen had given him and take her betony potion.

The day had continued dark and overcast, but still it seemed too bright to Hugh. He closed his left eye.

"What is it, Hugh?" he heard Thomas ask him anxiously.

There was no way he could disguise his distress. He was going to have to lie down the moment they reached Evesham.

Pray God that he didn't throw up.

"I have a headache," he said, his voice short and staccato-sounding.

He felt Thomas looking at him.

"Can you go on?" the young knight asked. "Do you want to stop for a while?"

Hugh thought briefly of stopping until the headache had passed. But it could last for eight hours and the air smelled of rain. Concealing his disability from those at Evesham did not seem worth hours of making the knights and the horses camp out in the cold and the rain.

He wished, for the hundredth time since he had left Somerford, that Cristen had let him travel alone.

"No," he said. "I will be all right."

"Can you see? Do you want me to take your reins?" Thomas asked next.

Hugh, who knew he could trust Rufus, said once again that he would be all right.

The headache raged for the remainder of the ride, but even though Hugh's stomach was queasy, he did not feel as if he were going to throw up.

Cristen's medications must be having some effect.

It began to rain and the knights pulled their hoods over their heads and rode on.

At last the walls of Evesham came into view. Hugh removed his helmet and was once more recognized by the men at the gate and allowed to enter.

In the outer bailey he met Philip Demain, who was leading a large black stallion in the direction of the stable. The horse's coat was wet from the rain.

Philip stopped dead when he saw Hugh.

The pain was like the edge of a sword repeatedly stabbing through the left side of Hugh's head.

"What are you doing here?" Philip demanded.

Hugh half closed his left eye. Standing there, Philip looked tall and blond and splendid, rather like the archangel Michael guarding the gates of paradise from sinners, Hugh thought a little hysterically. He managed to say, "I have come to see my mother."

The two men regarded each other through the falling rain.

Philip frowned. "You look peculiar."

"He's ill," Thomas said.

Hugh felt his stomach heave.

*No,* he thought. He closed his eyes and forced the nausea down. Sweat broke out on his forehead.

"You had better come with me," he heard Philip saying in a clipped tone.

Stableboys appeared out of nowhere to take their horses, and Philip turned to lead the way to the castle.

Hugh dismounted and once more his stomach heaved.

Thomas said worriedly, "Do you want to take my arm, Hugh?"

"No," Hugh said.

Putting one foot after the other, he crossed the bailey, fighting nausea the whole way.

He lost his battle in the inner courtyard. Abruptly he turned away from the others, bent over, and began to retch.

"I'm sorry," he said when it was over. He was trembling with pain and exhaustion and humiliation.

He felt an arm come around his shoulders. "Don't worry about it," Thomas's voice said in his ear. "Let's just get you to bed."

They went up the castle ramp and into the Great Hall.

Philip sent a page to fetch Lady Alyce.

Hugh held himself very straight. The taste of bile was in his mouth and he was horribly afraid that the nausea was coming back.

He could feel Philip looking at him, but he kept his eyes trained on the fireplace.

At last Lady Alyce came sedately down the stairs. Hugh watched her cross the floor in his direction.

"Back again?" she asked him sweetly.

Philip spoke before Hugh could reply. "He's ill, my lady. Perhaps you could show him to a bedroom."

"Ill?" Alyce looked at her husband's nephew suspiciously.

"Aye, my lady," Thomas said respectfully.

"What's wrong with you?" Alyce asked Hugh.

"I have a headache and it makes me sick to my stomach," Hugh said.

"He vomited in the courtyard," Philip informed the lady of the castle.

"Oh dear." Alyce's motherly instincts awoke. "You had better come with me, Hugh. I'll get a squire to disarm you."

The last thing Hugh wanted was some strange boy hovering over him.

Thomas said, "I'll take care of him, my lady. There's no need to call one of your squires."

Hugh felt a flash of gratitude.

"Very well," the lady Alyce said. "Come with me."

They crossed the floor to the stairs and followed her up to the next level. The door to the ladies' solar was partially open and the sound of feminine voices drifted out into the passageway as they went by.

Hugh wondered if his mother was inside.

Then they were in front of the room Hugh had occupied on his earlier visits to Evesham. Alyce pushed the door open and went inside.

Hugh and Thomas followed.

Alyce went over to the bed to check that it had sheets on it.

Satisfied that it was properly made up, she turned around. "I'll send a page with water."

"Thank you, my lady," Hugh said.

"I hope you feel well soon," she said pleasantly, and left.

"This will just take a minute," Thomas said, and quickly and efficiently, he got Hugh out of his wet cloak, his sword belt, his mail, his spurs, and his boots.

Another wave of nausea swept through Hugh.

"Is there a basin?" he asked Thomas desperately.

Thomas grabbed the empty washbowl and handed it to Hugh, who was sick once more.

Once it was over, he crawled into the bed and curled up on his side under the fur cover.

The pain stabbed on.

He shut his eyes. "I'll be all right," he said to Thomas. "You're wet and hungry. Go downstairs and join the others."

"There's nothing else I can do for you?"

"No."

"All right, then," Thomas said hesitantly. "Try to get some sleep."

"Aye," Hugh said, although he knew that sleep would be impossible until the pain subsided.

Finally he was alone.

Lying in the big bed under the rich fur cover, Hugh settled in to endure.

It was late afternoon when the sharp stabbing agony finally muted to a dull ache. Gradually that too subsided, until only a faint tenderness remained in the muscle on the left side of his neck.

Slowly Hugh sat up in bed, linked his arms around his legs, and rested his pain-free forehead on his knees.

*God, what an entrance,* he thought bitterly.

The bedroom door opened and a page looked in. Hugh had heard the door open and close periodically while he was lying in bed, but he had kept his back to the door and lay still. Now the page saw that he was awake, however, and advanced into the room.

"Are you feeling better, my lord?" he asked courteously.

"Aye," said Hugh.

"The household is at supper. If you wish to join them I will help you make ready."

Hugh moistened his dry lips with his tongue. "Is . . . is the lady Isabel at supper in the hall?"

"No, my lord. Lady Isabel takes her meals in the ladies' solar."

Hugh felt wrung out and exhausted. A headache always left him in this condition. But he could put this off no longer. It had to be done now.

He said steadily, "Will you go and ask the lady Isabel if she will see me?"

"Aye, my lord," the page said. He hesitated, as if he would add something, then changed his mind and left the room.

Hugh got out of bed and looked down at his clothes. His shirt was a mass of wrinkles, and his hose were stained with the mud the horses had kicked up from the wet road.

*Adela would be furious with me if I presented myself to my mother in such a state,* he thought.

The automatic reflex of never doing anything Adela would not like sent Hugh first to the washbasin and then to the wooden chest along the wall. Someone had folded his spare clothes into it, and he lifted out a clean linen shirt and began to change.

The page returned with word that Isabel would see her son. The boy helped Hugh finish dressing and then knelt to tie the leather cross-garters around his hose.

Finally there were no more excuses to delay. Hollow-eyed and pale, Hugh left his bedroom and went down the passage to the ladies solar.

He was admitted by a serving woman, who slipped out the door as soon as he entered, leaving him alone with the woman who waited for him inside.

The solar was large and well-furnished, with pieces of sewing and embroidery spread out on a large table along one of the walls. The room was well-lit by candles. A charcoal brazier gave off a glowing heat and the floor was covered by a rug. Isabel was sitting in a heavily carved chair in front of the window, whose shutters were closed against the cold November rain.

Hugh advanced toward her slowly. His heart was hammering so loudly that he thought for certain she must hear it. He stopped when he was yet four feet away from her.

"My lady," he said. "I am glad to find you safe."

She didn't answer, just looked at him as if she could not believe that he was really there.

Her eyes were dark, dark blue. That was what Hugh saw. Not the beautiful bone structure that was so like his own, but the eyes.

He remembered them.

His lips parted, but no words came out.

Isabel said, "Hugh." Her voice was faintly husky. Wonder and joy shone in the deep blueness of her eyes. "Hugh, it is really you!"

He swallowed. "So it seems."

"I have prayed," she said. "For so long I have prayed that you were still alive." She laughed shakily. "But to actually see you again . . . "

The blue eyes filled with tears.

"Don't cry," Hugh said hoarsely. "Please don't cry."

He, who never felt physically awkward, did not know what to do with himself.

Isabel gestured to the footstool that was in front of her chair. "Will you sit here, so we may talk?"

Hugh crossed the remaining space that separated them and cautiously lowered himself to the stool. It put him at a lower level than her chair, so he had to lift his eyes to look at her.

He felt like a child again.

He said, "I am sorry that I did not stay to see you the last time you were here."

He didn't try to explain why he had run away.

She shook her head. "You have nothing to be sorry about, Hugh." Slowly she reached out her fingers and lovingly touched his cheek. He remained perfectly still under her gentle caress.

"They tell me that you have lost all memory of your childhood," she said.

"Some of it is coming back," he said. His nostrils quivered slightly. "I remember your eyes."

Her face lit as if he had just given her the most precious gift in the world. "Do you?"

He nodded.

She took her hand away from his face and said anxiously, "You were ill when you arrived this morning? Are you well now? You still look very pale."

"I had a headache, that is all," he said. "I'm all right now."

Her delicately arched brows drew together. "What kind of a headache?"

He shrugged. "Just a headache. It makes me sick to my stomach, however, so I need to keep to my room until it goes away."

Her frown did not lift. "When did you start getting headaches? You did not have them when you were a child."

He made a dismissive gesture with his hand. "They started just recently. They're a nuisance, that is all."

Isabel regarded him somberly. "I get headaches like that," she said.

His eyes widened in surprise.

"A fine heritage I have bequeathed to you," she said. In her voice was a mixture of sorrow and bitterness.

Hugh did not know what to answer.

She folded her hands in her lap. "Will you tell me something of your life since . . . since you left Chippenham? I hear you were fostered by the Sheriff of Lincoln."

Hugh could talk about Ralf and Adela. He told her how Ralf had found him and brought him home. He told her about Adela and how she had insisted on keeping him. He told her about his life with them.

"You loved your foster mother very much," Isabel said quietly when Hugh had finished.

"Aye," said Hugh.

"I'm glad, Hugh." Her voice ached with love and with sadness. "I'm so glad that you had someone like Adela to take care of you. And this Ralf sounds as if he was a good man."

"He was a very good man," Hugh said quietly.

Her smile was full of pain. "You were more fortunate in your foster parents than you were in your natural ones."

Hugh dropped his eyes.

For a long moment, the only sound in the room was the drumming of the rain against the shutters.

Then Hugh said resolutely, "My lady, there is something I need to ask you." He met her eyes directly and brought it out. "Do you know who killed your husband?"

The lovely rose-colored flush that had been blooming in her cheeks drained away. "Hugh," she said. "Leave that alone."

"I cannot," he said. "I think I was there when it happened."

She went ashen. "Why do you say that?"

"I remember seeing his body. I remember blood . . . "

He shook his head as if to clear it.

"It was Walter Crespin who killed your father," his mother said. "I thought everyone knew that."

"Why would a mere household knight want to kill his lord?" Hugh said steadily. "What would he have to gain by such a dreadful deed?"

Isabel looked away. She shook her head. "I do not know," she said in a constricted voice.

Hugh made the discovery that he was incapable of taxing his mother with the story he had heard at Chippenham.

He said instead, "Two days ago I was on my way to Winchester to see Father Anselm. I only turned back because I heard rumors that Gloucester was on the verge of attacking Worcester."

A spark of hope awoke in her deep blue eyes. "Were you perhaps worried about me?"

"Aye," he said.

"Oh, Hugh. Oh, my darling son." She leaned forward, reached her arms around him, and drew him close so that his head was pressed against her breast.

Hugh let himself be held.

She was crying. He could feel her tears wet his hair.

*She doesn't want me to know,* he thought. *Why?*

At last her grasp on him loosened and she sat back in her chair. The tears, which he knew had been genuine, had not reddened her eyes or her nose. Her face was as beautiful as ever.

He said soberly, "I am still going to see Father Anselm."

She wrung her hands. "Why can't you be satisfied with what you already know? You can't change anything, Hugh! Your father has been dead for fourteen years."

He said to her what he had only ever said to Cristen. "I feel as if I am but half a person without my memory. I feel as if I am a cripple. I have to know what happened to me if I am ever going to be whole again."

She looked into his eyes, long and deep. Then she shuddered. "All right. But I cannot tell you, Hugh." Her face had a haunted look. "You will have to talk to Father Anselm."

"Then that is what I will do," said Hugh.

# 23

After leaving his mother, Hugh returned to his room, ripped off his clothes, tumbled into bed, and dropped like a stone into the sleep of utter exhaustion. He awoke to the morning light streaming through the partially opened shutter at his window. The bedroom was freezing. His stomach felt perfectly steady and he was hungry.

He dressed himself and made his way down to the Great Hall for the breaking of fast.

The first person he saw when he came into the room was Isabel, seated at the high table next to Simon. Hugh hesitated, then slowly made his way through the tables where the rest of the household were eating. As he passed the table where Thomas was sitting, he gave the young knight a brief, reassuring smile.

He reached the high table and took the empty seat at Isabel's side. They exchanged restrained good mornings.

Simon leaned a little forward so he could see around his sister and said, "I hope you are feeling better this morning, Hugh."

"Thank you, sir. I am."

"I understand that you were in Worcester shortly after the attack."

"Aye," Hugh said. He waited while a page put a cup of ale in front of him. "We arrived toward evening, after Gloucester's troops had left the area."

Simon frowned. "What condition was the city in?"

"It was as you might expect," Hugh replied. He picked up his cup of ale. "The livestock had been driven off, women raped, men murdered, and fires were burning everywhere."

A little silence fell as those at the high table digested this horrific news.

Hugh took a thirsty swallow of his ale.

Then Isabel asked fearfully, "How did the convent fare?"

"It was stripped of most of its furnishings and the outbuildings were burned," Hugh said. He forbore to mention the novices who had been kidnapped. She could find that out from someone other than her son.

Simon said defensively, "Miles of Gloucester is waging war just as Stephen is. The only difference is that Miles is more successful than the king."

"Really, Simon," Isabel protested indignantly. Spots of color burned in her cheeks. "To rob and burn a convent! How can you possibly justify that? Even in times of war, the Church should be sacrosanct."

"I understand that the soldiers were drunk," Hugh said.

"The poor sisters," Isabel mourned. She turned to her brother. "I should never have let you talk me into leaving them. I should have remained in Worcester. I could have helped."

"You were right to leave," Simon said forcefully. "And the sisters should have had the sense to leave with you. I offered them the shelter of Evesham."

Juliana, who was seated on Hugh's other side and who had been listening to the conversation with avid curiosity, now said earnestly, "I hope you will remain here with us at Evesham, Aunt Isabel."

Lady Alyce seconded this invitation from her seat on the far side of Simon.

Isabel was looking very distressed. "Thank you, but I feel that I must return to Worcester."

"Really, Isabel, you might think of us for a change. It's not as if you were indispensable to the convent, you know," Simon said angrily.

She flushed. "I know I am not indispensable, but at least I can be another pair of hands."

"Men from the town were helping the nuns set things to rights," Hugh said mildly. "I do not think that you should return to Worcester until things have settled down, my lady. I have little doubt that the king will send troops to reinforce the garrison there and with the way feelings are running in the town, it is no place for the sister of a known supporter of Gloucester to be found."

"Hugh is right," Simon said. "You had much better remain here, Isabel, where you will be safe."

She shook her head slightly, as if in refusal.

"Please," said Hugh.

She turned and her eyes met his. After a moment, she bit her lip and said unwillingly, "All right, Hugh. If you really think that is best."

"I do," he said.

"Are you going to stay with us as well, Hugh?" Juliana asked brightly.

Hugh continued to hold his mother's gaze. "No," he said. "This morning I leave for Winchester."

The day was cold and the sky was a hard clear blue when Hugh and Nigel's three knights rode away from the great stone walls of Evesham. They pushed forward steadily and after several hours had crossed the border of Gloucestershire and entered Wiltshire.

That was when Hugh informed his escort that he planned to make a brief stop at the castle of Abrille.

"Abrille?" Thomas said in surprise. "Why do you wish to go there, Hugh?"

"I have some questions I'd like to have answered," Hugh replied evenly. "It isn't far out of our way and my business won't take long."

Thomas exchanged a look with his fellow knights. Clearly Hugh was not going to tell them anything. Shrugging his shoulders, Thomas resigned himself to the delay, settled into his saddle, and followed Hugh without comment when he turned off the main road to ride east along a narrow woodland path.

At least it wasn't raining.

When Abrille finally rose before them, Thomas saw that it was an old-fashioned wooden motte and bailey castle that was smaller than Somerford. It was situated on a small river but, oddly enough, it was not surrounded by a moat.

The guards at the main gate challenged Hugh's party and asked them to state their business.

While Hugh talked to the sentry, Thomas cast his eyes over the castle and its environs. He figured it could be reduced by siege in a matter of two days.

The sentry sent someone to the castle with a message. Hugh and the knights waited.

The messenger returned and at last they were admitted through the gate and into the outer bailey.

Utterly mystified, Thomas and his companions dismounted and allowed grooms to take their horses. Then they trailed after Hugh as he crossed through the inner gate and into the inner bailey.

The baileys were in good order, Thomas admitted to himself. And the men seemed to be well disciplined.

*What the devil is Hugh doing here?* he thought as they were met by a squire, who escorted them up the ramp and into the Great Hall of the castle. A small group of men were seated before the fire, engaged in a game of backgammon.

The squire led Hugh up to the gray-haired man with the aquiline nose who was sitting closest to the fire and announced, "Sir Hubert, here is Hugh Corbaille of Keal."

From his position a few feet behind Hugh, Thomas could see how all of the men around the fire were staring at Hugh. Evidently his resemblance to Guy was not going unnoticed.

"I am very sorry to trouble you, Sir Hubert, but I have a very important matter to discuss with you."

Hugh's voice was quiet but underlined with unmistakable authority.

The older man lifted his splendid nose. "Aye? And just what is this matter, Hugh *Corbaille?*"

"It is something private," Hugh said. "May I speak to you alone?"

Sir Hubert frowned, and for a moment Thomas thought he was going to refuse. Then, moving painfully, as if his joints were hurting, he got to his feet. "Come along to the solar with me," he said grimly.

"Thank you," said Hugh.

The two men crossed the floor in the direction of a door that was set into the hall's east wall.

The castle was laid out very similarly to Somerford, Thomas thought. It was just built on a smaller scale.

Hugh and Sir Hubert disappeared.

The squire who had escorted them said courteously to Hugh's knights, "Would you care for some wine?"

"Thank you," Thomas replied. "That would be refreshing."

The knights who had been playing backgammon gestured for them to take a seat.

Thomas sat down, stretched out his legs, and resigned himself to answering questions about Hugh's resemblance to Abrille's over-lord.

Twenty minutes later, Hugh and Sir Hubert were back. Both men looked very grave.

When Hugh saw his men sitting around drinking wine, he made an impatient gesture for them to rise.

"Won't you stop for some wine yourself?" Sir Hubert asked with stiff courtesy.

"No, thank you, sir," Hugh returned. "We must be on our way."

Sir Hubert did not press him to change his mind.

Ten minutes later, Hugh and his escort were riding through the gate of Abrille and heading back toward the road to Winchester.

The rest of the journey went smoothly. They spent the night in an abbey stable, as the monks' guest quarters were already filled to capacity by refugees from Worcester. They left the abbey as soon as the sun was up, and by late afternoon they were riding through the Kingsgate into Winchester.

They proceeded directly to the cathedral. The knights waited in the courtyard with the horses while Hugh went into the church to see if he could locate Father Anselm.

He entered through the large front doors, walked down the side aisle, and stood quietly, looking around.

A priest who was too short and thick to be Father Anselm was kneeling in front of a statue of the Virgin. A young man dressed in the garb of a prosperous merchant knelt in one of the front pews, his head lowered into his hands. A number of old women were scattered here and there about the church, their lips moving in prayer.

The scent of old incense and burning candles hung in the cold air.

There was no sign of Father Anselm.

Hugh left the church and inquired in the courtyard for the residence of the priests. The building pointed out to him was an ordinary stone townhouse standing at the edge of the cathedral grounds. It in no way resembled the magnificent palace at Wolvesey that housed the Bishop of Winchester—who also happened to be the papal legate and King Stephen's brother.

Hugh knocked at the residence door, which was answered after a minute by a woman who was obviously the housekeeper. She was short and heavy and had three distinct chins.

Father Anselm was not in at the moment, she told Hugh, but she expected him back for supper.

"I wonder if you would give him a message for me?" Hugh asked.

She nodded encouragingly, causing the three chins to wobble. "Of course."

"Please tell him that Hugh de Leon desires speech with him. I will return later." Hugh stepped back as if preparing to leave, but then he had a further thought. "Perhaps you could also say that I come with the blessing of the lady Isabel."

The housekeeper's small button eyes glittered curiously as she pondered this enigmatic message. "I will tell him," she said.

"My men and I will find lodging in the city and I will return at suppertime to see Father Anselm," Hugh repeated.

She smiled broadly, revealing teeth that were startlingly white. "I will tell him."

"Thank you," Hugh said, and left.

He and the knights found an inn not far from the cathedral, and by the time they had seen to the stabling of their horses and eaten supper the day was growing dark.

Hugh left the knights to the warmth and camaraderie of the inn's taproom and went out into the cold November air to return to the cathedral. He left his mail and his sword behind at the inn, but took the precaution of tucking a dagger into his belt. He did not want to be surprised again while he was unarmed.

The same housekeeper as before answered the door of the priests' residence, and this time she told him that Father Anselm was in.

As soon as Hugh stepped into the house, he saw that it was built in similar fashion to Ralf's townhouse in Lincoln. The front door opened onto a small landing, which had stairs going up to the residence's main level. Also on the landing was a closed door, which Hugh knew hid the stairs that led to the basement.

The housekeeper took him up to the main floor. At the top of the stairs she turned left, leading him into a small unoccupied chamber.

"I will tell Father that you are here," she said.

The candles in the room had not been lit and it was quite dark. Hugh peered around and saw that the furnishings consisted of two chairs, one stool, one charcoal brazier, and two small tables upon which reposed two half-burned-down, unlit candles.

The brazier was also unlit and the room was frigid.

The sound of male voices drifted to Hugh's ears. The priests must still be at supper, he thought.

The housekeeper waddled back into the room with a taper and proceeded to light the candles on the two tables. She also lit the charcoal in the brazier and fastened the window shutters.

"Father is finishing his supper. He will be with you shortly," she told Hugh kindly.

"Thank you," he said.

Alone again, he could feel tension in every muscle of his body. His chest felt constricted and breathing was an effort. The pork pie he had eaten for supper was not sitting well in his stomach.

He stood by the brazier and stared down into the coals, which had not yet begun to give off any heat. He was shivering, but it was with tension, not with cold.

Finally he heard steps approaching, and then the tall figure of Father Anselm appeared in the doorway.

"Hugh," the priest said. His voice was husky with emotion.

"Father," Hugh returned. He was relieved to hear that his own voice sounded fairly normal.

The priest advanced slowly into the room. There was a strained look in his brown eyes and his fingers rubbed nervously at the cord around the waist of his brown robe. He looked at Hugh and said, "Mistress Alney said you wished to speak to me."

Hugh said, "I have come to you, Father, because I am trying to find out about my past and I think that you can help me."

For a long moment, Father Anselm stared at him in silence. The strain on the priest's face was unmistakable. "I will give you some good advice, Hugh," he said heavily. "Leave the past alone."

Hugh shook his head. "I can no longer go on living with only half a life. I need to find out about my childhood."

The priest moved to one of the chairs and sat down. His movements looked indescribably weary. "Haven't you seen your mother? Surely she can answer your questions better than I."

"She sent me to you."

A spasm of some undefinable emotion crossed the priest's face.

"How is Lady Isabel?" he asked. "I have been thinking about her and this raid on Worcester. Is she safe?"

"Aye. My uncle fetched her to Evesham before Gloucester's men arrived."

Father Anselm's eyes closed briefly. "Thanks be to God for that."

Hugh moved to the other chair, sat, and rested his hands carefully on the smooth oak arms.

Father Anselm asked painfully, "Why did the lady Isabel send you to *me*?"

Hugh said, "You were the chaplain at Chippenham when I was a child. You must know the things that happened in the household."

"What things do you want to know about?"

Hugh thought that the priest sounded afraid.

A little heat began to radiate from the brazier.

Hugh said, "I want to know about my mother and Ivo Crespin."

The priest's head jerked up. His back went rigid. "Where did you hear about Ivo Crespin?"

"I spoke to Alan fitzRobert, one of Roger's old knights who is still in service at Chippenham. He told me about it."

The silence in the room was taut with tension.

Hugh went on doggedly, "Alan told me that Ivo and my mother were lovers. He told me that when Roger found out about them he had Ivo castrated. He told me that Ivo killed himself."

Still the priest said nothing. In the light of the candle burning on the table next to his chair, his face looked cadaverous, his brown eyes sunk deep into their bony sockets. His body was still rigid with some emotion, which Hugh more and more suspected to be fear.

"I want to know if Alan's story is true," Hugh said.

There was a long silence, which Hugh did not try to break.

Finally Father Anselm replied in a hoarse voice, "God help us all, it is true."

Hugh's fingers tensed on the arms of his chair. "For God's sake." Despite himself, a tremor crept into his voice. "What kind of a man would do such a thing?"

It was clear to Father Anselm that Hugh was not talking about Ivo.

With an obvious effort, the priest made himself meet Hugh's eyes. "Your father felt that he was justified in doing as he did. Remember, he was Ivo's feudal lord, and Ivo had betrayed him."

"What Roger did was vicious," Hugh said. He was white around the mouth. "Was he a vicious man then?"

"No." The priest's voice was thin and strained. "No, I do not think that he was vicious, Hugh."

"Under the circumstances, that is a little difficult to believe." Hugh's fingertips were white, he was pressing them so hard against the arms of his chair.

"He felt he had been betrayed," Father Anselm repeated.

Hugh said, "And what of my mother?"

The priest wet his lips with his tongue. "What do you mean?"

"Why did my mother commit adultery with Ivo Crespin?"

Father Anselm winced. "You don't understand, Hugh. You don't understand how it was."

"That's right," Hugh said starkly. "I don't understand. That is why I am here, Father."

"You didn't . . . you didn't ask your mother about Ivo Crespin, did you, Hugh?"

The priest's eyes pleaded with him.

Hugh inhaled, then let the breath out slowly. "No," he said a little bitterly. "I didn't have the nerve."

"Thank God for that," the priest said. "Lady Isabel has enough to bear without knowing you have learned about *that.*"

Hugh leaned back in his chair and shrugged his shoulders, as if to exorcise the tension that was making him hold them so stiffly. He said, "Obviously my mother did not love or respect her husband. What of Roger, though? Did he love Isabel? Was that why he exacted such terrible retribution from Ivo?"

The priest replied with ineffable sadness, "I don't think Lord Roger loved anyone but God."

Hugh rested his dark head against the high back of his chair and regarded the priest with somber eyes.

"Your father was a great crusader," Father Anselm said, still with that note of sadness in his voice. "It is a thousand pities that he was forced to return home and take up the burden of a family. He was not the kind of man who should have had a family. He should have been a priest."

"He had a younger brother," Hugh said. "He did not have to marry. He could have left the earldom to Guy."

The priest shook his head. "Roger was incapable of turning his back upon what he perceived to be his duty. If God had called him to be the Earl of Wiltshire, then he would take up that responsibility, no matter how personally repugnant he might find it."

"*Personally repugnant?*" Hugh repeated.

"Think of this, Hugh," Father Anselm said gently. "Your mother was fifteen years old when she was wed; your father was a man in his late forties. It was not easy for her—so young a girl, and so very very lovely—to be wedded to a man who was not interested in her."

Silence fell as Hugh digested this information.

"So she turned to Ivo," he said.

Father Anselm lifted his hands. "It was wrong. It was adultery and it was wrong. They were wrong. But . . . I can understand how it happened."

Hugh regarded the priest with interest. "You did not condemn her, then?"

"No! No, of course not." Father Anselm seemed to realize that he was being too vehement, and he moderated his tone. "Christ did not condemn the woman caught in adultery either, my son. It would be well for you to remember that."

A strained silence fell between them. The room was still quite cold and the priest folded his hands into his sleeves to keep them warm.

Hugh shifted the line of his questioning. "Was Roger as indifferent a father as he was a husband?"

Father Anselm's sharp intake of breath was audible in the quiet of the room.

Deliberately, Hugh relaxed the pressure of his fingers on the arms of his chair. Once more he made a shrugging motion with his shoulders. He waited.

At last the priest said cautiously, "He cared about you, Hugh. In his own way, he cared about you."

Hugh lifted his brows. "'In his own way'? What do you mean by that?"

Father Anselm removed his hands from his sleeves and reached up to rub his eyes. "Are you quite certain that you want to know all this? It can only cause you pain."

"I am quite certain," Hugh said, his voice very clipped.

"Very well, then. Perhaps it is best that you do know." The priest linked his fingers together and rested them in the lap of his brown wool robe. He did not look at Hugh but instead fixed his eyes on the reddening coals in the brazier.

When he spoke his voice was firmer than it had been all evening.

"When you were a young child, you were quick and bright and fearless and Lord Roger was proud of you. He put you on a horse when you were two years old and you loved it. Nothing ever made you afraid.

"After the incident with Ivo, however, everything changed."

Hugh's fingers began to tense again.

Father Anselm rubbed his forehead as if it ached. "Lord Roger felt that his wife had shown that she was sinful and lustful and he was afraid that she might have passed those traits along to you. So he started you on a program that he felt would stamp out any of your mother's weaknesses, a program that would ensure you grew up strong and pure."

Hugh said a little incredulously, "I was six years old."

"He was afraid for you. He was afraid that you were tainted. He felt that it was his duty to save you."

For a brief moment, the priest's eyes flicked from their contemplation of the brazier to Hugh's face. "He really did think that, Hugh. It was not a subject on which he was completely rational."

The priest went back to staring at the coals. "He separated you from your mother. She was not to be allowed to see you anymore. He did not want her to influence you in any way."

Hugh's heart began to beat more loudly.

Unmistakable pain crept into Father Anselm's voice. "It was terrible for Lady Isabel. Your mother loved you very much, Hugh. You must always remember that."

Hugh sat, rigid as stone, and listened.

"Next, Lord Roger took over your education himself. You were no longer allowed to play with the pages or the other children in the castle. You were kept away from the knights. Lord Roger isolated you completely."

A chill began to seep into Hugh's bones.

"He made you spend hours and hours on your knees in the chapel."

Hugh remembered how he had recognized the window in the chapel at Chippenham. He swallowed.

"He would pray with you for a while, and then he would leave you there by yourself. You had to kneel upright and never move. Sometimes you were there for five hours at a time."

*I was six years old,* Hugh thought.

"I knew that what he was doing was wrong, and I tried to get him to stop it, but he would not listen." The priest gave Hugh a wretched look. "I was very young and he was the greatest crusader of his time. Why should he listen to me?"

Someone knocked upon the door and then it opened. The housekeeper peered in. Her small bright eyes went curiously from Hugh to the priest. "Would you like me to bring you anything, Father Anselm?"

The priest turned his head to the door. "No, Mistress Alney. Thank you."

She flashed her white teeth at them, and her three chins jiggled. After one more curious look, she retreated, leaving them alone once more.

As soon as the door closed, Hugh said harshly, "Did I never see my mother again?"

"At first you used to sneak in to see her." The priest rubbed his forehead once more. "God help me, but I aided and abetted you. Then one day he found you in her room. He beat you in front of her, which distressed her unbearably. After that you didn't try to see her again."

Hugh's mouth was very dry. He said with difficulty, "I thought you told me he wasn't vicious."

"I have thought about this for many years, and I understand now that he truly thought he was doing what was in your best interest."

Hugh made a sound indicative of contempt.

The priest looked at him sadly. "Perhaps I am making a mistake by telling you this."

Hugh shook his head in disagreement. His face did not look young at all. "I need to know," he said.

Father Anselm shut his eyes, as if he were trying to hide from a vision he did not want to see.

"During the course of the year, you changed." The priest's voice was very low. "All the brightness left you and you became quiet and withdrawn.

"I blame myself," the priest said wretchedly. "I should have done something. Your mother was helpless. I should have gone to her brother and told him what was happening. I should have done *something*. I know that. I knew it then. But . . . I was afraid of him."

Hugh looked incredulous. "Afraid of Simon?"

"No, of Roger. He was so cold, so convinced of his own right-eousness. And he was such a powerful man."

"Because he was the Earl of Wiltshire?"

"It wasn't just his position. It was something in himself, in his personality." Father Anselm looked directly at Hugh. "You have it, too," he said.

Hugh stared at the priest. He was very pale.

"There is something . . . compelling . . . about you that makes other men look to you for leadership. It is hard to explain, but it is most assuredly there."

"You are mistaken," Hugh said tightly. "I in no way resemble Lord Roger."

"In this way you do," Father Anselm contradicted him. "Nor is it a bad quality, Hugh. In fact, it is a good quality, if it is put to its proper use. It is what made Lord Roger such a great soldier."

Hugh did not reply. He was once more gripping his chair arms with white-tipped fingers.

The priest continued, "Roger's great flaw was that he would listen to no one but himself. He was guilty of the oldest sin in the world, the sin of Lucifer, the sin of pride."

Hugh inhaled deeply. When he spoke again, his voice had hardened. "I understand, Father Anselm, that you were the one who found Roger's body."

"Aye." The priest's voice was cautious.

"Tell me about it," Hugh said.

Father Anselm looked uneasy. "There is nothing much to tell. I came into the chapel and found him lying on the floor in front of the altar. He had been stabbed in the chest."

"It must have been quite a shock to you, to find him like that," Hugh said neutrally.

"Aye." The priest swallowed. "That it was."

"What did you do then?"

"Well . . . I raised the alarm, of course. None of us could imagine who might have done such a thing. Then . . . then the guards reported that Walter Crespin had ridden out earlier, with you on his saddle. That is when we knew that Walter must have exacted his revenge for Ivo."

Someone walked past the door and went down the stairs.

"What I don't understand is why *I* did not raise the alarm," Hugh said. "After all, I was in the chapel when it happened. And if Walter did indeed kill my father, why would I have gone off with him like that?"

Father Anselm went rigid. Every ounce of blood drained from his face. "You weren't in the chapel!"

"I remember being there," Hugh said. "I remember seeing my fa . . .—Roger's—body laying on the floor. I remember being afraid."

The priest was staring at him, looking both frightened and appalled.

"Walter Crespin didn't kill my father, did he?" Hugh said.

"Of course he did!" Father Anselm cried. "I was there! I saw it happen. Of course it was Walter Crespin! Who else could it possibly have been?"

Hugh's eyes were cold as they rested on the priest's face. "You were there when it happened?"

"God help me," the priest muttered. Visibly, he tried to pull himself together. "Aye. I was there. I saw it happen. I saw Walter Crespin draw his dagger and stab Lord Roger in the chest. Walter couldn't bear to see the way Roger was treating Lady Isabel, and so he killed him."

The priest's face looked like a death's head.

"I told Walter that I would give him time to get away. That's why I delayed my discovery of the body."

"And did you also arrange for Walter to take me with him?"

Father Anselm looked hunted. "He was taking you to Evesham, to your mother's brother."

"Why?"

"So you would be safe, of course."

"Why wouldn't I be safe at Chippenham? From what you have just told me, Roger was the only danger to me and Roger was dead."

The room was still cold but sweat had broken out on the priest's forehead. He said, "We . . . that is, *I* . . . thought it was best to get you away. The castle was going to be in turmoil once Lord Roger was found."

Hugh's straight dark brows lifted. "And so you entrusted me to the care of a murderer?"

The drops of sweat on the priest's forehead were very noticeable. "Walter was a good lad. He loved Lady Isabel. What he did he did to protect her. I knew you would be safe with Walter."

For a long moment, Hugh stared into the priest's agitated face.

"I don't believe you," he said at last. "I don't believe that is what happened."

"What do you mean? Of course that is what happened. I was there."

Hugh shook his head. "I don't believe that Walter Crespin was the one who killed Lord Roger at all."

The priest was staring at Hugh with fascinated horror.

Relentlessly, Hugh's voice went on. "There was another reason why you thought it was so imperative to get me away from Chippenham that day, wasn't there?"

The priest's lips barely moved. "What reason could that be?"

"I was the one who did it, wasn't I?" Hugh said. "I was the one who murdered my father."

# 24

Hugh lay awake in the bed he was sharing with Thomas. A dagger's width of moonlight streamed into the inn bedroom through a warped window shutter, giving enough light for him to make out the shadowy outlines of Thomas laying beside him and of the two knights who were sharing the other bed. The men were asleep. Thomas, who still had the remnants of a cold, was breathing noisily through his mouth. Otherwise the room was quiet.

More than anything in the world, Hugh wanted to be alone. There was nowhere for him to go, however, so he remained in the bed, holding himself very still so that he would not awaken Thomas.

Wisps of memory floated before his eyes:

The chapel at Chippenham, with its half-circle window set into the stone wall over the altar.

A man's body sprawled on the floor in front of him.

*My fault. It's all my fault.*

Blood.

Horror.

Hugh's stomach heaved.

*I must have hated him very much,* he thought.

Lying there in the dark, he had worked out for himself how it must have happened. He had stabbed his father to death, and either Father Anselm had walked in upon them or he had gone to the priest and told him what had happened. To protect him, Father Anselm, and probably his mother, had asked Walter Crespin to take him away, to Simon of Evesham, his mother's brother. Then Father Anselm had pretended to discover the body.

Had the priest planned all along to let Walter Crespin take the blame for the murder? Or had he just allowed Walter to become the scapegoat once it became clear that Ivo's brother was dead?

*No wonder I couldn't bear to face my mother,* Hugh thought bitterly. *She must know the truth about me.*

He thought of her words to him when he had spoken to her in the ladies' bower at Evesham: *You have nothing to be sorry about, Hugh.*

Certainly she could not have been unhappy to learn that her husband was dead. But it must have been a fearful thing to discover that her seven-year-old son was a murderer.

No wonder she and Father Anselm had not wanted him to pursue his past.

They were still denying the truth to him. His mother had sent him to Father Anselm to be told the exact story the priest had told him tonight. And Father Anselm had done his duty. Even when the blinders finally had been ripped away from Hugh's eyes, and he had recognized his own guilt, the priest had continued to blame the hapless Walter.

But there was no other explanation for the feelings of guilt that had assailed Hugh so vividly in the chapel at Chippenham.

*My fault. It's all my fault.*

Walter Crespin hadn't murdered Roger de Leon; Roger's son had.

Hugh knew what he had to do next. He had to return to the Chippenham chapel. Now that his mind was no longer trying to hide his own guilt from him, he might be able to remember exactly what had happened on that fateful morning. More than ever before, Hugh needed to know.

Had Roger done something to provoke him, or had he stabbed his father in cold blood?

Earlier, when he had told the priest that he was going to Chippenham, Father Anselm had protested.

"You're wrong about this, Hugh. You won't remember killing your father because you didn't do it."

But Hugh knew that he was lying.

Tomorrow morning he would send the knights back to Somerford, and he would ride by himself to Chippenham. He had a feeling that this time his memory would return.

Early the following morning, Father Anselm presented himself in the inn stable and told the stableboy on duty that he had been given permission by Hugh to borrow one of the knights' horses. The boy, who knew Father Anselm from the cathedral, cheerfully saddled up the roan stallion that had once belonged to Geoffrey and now was Thomas's. Twenty minutes later, the priest had ridden out of Winchester and taken the road to Evesham.

Thomas was furious when he learned what had happened. After excoriating the stableboy, he reported the theft to Hugh. To his surprise, Hugh took the news calmly.

"You will get your horse back, Thomas, I promise you. The priest has merely borrowed him."

"When you borrow something, it means you have the owner's permission," Thomas snapped. "Taking another person's possession without his permission is stealing."

The men were in the inn bedroom, where Thomas had found Hugh putting on his mail.

"I believe the priest is riding to Evesham," Hugh said. "He had no access to a horse and so he borrowed one of ours. He will return it."

Thomas took Hugh's spurs from on top of the chest and knelt to strap them on his feet. "So what am I supposed to do?" the young knight asked grumpily as he fastened a buckle. "Wait around Winchester until he decides to come back?"

"If you wish to return to Somerford immediately, I will hire a horse for you. Otherwise you can wait here in Winchester. I am quite certain that Father Anselm will return within the week."

After consulting with his two companions, Thomas decided that the three of them would remain in Winchester to await the priest's return. A horse was a knight's most valuable possession, and Thomas wanted to make very certain that he got his roan back.

So it was that later in the morning, Hugh set out for Chippen-ham by himself.

Father Anselm was not a great horseman, but he pushed himself and Thomas's stallion mercilessly, not stopping until darkness fell. By the middle of the following day, he was at the walls of Evesham Castle.

Just inside the gate he met Philip Demain, who was at the head of a contingent of knights on the point of riding out.

"Father Anselm!" Philip said in surprise. "What are you doing here?"

"I must see the Lady Isabel," the priest said. "It is a matter of the utmost urgency."

Philip hesitated, then turned to the man who was riding behind him and said, "Take charge of this lot, will you, Fulk?"

"Aye, Philip," the other knight replied.

"Come with me," Philip said to the priest. "I will take you up to the castle."

"Is Lady Isabel still here?" Father Anselm asked as his horse fell into step beside Philip's. "She has not returned to the convent in Worcester?"

"She is still here, Father."

The priest let out his breath in a sigh of relief. "Thank God."

Philip signaled to a couple of stableboys who were crossing the bailey and the boys came running. The men dismounted and the stableboys took their horses. Philip led the way to the inner court-yard of the castle.

"That is a nice horse you have there," he commented. "Haven't I seen him before?"

The priest had the grace to blush. "I borrowed it from one of Hugh de Leon's knights."

Philip lifted one blond eyebrow. "And where is Hugh now? I understood that he was going to Winchester to see you."

"He came to see me," the priest replied. "He was still in Winchester when I left."

Philip's other eyebrow went up, but he said nothing.

They went up the castle ramp and entered Evesham's Great Hall. The midday meal had been completed and a few servants were still cleaning up from it. Except for the servants and a group of pages who sat on a wall bench waiting to be sent on errands, the hall was empty.

Philip said, "Lord Simon is not in the castle at the moment. He went out hawking. Shall I send for the Lady Alyce? Would you like to wash before you see Lady Isabel?"

"No," the priest said tersely. "My business cannot wait."

Philip looked at him with candid curiosity. "Very well. I will send a page to ask if she will see you."

Philip signaled and in a moment a rosy-faced page was running for the stairs. Father Anselm stood in tense silence, waiting. Philip asked courteously if he would like a cup of ale, and the priest merely shook his head.

Finally the page returned.

"Lady Isabel will see you, Father Anselm," the boy announced. "If you will come with me, I will take you to her."

The priest nodded and stepped forward to follow the fair-haired boy.

The page took him first up the main stairs, and then up a small spiral staircase that had a single door at the top. He knocked.

Isabel's voice, well remembered even though he had not heard it in fourteen years, said, "Come."

The page opened the door. "I bring you Father Anselm, my lady."

"Thank you, Peter."

The page held the door so that the priest could enter. Then the boy stepped back out into the passage and gently closed the door behind him.

Father Anselm and Isabel were alone in what was evidently her bedroom.

"Father Anselm." Across the width of the room the two of them looked at each other, assessing what the years had done to each.

"I had you brought here because I assumed you wish to be private," she said.

The priest's cavernous dark eyes were devouring the woman's face. When finally he spoke his voice was not quite steady, "Aye, my lady. You were right. This is a matter that requires privacy."

Isabel wore a blue mantle over her tunic and her uncovered black hair hung in two long braids over her shoulders. Her face was taut with tension.

The priest made a visible effort to pull himself together.

"Hugh came to see me."

Isabel clasped her hands together at her waist and watched him out of fear-filled eyes. "I did not know what I should tell him, so I sent him to you."

The sun from the window glinted on the blue-black of her hair.

The priest said painfully, "This is difficult for me to tell you, my lady, but . . ." Father Anselm took a deep breath. "He asked me about Ivo."

Isabel flinched as if he had struck her.

"Oh, God. He knew about Ivo?"

Father's Anselm's face was perfectly white.

"Apparently he heard the story from Alan fitzRobert, who is still in service at Chippenham," he replied.

Isabel said in a choked voice, "He said nothing about Ivo to me."

In a low tone, the priest replied, "I can see where he might have found that somewhat difficult."

"And what did you tell him, Father?" Isabel asked.

She had bowed her head and was refusing to meet his eyes.

"I confirmed Alan's story," Father Anselm said in the same low voice as before. "I felt that I had no choice."

"I suppose not," Isabel said despairingly.

"My lady, he was going to have to know about it. It was the only way to make him believe that Walter Crespin had reason to kill Lord Roger."

Isabel lifted her head and stared at the priest for a long, silent moment.

"I am so sorry, my lady," Father Anselm said wretchedly. "I just did not see any other way . . . "

Isabel gestured for him to stop talking. "It was not your fault. I should not have laid this burden on you. I should not have sent Hugh to you. God knows, you have already done enough for me."

The priest's reply was deeply bitter. "I have done nothing for you, my lady, except to make your life more painful."

Isabel shook her head in disagreement.

"My lady, I am afraid that I have more bad news. Hugh still does not believe that Walter killed his father."

Isabel's eyes widened. "But why? If he knew about Ivo, why shouldn't he believe Walter guilty?"

The priest took a step farther into the room. His face was stark as he replied, "My lady, he told me that he remembered being present in the chapel when Lord Roger was killed."

Isabel's eyes were almost black with pain and fear. "He told me that, too. But he doesn't remember what happened!"

"My lady . . ." The priest looked away from her, as if he could not bear to see her face when he imparted his news. "It grieves me more than I can say to have to tell you this, but Hugh has come to the conclusion that it was he who murdered his father."

Her breath hissed audibly in her throat.

*"Why should he think that?"*

The priest shut his eyes at the pain in her voice. He said wretchedly, "I made an error and told him about the way Roger treated him after Ivo's death. It was a mistake, I see that now, but I thought it would explain to him why he had such evil feelings about the Chippenham chapel. All it did, however, was to show him that he had reason to wish his father dead."

Isabel's hands were pressed to her mouth. "Oh my God," she moaned through them. "Oh my God."

"He deduced that the reason we had Walter take him away from Chippenham was to safeguard him from discovery."

Over her hands, Isabel's eyes were appalled.

"You did not tell him the truth?"

"He would not have listened." The priest took another step forward. "My lady . . . the reason I came here in such haste is to tell you that Hugh is on his way to Chippenham. He thinks that if he goes into the chapel with this new knowledge, he will be able to remember."

"Then we must go to Chippenham as well."

Isabel rose from the window seat.

"I think we must," the priest agreed somberly. "He cannot be left to remember the truth alone. We must be there to try to explain . . ."

A spasm of pain passed across Isabel's face. She breathed in and out once, with great care, then said, "How long will it take us to reach Chippenham if we leave right away?"

"If we leave immediately we can stay over the night at the abbey in Cirencester and be at Chippenham by tomorrow afternoon."

"We'll do that, then," Isabel said decisively.

"We will need an escort," the priest said.

Isabel shook her head. "I don't want an escort, Father Anselm. The fewer people who know about this, the better it will be for Hugh."

"With two armies in the area, the roads are not safe. I don't mind traveling alone, but I am not a knight." Father Anselm flushed. "I am not capable of defending you, my lady."

Isabel made an impatient gesture. "You are a priest. No one will bother you."

"That may be so, but I cannot guarantee that they would not bother you."

"I don't want an escort of knights," Isabel repeated. "I want to keep this quiet."

"What about Philip Demain?" the priest suggested. "He is a very capable young man and he knows Hugh. I am sure he can be trusted to keep his mouth closed."

After a moment, Isabel said crisply, "All right, but just Philip, no one else."

"I will speak to him," Father Anselm said. "When can you be ready?"

"I will be ready in half an hour," Isabel said.

"I will find Philip and ask him to have horses made ready for us," said the priest.

It was two in the afternoon when Philip Demain set off from Evesham with his two charges. It had taken quite a bit of talking from the priest to convince him that it was necessary for Isabel to leave for Chippenham without waiting for her brother's return.

"If you won't escort us, Philip, then we will go alone," the priest had said.

Philip had seen that he meant it, and had given in. Which was how he found himself cantering through the forests of

Gloucestershire with a tired but determined woman and an exhausted but equally determined priest.

Philip had left Thomas's roan behind and given Father Anselm one of the Evesham stallions, so at least the horses were fresh. The priest had been in the saddle for two straight days, however, and Philip could see that he was aching and sore. And Isabel, who had spent the last fourteen years in a convent, was not accustomed to the exertion of a long ride either.

Neither of them complained, however. In fact, whenever Philip suggested that they might stop for a rest, his companions stubbornly insisted that they push on.

Nothing could have shown Philip the urgency of their errand more vividly than their determination to continue despite their obvious physical discomfort.

They cantered on.

They arrived in Cirencester an hour after vespers, and asked for lodging at the abbey there. Philip saw his two charges taken into the care of the monks before he went to the stable to make certain that the horses were taken care of properly. By the time he returned to the abbey guest house for a meal, it was almost time for compline.

Few travelers were on the roads these days because of the war, and they were the only guests at the abbey this night. Consequently Philip had a room to himself and did not see Father Anselm until the following morning, when he went downstairs for breakfast.

Isabel was already sitting at the table and Philip took the bench across from her. It was sheer physical pleasure just to look at her, he thought.

"Good morning, my lady," he said politely. "Did you sleep well?"

"Aye, thank you," she said.

She did not look as if she had slept well, however. There were shadows under her beautiful eyes.

At this moment, Father Anselm entered the refectory. Isabel's eyes turned to him with a look of unmistakable urgency.

"Eat something, my lady," the priest said, looking at the untouched bread that lay in front of her. "It will not help Hugh to have you fainting from hunger."

Isabel frowned, but she picked up her bread and bit off a small piece.

Father Anselm sat down next to her.

Philip looked at them from the other side of the table. He remembered very well Isabel's words when he and Simon had first brought her the news that Hugh might be alive.

*For fourteen years I have done penance for my wrongs to my son.*

And the priest, when he had learned of Hugh's existence, had said, *Am I to be given the chance to make up for all the wrong that I did to that boy?*

Whatever it was that lay in the past was evidently about to be brought to light.

Hugh's face rose before Philip's mind's eye.

*Poor bastard,* he found himself thinking. *I don't think he's in for a very pleasant afternoon.*

# 25

Hugh was halfway across Salisbury Plain when the headache hit. He spent the night in an empty shepherd's hut, waiting for the agony to pass. By daybreak he was wrung out and exhausted, but his head was clear of pain. He made himself sleep for a couple of hours before he started out once more for Chippenham.

It was midafternoon by the time Hugh reached the open field where the tournament had been held two months before. He halted Rufus and stared for a moment at the great battlemented curtain wall of Chippenham, so gray and forbidding under the cold blue sky. Next his eyes moved to the high stone towers from which flew the crimson flag with its insignia of a golden boar. The flags were rippling in the chill November breeze.

*This is where I spent the first seven years of my life,* he told himself.

He squeezed his calves gently against Rufus's sides and the stallion walked forward, carrying him ever closer to the high twin towers that guarded the main entrance to the castle.

The men at the gate recognized him and let him ride under the raised iron portcullis without question.

Hugh was deeply surprised when no one insisted upon escorting him to the earl.

Security at Chippenham was very loose, he thought with stringent disapproval.

There was no doubt that the guards' carelessness was convenient for his own purposes, however. Unimpeded, Hugh rode Rufus to the stable in the outer bailey and gave the stallion into the hands of a stableboy with instructions about how to feed him. Then he proceeded on foot to the second gate that barred the way to the inner courtyard.

Once again he identified himself to the men on guard at the gate tower and was allowed to pass under the portcullis.

Once again Hugh frowned at the lax discipline that appeared to prevail among Guy's retainers. He had passed a number of knights and men at arms in the outer bailey, and not one of them had stopped him to ask his business. Even now, as he approached the great square stone keep of Chippenham, with its four towers and its separate forebuilding, no one intercepted him to demand his credentials.

*This is disgraceful,* Hugh thought as he walked up the wide stone ramp that led to the main entrance of the castle. He went through the heavy door and found himself alone on the stone-floored landing. Instead of taking the stairs to the Great Hall, he turned into the forebuilding, which housed the chapel.

Hugh had no intention of seeking out Guy if he did not have to. He wanted to do this alone.

It was late in the afternoon by the time Philip and his two charges reached Chippenham. Unlike Hugh, Philip's face was unknown and he was stopped at the gate and questioned about his business.

"We are seeking Hugh de Leon," Philip replied.

"Have you seen him?" Isabel asked anxiously.

"Aye, my lady." As she spoke, Isabel had pushed back the hood of her cloak and now the guard stared at her with dazed recognition and admiration. "He arrived about two hours ago."

Father Anselm said in surprise, "I thought he would be here much sooner than that."

"Something must have detained him," Philip said.

"I will be glad to escort you to Lord Guy, my lady," the guard said respectfully, his eyes still glued to Isabel's face.

"Thank you," Isabel replied. "Do you mind if we hurry?"

The knight left the gatehouse and signaled to a squire to bring his horse. Then, with a showy move he had obviously practiced, he leaped into the saddle from the ground.

Before he moved off in front of them, he cast a quick glance at Isabel to see if she had noticed his athleticism.

She was staring at the chapel window in the castle forebuilding.

"Follow me," the knight said gruffly, and led the way across the bailey to the gate in the castle's inner walls. Once in the inner courtyard, they all dismounted and servants took their horses. Then their escort led them up the ramp, through the door, and up a flight of narrow stairs to the Great Hall.

Philip looked at Isabel with alarm as they walked into the hall. She was white to the lips.

*She was once the mistress of Chippenham*, he thought. *Returning here must bring back memories.*

The dinner hour was approaching and servants were beginning to set up tables in the hall.

"Come and warm yourself before the fire, my lady," their escort said respectfully. "I will send someone to tell Lord Guy that you are here."

"Thank you," Isabel said, and she preceded the men across the floor to the great stone fireplace. Philip could not help but notice how stiffly she walked. The long hours in the saddle had taken their toll on her.

Father Anselm and Isabel waited in tense silence while Philip struggled to reply politely to the guard's questions. When at last Guy came down the stairs from his private solar, he was obviously stunned to see his sister-in-law.

"Isabel!" he said. "Whatever brings you here?" The gray eyes that were so like Hugh's flicked from Philip to Father Anselm. "And with so small an escort!"

"Hugh is here, Guy," Isabel said tersely. "Did you know that?"

The gray eyes widened. "No. No one told me. When did he arrive?"

"A few hours ago, I believe," Isabel said.

Guy did not look pleased. He cast his eyes around the busy hall, as if searching for someone. "Where is he?"

"I believe he is in the chapel," Isabel said.

Guy slowly returned his eyes to his sister-in-law. "In the chapel?" A deep line indented his forehead. "Again?"

"What do you mean, 'again?'" Isabel asked sharply.

"He was here once before. He told me he was trying to recover his memory." Guy shrugged his heavy shoulders. "He was not successful. Has he decided to try again?"

"Aye," Isabel said. "And I have come to help him." She laid her fingers on Guy's blue wool sleeve. "With your permission, my lord, Father Anselm and I would like to go to the chapel to join Hugh."

There was a moment's silence as Guy looked from Isabel to the priest, then back again to Isabel. Then he said grimly, "We'll all go."

"No!" Father Anselm protested.

"We'll all go or no one will go," Guy said adamantly. "Hugh is not the only one who would like to know what happened the day my brother was murdered."

Isabel turned to the priest. "It doesn't matter," she said. "All that matters now is Hugh."

After a minute, he nodded reluctantly.

She turned back to Guy. "Very well," she said. "But let us go immediately. He has been alone there for too long."

Guy offered Isabel his arm. "Come along then."

She took it and the two of them led the way back across the Great Hall to the stairs. Father Anselm fell into step on the other side of Guy, and after a moment's hesitation, Philip followed them.

Hugh had been kneeling in the chapel for hours.

*This is what my father used to make me do,* he thought. *I used to kneel here, and look at the window and the sunlight coming through it. I used to wish that I was outside in the sun, not inside here in the cold and the damp.*

He remembered that. He remembered those feelings.

He remembered the guilt and the terror.

But he could not remember what had happened.

He shut his eyes and turned his thoughts to the one person who had never failed him.

*Adela,* he thought. *Help me. I need to know this. Please, please help me.*

Nothing. Only the smell of damp and old incense. Only the chill of the unheated stone. It was growing dark outside and the interior of the chapel was becoming dimmer and dimmer.

It wasn't going to work. He wasn't going to remember. He was doomed to spend the rest of his life like this, not knowing.

He bent his head and covered his face with his hands.

He had shut the door behind him when he entered the chapel earlier, and now he heard the sound of the heavy oak door being pushed open.

Hugh's hand immediately went to the dagger at his belt.

He didn't look around. Instead he continued to kneel upright, his eyes on the crucifix that hung above the altar.

He listened intently to the noises behind him.

He heard the sound of more than one pair of feet. Several people were coming down the aisle.

A muscle flickered along Hugh's jaw and he spun around in the pew, his hand still on his dagger.

A woman's voice said, "Hugh, are you all right?"

With astonishment, he recognized the voice as belonging to his mother. His hand dropped away from the knife.

She was standing at the end of the bench where he was kneeling, and behind her was Father Anselm. Dimly, Hugh was aware of the presence of two other men, but his eyes were all for Isabel. He didn't answer her question.

"Have you been able to remember?" she asked gently.

He shook his head. He didn't think he was capable of speech.

"Then I will help you," she said.

His fingers went to the bench in front of him, and then he levered himself to his feet. He had been kneeling for so long that his legs felt unsteady. He had a pain in the small of his back.

"How?" he croaked.

"Father Anselm and I were both in the chapel with you on the morning your father died," she said. "We'll show you how it happened."

Hugh stared at her out of haunted eyes. "You were there, too?"

"I was there," she said, "and Father Anselm and Walter Crespin and you. And, of course, your father."

"Don't try to tell me that Walter Crespin killed him," Hugh warned harshly.

"No." Slowly she shook her head. "I am not going to do that."

Whoever was standing toward the back of the chapel was carrying a candle, so the central aisle was dimly illuminated. Hugh was able to see his mother's face.

"Then you admit that Walter didn't kill him?" he demanded.

"Walter didn't kill him," she agreed gently.

Hugh swallowed hard. "Who did kill him then?"

"Let us see if you can remember," she said.

She held out her hand to him. "Come here."

Slowly Hugh edged his way out of the bench until he was standing at his mother's side. She took his hand into hers.

"This is how it happened," she said.

He stared down into her face. His breath was coming short and shallow.

"Do you remember what Father Anselm told you about the way your father separated us and about how he made you kneel in the chapel for hours, praying that you would not turn out like me?"

Hugh nodded tensely.

"It went on for a year," she said. "Then, when Roger showed no signs of changing his fanatical course, I knew that I had to do something. I deserved to suffer, but I could no longer bear to see what was happening to you. So I asked Ivo's brother if he would take you away from Chippenham, to the protection of my brother, Simon. Walter said that he would."

Isabel was still holding Hugh's hand in hers. Her ringless fingers were icy cold.

She went on calmly, "That morning, Walter and I came to the chapel together. I knew I would find you here and I knew that you would not go with him unless I told you to."

She glanced at the bench beside them.

'When we came into the chapel, you were kneeling in the very same place you just were. You weren't alone, however. Father Anselm was kneeling with you."

Hugh flicked a glance at the priest.

Isabel's fingers tightened around his. "I told you what I wanted you to do. At first you refused to leave me behind, but I convinced you that you had a much better chance of reaching Evesham alone. I told you that my only real hope of rescue was for you to tell my brother what was happening at Chippenham.

"Finally you agreed to go with Walter."

She tugged at his hand and walked with him the rest of the way down the aisle. They stopped before the altar rail. Then she put her hands upon his shoulders and placed him in a specific spot.

She motioned to Father Anselm, who came forward and took up a place at a little distance from her.

"This is how we were all standing when your father came into the chapel," Isabel said. "Walter was behind Father Anselm."

Hugh felt a terrible pressure beginning to build inside his head. *Not another headache*, he thought despairingly. *Not now.*

But the sharp pain of a headache did not follow. It was only the pressure, building and building, until he thought his skull would explode with it.

A deep voice rang in his ears.

*What are you doing here, Isabel?*

"He was enraged," his mother's voice said. "I was not supposed to talk to you at all."

A presence seemed to rise before Hugh. A presence that was huge and angry and terrifying. It blocked the space between him and his mother so that he could no longer see her.

*Do I have to lock you up to keep you away from the boy?*

The pressure in Hugh's head was excruciating. He couldn't see the chapel, or his mother, or the priest who was standing close beside them. All he saw was darkness. All he felt was this fearful, towering presence.

His father.

Isabel's voice floated to his ears. "He threatened me, Hugh, and that made you try to protect me."

Now it was a child's voice that sounded inside Hugh's head.

*Leave my mother alone! You're not a good man, you're an evil man. God doesn't love you. God wouldn't love a man who does the things that you do!*

Hugh's heart and pulse were racing. He struggled to suck air in and out of his lungs. He felt terror right down to the marrow of his bones.

The presence turned on him.

*What did you say?*

Again came that defiant child's voice.

*I said you were evil. You're evil and I hate you. Leave my mother alone!*

A huge hand was lifted. A fist smashed into his face and he crashed to the ground.

Blood poured down his face into his mouth.

A woman's voice screamed, *Don't touch him! Don't you dare touch him!*

Everything was dark and blurry. His head was ringing. The presence was still looming over him. Desperately he tried to scramble to his feet.

Then he saw her coming with the knife.

He screamed.

*No, Mama. Don't!*

She said hysterically, *You'll never touch him again!*

The presence swung around to face her, and she struck.

His father fell to the ground.

Except for the sound of Hugh's labored breathing, the chapel was deadly silent. He stared with horror into his mother's eyes. She was crying.

"I didn't want you to know, Hugh. I didn't ever want you to have to live with the knowledge that your mother was the one who killed your father."

He felt tears sting behind his own eyes. He began to shiver.

"It's all right, Mama," he said. "It's all right."

She took a step toward him, and he lifted his arms. In a moment she was in them, sobbing brokenheartedly against his shoulder.

"I didn't want you to know, but I couldn't let you go on thinking that it was you."

He cradled his mother's slim, shaking body in the shelter of his arms. Her warmth made him stop shivering.

"It's all right, Mama," he repeated. He patted her narrow back gently. "Don't worry. Everything is going to be all right."

# 26

It was Guy who stepped forward and said, "I think we had all better repair to someplace where we can discuss this matter privately."

In silence, the rest of the party followed Guy down the chapel stairs, across the landing, and then up a narrow spiral staircase that ascended to one of the towers. The room at the top of the stairs was well furnished and comfortable and adjoined a small bedroom. Guy told them all to sit down, then went around the room lighting the candles.

It was little wonder that Hugh had lost his memory, Philip thought, as he took a stool at a little distance from the rest of the group. His mind had been trying to protect itself from an almost unbearable knowledge.

Hugh and Isabel had seated themselves side by side upon the wide window seat, and the closed wooden shutters acted as a frame for their elegant dark heads.

Guy finished lighting the candles and took his own chair.

They all looked at each other.

It was Hugh who finally broke the silence.

"So." His voice sounded composed, although his face was still very pale. He said to the priest, "When did you decide to place the blame on Walter Crespin?"

Father Anselm's eyes were urgent as he looked back at

Hugh. "It was never my plan to blame Walter," he returned. "After it happened, Walter and I decided that the best thing would be to follow Lady Isabel's original plan and get you away from Chippenham. You were understandably shocked, and we did not want you to have to answer questions. So we all agreed that Walter would escort you to Evesham."

Philip glanced at Isabel. She was looking at Hugh with naked longing in her eyes.

Father Anselm continued speaking to Hugh. "I don't know what happened on that journey except that you must have been set upon by outlaws. The following day, instead of hearing from Lord Simon that you were safe, we learned that Walter had been killed and you were missing."

Isabel suddenly lowered her head.

Father Anselm said, "You can imagine how your mother felt when she heard that news."

*My God,* Philip thought in horror. *What a tragic sequence of events.*

Isabel said, "Do you have any memory at all of what happened on the road, Hugh?"

A flash of something glinted in Hugh's gray eyes, and then the familiar shutters came down. He shook his head and said regretfully, "I remember nothing of what happened to me until I met Ralf."

*He remembers, all right, but he is not going to tell her,* Philip thought.

The priest went on with his story. "I gave Walter a few hours' start and then I pretended to discover Lord Roger's body. I am being honest when I tell you, Hugh, that it never occurred to me, and I'm sure it never occurred to your mother, to cast the blame on Walter."

Silently, Isabel shook her head.

"It was the knights at the gate who had let Walter and you out who first raised the cry against him. I persuaded Lady Isabel to keep silent until we were certain that the two of you had arrived safely at Evesham."

For the first time, Guy spoke, his voice heavy with sarcasm. "Just who *were* you going to blame for Roger's death? I presume that Isabel was not going to confess."

"I would have confessed to the crime myself," the priest said quietly. "I knew that I was greatly to blame. I should have sent for Lord Simon months before."

Philip stared at the priest's tortured face as he looked at Isabel and made a discovery. *He loves her.*

"I would never have let you do that, Father Anselm," Isabel said firmly. She gave Guy a level look. "I would have confessed rather than stand by and see an innocent person blamed."

Guy looked skeptical. He opened his mouth as if he would speak, but Father Anselm was before him.

"Our first priority was to get Hugh under the protection of his uncle. I know that I, at any rate, was hoping that Lord Simon would tell us what we should do next."

The priest looked again at Hugh. "Then the news came that Walter had been killed, and shortly after that his body was returned to Chippenham. He had been stabbed to death." Father Anselm looked very tired. "As you can imagine, Lady Isabel was in no state to make any decisions at all, she was so distraught by the news of your disappearance. When Lord Simon arrived, I told him the whole, and he and I deemed it best to allow Walter to take the blame. He would not have minded. He would have been glad he could do something to protect Lady Isabel."

Isabel made a small sound, like an animal in pain.

Hugh's face was like stone.

"A convenient conclusion," Guy said with heavy irony. "There is only one part of this story that has never made sense to me. What reason would this Walter have for wanting to kill my brother and kidnap his son?"

The room was utterly silent.

Then Isabel said quietly, "A year before, I had had a love affair with Walter's brother, and when Roger found out about it, he had Ivo castrated. Then Ivo killed himself. So you see, Guy, Walter had good reason to wish Roger dead."

The look of horror on Guy's face echoed the horror that Philip knew must be engraved on his own features.

*Castrated. Dear God. What kind of man had Roger de Leon been?*

Isabel clasped her arms even more tightly around herself. Hugh appeared to be staring intently at his boots.

"Who knew about this?" Guy said harshly.

"All of the castle knights knew," Isabel replied. "That is why they were so quick to point a finger at Walter. They all knew that he had a reason to wish Roger dead."

"I cannot believe that I never heard a word of this," Guy said.

"The household wished to protect Lady Isabel," Father Anselm said. "No one wanted to see her suffer any more than she already had. The knights all held their tongues."

Guy shifted his heavy frame in his chair. "Unfortunately, the result of all of this concern for Isabel's reputation led to blame being cast on me. You are aware, I presume, that for years I have been suspected of having paid Walter Crespin to kill Roger so that I could assume my brother's honors?"

"Perhaps there was suspicion, but there was no proof," the priest said. "We knew there never would be proof, because there was none to be found."

The candles in the room all flickered at once, as a chill breeze came into the room from under the closed door.

For the first time in a long while, Hugh spoke. "It seems to me that you came out of this tragedy the best of us all, Uncle. You became the Earl of Wiltshire, one of the most powerful men in the kingdom. On the other hand, my mother locked herself away in a convent for fourteen years, and I lived for most of my life without knowing who I was. I cannot find it in my heart to feel sorry for you."

His voice had an edge that could cut glass.

Guy's head jerked up and the two pairs of gray eyes met and held.

"I am still the Earl of Wiltshire," Guy said grimly. "And I intend to remain so."

Hugh's eyes were cold as the winter sky. He looked back at Guy and did not reply.

Philip, staring at Hugh's still, dangerous face, thought, *After all, he is his father's son.*

He shivered at the thought.

Suddenly Philip remembered another death.

"You may not have been responsible for the murder of your brother, my lord, but what of the knight who was killed at your tournament?"

Guy swung around to stare at Philip. "I had naught to do with that. It was a mêlée, for God's sake. Men get killed in mêlées all the time."

"I saw it happen," Philip said. "Geoffrey was pushed from behind."

Guy's face flushed red with anger. "Well, I was not responsible!"

Philip's eyes narrowed in disbelief.

Hugh said, "I believe I might be able to clear this particular matter up, my lord, if you will send for Aubrey d'Abrille."

All eyes swung toward Hugh.

"Who the devil is Aubrey d'Abrille?" Philip demanded.

Guy answered without removing his gaze from Hugh's face. "He is one of my household knights. What does he have to do with this matter, Hugh?"

"Send for him and we shall see," Hugh returned calmly.

Guy swung around to face Philip. "Go down to the hall and ask a page to fetch me Aubrey d'Abrille."

Philip unfolded his considerable length from the stool upon which he was sitting and left the room.

The household was still at supper when he arrived in the Great Hall. Guy's place of honor at the head table was conspicuously empty. Philip beckoned to one of the pages who was carrying a platter of meat and relayed Guy's order. The boy took his platter over to a table of knights and said something.

A tall man with distinctive chestnut-colored hair rose and accompanied the page back to Philip.

"Lord Guy wishes to see you," Philip said abruptly. "Come with me, if you please."

The knight's face was very still. He didn't say a word. He merely nodded.

The two men climbed the spiral stairs that led to the tower room where Guy and Hugh awaited them.

The room was silent when Philip reentered.

"My lord," he said to Guy. "Here is Aubrey d'Abrille."

He felt the knight beside him stiffen and turned to look at him. The man was staring at Isabel.

Hugh spoke from her side. "Good evening, Aubrey. I'm afraid I entered Chippenham without your knowledge this time. I apologize for depriving you of another opportunity to try to kill me."

Isabel's breath caught audibly.

The red-haired knight scowled and forced his gaze to Hugh's face. "I don't know what you're talking about."

"I think you do," Hugh replied. "You tried to kill me twice. The first time, at the tournament, you were successful in killing the man who was riding my horse. Your second attempt was less satisfactory, although you came very close."

"What are you talking about, Hugh?" Guy demanded angrily. "Why should Aubrey want to kill you?"

Hugh's expression was perfectly contained.

"Ask him what name he was born with," he said.

At those words, the knight took a step backward. Philip moved to put himself in front of the door.

Hugh's voice went on, calm and steady. "He grew up in the castle of his maternal uncle, Hubert d'Abrille, and when he came to Chippenham he took his uncle's name. But he was born Aubrey Crespin, younger brother to Ivo and Walter."

Isabel cried out in pain.

"Is this true?" Guy demanded of his knight.

He lifted his chin and replied defiantly, "Aye, it is true. I am Aubrey Crespin."

"Oh my dear God," said Isabel.

The knight stared at her. "You were the reason both my brothers died," he said bitterly. "I wanted to hurt you the way you hurt me."

Isabel's mouth was quivering.

"You're Ivo's brother?"

Her voice was a mere thread of sound.

"I am Ivo's brother. And Walter's brother as well. Don't forget Walter, who sacrificed both his life and his reputation on your behalf. *My lady.*"

He spoke the last words as if they were a curse.

It was Hugh who answered the accusation. "It was my father, not my mother, who was responsible for the death of your brother, Ivo. And it was outlaws on the road who killed your brother, Walter. Your vengeance has been misplaced, Aubrey."

The knight's light green eyes burned in his pale face. "I don't think so. You are his son as well as hers."

"My son," said Father Anselm in a gentle voice. "I knew both your brothers. They were brave and honorable men. They would never want you to exact this kind of revenge."

Aubrey stared at the priest and did not reply.

"Walter gave his life trying to keep Hugh safe," Father Anselm went on. "Do you think it would give him joy to know that his own brother was the cause of Hugh's death?"

The knight's breathing was harsh and audible in the quiet of the room.

"My mother has been punished enough," Hugh said. "There is no necessity for you to add to the burden she already bears."

Tears began to pour down Isabel's face.

"You have Ivo's eyes," she said to Aubrey. Her voice caught on a sob and she pressed her lips together hard.

"Go back downstairs," Guy said to the knight in a hard voice. "I will deal with you later."

Without replying, Aubrey turned and strode toward the door.

Philip stepped aside and allowed him to pass.

Once the door had closed behind him, everyone looked at Hugh.

"How did you know who he was?" Guy demanded.

"I stopped at Abrille on my way to Winchester and spoke to Sir Hubert," Hugh said. "He told me who his nephew really was."

"But why did you even suspect him?" Philip asked. He was still standing by the door.

"It was easy enough to see that he hated me. I had never seen the man before in my life, and I could not imagine what I might have done to engender such fierce enmity. Then it occurred to me that perhaps it was not I whom Aubrey hated, that perhaps he saw me as a means of getting back at someone else."

Hugh shrugged. "After that, it was simple enough to conclude who Aubrey might be. I went to Abrille for confirmation of my suspicion, and I got it."

"I thought you believed that I was the one who was trying to kill you," Guy said ironically.

"The thought did cross my mind," said Hugh. "But I did not think you were stupid enough to kill me in your own castle."

"Thank you," Guy said with heavy sarcasm.

Hugh nodded coolly.

Once more the eyes of the two men who had claim to be Earl of Wiltshire locked together.

The room was thick with tension.

Guy shifted in his chair.

"What would you say if I offered to name you my heir?" he asked in an abrupt voice. "Would you promise to recognize my position as earl if you were guaranteed to succeed me after my death?"

Hugh continued to look at him and did not reply.

Guy's voice hardened. "You would have to promise not to seek assistance from the empress or Gloucester, however."

Hugh's face was wearing its most shuttered look.

"And if I did that, you would recognize me as your heir?"

Guy hesitated before saying firmly, "Aye. If you formally swear not to seek support against me, I will recognize you as my heir."

Hugh asked, "What about the king? Would he agree to such a contract?"

He might have been discussing the price of hay, so disinterested did he sound.

Guy snorted contemptuously. "Stephen needs me too much to balk at anything I might suggest."

"Stephen would know that such a promise on my part would free you from having to rely on him for support," Hugh pointed out.

"We can work out the details," Guy said impatiently. "What I want to know is . . . are you interested?"

Everyone stared at the cold, capable, guarded young man who was sitting on the window seat.

At last, "I might be," Hugh said slowly.

"You won't get Wiltshire any other way," Guy said. "I am too firmly entrenched for you to turn me out. And I have the king's voice."

"Perhaps that is true," said Hugh. "But I would still have the option of going to the empress."

"She is not going to win this war, nephew. Gloucester has not been able to command enough support."

Hugh lifted one level black eyebrow. "That remains to be seen."

Guy stared at his nephew, his face hard.

Hugh stood up.

"I will think about what you have proposed, my lord, and I will let you know."

"Very well," Guy said grimly. "Don't take too long, though, Hugh. I might change my mind."

Philip stood by the door, rigid with dismay. This plan of Guy's would undermine all of Gloucester's hopes of attracting Hugh to his side.

*I have to get Hugh back to Evesham so that Lord Simon can talk to him,* he thought desperately.

The last thing Philip wanted was for Hugh to settle for being Guy's heir.

* * *

Much to Hugh's surprise, that night he slept. He had fully expected to get a headache, but his head continued to remain clear. Nor did he lie awake for hours, revolving what he had learned around and around in his tired brain. Instead, five minutes after he had crawled into bed and pulled the fur coverlet up over him, he dropped into the deep and dreamless well of healthy sleep.

He awoke in the morning with one thought on his mind.

*Cristen.*

All that he had learned in the last twenty-four hours, as well as the decision he must make about his uncle's offer, he needed desperately to discuss with Cristen.

Philip, Isabel, and Father Anselm were as anxious to depart from Chippenham as Hugh, and so shortly after they had broken their fast, the four of them met in the bailey and mounted up.

Guy did not show himself to bid them farewell.

Father Anselm was returning to Winchester and was the first to break away from the group. As soon as they reached the main road, he turned south while Hugh and Philip and Isabel continued on northward.

Hugh planned to accompany Philip and his mother as far as Malmesbury, at which point he would turn off the road to ride to Somerford, while the others followed the road north into Gloucestershire.

The town of Malmesbury was not very far from Chippenham, and for most of the short ride Philip tried to convince Hugh to change his mind and continue on with him and Isabel to Evesham.

Hugh was happy to have Philip monopolize the conversation. He even asked him a number of leading questions to encourage him to go on talking. He also reminded Philip to have Thomas's stallion sent back to Somerford.

Father Anselm had been charged to tell Thomas to hire a horse and return to Somerford, where he would be reunited with his precious roan.

The sky was heavy with clouds and Isabel huddled inside her cloak to keep warm. She spoke very little.

When at last they had reached Malmesbury, Hugh knew that he had to say something to his mother. He understood that she needed some sign of affection from him, but his own feelings for her were very conflicted.

All the while that he had been pretending to listen to Philip, he had been thinking about what had happened in the Chippenham chapel fourteen years ago.

*She killed my father to protect me.*

That was why he had always felt so guilty. He had provoked Roger's rage, and that in turn had caused Isabel to strike out at her husband.

*It's all my fault.*

That's what he had thought, and in a sense he supposed it was true. But his adult mind was able to perceive what his child's mind had not: that the gravest fault of all had belonged to his father.

If he and Isabel bore any guilt for Roger's death, they had surely paid for it.

*She killed my father to protect me.*

Why, then, was he so angry with his mother?

Dimly, he perceived that it had something to do with the terrible thing that had happened to Ivo.

Even more dimly, he sensed that he couldn't forgive her for turning to Ivo, that he hadn't been enough for her.

Isabel wasn't his real mother, he told himself, as he rode along, nodding at whatever it was Philip was saying.

Adela had been his mother.

But Adela would want him to be kind. So when it came time for him to part from Isabel, he took off his helmet and leaned over from Rufus's back to kiss her soft cheek.

"Goodbye,"—he started to say *my lady*, then changed the words to "Mother."

She gazed at him as if she were trying to memorize his face. "Shall I see you again?"

He made himself smile. "Of course. I shall come to Evesham."

She bit her lip and looked undecided. "I may return to the convent in Worcester."

He said instantly, "Do not do that. No one who is a member of Simon of Evesham's family should show their face in Worcester. The feeling there is very strong against Gloucester and his supporters. You would not be safe."

"I am only a woman, Hugh," she protested. "And I would be in the convent."

"Don't go, Mama," he said sharply. "It isn't safe."

He heard his own words and his frown deepened.

After a moment she said mildly, "All right, Hugh. If it will make you feel easier, I will remain at Evesham for a while."

His eyes were as stormy as the gray clouds overhead. "Good," he said.

"I will see that the Lady Isabel is safely delivered to her brother," Philip assured him.

Hugh put his helmet back on. The noseguard effectively concealed him from the eyes of the other two.

"God go with you," he said with invincible courtesy.

"God go with you, my son," Isabel returned. Then she lifted her reins, clucked to her mare, and moved away from him.

Her back was very straight.

Hugh had a horrible feeling that she was crying.

*There's nothing I can do about it,* he thought desperately.

He turned Rufus and cantered away down the other road.

The closer he got to Somerford, the lighter his heart grew.

Soon. He would see her soon.

A few flakes of snow drifted out of the gray sky, and Hugh took off his helmet and held his face upward to feel their cold, feathery kiss on his bare skin. He smiled.

It never even crossed his mind that snow would be a hindrance for Philip and Isabel. All his thoughts were centered on one thing only.

Cristen.

He wanted her to be in the herb shed. He wanted her to be alone. He didn't want to have to meet her in a room full of people, or in front of her father.

He wanted to be able to hold her.

He sent her a message with his mind. *Go to the shed, Cristen. Go to the shed and wait for me.*

He realized what he was doing, and he laughed at himself.

*It doesn't matter where I see her,* he thought. *Tonight we will be alone.*

At long last the forest fell away and the outer walls of Somerford came into view. He remembered how big he had thought the castle when first he had come here.

Compared to Keal, Somerford had been enormous; compared to Chippenham, it was small.

The two guards at the gate shouted a welcome as Hugh rode up. They had recognized Rufus as soon as horse and rider had come into their view.

Hugh stayed at the gate for a few moments, answering questions about Thomas and the other two knights he had left behind in Winchester.

Brian came running. "I'll take care of Rufus for you, Hugh!"

Hugh dismounted and gave the stallion into the care of the boy. Then he began to walk across the bailey under the lightly falling snow. The men at the gate watched him. His mail coat swung to his knees as he walked and his spurs jingled. He was carrying his helmet under his arm.

As they watched, Hugh veered away from the inner walls and crossed the bailey toward the herb garden. He passed through the fence and out of their view.

The guards turned back to the gate and Brian began to walk Rufus to the stable.

Hugh stared at the shed. The door was partly open and he could see the glow of the charcoal brazier inside.

She was here.

His heart began to hammer in his chest.

He pulled his mail coif away from his head and walked along the path to the shed.

He opened the door.

She was standing close to the brazier, waiting for him.

Her brown eyes searched his face.

"Is everything all right, Hugh?"

He took two steps, and she was in his arms. He could feel the small, delicate bones of her back beneath his fingers, but his mail coat kept him from feeling her softness pressed against him.

No matter. Tonight there would be nothing between them.

"Aye," he said huskily. "Everything is all right, now that I am with you."